Praise for Philip Hook's previous novels:

The Stonebreakers

'The cleverness lies in his being able to elevate paintings to such a level as to make us believe that it is worth chasing halfway around the world for them. Courbets, Klimts, Renoirs and Corots acquire the importance that other thrillers give to Russian spies and pieces of intelligence that will end the Cold War'
Literary Review

'Hook's art-world thriller revolves around a simple but imaginative premise . . . Hook certainly knows his stuff and it is his convincing re-creation of the insular and often petty-minded art world that sets this book apart'
The Sunday Times

'He writes better about the physical nature and impact of painting than anyone I have read for years, as well as the Australian critic Robert Hughes'
Grey Gowrie, *Daily Telegraph*

'An excellent novel by an enormously underrated author . . . It is intensely enjoyable'
Nicholas Coleridge, *The Week*

The Island of the Dead

'Philip Hook's expertise in the art world provides the background to his entertaining novel. The story flows stylishly . . . the characters are convincingly drawn'
Sunday Telegraph

'His masterful new novel offers a diverting new genre of mystery in the form of an insider's view into the international art world'
Birmingham Post

'A classic thriller . . . It's easy to get hooked on Hook'
Northern Echo

'A most imaginative and unusual novel'
Manchester Evening News

Also by Philip Hook

The Stonebreakers
The Island of the Dead

About the author

Philip Hook is a senior director of Sotheby's and appears regularly as pictures expert on BBC tv's *The Antiques Roadshow*. He has the unusual distinction of having also been a director of Christie's, which he joined in 1973 straight from Cambridge University, where he read History of Art and won a soccer blue. In between the two auction houses he founded London art dealers the St James' Art Group. He is the author of *Popular 19th Century Painting* (1986) and a comic novel *Optical Illusions* (1993), as well as two thrillers, *The Stonebreakers* and *The Island of the Dead*, both available in Coronet paperback.

The Soldier in the Wheatfield

Philip Hook

CORONET BOOKS
Hodder and Stoughton

First published in Great Britain in 1998
by Hodder and Stoughton
First published in paperback in 1999
by Hodder and Stoughton
A division of Hodder Headline PLC
A Coronet Paperback

10 9 8 7 6 5 4 3 2 1

A CIP catalogue record for this title
is available from the British Library

ISBN 0 340 68217 5

Typeset by Hewer Text Ltd, Edinburgh
Printed and bound in Great Britain by
Clays Ltd, St Ives plc

Hodder and Stoughton
A division of Hodder Headline PLC
338 Euston Road
London NW1 3BH

To my parents

ACKNOWLEDGEMENTS

My thanks are due to many people in various different countries who have helped me in the writing of this book. There is not room to list them all here, but I want to record my particular gratitude to Dorothee von Hammerstein-Equord, Georg von Oppen, Bernd Freiherr Freytag von Loringhoven, Boris Asvarisc and Amy Page. Their help and advice have been invaluable; any deviation in the narrative from historical fact, intentional or unintentional, is entirely my responsibility.

PART ONE

December

ONE

Fedorov ducked into the doorway and paused, glancing up and down the pavement behind him. Snowflakes swirled in the unhealthy yellow light cast by the streetlamps, and the looming facades of the buildings stared blindly down at him, their windows unlit. Not a soul. But then you didn't venture out after dark in this part of St Petersburg in December. Not unless you had a very pressing reason. Not with the temperature at minus twenty-two degrees centigrade, and a cruel wind blowing in from the sea.

Reassured, he drew his jacket about him and pulled his cap down further over his eyes. With the back of his gloved hand he brushed away the flakes that had settled on his moustache, and pushed through the door into the courtyard. Once inside he stood still again, listening, taut with anticipation. He saw the light burning from the window immediately round the corner and pressed himself right up against the wall so that he could approach and look in without being seen. One glance was enough. A corpulent man in a leather jacket sat slumped in a chair snoring. At a table on his right stood a three-quarters empty bottle and a glass. And in front of him flickered a bank of six television screens.

As he stooped to ease himself beneath the window and into the courtyard proper, Fedorov considered those screens. OK, the drunken slob in front of them was asleep, but what were they doing there? They struck him as simultaneously a threat and a stimulus. This was a building that contained things that needed protection. There was a security system in place. He would have to go carefully. But on the other hand it also made it a building worth penetrating. The rewards were potentially greater.

He remembered what Igor Antonovich had once told him and took courage. There were tracks in life: fast tracks, slow tracks. You just had to make sure you manoeuvred yourself on to the fast track, the lane on the highway where it was you who did the overtaking. There was a real fast track in Russia now, Igor had said, there were fabulous opportunities for those prepared to reach out and grab them. Fedorov could feel his own life accelerating. He was going to grow big in this town. He was going to get rich. Like Igor, who owned his own car. Or one day, perhaps, like the man he'd met last night, the one with the sharp black suit whose eyes had been hidden behind dark glasses. The man who'd made him a business proposition and then driven away in a gleaming, nearly-new Mercedes.

The cold didn't bother him tonight because he was on the up, wasn't he? He could sense it all coming together for him. He'd always lived by his wits. Sometimes he sold souvenirs in the markets: old Red Army caps, badges, holsters, hip-flasks. And last winter he'd made a fair bit of extra money out of incredulous tourists by hacking through the packed ice of the Neva to the water beneath, stripping off to his underpants, and jumping in for $5 a time.

You had to be inventive to get on in this town. Keep your wits sharp. He was no fool. He wasn't going to be pushed around. Not by Igor. Not even by the guy with the sleek, nearly-new Mercedes. The guy who had deigned to talk with him for six highly-charged minutes in the back of that glorious car last night. The man whose eyes Fedorov had never seen.

'Dimitry Abramovich Fedorov, this is your lucky day, my son.' It had been Igor accosting him with mock formality last night in the bar. In Svetlana's bar, where the proprietress, a mountainous Ukrainian woman, simultaneously dispensed obscenities and large measures of home-brewed alcohol. 'There's a man outside who wants to meet you. A very important man.'

'Why doesn't he come in, then?' Fedorov had demanded truculently. This was Dimitry Abramovich Fedorov in the fast lane, warmed by four glasses of Svetlana's cheapest vodka. 'If he wants to meet me, he can come in here, can't he?'

'Don't be a fucking idiot.' Igor's red face was suddenly very close to Fedorov's. His tie was undone, almost adrift from his collar. He was angry. But he was anxious too. 'Mr Kuslov is not the sort of man who comes into a place like this to meet people like you. If he asks to see you, then you get out there. Bloody quick.'

'Who is this Kuslov?'

'A business associate of mine.' Igor stood up to his full height and fiddled with his tie; straightening it, as if out of deference to Kuslov. 'Important guy. A big guy. Look, I'll tell you something for free: if you know what's good for you, you keep in with guys like Kuslov. And don't hang about, because the Kuslovs of this life don't often come knocking at your door: he's richer than you could ever dream about.'

Fedorov got up. But slowly. Taking his time. He wasn't going to be pushed around. He reflected that when he'd first met Igor, he'd been in awe of him. But he was less so now. Less so since he'd done that business with him with the Sony Walkmen, known the power of having Igor momentarily dependent upon him, held out for and got the extra thirty dollars to make the three hundred.

And less so since he'd seen his anxiety tonight.

So he followed Igor out of the door of Svetlana's hovel-like bar, pushing past the steaming bodies of the dockyard workers and the sad old whores, a rancorous and malodorous agglomeration of humanity all huddled together as much for warmth as camaraderie and saw it there, parked across the street, like a vision of heaven after the certainty of hell: the biggest, sleekest Mercedes car he'd ever been close to.

It might have been a year or two old, but it was without doubt the most luxurious car he was ever likely to sit in. Because that was what seemed to be happening now. The windows were darkened, but a door opened and a hand was beckoning him inside.

And now he was in there, alone with the man he took to be Kuslov. And Igor wasn't even allowed in there with him. Igor was told to wait outside, stamping his feet in the cold. Fedorov caught his breath with excitement, and an extraordinary thought occurred to him: could it be that he was now in a faster lane than Igor?

Kuslov wore dark glasses, so he couldn't see his eyes. Fedorov noted, however, that his suit was very sleek, like his car, and that his tie was done up and adhered to his collar in a way that Igor could never manage to achieve, no matter how he knotted it. These were problems which did not yet concern Fedorov personally, because he never wore a tie himself, had not yet reached that level of aspiration. But if things went on like this, it might not be long before he did. As he couldn't see his eyes, Fedorov's gaze was drawn to Kuslov's wrists: on his left he wore a watch that was clearly extremely expensive. And on his right he wore a gold bracelet. A very thick gold bracelet.

Fedorov took a seat next to Kuslov, as instructed.

'So,' said Kuslov. There was silence for a moment. Fedorov suddenly wished that he hadn't had the fourth glass of Svetlana's vodka. His brain felt less sharp than it should. He sensed that his brain had to be sharp in order to cope with this man. Fedorov ran his hand along the light-coloured leather of the upholstery of this car and subconsciously marvelled. He had never sat on anything quite like it.

'So, Dimitry Abramovich,' repeated Kuslov, and paused again, weighing him up. Fedorov felt uneasy and yet expectant at the same time, not sure if he was to be offered a beating or a treat. Then Kuslov went on: 'I believe you to be a man who knows a good deal when it is proposed to him.'

Fedorov agreed eagerly with the assessment.

'How would you like to do yourself some serious good? Get on in life?'

'I would like that,' said Fedorov rather too quickly.

'Then I have a proposition to put to you.'

Fedorov nodded, trying to rein in his enthusiasm. The vodka told him that anything this splendid gentleman in his wisdom and generosity was prepared to let slip to him from the majesty of his table should be accepted as a gift of extraordinary good fortune. But through the fog of euphoria, another voice told him to be careful.

'I think that you are good at finding unconventional entrances into places.'

Fedorov stroked his straggly moustache. 'Could be. What sort of places?'

'Your friend Igor Antonovich told me about some personal stereos that came your way. I think that you – how can I put it? – liberated them from a place of confinement with a very narrow access?'

Fedorov considered the question, recalling the excitement of the enterprise, torn again between pride in his achievement and an instinct that it was advisable to keep a certain amount hidden from Kuslov. To be economical with information. Because with a man this powerful, you needed something to trade, otherwise he would consume you entirely, and God knew Fedorov had little enough with which to barter. He mustn't reveal it all at once. He remembered the facade of the big grey building. He remembered the window at the back, open just ajar, and the grille through which he had managed to insinuate his short, thin and extraordinarily supple frame. He remembered picking the lock which led him through into the small warehouse where they'd been stacked up to the ceiling, hundreds of them, Sony Walkmen in their boxes. He remembered how he'd got away with fourteen of them, not being able to carry any more, not being able to prise any more through the grille on his way out. And he remembered the three hundred dollars he'd finally prised out of Igor for them. But all he said to

Mr Kuslov now was, 'Yeah, I had a bit of luck with those stereos.'

'I am a generous man.'

Fedorov agreed. He had no reason not to.

'If you find things in future that you think may interest me, I want you to come to me first. I will pay the best prices. Always the best prices, you can rely upon it. I will look after you. Have a drink?'

Before Fedorov knew it, Mr Kuslov had produced a bottle of top-notch Russian vodka, loosened the cap, and passed it to him. Fedorov swigged without thinking, and felt warm again to Mr Kuslov, particularly when he told him he could keep the bottle.

'Just occasionally,' said Mr Kuslov slowly, 'there may be special jobs I ask you to do. Special things I need you to get me, from specific places. Not often. Just occasionally. Will you do those jobs for me, Dimitry Abramovich?'

Fedorov took another long draft from the bottle and nodded vigorously. A sudden desire overwhelmed him, a desire to impress the man in this superb car, to produce something that would really make him sit up and take notice, convince him once and for all that Dimitry Abramovich Fedorov was firmly set on the fast track. He resolved to bring him fifty Sony Walkmen. No, a hundred.

Fedorov was about to take leave of his new friend. Clutching his bottle, he was about to open the door when Mr Kuslov laid a hand on his forearm and gave him something else. 'Here,' he said, 'take my card. My telephone number's on it.' And then he added, as an afterthought, 'Oh, and by the way, from now on if you trade with anyone else except me I'll break your legs. Both of them. Understand?'

He edged forward to inspect the basement windows in the courtyard, dropping to his knees in front of each one, clearing the snow away to get a closer look. He moved purposefully, carefully; but there was an increasing edge of desperation at

THE SOLDIER IN THE WHEATFIELD

each disappointment, at each grille securely in place, at each lock engaged.

The evening had begun with optimism. He had spent the day bouyed up by an awareness of his new association, of the status conferred upon him by his new business arrangement with Mr Kuslov. And the snow coming had been an extra bonus. He liked the snow. It meant there were less people about, that he was less likely to be interrupted in his activities. It was an extra cloak of secrecy. He'd set out determined to achieve something, to return with some trophy to lay at the feet of his new benefactor. Hadn't the man promised the best prices? Hadn't he said he would look after him? He ached to test out the claim. So Fedorov had been drawn back to the big grey building near the docks, the scene of his former success. He was driven by the idea that there remained a pile of Sony Walkmen awaiting liberation, and he carried with him in his jacket a folding but capacious bag in which he aimed to transport rather more than just fourteen of them. But when he had got there half an hour ago, things had changed. The window through which he had gained access was now locked and the grille replaced with something stronger and narrower through which even he could not pass. Regretfully he had had to move on. To find something else.

So now here he was, in this unknown courtyard. On the prowl. Looking for the half chance.

He was three quarters of the way down the third side of the quadrangle when he saw what he was looking for. The window was closed but its lock was not engaged. He pushed the snow away to get a clearer view. The flakes were still drifting down incessantly. Drifting down like dollar bills.

He leant forward, put his gloved hands to the window frame, and pushed. Nothing happened. He pushed again, harder, and with a sudden shudder it eased upwards, wide enough for him to squeeze through. When he picked himself up from the floor inside, he found he was trembling. It wasn't fear. It was elation. He was going to strike lucky again. He was going to find something to offer Mr Kuslov. Something wonderful. Soon he'd be able to afford that car.

The room he was in seemed to be some sort of office: bare, apart from a row of battered files on a shelf. And a desk. He pulled out a drawer. It was empty. He tried the second drawer. Nothing except an empty packet of cigarettes. He opened the door to the corridor. As he walked softly through he noticed that the snow from his boots was melting on the linoleum floor. It vaguely disturbed him, but he pushed on. Determined to get to the Sony Walkmen.

He tried four doors and they were all offices. His anger was rising. What did he want with files? The fifth was a heavier door, a steel door, but it yielded to his shoulder, and inside it was different. It was a dimly-lit store-room, because there were wooden racks, but he could not at first make out what they contained. Thin, oblong objects, like trays or blocks of wood. He wasn't inclined to risk turning on a light even if he could have found the switch. But he reached forward, curious, and took one out. It was a wooden panel, about forty centimetres by fifty. He couldn't see it very clearly but he thought it might be painted and it suddenly came to him that it was an icon. Icons could be valuable. Mr Kuslov was the sort of man who might be interested in icons.

He opened up his bag and found that it contained the panel comfortably. There was another in the rack of a similar size and he slipped that one in as well, noting only that the surface of this second icon was of a different texture from the first. To a certain extent he was on unknown territory here: Sony Walkmen were one thing, of a definite and calculable value. Icons were another. But what the hell, these were the best he was going to do tonight.

When he'd been in the habit of easing himself between the ice down into the River Neva, the shock of the water had never been that bad partly because it was warmer than the ice above and partly because he'd always been braced, expecting it. But the sudden noise he heard now in the passage outside almost gave him a heart attack. There was a crackle of short-wave radio, and then the man's voice, very close by, calling control. Routine Patrol, said the voice. Sector Five. He lay his weight against the door, his blood pounding. How long before the guard noticed the wet footprints? How long before the alert for a suspected intruder was flashed round the building? In the distance he heard a dog barking. Shit. Radios. Dogs. This was serious security. What were they protecting here, for God's sake? How many of them were there? He wanted to get out: and yet even now he was loath to do so without some trophy. Something to justify all the effort. Something to reassure himself that he was still in the fast track.

He eased the zip up on his bag and listened, tense.

He heard the guard's footsteps receding along the passage. Why hadn't the man seen the melted snow on the linoleum from Fedorov's boots and raised the alarm? He opened the door a fraction, and there was the answer: the guard himself must just have come in from outside, and his own feetmarks were mixed in with Fedorov's, destroying the evidence. Gratefully Fedorov saw his line of escape clear, and scampered back to the original office where he had come in. He closed the door quietly behind him and wriggled out of the window, landing with his face in the snow, the bag somehow having passed through with him. He stood up, dusted himself down, and edged back out of the courtyard into the street. It was snowing harder now. The imprint of footsteps would last no more than a few minutes before being lost forever.

He clutched the bag of icons to him and ran for it.

Here was Dimitry Abramovich Fedorov at his own front door. Fedorov wet and cold, with his wispy moustache almost frozen to his face, but Fedorov triumphant, a believer in his own myth: the bedraggled rodent elevated momentarily to King Rat. He pushed through the ramshackle doorway of the apartment block overlooking the Neva which has been his home off and on for the past two years. It had once been a very grand apartment block, two apartments per floor, ten rooms per apartment, high ceilings, elegant windows. But that had been many years ago. Now the ten-roomed apartment in which Fedorov had his base was home to seven other households as well, each household a separate human drama compartmentalised into its room or two, an uneasy community of nation states all craving independence yet forced to share the same sanitation.

He heard old Yashin coughing his guts out from the first door on the right and the music from the transistor radio that blared incessantly out of Madame Balushkin's quarters, drowning whatever liaison the fat old tart was conducting in there with the latest client too drunk or short-sighted to notice the difference. He tiptoed past the stertorous snoring of old Mrs Irinovsky, the poor old bat who eked out an existence on her forty dollars a month state pension, and had converted her room into some sort of shrine to her three-years-dead husband, the walls adorned with his photographs, his medals on display, even his underwear still not thrown away. And then he was at the door of his own room. He got out the key and braced himself for Ludmilla.

She was half undressed, lying on the bed reading a magazine and smoking a cigarette. She looked up, coarse-featured, abrasive. Sensual. She was taller than Fedorov. Certainly she weighed more. But that was part of her attraction. There was so much of her. Sometimes Fedorov thought he was going to drown in her.

'Are you crazy going out on a night like this? Look at the state of you.' But she didn't get up or help him out of his coat. She just took a drag on her cigarette and contemplated him through the smoke.

He didn't speak at once, but laid his bag carefully against the wall and went over to the stove to warm his hands. Taking his hat and coat off now and hanging them next to the stove, he said, casually: 'I've been doing business.'

'Business? What sort of business?'

He reached into the cupboard for the bottle of vodka. Kuslov's vodka. The seal of their deal. He poured himself some into a chipped glass and noticed as he did so that the bottle, over half full when he'd left this afternoon, was now three quarters empty. He wouldn't make an issue of it, he decided. Instead he said, 'Very good business, as it happens. I've got this new partner.'

'What, you mean you've found some other crooked bastard besides Igor to rip you off?'

The dumb bitch had got it all wrong, of course. She didn't understand he was in a faster track than Igor now. 'I don't let Igor rip me off.'

'How you can stand there and give me such crap I don't know. Letting him have those personal stereos for a hundred and twenty dollars. That's less than ten dollars each. You shouldn't be allowed out alone, you know that?'

Of course he'd had to say a hundred and twenty to her, hadn't he? If he'd told her the full three hundred she would have had most of it off him, wouldn't she? But he was uneasily aware that the price of his financial independence was a lowering of his competence in her eyes.

'Look,' he said, 'those stereos were difficult to place anywhere else. You don't know the full circumstances. But I tell you something: big changes are coming in my life. The guy I'm in with now, this Kuslov, he's promised me the best prices in town. He's renowned for it. And he's a big operator. You should see the size of his fucking Mercedes.'

'You don't get to drive a Mercedes through giving the best prices in town.'

'What do you know about it?'

'More than you do, anyway.' She flicked the pages of her magazine.

He poured himself more vodka and lit a cigarette. The action gave him time to consider the situation. Ludmilla had this knack of aggravating him but simultaneously imposing herself on him. Of course he knew bloody more than she did about how to handle men like Kuslov. But he needed her, so he wasn't going to make an issue of it. What he couldn't understand was why he needed her. She lay there like a fat doughball, smoking his cigarettes and drinking his vodka. Fat doughball spending his money. Fat doughball engulfing his body with her voluminous flesh, offering him a cheap-scented glimpse of paradise.

'I'm going for a piss,' he said a little later and set off on the well-worn route from their doorway to the evil-smelling lavatory at the end of the corridor. The sodding thing wouldn't flush. It was probably frozen again. He retraced his steps and realised he was very tired, ready for bed. On balance it hadn't been a bad day. The first day of his new, accelerating life.

When he got back he found Ludmilla sitting on the edge of the bed with his bag in her hands about to unzip it.

'What have you got in here, then?' she demanded.

'Icons,' he told her.

'What do you want with icons?'

'I'll get good money for them.'

'What, from your new friend? This famous Kuslov?'

'That's right. Kuslov. He's particularly asked me to lay hands on icons. He's got the market for them. Fucking controls it.'

Having executed this embroidery on the truth, he leant across and helped her pull the zip the whole way across and manoeuvre the contents out. She took a glance at them and frowned. Then she turned away. Disdainful. Wordless. No longer interested. For a moment the resentment bubbled to the surface and he felt like hitting her.

But it passed. Instead he slid into bed next to her and smoked a final cigarette, contemplating the discoloured, flaking paint on the ceiling. Later she reached to switch off the light and the last thing she murmured before she rolled over and went to sleep was, 'Bloody funny icons.'

TWO

The same December evening it was milder in Geneva, but there was still a nippy wind and rain in the air. Heinrich Stahler sat in the bar at the Hotel Richemond protected from the weather. He was rich enough to be protected from most unpleasantness, if he chose. He took a drink from his glass and contemplated his companion Kracht. He was intrigued by the man, simultaneously impressed and a little repelled.

Kracht, with his heavy spectacles, his untidy hair, and his cumbersome, overweight body, balanced uneasily on the chair, his brow furrowed in the effort of concealing his own oddness. Kracht was out of place here, ungainly amid this elegance, watchful as if at any moment he might make some maladroit movement and break something fine. Kracht belonged in an office, in front of a computer screen. He belonged on a telephone, in shirtsleeves and braces, or at the other end of a fax machine. Kracht should be heard and not seen. He sipped mineral water and blinked at the unfamiliar surroundings, like a badger caught in a car's headlight. Stahler reflected that he has never seen him drink alcohol. Normally Stahler had no patience with such abstinence, saw in it not strength but weakness. But Kracht was different. Stahler had never come across such an incisive brain. It was entirely plausible that alcohol could indeed impede its icy efficiency.

Stahler was svelte and self-possessed. His suit and tie were expensive. He was used to being looked at, to making a public impression. He was also a bully. He expected to be listened to rather than to do the listening. He had acquired the habit of unthinking self-assertion, and the impatience that goes with this presumption of leadership.

'So we find someone bribable,' he said. 'Buy them, you mean?'

'No.' Kracht spoke thoughtfully but with complete confidence. 'I think not, in this instance. Better that we look for an upright man.'

There was a novelty about being with Kracht. About being told things by this mountainous hobbledehoy that he hadn't thought of himself before. About tapping into someone else's intelligence and deriving benefit from it. 'An upright man?' queried Stahler.

'It's the upright ones who fall the hardest,' Kracht explained. 'The others, the ones who are used to slipping up, they have learned how to break their falls. Therefore they bruise less. We need a heavily bruised man, one whose sensitivity makes him malleable.'

'What do you mean by bruising here?' asked Stahler, setting down his Scotch on the table in front of him.

'I mean that we need to create in our man a certain susceptibility.'

'Susceptibility to what?'

Kracht paused. It was not that he was uncertain about the answer, merely that he seemed surprised that Stahler needed to ask the question. 'Guilt,' said Kracht. 'The need to make amends.'

Kracht knew. Kracht had experience of the darker side of men's minds, an instinct for the exploitation of their weaknesses. It all stemmed from knowing so much about money. If you understood as much about money as Kracht did, you were expert in one of the mainsprings of human motivation. It gave you a peculiar insight into desire. If Kracht were asked his profession, he would probably have answered 'accountant'. It would have been an utterly inadequate description of his talents, like classifying Tolstoy as a farmer or Hitler as a painter. Kracht had learned the art of human manipulation. He knew very well that this was why Stahler had turned to him, why Stahler was prepared to deploy his wealth to retain Kracht at an enormous fee to act for him. Kracht, besides being expert in every aspect of discreet commercial transaction, also had one further invaluable ability. He knew how to persuade people to do things against their will. The measure of his refinement was that he had learned when to achieve his aim by applying financial pressure, and when to exert compulsion of another kind.

'You see,' added Kracht, 'a man who has been bought is the servant of the highest bidder. In the end he is neither loyal nor reliable. But a man bound to you by the bond of guilt is yours completely. Yours, until you allow him expiation.'

'Do you have such a man in mind?' inquired Stahler. 'Have you identified someone suitable?'

Kracht nodded his large head slowly. 'I have had discreet inquiries made. I do not anticipate a difficulty.' He paused, then added, 'It is extraordinary how it is men, rather than women, who are the most truly vulnerable to flattery. There is never a shortage of raw material.' Kracht shrugged almost sadly, as if the knowledge gave him no comfort. It was just one more human weakness whose understanding gave him power, one more weapon in his secret armoury.

Stahler's patience was not limitless. He was a busy man. He had policies to formulate, orders to give, issues on which to pontificate. He had to catch the last flight back to Düsseldorf this evening. His driver was waiting outside.

'No shortage of upright men, then, here in Geneva?' he said with a little laugh. And he got up to go.

'I only need one,' Kracht assured him. 'One, suitably positioned. He is out there. In fact my people think they may have already found him.'

Alphonse Baugniet was that upright man. He was a model citizen in a country of model citizens. He lived in the Servette

17

region of the city, not far from the football ground. It was not a bad little house. It had four bedrooms and a small balcony. As he worked its neat handkerchief of garden on Sunday afternoons, he could hear the planes landing at Cointrin a few kilometres to the north, and he derived pleasure from their proximity. He was employed in the transportation industry, and he liked planes; he liked the romance and adventure that their inward and outward journeys brought to his life. The huge distances that they travelled gave a thrilling perspective to his imagination. He enjoyed handling the goods brought half way round the world. There was a satisfaction simply in the labels on the packing cases.

Baugniet was 45, married to a wife whom he worshipped, with whom he had three delightful children. He had always recognised that his wife was exceptional. Estelle Baugniet ran the household with exemplary efficiency; she brought the children up firmly but kindly. She did good works. She was a rock of dependability. There were those who even suggested that she was a modern-day saint. It is not always easy to be married to a saint, and mixed in with Alphonse's adoration of her was a certain reverence, sprinkled, perhaps, with a tiny seasoning of fear, the sort of fear felt by one human being as they become increasingly aware of their dependence upon another of demonstrably greater strength of character.

Estelle was religious, a good Catholic. She went to church every Sunday. Although there were times when he might have preferred to stay in bed, Baugniet generally found himself accompanying her. She was his moral conscience. It wasn't that she said anything. It was just the way she looked at him.

And she was an excellent mother. His children were testament to that. Baugniet exulted in them, in their physical and mental prowess. He relived his life through them, was able to recast his own shortcomings as their successes. Gabrielle's ability as a mathematician redeemed the memory of his own more pedestrian academic progress. He watched with pride as eleven-year-old Martin performed on the ski slopes for his school; he slalomed every corner with him on his triumphal progress to the prize that Baugniet himself had often aspired to and never won. And at eight, Marie-Christina's soft-skinned, doe-eyed beauty was a constant delight to him. Sometimes he sat at home watching the three of them as they watched television, marvelling at how lucky he was in them. These children were his monument. In them he had achieved the sort of fulfilment that others seek in their work or in their art, and he knew enough about life to recognise that such achievement is not given to every man.

His work? Yes, he was happy enough at his work. He was meticulous and industrious rather than inspired. He was never going to be the highest of flyers, but he took trouble over things in a business where detail mattered. He was chief foreman at the internationally renowned Geneva-based shipping and storage agents, Bartsch AG, where he organised the warehouses. He had been doing it for twenty years, and he was good at it. He could see his way round logistical problems quicker than most people. And he inspired confidence in clients, gave them a sense of his own appreciation of the value of their property. Equally important, he impressed them with his discretion. When you worked in the Free Port, as he did a lot of the time, clients especially valued discretion. Baugniet handled their secret things, the things that they wished to keep beyond the jurisdiction of the authorities. The Free Port was a place of sanctuary, an area set apart beyond the reach of the customs inspector, beyond the hands of the taxman, too. The people who moved in this shadowy hinterland, the clients who made use of its facilities were often nervous men, and Baugniet knew how to deal with them. Tactfully, gently. How to inspire in them trust in the ultimate security of their property.

Baugniet was a creature of habit. On Friday evenings he invariably went for a drink with a few of his workmates, in a ritualistic celebration of the imminent weekend. They would drive down to a bar called the Antelope, in the lee of the Central railway station. There he generally drank two glasses of wine. On one occasion he had drunk three, and upon his slightly later than usual return home had had to bear that look again from Estelle. That wounded, betrayed expression. Not that she had said anything. But nonetheless he had felt that he had somehow wronged her. And he had hated himself for it.

But this Friday was different. This Friday his wife had taken the children by car to Neuchatel to visit her brother. She was staying the night there. The next day was her brother's oldest son's first communion. Baugniet had agreed to join them for the ceremony next morning, got Estelle's dispensation not to make the journey till tomorrow. 'Come in the morning by train,' she had told him. 'You'll be tired on Friday after your day's work. Take it easy, have a good night's rest.' It meant that he was alone in the house tonight; alone in the house for the first time for as long as he could remember. So when Ricki, the longest-serving porter and his friend for fifteen years, asked him if he was ready to come down to the Antelope Bar, Baugniet's first thought was that for once he might with impunity allow himself that third glass.

By 8.30 he was actually on his fifth glass of wine. Ernesto the van driver was in the middle of an account of the extraordinary amounts of money his brother-in-law in Turin was raking in as an insurance salesman. Ernesto's existence was circumscribed by a range of relations whose financial success was greater than his own. At first Baugniet had read only envy into his colleague's stories; but latterly he had been inclined to wonder whether Ernesto was not in fact sustained by them, deriving vicarious glory from their telling. It was at this moment that Baugniet felt an unfamiliar hand on his arm.

He could not have said at what point she had come in with her friend and sat down at the table next to them. Certainly they had not been there when Baugniet and his party had arrived. But there she was now, touching him, demanding his attention: dark-haired, olive-skinned and long-legged; or maybe it was just that her leather skirt was very short. With a slow stirring of excitement, he dimly recognised her. It was the same woman that he'd noticed here last week, and even, come to think of it, the week before. He remembered her because on one occasion their eyes had met across the room, and he'd half imagined she was smiling at him. Last time he'd done nothing about it; but now she was actually next to him. He saw that she was in her early thirties; not beautiful, exactly, but sensual, with a wanton mouth.

Sensual. That was how she looked, anyway, to a forty-five-year-old man on his fifth glass of wine. On a Friday evening when his wife and children were safely packed away to Neuchatel.

She had a cigarette between her lips and was asking for a match. He had a lighter, and when he flicked flame to the tip, she thanked him. And winked. Winked, before going back to conversation with her friend.

'I think you're in there, mate,' Ricki announced in a whisper thick with alcohol and envy, and they laughed as men do in bars when they have just consumed their fifth glasses of wine.

Alphonse felt suddenly good. He felt young again. Elated, almost triumphant in his recaptured youth. Maybe his greying hair was thinning on top, but his body was still trim and muscular, kept in condition by the periodic necessity to roll up his own sleeves and shift heavy packing cases. He was aware of her now. He kept looking surreptitiously in her direction. A couple of times he caught her eye. She smiled back at him. And for a brief moment in her smile he glimpsed the thrilling new world opening up for him. A world in which you didn't get your kicks from merely reading the labels on the packing cases. A world in which you actually got to go to those exotic places yourself.

There was another bottle. There was the reluctant withdrawal of first Ricki then Paul, the senior clerk, summoned home by domestic duty. Only Ernesto was left, mumbling an unlikely story about a nephew in New York who was making a fortune at a merchant bank. Alphonse took the bottle in his hand and turned to her. 'Won't you both join us?' he said, looking only at the dark one. The dark one who fancied him.

It was madness, of course. A little later her blonde friend had gone home. Ernesto had gone home. Or rather he had departed to relieve himself and never come back. She was called Sandra, she said. They pulled their coats on and stumbled out of the bar together, into the back-street full of cheap hotels. She tottered and grabbed his arm to steady herself, giggling that the wine had gone straight to her head. 'You're going to have to be a gentleman and walk me home,' she told him.

When they got there she said he could come up and she'd make him some coffee as a reward. It was the least she could do. There didn't seem any reason to refuse. Once inside, he glanced about him, registering the open door to the bedroom, the pink shades on the bedside lights. He was surprised by how soon after she came back with the cups that she drew him on to the sofa and started kissing him. He could no more have stopped himself then than he could have stood in the path of an aircraft landing on the runway at Cointrin and turned it back.

She had a mirror set at right angles to the bed. Out of the corner of his eye he suddenly caught sight of himself, his naked white body straining against her body, her legs wrapped round him like a gymnast or an acrobat. It was suddenly unreal. That's not me, he assured himself. That's some actor in a film.

At his nephew's first communion in Neuchatel next day, he felt strangely divorced from himself, as if everything that had happened to him last night had indeed been no more than a film. True enough, he had a substantial hangover as tangible proof of a certain sort of excess. But the woman? Sandra? His involvement with her hovered in a no-man's land somewhere between fact and fantasy. He concentrated very hard. He sensed salvation in letting the memory of the evening uncouple from reality, in convincing himself that the sequence of events faintly recalled had not actually taken place. They were no more than some protracted erotic fantasy, an extended wet dream over which he was exonerated from any real responsibility. After all, was it likely that he, Alphonse Baugniet, happily married to a universally admired wife, blessed with three delightful children, would be standing here in the midst of his family at one of the holiest rites of the Catholic Church if but a few hours earlier he had been making passionate love to a casual pick-up from a bar? No, it was unthinkable. He clutched the back of the pew in front of him to steady himself. His wife reached out a gloved hand and covered his own in a momentary gesture of tenderness. He smiled quickly at her, and breathed a sigh. A sigh of expiation and relief.

By Monday the exercise in self-persuasion was all but complete. 'Oh, that girl?' he replied to Ricki's knowing inquiry with a dismissiveness that almost convinced himself. 'No, she left with her friend soon after you did.'

'Better luck next time,' leered Ricki.

Baugniet just shrugged and smiled and went on sorting out the shipping dockets he had in his hand. What was Ricki on about? He was a happily married man, for God's sake.

And then on Tuesday the photographs arrived.

They arrived at Baugniet's neat four-bedroomed house in Servette. They arrived in a plain brown envelope addressed to him, marked Personal. He opened it in the hallway as he was about to leave the front door for work.

There he was again, the man he had glimpsed in the mirror. His naked white body arched against hers in the squalid melee of the sheets. The cruel light cast by the cheap bedside lamp with the frilly pink shade illuminated his features with unforgiving clarity. There could be no dispute. The man in the photographs, his face sometimes contorted in a rictus of passion, at others slack with drunken stupidity, was unmistakably Alphonse Baugniet. Alphonse Baugniet, model citizen. Alphonse Baugniet, happily married father of three.

He stood there for a moment in the solitude of the hallway, unable to propel himself in any direction. The power of movement had temporarily gone from his legs. He felt sick at the grotesque intrusion into the dark places of his privacy that these photographs so effortlessly achieved. He felt sick at the idea that Estelle might conceivably have set eyes upon the contents of this envelope before him. In the past she had frequently opened his mail. She had always made it seem like one of the more delightful rites of marital intimacy. 'You don't mind, chéri, do you?' she had asked him. 'There are no secrets between us.'

But what struck him as most nauseating of all was the possibility that his children might somehow have seen these photographs. If they had laid unwitting hands on this slim brown package. If he hadn't by chance got to the letter box first.

And then finally he drew from the envelope the message, written in simple capitals on a cheap, otherwise unmarked piece of writing paper. In order to prevent wider circulation of these photographs, he was informed, he must ring a certain number in Geneva at four o'clock the following afternoon. At some point in the future, the owner of the negatives required from him a very small service, the details of which would be given to him. Once that service had been performed, the negatives would be destroyed.

He could rely on that destruction. He could trust that there the matter would end. Just so long as he did what was required of him.

Summoning every reserve of strength to his body, he pushed through the front door. He tried to call out his customary farewell as he departed, but no sound came. In silent concentration at the effort of putting one foot in front of the other, he walked slowly towards the car to drive to work.

*   *   *

When Kracht received the news, he grunted. He was not a great communicator, or rather he did not waste words, did not use them just for decoration. But the grunt indicated a reasonable level of satisfaction at the success of the enterprise so far. He was a patient man. He filed the information away for when it would be required, and poured himself another glass of mineral water.

PART TWO

February

THREE

London, in February: a cold, dead, damp month, when the sky presses down on the roofs of the city like a shroud, and the difference between night and morning is only a marginal shading from black into grey. A bad month for hangovers. Parnello Moran glanced out at the rain beating against his window, then unwound his tall, thin frame lengthways on to the sofa, arranging himself as horizontally as possible. He felt fragile. Lying back in the red-brocaded drawing room of his elegant but decaying Edwardian mansion flat, he tried not to think too much. From this flat, at the top of four flights of very steep steps in Jermyn Street, St James's, he ran a sporadic picture-dealing business. It was a bad month for selling things to people, too. He suspected that today was going to be one of his less dynamic days.

Beneath longish, unkempt fair hair, his face even in solitude wore a self-quizzical look, which was partly due to the way his unusual green eyes drooped naturally into that expression, and partly in acknowledgement of the essential irony of life, the absurdity of its perpetual frustrations. On the superficial level he liked to give the impression of taking nothing very seriously. This was to hide the fact that on another, deeper level he took everything much too seriously. Indeed, in certain moods he was inclined to see himself as the dying twentieth century's reincarnation of Lord Byron, waging an unequal struggle against a range of antagonists some of which would have been familiar to the great Romantic poet, others less so: duplicitous fellow-dealers, parking wardens, clients of irredeemably suburban taste, tax inspectors, and girl-friends who constantly misunderstood him.

It was nearly midday. Parnello reached for one of the cheap Spanish cigarettes which he habitually smoked as an antidote to the morning after. He lit it, and through the smoke ran a rheumy eye round the drawing room which doubled as his gallery, contemplating his stock, the works of art hanging discreetly for sale on the walls. They were good, his pictures. Above the fireplace was a magnificent early Corot, the landscape whose horizons, he'd recently told an uncomprehending Mr Kuprowsky of New Jersey, were 'deliquescing in its own pellucid atmosphere'. On one side of it hung an extraordinarily powerful Géricault, a macabre and shadowy little oil sketch of a tortured male nude wrestling with a serpent, and on the other a Delacroix watercolour, miraculously unfaded, showing two arabs squatting in a market place. Elsewhere there was a Boudin beach scene, an Edward Lear of Athens, and a Vuillard interior; in the drawers of his cabinet, lying in darkened, tissue-wrapped seclusion, were works on paper by Caspar David Friedrich, Tiepolo, and Gauguin, a wonderful study of the head of a Tahitian girl.

Around Parnello lay the debris of the night before. Dirty glasses, unemptied ashtrays, a half eaten smoked salmon sandwich. Across one chair was draped a woman's scarf, an expensive silk scarf he could connect with none of the guests he remembered. But now he came to think of it, a group of people, friends of friends, had turned up sometime after midnight and he had only a confused memory of how many, let alone of who they had been. Some evenings Parnello Moran demanded unbroken solitude, was fit company only for himself. And then there were others, like last night, when he needed people, when he threw parties, when the guests ranged from models to taxi-drivers, from tattooists to members of parliament. It was one of the ways of keeping February in London at bay.

He heard keys in his front door, followed by its slamming, and a few seconds later Brenda stood in his drawing room, taking off her wet coat, a cigarette clamped tenaciously between her heavily-painted lips. Brenda fulfilled a role in his life somewhere between secretary, charlady and analyst. She was an elderly woman of superb vulgarity and fathomless street-wisdom, the product of forty years' service as a West End actress's dresser.

'Blimey!' she exclaimed, still not removing her cigarette from her mouth. 'What happened here last night? Holding a rave, were you?'

'A few people came round.'

'Too much to expect that you could have done a bit of clearing up yourself, of course. And what's this?' She picked up the Hermes scarf. 'One of your fancy women, I suppose? Still here, is she?' She cast a hopeful glance in the direction of the bedroom door. For Brenda, life's justification was that it should imitate theatre. Existence could be conceived most satisfactorily in terms of a continuing comedy of sexual manners.

'I'm entirely alone, I assure you. More's the pity.'

She shook her head. 'It's squalid here, that's what it is. No woman in her right mind would want to spend the night here, anyway.' She bent to pick up a coffee cup which had upset its contents over a pile of auction catalogues. 'Strewth, Mr Moran, what a disgusting mess. And these are next week's New York old master sale catalogues. Have you looked at them yet?'

'Not yet,' he admitted.

'I don't know. I do what I can. It's not so much that you're helpless as unhelpable.'

'But it's not help I'm looking for.'

'What are you looking for, then?'

He inhaled deeply on his cheap Spanish cigarette. 'Passion,' he replied.

Brenda guffawed. She picked up an empty vodka bottle from the floor and contemplated it. 'You know what you've got, don't you? You've got a drink problem.'

'Look, it's not so much a drink problem as a life problem. Most people have it, in one form or another.'

'What you need is to organise your time better.'

'Please. Not another lecture. It's too early in the morning.'

'I mean it. I know for a fact that Lord Humber came round yesterday afternoon and you weren't in. There was a message on the answerphone. He probably would have bought your Edward Lear if he'd been able to see it.'

He shook his head and smiled back at her, gently, as if explaining something very simple to a child. 'Brenda, darling: I am not a shopkeeper.'

It was true: he was nothing so prosaic. If he believed in one thing, it was that the individual was more important than the system. That it was better to fail gloriously doing something eccentric than to wind up chairman of Unilever. His substantial private income was simultaneously an enabling and a corrupting force in this respect, allowing him to indulge his exceptional intelligence in the ever more abstruse, forever distracting him from the practicalities. He was recondite in the most unexpected and unproductive ways. He was an investigator of the hidden cul-de-sacs of history, his mind a repository of unlikely facts and fantasies. He was a compiler of lists: of eminent men of the twentieth century with famously large members; of Hollywood film stars who had also played first-class cricket; of nineteenth-century bibliophiles who had died falling off library steps. He could tell you which bird had the longest eyelashes and the name of the species of flea that had been the carrier of the Black Death to Britain. He was an expert in the only English artist of the eighteenth century to have been banned from the city of Florence for gross moral turpitude. And what fascinated him almost as much as the landscapes of Claude Lorraine was the fact that the painter had started life as a chef specialising in puff pastry.

'I must get on,' said Brenda, frowning at her watch. 'Do me a favour, will you?'

'What's that?'

'Have a look at these New York catalogues when they've dried off. You may be missing something.'

'I doubt it.'

'You won't know if you don't look.'

'You're a slavedriver.'

'Are you going out to lunch? You really should eat more, you know that?'

'Maybe later. I'm waiting for a call from America. A client.'

'I thought you said you weren't a shopkeeper.'

'I'm not,' said Parnello, stretching out his long body and yawning. 'I'm a "marchand-amateur".'

'What's that when it's at home?'

Parnello considered the question carefully. 'A man for whom passion is ultimately more important than money,' he told her.

'Oh, you mean a bankrupt,' said Brenda, and disappeared into the kitchen.

Twenty minutes later the client from New Jersey rang. Parnello, who had been dozing, sat up and composed himself before lifting the receiver. He could hear Brenda in the distance, clattering glasses.

'So, Mr Kuprowsky, have you had a chance to think about it?' Parnello spoke casually down the telephone. As if it didn't really matter one way or the other.

'I guess I have.'

'What do you feel?' It didn't do to pressurise, to threaten.

'Mr Moran, I've gotta tell you. That's one hell of a picture you've offered me.'

'It's beautiful, isn't it? The best early Corot I've ever had.'

But even then Parnello wasn't sure, had detected some reservation in the other man's tone. Art dealing is like angling. You spend long tracts of time immobile on the riverbank, your line baited, waiting. Maybe 'deliquescing horizons' had been the wrong bait in this case. Beyond a certain point, you can't force the issue, anyway. It's up to them. It's up to the fish. There's no telling when you'll get a bite, when the exquisite work of art that you have discreetly made available to a number of discriminating collectors will finally attract an offer. You have to be patient. Sometimes days and weeks go by without any movement, without any murmurs on the fly. And then you finally see it bobbling, you wind the line in, and what have you caught? A twelve pound pike, or a bit of riverweed?

'You see, Mr Moran, if it were just up to me I'd take that picture like a shot.'

Oh, God. That first uncertainty. It was going to be riverweed after all.

'Like a shot,' he repeated, then paused. Ominously. 'Problem is that Mona's not so keen.'

'Mona?'

'My wife. One determined lady, I can tell you. She wants something with a bit more colour in it. It doesn't fit the decor of our salon.'

'Would it help if I sent it over to you? So you could hang it up for a few days, live with it?'

'She's darned obstinate, Mr Moran. Believe me, once she's decided against something, she won't turn around. It's a shame, but there you go.'

'I'm sorry,' said Parnello, reflecting that one of the few advantages of having a wife would be the convenient excuse she often gave you for not doing something.

'There you go,' repeated the man. Like some sort of mantra. As if that made everything all right.

Parnello replaced the receiver and walked thoughtfully to the window. Then he shook his head, and poured out a small glass of vodka. He had promised it to himself as the telephone rang in celebration of a deal concluded. Now it seemed only right to drink it as a consolation. He leant on the window sill and reflected that there were aspects of his trade which jarred with his own character. He was a taker of risks, a follower of instinct. The inactivity of waiting, the passivity of subjecting yourself to the client's whim, was alien to his nature. But most of the time his sense of humour carried him through. That and the vodka bottle. He could still laugh. He didn't take it all too seriously. Most of the time.

He watched the rain falling outside, running in eager little rivulets down the glass, gathering in drops on rims, creating pools in crevices. This was an insistent, pervasive rain, seeking out the weak places in the guttering and brickwork, infiltrating the cracks and spreading damp where it had no right to penetrate. It induced an inertia, this rain, a seeping paralysis. From his vantage point he followed the progress of the tops of various umbrellas hurrying along Jermyn Street below. How had it happened, he asked himself? How had it come about that he, Parnello Moran, an intelligent thirty-five-year-old single male, for whom any number of worthwhile, fulfilling careers would have been viable, had ended up an art dealer? Ended up circumscribed by people who, if they had the discrimination to see that his pictures were glorious, lacked the wealth to acquire them, and, if they had the wealth, lacked the requisite discrimination?

'Pearls before swine,' he said out loud, and splashed a little more vodka into his glass.

It had been Marvel who had done it. A girl called Marvel Morenes.

She had deep brown Hispanic eyes and lustrous hair the colour of caramel. She was earnest, anxious and tenacious in the way that people are who take themselves desperately seriously. Imprisoned in the body of a voluptuary, she nursed the spirit of a neurotic librarian.

It was 1984, the year after he had come down from Cambridge garlanded with the honour of a first in English, but unable to work out for what career exactly this close familiarity with the Romantic poets in general and minute knowledge of Lord Byron in particular had actually prepared him. 'A man must travel, and turmoil, or there is no existence,' wrote Byron. Parnello was inclined to agree. So he had traversed South America, working first in a bar in Valparaiso and then driving a taxi in Caracas. There had even been a short period employed in an abbatoir in Mexico City. He had ended up, like so many others in feckless pursuit of their own identities, on the west coast of America.

'Would you agree that the gap between aspiration and achievement is the essence of all tragedy?' Marvel demanded of him over a drink in a bar in Venice. Venice, California.

'I'd say it was the essence of all comedy,' he told her.

'That's typical of you, you'll never take anything seriously, will you?' She paused, angrier than she wanted to admit. 'And Parnello? What kind of a name is that, anyway?'

He considered pointing out the incongruity of this question coming from someone christened Marvel, but he did not want to provoke her. 'It's Irish,' he says. 'An ancestor of mine acquired it on the Grand Tour to Italy about 1770. He set off from Donegal just plain Parnell. When he got back he was so transfixed by all things Italian that he'd become Parnello. My mother came across the name in the family annals and rather liked it, so she revived it for me.'

She frowned. Marvel did a lot of frowning.

'You're a funny guy, you know that?' she informed him. 'Don't tell me: you're Aquarius, aren't you?'

Parnello paused. He was Capricorn, but he didn't want to upset her. 'How did you guess?' he smiled at her.

'I always know,' she sighed, Cassandra-like.

He arranged to meet her on the steps of the Los Angeles County Museum the next day, but couldn't remember whether he'd said two or four o'clock. When she wasn't there at two, he decided to go inside and have a look around. He could not recall ever having voluntarily gone into a picture gallery before. It wasn't that he had any particular preconceived antipathy for art: merely that his education had been literary rather than visual, to do with words rather than images. He had never properly looked at pictures; there was no tradition of it in his academic genes.

His grandparents' house in Ireland was hung with tenebrous family portraits at which no-one ever granted more than the most cursory of glances. The scholarly discipline for which such things might constitute the raw material would only have been conceivable to him as some debased form of the pure metal of the study of history.

But the paintings he saw now were suddenly fascinating. Their impact was aesthetic rather than intellectual. The revelation which they brought to him was that artists had different and distinctive handwritings, that they handled paint in as personal and idiosyncratic a way as other people inscribed words in pen on a page. He could tell at once why these two Rubenses were both by Rubens. They were by the same man because both were executed in the same unmistakable handwriting.

He told Marvel about it when she turned up at four. She was majoring in the history of art, and became rather proprietorial about the pictures when Parnello started holding forth about them. There was a loan exhibition of nineteenth century French painting on view, and he showed her a Géricault of a horse in a stable which he maintained could not be genuine.

'Why?' she demanded.

'Because it's not by the same artist as this one,' he said, indicating a prancing horse taut with nervous energy, the sheen of its flanks rendered in a flickering salvo of brush-strokes. 'This one says it's by Géricault, too, and I presume it must be, because it's so bloody good.'

'So you know better than the curators, huh?'

'I think I probably do.' He smiled back at her. She was clever enough to suspect irony in his tone, but not quite clever enough to realise that on this occasion there wasn't any.

'Where can I see more of these?' he asked her.

'What, works by Géricault?'

'Yes, and Delacroix, too. All this amazing Romanticism. It's like Byron in paint.'

'You could try the Louvre.' Marvel offered the information with a studied casualness which betrayed a secret pride in her own expertise.

'In Paris?'

'In Paris, France.'

'So let's go there.'

'What, now? Today?'

'Why not? There's probably a flight tonight. We could be having dinner in Montmartre tomorrow.'

'Jesus, you're not kidding, are you?'

Parnello shook his head. He would have been the first to acknowledge that such spur-of-the-moment decisions were easier for him since his grandfather had died six months ago and left him a substantial amount of money. But he probably would have done it any way.

He took off alone that evening. He was sad to leave Marvel behind, but on the other hand it had become clear to him that this was one more girl from whom parting was inevitable sooner rather than later. One more girl who didn't really understand him. But he was grateful to her, too, in a way, because through her something else had become clearer to him: that he wanted to be involved with pictures. That the works themselves were of riveting fascination. That he had a talent for them. That he had an 'eye'. Perhaps he even sensed then that what he'd been through so far in his life, the haggling with customers in his cab in Caracas, the lotus-eating in Beverly Hills, the moment of revelation in the Los Angeles County Museum, these were all part of a preparation for something. Perhaps it was already inevitable that he would become an art dealer. What other way of life, short of becoming a mercenary, would have offered him the opportunity to continue to travel – and turmoil – without which Byron said there was no existence?

The strange thing was that Marvel had become an art dealer, too. In 1986 she had moved to New York and, armed with a wad of transparencies of other people's pictures, set up in a gallery on East 79th Street. He had come across her

again at an auction in Monaco three years
frowned a lot. She was still inclined to assert he
by turning the conversation at every opportunity
issues. But she was doing rather well. Her tenacity
in good stead.

Parnello turned away from his window in Jermyn Street. It
was half past twelve: too late in the morning to dispel his
disappointment in the baiting of another line and its casting
out upon the waters. It was a dead, wet day. He was inclined
to spend the rest of it reading a novel, or perhaps going to
the cinema round the corner in Piccadilly. He lay back down
on the sofa, but then, his conscience pricked by the sound of
Brenda singing tunelessly as she hoovered in the bedroom,
he reached out for the New York catalogue. It was still sticky
from the coffee but he began to look through it. Simply to
pass the time.

He was not methodical. He subscribed to the catalogues for
all the main picture sales in both London and New York, but
he didn't necessarily look at them. Sometimes Brenda filed
them away unread, past their sell-by date. Parnello reflected
that there are few things so ephemeral as an auction catalogue;
before the date of the sale which it advertises it is a repository
of dreams, of fantasy, of speculation: which ill-considered
trifle will transmogrify into a masterpiece; which masterpiece
through someone's chance stroke of good fortune will be
acquired for a pittance? But once the hammer has fallen
on the final lot, the auction catalogue dies. Its corpse is
embalmed as a document of record, but the spirit has gone
from it, the fantasy evaporated. The picture in the catalogue
that you notice and fall in love with after the sale has taken
place is a woman you will never possess satisfactorily. If
you do manage later to track her down, the moment has
passed. She is devalued through having been spotted first
by someone else, having passed through their hands. Her
freshness is gone; she is tainted.

The sale was in four days' time. He leafed through the

39

pages casually, with relief that his eye did not fall upon anything demanding attention or action.

Until lot 147.

It was only a black and white illustration, a small one, too, just a quarter of the page, but the moment he noticed it he took his feet from the sofa arm and sat up to look at it more closely. There was a shock of recognition, like seeing a familiar face suddenly in a large crowd of otherwise anonymous people. His eye was drawn to it instantly.

First of all, the subject was intriguing: a bend in a river, one bank of which rose up steeply into a wooded hillside. Exquisitely situated towards the top of the hill was an elegant villa with a balustraded balcony. You could tell the view from that balcony was sensational, over the river and across the plain to the right, the plain chequered with fields in which untended bonfires burned beneath a setting sun. On the river itself a ferry worked a laboured passage, manned by two perspiring men in breeches. Vespertine. That was the word to describe the elegiac quality of this evening light.

German School, early nineteenth century. That was the catalogue description. The date at least was accurate: from the costume of the ferrymen, from the way the paint was handled, Parnello put it at about 1820. But that was as far as the auction house's experts had got. They had peered at this unsigned picture, studied it briefly, probably turned it over to see if there was any name inscribed upon its reverse, and, finding nothing, had put it to one side undeciphered, nameless, without even an attribution to an artist. Parnello's heart gave a little butterfly beat of excitement. He knew. He had extracted the single envelope from a bundle of letters and known who it was from without opening it. Known from the handwriting.

German School, early nineteenth century. They were half right in its nationality. This was the work of Johan Christian Clausen Dahl, born in Norway in 1788 but a pupil of the great German Romantic painter, Caspar David Friedrich in Dresden. From then on Dahl painted largely in Germany.

40

Obscure; but not that obscure. An artist for whom collectors – and even museums – might compete. Once that artist had been identified. It was ironic the way a picture's merits were increased by attribution, thrown into higher relief by the knowledge of the individual creative force which shaped them. And Dahl was no mean painter. He had the romantic's innocent entrancement with nature, the awed wonder at nature's extremest manifestations. Parnello remembered a spectacular eruption of Vesuvius, and a cascading mountain river plunging vertiginously over gigantic rocks. This was the landscape of the artist's imagination. These things he painted well. With feeling.

Parnello ran his eye down the entry for lot 147, checking, praying that the cataloguer had not noted any chance piece of information which would give the game away. No, the cataloguing was reassuringly bland: German School, early nineteenth century. A river landscape with a ferry, oil on panel, 48 by 61 centimetres. No provenance recorded; no exhibitions; no literary references. A victim of historical negligence, a picture fated to sink in the sea of ignorance. Until Parnello had noticed it.

He was the salvage expert. He was the man who could dredge it back from the seabed and restore its identity.

Then there was the business side of the proposition, the estimate published below the catalogue entry. Eight to twelve thousand dollars, he read. A fence-sitting estimate, an estimate which lacked the courage of its conviction. An estimate that was both too much and too little, acknowledging the quality of the execution without admitting to the fantasy of who might actually have painted it. An estimate to set Parnello's pulse racing. If this was indeed an undisputed work by Dahl, then Parnello had an intelligent idea of what he could sell it for: something in excess of 100,000 dollars. But in order to achieve that price, the attribution must be cast-iron.

Parnello knew it was right, knew it was genuine. But he also knew that he needed more conclusive evidence than his own instinct to satisfy the doubting punters. To satisfy the Kuprowskys of this world.

He took his coat and prepared to set out into the rain.

'Where are you off to?' demanded Brenda from the kitchen where she was leaning against the fridge, still smoking indolently. 'Sneaking off to some love-nest, I suppose?'

'You keep your disreputable fantasies to yourself.'

'Hark at him, all prim and proper. But I know what you get up to. Fancy-women all over Belgravia.'

'I'm actually off to do some research.'

'Is that what they call it now?'

'I'm going to the Courtauld Institute.'

'Oooh, the Courtauld Institute. So the Rapacious Knight of Commerce is off to plunder the Sleepy Virgins of Academia.'

'I suppose you could put it like that.'

Brenda's trouble was she couldn't quite decide whether she was Shakespearian or vaudeville. Dame Edith Evans or Barbara Windsor.

'You men, you're all the same,' she called fondly after Parnello as he closed the door behind him and trotted down the stairs.

It was still raining heavily. He walked through the puddles along the borders of Soho and Covent Garden, heading towards Somerset House. As he crossed Aldwych, he caught the brief tang of the river in his nostrils, heard the distant calling of seagulls even over the throb of the traffic. For a moment he was reminded of distant ports, of Valparaiso, and he felt a shot of neat wanderlust surge through his veins. Then he passed through the gateway of the Courtauld Institute and loped down the stairs to the Witt Library.

Pushing through a doorway, he was there. In amongst the green box-files, shelf upon shelf of them, stretching into chamber after chamber, storey after storey, organised by nationality and filed alphabetically under artist's name. This was a library of images, of photographs of paintings. A record of just about every painting in the world that had ever been photographed. You had the feeling that if you delved here long enough, all mysteries might finally be solved, all deceptions uncovered. Except perhaps the ultimate deception, the illusion of the eye into seeing reality in paint.

It was just a question of knowing where to look. And that he did know now. He was set on one thing: the confirmation of his instinct. He found the Scandinavian section, and then the green box marked 'J. C. C. Dahl, horizontal landscapes with rivers'. He carried it away to a private alcove where he drew up a chair to a table and set himself to examine each photograph in the file.

There were a large number of them, photographs from museum archives, from auction and exhibition catalogues, from fine art magazines; photographs of a wide variety of qualities and ages, too. Each one was pasted on to a separate A4 sized card, and inscribed below with the details of the picture shown. Each one was a piece in the huge jigsaw that was an artist's oeuvre, his total artistic output. Get the jigsaw right, and you understood the artist. His life. His aspirations. And how far short of them his achievement fell.

He flipped through many views of rivers, most often the Elbe. Sometimes the distinctive skyline of the lovely city of Dresden featured, sometimes other unidentified groups of buildings. And when he came across it, the image he was seeking was attached to one of the oldest pieces of card there, and the photograph itself looked faded, cut from a yellowing catalogue. But it was clear enough to see that it was the same picture as lot 147 from next week's New York sale, he was sure of it. There was the house, set in the wooded hillside. There were the perspiring ferrymen, and the smoking bonfires. More important, the measurements corresponded, and the fact that the picture was painted on panel. Parnello pulled the New York catalogue from his pocket and opened it up to check: yes, there could be no doubt. The wispy patterning of brushstrokes transcribing scudding clouds across the setting sun were identical. Not just the same handwriting, but the same picture. You couldn't duplicate exactly that chance delicacy of brushwork, that arbitrary felicity of the handling of paint.

Where had this illustration come from? He looked about him. No-one moved in this area of the library. Twenty yards away, barely visible in her alcove, a girl bent studiously over her work. She wasn't looking in his direction. Surreptitiously he prised a little of the photograph away from the card, until he was able to read what was printed on the reverse. It was in German. Weber, Berlin, he could make out: that was the auction house. And there was the sale date, 23rd May 1931. An auction catalogue, then, and the number 34 printed beneath the photograph was presumably the lot number of this picture in that sale. Parnello made a note of all this information, and then sat back and thought it out.

Weber, Berlin, in 1931. A highly reputable auction house of the time. Who had been the seller, he wondered? How much had the picture made? Who had borne it home in triumph after the fall of the hammer? The answers to those questions would have to wait. But at least he knew now. He had had his instinct confirmed. The pre-war Berlin sale provenance established it. Lot 147 in the upcoming New York auction, catalogued simply as German School, nineteenth century, was actually the work of Johan Christian Clausen Dahl.

He heard soft footsteps behind him and hurriedly slid the card back into its folder and closed the file. He turned round as casually as he could and said, 'Hallo, Shagger.' The man was heavily built, shrouded in an opulent overcoat, and yet there was something feline about the softness of his movement. He stopped and leaned against the shelf marked 'Scandinavian, D-F', contemplating Parnello, sizing him up.

'Wotcha mate,' he said. The cockney was an affectation. Shagger actually hailed from a family of perfectly respectable stockbrokers in Surrey, but he liked to operate from behind such facades. 'On to something, are you?'

'On to something?'

'Made a discovery, have you?' Shagger gestured to the file.

'Could be,' said Parnello brightly. As he spoke he slid the New York catalogue deeper into his coat pocket.

'Going to make you loads of wonga?'

'Loads of it.'

'Fancy cutting me in for a half share?'

'I hadn't thought of it, no.' Parnello gave him an amused grin.

Shagger nodded. Digesting the information.

'Don't blame you, I suppose,' he admitted. There was a pause. 'So are you going to New York next week?'

'I haven't decided yet.'

'Anything you fancy in the sales?'

'Not specially. How about you?'

Shagger shrugged. 'Load of crap, old son, if you ask me. It's a bloody disgrace how those auction houses get away with calling their sales "Important" when they're stuffed full of such dead-beat pictures.' He laughed, but his eyes were watching Parnello carefully, trying to read him.

Parnello smiled back at him. 'Outrageous,' he said. 'So you won't be going over yourself, then?'

It was a game, they both knew it. Shagger assumed an expression of heavy responsibility. 'I might have to go and execute a couple of bids for clients. I'm not sure yet.'

'So we may see each other there, then. Or we may not.'

Shagger sighed and shook his head. 'Do you know something, Moran? You can be a shifty bastard when you put your mind to it.'

'Shifty?'

'You look as though you're hiding something, my son.'

Parnello laughed. 'I'm not hiding anything from you, my dear Shagger. I'm an open book, I assure you.'

'Bloody Irish. Charm the birds of the trees, wouldn't you?' But there was a sneaking regard in Shagger's tone. If there was one thing that Shagger responded to in life it was deception. He was a connoisseur of the feints and dummies of the art world, its bluffs and intrigues. That was what made him such a good dealer. Parnello liked him, had done business with him in the past. But he knew you had to watch him.

Parnello got up and walked over to replace the file. He didn't hurry. Only when it was back on its shelf did he glance at his watch. 'Is that the time? I must be on my way. And don't let me keep you from your massage parlour.'

As he sauntered back up the stairs he felt suddenly elated. His grasp tightened round the catalogue in his overcoat pocket. Possessively. It was absurd, really. It was only a painting. But it was his. His discovery. And for the moment its acquisition was more important than anything else in the world.

It wasn't so much the money. It was the thrill of an incipient passion. The thrill which, rather like the excitement at the start of a love-affair, made it difficult to tell whether he had found the object of his desire or if, in some mysterious way beyond his immediate comprehension, it had found him.

FOUR

Parnello watched the girl curiously, with a kind of proprietorial jealousy. Not so much because of her, but more because of what she was looking at.

He tried to reassure himself that there were, of course, any number of innocent reasons why a spectator might stop in front of a picture on public exhibition in a pre-sale viewing at a leading New York auction house. He himself had arrived in the galleries a few minutes before, and circled the rooms with every affectation of nonchalance. Out of the corner of his eye he had caught sight of the Dahl. But he had deliberately not gone up to it at once. He had ambled round neighbouring pictures, feigning interest in them, as if engaged in some arcane courtship ritual with the true object of his attention. And then when he finally returned to the alcove where the river landscape with a ferry was hanging, he had found her in the way, peering at it, obstructing his view. He retreated again, keeping her in his line of vision. Her interest in the picture meant nothing, of course; but he felt a mild unease that someone so attractive should by her proximity to the work be drawing attention to it. If Shagger Parks came in now his eye would inevitably be drawn to her, and by extension to the painting she was looking at, the painting whose anonymity Parnello was so anxious to protect.

She was tall and fair, and wore a dark blue jacket over a polo-neck and tight black trousers. As she bent forward to look closer at the panel, she fingered a strand of long blond hair back behind her ear. From where he was standing, twenty feet away, pretending to examine an undistinguished Italian landscape, he wondered idly how old she was. Late twenties, perhaps. Not more than thirty, anyway. Of course she was attractive, but he knew her type: healthy, clean-limbed. Too perfect. Her smile would reveal a set of gleaming white, immaculately architectured teeth. Her laughter would be a substitute for a point of view. He provisionally put her down as a girl with a job on the fringes of the art world. A receptionist in a Madison Avenue gallery, perhaps, whiling away her lunch hour in the saleroom. Normally she would have had a date, with a girlfriend or an admirer. Other lunchtimes maybe she worked out in the gym. But today she had come here, and her eye had been caught by the Dahl. Parnello's Dahl. Why? he wondered. Maybe it was the frame. Maybe it was the landscape. Maybe there was something about the bend in the Elbe that reminded her of her grandparents' house near Rhinebeck on the Hudson River.

He moved on to the next room to browse amongst the other pictures in the sale. Surrounded by paintings, he was in his metier, absorbed, fulfilled. Here he could bring to bear his 'eye', his outstanding gifts of visual discernment, analysing passages of paint, detecting similarities, recognising characteristics, summoning up from his extraordinary visual memory significant points of comparison by which to verify or disprove attributions. He paused at a little David Teniers interior. It was very worn. The signature was probably strengthened by a later restorer. But on balance he was prepared to believe that it was genuine. Or had been, many years ago. But it didn't interest him, not this routine view of peasants carousing in a tavern. The handwriting was authentic, but the content was dull and repetitive. It was like receiving a letter from a familiar correspondent and finding he had nothing to say.

Parnello turned the pages of the sale catalogue once more, and took momentary pleasure in its distinctively archaic terminology. By deep-rooted auction house tradition, the subject matter of old master pictures must always be described in its own unchanging language. There were winter landscapes, river landscapes, harvest landscapes; they could be wooded, mountainous, or coastal, Italianate, classical or capriccio; when particularly panoramic they were deemed extensive; their populations – staffages, rather – comprised countryfolk, rustics, cowherds, shepherds and ferrymen. In taverns and inns, peasants caroused or made merry, while outdoors disreputable dogs 'favoured' treestumps. Further up the social scale, elegant companies held levees, banqueted, or ranged the countryside as hunting parties. History melted into mythology: here were beggars and bacchantes, alchemists and sportsmen, clerics and quack doctors. Magdalenes were penitent, Scipios were continent and Venuses recumbent. Nymphs were surprised by satyrs and putti disported in painted cartouches. Thus an Arcadia was brought to life, here in the unlikely surroundings of upper East side Manhattan. Thus the past asserted its power over the present.

He closed the catalogue and turned back into the first room to see if she was still there. No. She had gone. He felt relief, and simultaneously an absurd murmur of regret. Now. At last. He wandered back to the Dahl and ran his eyes over it, furtively, as if he himself were being watched. There was no doubt about it. The picture was all that he had hoped it would be. The handwriting gave it away. The handwriting in paint again. What he had not been prepared for was the beauty of the colouring. The landscape was suffused with the crimson glow of sunset, tinging the clouds, reflecting in the water of the river. It was romantic. Elegaic. Vespertine. And when he turned it over to look at the back of the panel, he found something else. Something exciting. On a small, yellowed label, in a distinctively Germanic script was written in faded ink the number 34. Insignificant at first sight. Unless you happened to have seen the catalogue of a sale held at Weber in Berlin in May 1931. And remembered the lot number of the Dahl offered then. 34.

There was other writing, too, on the reverse, scribbled in

pencil directly on to the very wood of the panel. Parnello strained to decipher it, holding it so that the light raked across it reflecting in the shiny surface of the spidery lead lines. 'Links neben dem Kamin im Arbeitszimmer,' he read. For a moment he thought he had stumbled upon some topographical identification of the scene depicted. Then he smiled to himself. It translated as 'left of fireplace, study'. It was no more than a notation of where in some long-forgotten room the picture had once hung. Some long-forgotten room, whose geography was for a fleeting moment brought poignantly to life.

Parnello left the auction house, running down the stairs to street level. The February air was bitter as he pulled his coat about him and hurried across town towards Fifth Avenue. But he felt a surge of pure excitement; the excitement of the jagged silhouette of the New York skyline, the breathtaking vertigo of all that glass. It was the excitement of being in a different city, on another continent. The satisfaction of his craving to travel. Last night, as the taxi swung across the Triborough Bridge, Manhattan had come into view lit up across the water, the same gigantic, impossibly beautiful stage-set, an infinity of coloured lights in serried ranks held at different levels like some celestial bar chart. Here was a man-made wonder to set against any of nature's, the ultimate triumph of the artificial over the natural landscape. A subject to tempt a modern Romantic, perhaps. A subject for the brush of a latter-day Dahl.

They had arranged to meet at nine at an Italian restaurant in Greenwich village.

'There'll be a bunch of people joining us,' she had said on the telephone. 'You don't mind, do you?'

'Marvel, it will be a pleasure to see you again. And to meet your friends.'

She was alone as he arrived in the restaurant; he caught her snapping shut a mobile telephone and surreptitiously sliding a transparency back into her Louis Vuitton bag.

'Do you never rest?' he asked as he kissed her and took a

seat. 'Still doing business at this hour? I'm very impressed.' Her figure was thinner now, less voluptuous; as she removed her spectacles, he saw that the frown lines had become more deeply etched on her face, and her mouth was set harder.

She shook her head. 'Jesus,' she said, 'why are the only clients I get to deal with all such walking personality disorders?'

'No-one ever said art dealing was easy.'

'I'm offering this guy this Sisley, right? It's not as if he can't afford it, he just sold his pharmaceutical business last year for 650 million bucks. I'm only asking seven hundred thousand. But everything's a problem for him: the price, the condition, the size, the colours. And you know what he just asked me? He said, "How come this guy Alfred Sisley's a French Impressionist when he's got a British name?" '

'Maybe you're not asking enough?'

She glanced up at him, horrified at the suggestion. When she saw he was laughing, she allowed herself a brief smile.

'There's a name for my condition, you know,' she said.

'What's that?'

'Client abrasion.'

'I recognise it, it's painful. What's the treatment?'

'I don't know. Intravenous prozac?'

'Let me apply a little alternative medication.' He refilled her wine glass. She drank.

'So how are you?' she asked him.

He swept back the straggling strands of hair that had fallen forward over his eyes and began to tell her, in a general sort of way. About life in London. His flat in Jermyn Street. The pictures he was handling. Not about the Dahl, though. That was his secret. But she wasn't really listening, anyway. He could tell. Her mind was still on the Sisley.

A few minutes later two more people arrived. A husband and wife, introduced as Ryder and Nancy Onslow. He was short and tubby, but with the sort of surface sleekness that is the hallmark of wealth. She was in her early forties, marginally younger than her husband, a thin, opulent, immaculately groomed woman. There was a disrobing of expensive coats.

'Ryder and Nancy are my good friends and clients,' explained Marvel. They're mine, she was warning him. Don't even think of trying to sell them any of your pictures, OK?

Parnello shook hands. 'Marvel was just explaining how all her clients suffer from personality disorders. What a pleasure to meet the exceptions.'

Marvel frowned. Nancy looked momentarily perplexed, but her husband laughed. 'On the contrary,' he said, 'I'm right up there with the worst of them. In my case it's egotism, monstrous egotism.'

Parnello warmed to him at once.

'So who are we waiting for?' asked Nancy, regarding the fifth place at the table.

'Humphrey's joining us.'

'Humphrey?' asked Parnello.

'Yeah, Humphrey Gardener.'

'Oh, that Humphrey.' The head of the auction house old master department was a professional Englishman in New York. Parnello had first met him twelve years ago, in London. At that time Humphrey had been a diffident, scholarly figure, recently emerged from the Courtauld Institute, fond of ill-fitting sweaters and apparently owning only one pair of shoes, scuffed and upturned at the ends. Periodically Parnello had observed his development in the decade since his posting to America. Humphrey had left London speaking with a flat, neutral accent, here and there inflected by his native East Anglia. But his arrival in New York had intensified the Englishness of his voice, rounded it out into the plummy drawl that was now the delight of a hundred Park Avenue hostesses. His wardrobe had expanded too: immaculately cut Savile Row suits combined with florid bow ties, shoes exquisitely cobbled in St James's, all calculated to suggest a background of European, specifically British grandeur. In the hothouse of Manhattan he had bloomed like some flamboyant flower, a flower about which there lingered nonetheless the faintest suspicion of artificial colouring.

'My dear chap,' effused Humphrey to Parnello when he arrived soon afterwards. 'Simply splendid to see you.'

'And you, Humphrey.'

Humphrey kissed Marvel, and shook hands with Nancy and Ryder. 'I take it you're over for the sales,' he said to Parnello.

'I've had a look round.'

'We've got some particularly good things this time, don't you agree?' Humphrey surreptitiously examined his hair in the reflection of his knife and smoothed it into place. 'Isn't the Vernet a dream? It's a variant of the Chatsworth picture.'

'And there's another version in the St Simon Collection, of course.'

'Of course,' agreed Humphrey, vaguely. Parnello smiled to himself. The St Simon Collection was his own spur-of-the-moment invention.

'So what lots are the boys in the trade getting excited about?' probed Parnello. 'What's going to do well?'

'Oh, they all like the Vernet, that'll sail away.' Humphrey took a sip of wine. 'Then there's the group of Dutch pictures from the Ostreicher estate. Sublime little van Goyen.'

'And which one's the sleeper?' Now was the moment that Humphrey might be tempted into a revelation of uncertainty. If he had any. Perhaps to gauge Parnello's own reaction to the lot in question.

But Humphrey smiled at him with an expression of exquisite smugness. 'I don't think you'll find sleepers in my sale.'

Parnello grinned back. 'Maybe you're right.' He felt the Dahl securer in his grasp. Humphrey wasn't a fool. He just didn't know about Dahl. And no-one else had voiced to him speculation about lot 147.

'Will someone tell me what a sleeper is?' demanded Ryder.

'A sleeper is a picture by a desirable artist that passes unattributed through a sale,' said Marvel authoritatively. 'It's the one the auctioneers don't spot.' She still took pleasure in the display of her own expertise.

'In that case I guess that Humphrey would be the last person who'd be able to answer your question,' said Ryder to Parnello. 'Given that he was presumably responsible for the cataloguing of the sale.'

'That's not entirely true, if I may say so,' objected Humphrey, wrapping a blanket of advance cover about himself against any imputation of incompetence. 'Sometimes the best way to achieve the highest price is deliberately to underplay a picture. Then the trade think they've made a discovery, fall over themselves to bid on it and it ends up making more than it's worth.'

'I like that term "sleeper",' mused Ryder. 'It could apply to people as well as pictures.'

'What, you mean someone who amounts to more than they seem?'

'That. Or someone going through life in disguise. Someone with secrets to hide.'

Later Humphrey announced that he felt like champagne. 'You'll all join me, I hope. You'll have some, won't you, Marvel?'

Parnello watched Humphrey's hand stray across to rest lingeringly on Marvel's knee. Marvel continued to frown but did not immediately dislodge it. Perhaps she was still preoccupied with the recalcitrant buyer of her Sisley. Humphrey had always been a groper, remembered Parnello. A surreptitious fondler of secretaries in elevators. A man now so convinced of his own significance as to have constructed a myth of his own physical desirability.

Humphrey's eloquence was stimulated by the champagne. He proposed a toast to Marvel and Nancy, complimenting them on their wit and beauty. Parnello, feeling benign, proposed a further toast to the success of Humphrey's old master sale. Then Ryder raised his glass and drank to personality disorders.

Ryder, it emerged, was a historian. He lectured at Columbia University on the European twentieth century, specialising in German history.

'And does academic life allow enough opportunity for the expression of your monstrous egotism?' asked Parnello.

Ryder laughed. 'But of course: it's the perfect arena. I am paid to hold forth to all those eager young students who hang on my every word. I get to believe I'm divine. And then I'm supported by my wife's fabulous wealth. It all adds up to man's ultimate dream: power without responsibility.'

'You talk a lot of nonsense, Ryder,' said his wife fondly.

'Lucky devil,' drawled Humphrey, lacing his words with an urbane self-mockery. 'My professional life seems increasingly to consist of responsibility without power.'

'But while we're on the subject,' said Ryder to Parnello, 'you haven't told us what your own personality disorder is?'

'Maybe I haven't got one,' suggested Parnello. 'Maybe that's the reason why I could never aspire to becoming Marvel's client.'

'That's something you can't be allowed to get away with,' Marvel interrupted. 'Parnello Moran's got a personality disorder all right. His trouble is he can't take anything seriously.'

But Marvel was wrong. There were some things he took seriously. As he settled himself into the cab for the long journey back uptown to his hotel, he watched the teens of the cross-hatched streets turning into twenties and remembered what had happened that afternoon. Just before the saleroom closed, he'd gone back there for a final inspection of lot 147, a criminal revisiting the scene of his imminent crime, an illicit lover keeping a secret assignation. When he turned the corner to the alcove in which the picture hung, there she had been again. The tall, long-legged blonde girl. Leaning forward, looking at it intently.

At ten minutes past four: an inexplicably long lunch hour.

She'd realised she was being watched, and glanced sideways at him before walking off towards the exit. She could not help moving gracefully, but there was a resentment in her step, as if she was half inclined to turn back and remonstrate. As if the roles had been reversed from this morning, and she now treated his presence as an intrusion into something she regarded as her own personal, private preserve.

He'd been wrong about her. Her interest in this picture was more than casual.

More than casual. And yet not merely acquisitive, either. Parnello had watched many women standing in front of paintings that they want to buy. As status symbols. As items of decoration. Or simply as objects with which they had fallen in love. But that was not the case here. There was something in this picture which went deeper. Something that touched her in an unfamiliar way that he could not quite define.

Parnello took that seriously. Very seriously indeed.

FIVE

For Alexandra Hamilton, the visit to her mother on East 29th Street was a familiar journey. It was the journey back into her own childhood. Every step that she took was redolent with memories of the not-so-distant past. Good times. Bad times. After all, she had lived in this apartment herself from the age of ten to twenty-four, grown up in it. When she had finally moved out four years ago to share with a girlfriend, she hadn't gone far: she was only eight blocks away and she generally dropped by to check on her mother once or twice a week. But now, as she stepped off the downtown bus into the twilight, flinching at the sudden blast of cold February wind that cut through to her bones, she felt the same diminishing of the spirit that the area always induced in her. It was a throwback to the earliest days, to that traumatic time when they had first been compelled into residence here: a tearful, newly widowed mother and her mystified daughter, Alexandra, angry and uncomprehending as to why the upheaval in their lives had on top of all else meant the abandonment of their comfortable Park Avenue duplex. Was it some sort of punishment for the death of her father? Had she and her mother been somehow guilty of contributory negligence?

Her mother had tried to console her: 'It's not so bad. The areas round here have got such pretty names: look at them, honey – Gramercy Park, Kips Bay, Murray Hill.'

The names might have been pretty, but the neighbourhood

most emphatically wasn't when she first set eyes upon it, not after the upper reaches of Park Avenue. On the corner of their block there was a laundrette, its bank of machines churning forth clouds of steam tinged with the foul odours of other people's washing. Opposite, a Bangladeshi delicatessen spilled its wares and spices on to the street, a riot of equally alarming and unfamiliar sights and smells. What Alexandra, with all the perversity of a ten-year-old, had not been able to forgive her mother was the way she constantly tried to talk the area up. Who was she trying to kid? But of course she knew perfectly well: the person her mother was trying to kid was Alexandra herself. And that was unforgivable too. Particularly when Alexandra knew that her mother didn't believe what she was telling her, either. Not really. Not in her heart of hearts.

And then, a month or two after they had moved into their three-room apartment on the fourth floor, her mother had said, 'You know what, Alex? I seem to remember there's a decent hotel on East 29th Street. The Martha Washington. Ladies only, of course. It's where your Dad's Aunt Eliza always used to stay when she was in New York, so it must be good. Why don't you and I go and check it out? Have some tea there, treat ourselves.' Of course Alexandra knew that her mother was only doing it as an exercise in self-deception. To prolong for her daughter the illusion that the area still had some class. Even more important, to prolong it for herself. But when they got there they found that the Martha Washington had gone down market. It was now more hostel than hotel, some kind of a hang-out for weirdos: punks, pimps, transvestites and other exotic forms of metropolitan life. Mother and daughter took one look through the door and retreated. Under the circumstances, Alexandra might have derived some measure of sadistic satisfaction from this dashing of her mother's hopes. But suddenly she didn't. Suddenly she felt only the most desperate love and compassion for her. For the first, but by no means for the last time, she felt stronger than her mother.

She paused at the doorway now, seventeen years on, peering up to her mother's fourth floor apartment, checking to see that her lights were on. The front of the building was criss-crossed with the iron fire-escapes that in smarter parts of Manhattan were decorously hidden behind the scenes. It was as if the architect had given up, decided that the facade was already so irremediably ugly that its further defilement would not matter and might even save a few dollars in construction costs. She let herself in through the front door, and stood in the familiar hallway. Deserted. No uniformed porter here. Piles of junk mail littered the floor. The only decoration was a poster pinned to the wall: 'Recycle Now!' it said. 'It's the Law.' The elevator had the out of order sign displayed again, so Alexandra ran up the three flights of stairs to her mother's apartment. In one way it was better to know for sure that the crummy thing wasn't working; better at least than getting into it and having it clanking to a halt between floors as it had done several times in the past. And the exercise did her good, after all, stretching her long legs up those well-remembered steps. But it didn't alter the fact that the guys who ran this building were a bunch of crooks. A bunch of crooks who wouldn't get off their butts to fix even the most basic amenities. Not until you threatened them with court action.

She struggled with the three keys that security dictated she had to negotiate before entering her mother's front door, reflecting that even twenty-three locks would not have done old Mr Asanovic much good last week: they'd come with a sledgehammer, four of them, and been in and out of his apartment downstairs in ninety seconds, while old Mr Asanovic had cowered in his own bedroom. He'd been lucky, the cops had told him. Lucky to get away unhurt. He'd repeated it to her when she'd gone to see him afterwards, and found him almost marvelling at his own good fortune. It made her mad, hearing that the police had told him that. Implying that he was in some way blameworthy himself. Just by being there. Just by being old and alone and vulnerable.

She'd tried to keep the news from her mother, or at least play it down. After all, the poor woman spent most of her waking hours alone here. She went out less and less. Occasionally one of her friends might drop round for an afternoon game of canasta. But otherwise the only diversion was the television, or waiting for Alexandra to call by those evenings she could make it on her way home from work. Alexandra tried not to let too many days go by without checking on her. It was important to keep her mother's spirits up. Now she threw off her coat, dropped her bag on the chair in the small hall and called out cheerfully, 'Hi, Mom. How's your day been?'

'Quietish.' She smiled wanly from the sofa but didn't get up. She suddenly seemed very frail as Alexandra went over and kissed her on the forehead. As if looking at her for the first time. Alexandra noticed how thinly the skin was stretched over her cheekbones, how claw-like her hands had become. She glanced over to the table where the photographs stood, ranks of them. They were her mother's weakness, those framed photographs. Shrines to the past. Memorials to better times. And much, much worse ones. For a moment she sought out her favourite, the one of her mother taken in 1964, when she looked like a blonde Jackie Kennedy. That was the year before she'd married. She was almost a beauty, then.

'You know what we ought to do here, Mom? We ought to get together a residents association. Fight those creeps administering this building. Remind them you've got some rights, too. As tenants. They can't just take your rent and give you nothing in return. You need to stand up to them.'

Her mother shook her head slowly. 'It's no good, Alex, not here,' she said. 'That's not how it works. Maybe back on Park Avenue in the old days, when we had neighbours who counted for something . . .'

Alexandra hated it when that tired, hopeless look came into her mother's eyes. In the same way that she had once resented her false cheerfulness, she now detested her defeatism. She wondered again at her mother's power to evoke in her simultaneous feelings of irritation, guilt, pity and love. And apprehension, too. Just how ill was she?

It was so difficult to get anything out of her about her health. But a lot of the time she didn't look well, didn't look well at all. And these tests she was going into hospital for next week, what were they all about? Her mother had said vaguely they were just routine, something to do with the kidneys. Come on, Mom, she'd thought, you don't have to hold back on me. I'm your daughter and I'm a big girl now. You can tell me. But when pressed, her mother had merely looked perplexed and a little frightened. Perhaps she genuinely did not know. Did not understand. Did not want to understand. So Alexandra had called Dr Grabowsky herself that morning in search of information, but he hadn't been available. The secretary had said she'd get him to call her back, but of course he never had. She'd have to try again tomorrow. Now she said with determination, 'Why don't you try, anyway? Ring a few people's doorbells.'

'Whose doorbells? Mr Asanovic? That mad woman upstairs? The drug-pushers in the basement?'

Alexandra had to admit that the raw material wasn't promising, that you'd have your work cut out forming that collection of deadbeats and inadequates into a line, let alone anything resembling an effective Residents Association. But she wasn't going to allow her mother to win the point. 'We'll see about that,' she said briskly, and then she did what she'd been meaning to do the moment she got home and walked over to the table with the photographs and began to look through them. Casually. As if they'd just caught her eye by chance.

'My, look at you,' she said, picking up the Jackie Kennedy. 'Hardly changed at all.'

'Stop it with your nonsense, honey,' said her mother, but she blushed slightly and you could see she was pleased.

'What a glamour-puss,' persisted Alexandra.

'No, you're the one with the looks, Alex, you got all the beauty genes in our family.'

'And where do you think I got them from?'

'From your father.' She spoke with the dogmatism of the

61

fanatic. She worshipped that man, thought Alexandra with a sudden perspective of distance, as if for a moment the people she was observing were a pair of strangers and not her parents at all. She worshipped him; and since he's gone there's been nothing left in her life. God, I hope I never get that dependent on a man.

Her mother, suddenly animated, was asking her something again: 'Pass him over, that one on the left. Let me have another look at him. There. Such a handsome profile.'

Alexandra handed her the framed photograph and leant over the back of her mother's chair to look at the familiar image once more. He was handsome, that was true enough. He had a pipe between his teeth. He looked like one of those filmstars of the 1950s, perhaps a little like James Stewart. There had been a streak of vanity about him, too. She remembered the way he liked his hair always to be immaculately brushed; how annoyed she'd sensed him become when she ran her fingers through it as a little girl on his lap. Strange, that remembered tensing of anger in him as she did it. It was her most vivid memory of him. Wasn't a father meant to be so close to his daughter that she could wind him round her little finger? But she'd never really had that feeling with him. He'd been that much older than most fathers, anyway: 49 when she'd been born. Maybe that had made him different. And 59 when he'd died. That certainly had.

'I remember when I first met him he was smoking that pipe,' said her mother. 'He had such confidence.'

Such confidence that he had begun to believe the myth of his own infallibility. Such confidence that he'd entered the financial markets trusting nothing more than his own instinct. Such confidence that when he'd had the heart attack and been gone from one day to the next, all he'd left behind had been debts. The Park Avenue apartment had had to go. They'd ended up in these three rooms here. On East 29th Street. At the wrong end of town.

Sometimes Alexandra felt guilty that she had moved out

THE SOLDIER IN THE WHEATFIELD

from here once she'd got a job that paid enough to permit it. She was only eight blocks away. But she couldn't have stayed. She loved her mother dearly, but she would have gone crazy.

Alexandra put her hand over her mother's for a moment and squeezed. 'Good old Dad,' she said softly. She took the photograph back to its place and set it up again.

Then casually, as an apparent afterthought, she picked up the one in the black frame towards the back. It hadn't been touched for some time, to judge from the thin layer of dust on it. Mom wasn't that agile at dusting any more. Objects got missed. It was the one photograph up here in which there was not a single human being portrayed. It showed an interior. It showed things, not people. She remembered a time when her mother had been very fond of showing it to her, earlier in her childhood. 'These were things I knew so well when I was a little girl your age,' her mother had told her. And out of a childish empathy she had paid particular attention to them. There had been a time when she could close her eyes in bed at night and see just about everything in that photograph. And the details had stuck, welded into some back crevice of her brain.

Knocked loose now into the forefront of her memory. Even though the photograph had not been looked at for months.

She stared at it for about ten seconds very hard indeed. Long enough to convince herself that she had been right this afternoon.

Should she tell her mother about it? Should she risk trespassing into the forbidden area? Not yet, she decided, not yet. It would only upset her. Confuse her. God knew, Alexandra herself felt confused enough by it all. But she knew what she needed now, for final confirmation. She needed to see that album. The one that her mother kept locked in the second drawer of her bureau. The one that her mother had brought out just once to show her, and never let her see again.

* * *

Alexandra is fifteen. She understands everything and she understands nothing. Her world wobbles on a knife edge, half exhilarating and half intolerable. It's raining outside, it's Sunday afternoon. It's the hour of infinite tedium. She's sitting at the table dully applying herself to finishing her homework. And thinking about the party which she's going to next week. It's a school dance. It's a disco. What's she going to wear? Does she even want to go? Her mother is on her knees, sorting out papers. She always sorts out papers on Sunday afternoons. Pays bills. Answers letters. Worries herself sick. Now she burrows in the bureau drawer and suddenly picks out the album. It's old and battered, and Alexandra watches out of the corner of her eye as her mother opens it, begins to leaf through.

'Hey, Alex,' she says, getting up from the floor and clutching it under her arm. 'You want to know about the old days? Well, come and look at this.'

So Alexandra, grateful for any distraction, gets up and goes to sit next to her mother on the couch. She drapes herself there, tossing back her long blonde hair from her face. She is long-legged. Gawky. Half girl, half woman.

They turn the pages, looking at the antiquated, yellowing snapshots. They are precise, detailed records of objects: statues, porcelain, pictures. 'Look at these, Mom,' she says. 'I recognise some of them. They're the things in the photograph.' She means the photograph on the table. The one her mother's shown her so many times already.

'That's right, honey. They were all from our old home.'

They go on like this for a while, and then quite suddenly the next page is different. The next page shows a photograph of people, not things. It's a shock, this sudden encounter with humanity, with living beings. There's a father with two children on the beach. It's only a black and white print taken a long time ago, but you can tell it's a glorious summer's day. They're all in bathing suits. They've built a sandcastle and the children are smiling into the camera, mighty pleased with themselves. The girl is no more than five or six. The boy is maybe eight. The man is strong and tanned and has blond hair. He's not smiling, although Alexandra is impressed by his eyes. They are thoughtful; maybe even troubled. But there is a gentleness to them, too.

'Who are these guys?' enquires Alexandra lightly.

'Oh, God!' her mother breathes. There is a pause, then she says very softly: 'Don't you know who that little girl is?'

'No?' But she's beginning to suspect.

'That's me.'

'Gee, Mom. And is that your dad?'

'Your grandfather. My dad.' Her mother's voice is barely raised above a whisper. It is as if she has lost the power of her vocal chords.

'He was killed in the Second World War, right? Back in Germany?'

Her mother nods. 'I was eleven when he died.'

Eleven, calculates Alexandra, with the sublimely self-centred concern that is the hallmark of the fifteen-year-old mind. I was only ten when my dad died. So Mom can't have had it as bad as me. She shouldn't be too upset. 'And is that your brother?' she asks, pointing at the boy.

Her mother nods again, and suddenly her face is contorted with grief. It's like she's having a seizure. She closes the book and clutches it to her as she weeps, sobbing out loud, rocking back and forth in a blind motion of despair. It is terrible. Alexandra has never seen her mother cry like this before. She reaches out a hopeless arm to comfort her, and when it has no effect, she feels obscurely resentful. After all, she's never asked to look at the album, has she? It has all been her mother's idea.

A few minutes later, when her mother's a little recovered, she replaces the album in the drawer and locks it. It is the last time Alexandra gets to see it.

Sure, Alex learned a little more about her grandfather in the years after. Who he was, what he'd done. Her mother even finally told her about her brother, too, the little boy in the photograph. He died towards the end of the war as well, apparently. Got some sort of pneumonia; nothing very serious by modern standards, but there weren't the drugs in Germany to treat him. Not in Germany in February 1945. And then at the end of the war, they had got out, found sanctuary with cousins in America. Just the two of them, the two of them that were left: Alex's mother, aged eleven, and her mother with her.

Once Alex said to her mother: 'I guess this makes me half German, doesn't it, Mom?'

'No,' said her mother emphatically. 'You're American.'

'But you were born German.'

'Born German, maybe. But that was another world, and there's no going back to it. I don't feel German. No, I'm American too. Like you. Like your Dad.'

Just occasionally, as she grew older, Alexandra would speculate about it all. When she heard her mother say something with the tiniest inflection of a German accent. When the chance pronunciation of a word offered a sudden, fleeting insight into the past.

But Alexandra never asked to see the album again. And the opportunity was never again offered to her.

How to raise the matter now, she wondered? The past was perilous, forbidden territory, only to be navigated by the narrow path whose route her mother must point out herself.

'Why don't you fix yourself a drink?' suggested her mother. 'You must be exhausted. I guess it's bitter cold out there.'

'OK, I think I'll make some tea. Would you like something?'

'Not for me, honey.'

'You know where I went at lunchtime?' Alexandra called through from the kitchen. 'I went to that auction house on Park Avenue. You know, that real glitzy one where they sell Monets for twenty million dollars?'

'Buy anything nice?'

'I thought I'd save my money. You know pay-day's not till next week. No, I go in there quite regularly, I find it kind of interesting. You don't have to buy, you can just look around. They have amazing things in there: furniture, silver. And pictures.'

'Pictures?'

'Yeah. You know, paintings.'

There was a pause while the word hung there, suspended between them. Alexandra held her breath, waiting. Then her mother went on, in a gentler, reminiscent voice: 'In the old days we used to have such pictures, Alex. Such beautiful pictures . . .'

Now. Now Alexandra could ask her. This was the lead-in she needed. The start of the path into the past.

But somehow the words would not form themselves. Perhaps it was cowardice. Perhaps it was the image of her mother on that very couch, clutching herself, sobbing with impenetrable misery. Perhaps it was a sense of all the hidden, unknown things she might be unleashing. No, she needed to think it all over a little longer before she decided how to act.

Alexandra came in with the tea, sat down, and picked up the *New York Times*.

'Hey, look at this, Mom: *Singing In the Rain*'s on tonight. Channel 9, eight o'clock. Your favourite.'

'Let me see.' Her mother took the newspaper and reached for her reading glasses. She studied it and nodded with approval. 'That's my evening taken care of, anyway. You staying for supper?'

'No, I have to go, Mom.'

'Got a date?'

'Not tonight.'

'Who are you seeing these days? Is it still Barry? I like Barry.'

'Barry's in Los Angeles at the moment. No, I've got stuff to do.'

Her mother did not press her, and Alexandra was relieved, because she needed time to think.

It was not every day, after all, that the dead things of the past started coming back to life.

SIX

The day of the sale, anticipation mounting. Ten minutes to go before the first lot. People thronged into the auction house singly and in groups, clutching auction catalogues like communicants arriving at church with their prayer books. Yellow cabs and limousines pulled up at the doorway, spilling out sleek, moneyed buyers whose breath turned to scented steam as they traversed the few yards of clear cold February air between car and concierge. Once greeted and welcomed inside they hit a wall of heat. The auction houses had done their research. There was an optimum temperature most conducive to bidders raising their hands. It was sixty-eight degrees fahrenheit. Some of these people looked preoccupied; others almost unnaturally relaxed, deliberately nonchalant. Parnello, his drooping green eyes quizzical but vigilant, hovered between the two.

'Wotcha mate. So you made it over?' It was Shagger in a resplendent floral tie. Shagger, the self-roughened diamond.

'When I heard you were coming I knew there was something I shouldn't miss.'

Shagger ran a suspicious eye over him. 'You're up to something, Moran. I can tell.'

Parnello shrugged innocently and took his seat. He looked about him. Besides Shagger there were a number of familiar faces: other dealers over from London; New York dealers; dealers from Paris, Zurich and Vienna. A collector he knew slightly from Cleveland. The curator of a mid-Western public collection and his boyfriend, both wearing identical moustaches. And in addition to the trade and the museum representatives, there was the usual sprinkling of diverse humanity that peoples the saleroom on these occasions: elegant women who aren't quite as rich as they look; ramshackle men who are considerably richer. Criminals and connoisseurs. People drawn by a fascination with the past; people driven by a fear for the future.

The sale went well. Ominously well. The van Goyen made half a million dollars. The Vernet reached 350,000. Even the worn little Teniers fetched 75,000 against an estimate of 30 to 40,000.

And so on to lot 147.

Parnello sat back in his seat and stretched his long legs out into the aisle. There are intemperate but keenly-felt pursuits, said Byron, whose principal attraction is the agitation inseparable from their accomplishment. Gaming, thought Byron, was one; battle and travel two more. Parnello was inclined to add to that list bidding at auction. Inside he seethed with a mixture of exhilaration and trepidation as the picture of smoking bonfires beneath the crimson sunset was held up by the porters. But on the surface he looked relaxed, uninvolved. After all, it was not as if he had to do anything. Not the way he had arranged it. All he had to do was watch.

The bidding began slowly.

Five thousand dollars, said the auctioneer, in a tone intended to imply that such a ridiculously low starting point was a mere formality. He repeated the figure a little less confidently, unable to exclude a timbre of pleading from his voice. Then 5,500, he said suddenly. Not a real bid, of course. An invented one, in an attempt to get things going. 6,000. Still acting, Parnello could tell. No-one had actually come in.

6,500. Yes, there was one, a real bidder. You could tell from the flicker of relief that momentarily registered in the auctioneer's eyes. You could tell from the way that

Humphrey, standing just to the side of the rostrum, shifted his weight from one foot to the other and relaxed. Quickly Parnello shot a glance sideways and caught the end of the surreptitious movement that had signalled a bidder's interest. It was an unknown man on the end of the second row.

6,500: any more? Are we all done, then, at 6,500? 7,000, thank you.

The new bid had come from the sales clerk standing next to the auctioneer. Then the bidding rose in five hundreds to ten thousand dollars. Slow, staccato, stuttering little jumps; like a flame leaping, then dying. Dying. Or did it still flicker?

11,000, thank you, continued the auctioneer. A new bidder, standing at the back. Parnello glanced over his shoulder and identified him. Damn: the moustachioed mid-Western museum curator, glancing tight-lipped at his boyfriend as if for reassurance. Now the tempo suddenly quickened, and within a matter of seconds the bidding had jumped to 19,000 . . . 20,000 . . . 21,000. There it paused, then shot on again to 28,000 . . . 30,000 . . . and on in 5,000s all the way to 55,000.

'With you, sir,' said the auctioneer, 'standing at the back.'

Parnello looked over his shoulder again at the museum man: sweating slightly, tense, nervous. And then he saw her, two away from the bidder, standing there, long-limbed and blonde. Frowning. Absorbed.

Now Parnello raised his own hand. He'd hoped this would not be necessary: the sales clerk had had his confidential instructions to go up to 50,000 on Parnello's behalf. That should have been enough, to ensure both anonymity and success. But now he was compelled to break cover and join the fray there was something to be said for doing it openly. If he bid with transparent confidence now, he might unnerve the competition.

65,000 . . . 70,000 . . . 75,000. Still the standing man's bid. Still he was hanging in there. There was a good and bad side to bidding against this particular opponent. On the one hand the curator was probably knowledgable enough to have identified the Dahl. On the other hand his museum was notoriously underfunded.

80,000 said Parnello, affecting hesitation; and now his rival, too, wavered. Finally, after an eternity, he ventured, 82,000. That jump over the round figure into a new sequence was always psychologically dispiriting. Very well, said the auctioneer. But his look said, don't bother me with such small increments again.

90,000, called out Parnello airily.

The room experienced a little shock of excitement at such bravado. And that did it. The extravagance finally daunted the man at the back. Who knew where Parnello would stop? If he was going to take such giant strides, there was no point in running with him. Which was exactly the message Parnello had meant to communicate. He pursed his lips a little ruefully as the hammer came down, feeling that mixture of triumph and unease that always accompanies the expensive acquisition of something you knew you wanted but you did not know how much. He hadn't intended to go above 65,000. But it wasn't really the expense that he regretted. It was the fact that the pleasurable agitation was over; that the flame of excitement which had burned in his life for those few brief moments of competition was extinguished.

On his way out he saw her ahead of him, hurrying down the stairs. At the doorway she turned back briefly and caught sight of him. For a moment their eyes met and she looked at him with recognition. Recognition, followed by immediate and unmistakable hostility.

He was intrigued and followed her on down. The doorman held the door open for him and as he emerged on to the sidewalk and looked left he saw her again, striding quickly away, her figure diminishing against the distant backdrop of the teeming city. In a moment she would be lost in the serried infinity of changing traffic lights that receded as far as the eye could see, swallowed up into one of the myriad yellow cabs that snaked ahead in procession downtown. He began to run.

Ahead of him she crossed at the last minute, just as the lights changed against him and he was held back by an angry stream of traffic jostling for position to traverse Park Avenue. By the time the lights changed again in his favour, he couldn't see her. Had she made it into a taxi? He ran on, looking both left and right, alternately into shop windows and slow-moving cabs. By the time he reached the end of the block and hit the next lights, he knew he'd lost her. He stood still for a moment, surprised at his own desperation. He'd just bought the picture, hadn't he? He'd achieved what he'd set out to do that day. He laughed at himself. He should calm down a bit. The excitement of the sale had got to him.

And then there she was again, at the kiosk just round the corner, buying a newspaper. She looked up and caught sight of him again, then turned away quickly, but this time he was on her before she could escape, put out his hand to touch her arm.

'You were in the saleroom just now, weren't you?' he said.

She tensed, but didn't move away. Close to, she was very pretty indeed: long blond hair swept away from her face; a white teeshirt worn under a well-cut blue jacket; golden skin. Candyfloss. 'So were you,' she said. 'You bought that picture.'

There was still resentment in her tone. He smiled at her. 'Won't you let me buy you a cup of coffee so that we can talk about it?'

'What is there to talk about?' The anger was on the surface again.

'Well, you could reassure me, anyway.' He was already guiding her to the Italian cafe he'd noticed two doors away, and she was allowing herself to be directed. 'I keep asking myself: what have I done wrong? I've only bought a picture. In fair and open competition. And yet here's this beautiful girl furious with me. I haven't run over your cat or written you obscene letters. If you wanted the picture that badly yourself, then you should have bid against me.'

'Bid against you? Oh, that's great. I suppose you think I've got an extra 100,000 bucks to throw around.'

'Well, you look like . . .'

'Please,' she interrupted him. 'Just don't say a million dollars, OK?'

She sat down opposite him at the table in the cafe and stared back at him. Belligerent. He'd been wrong about her. She didn't use laughter as a substitute for a point of view. She wasn't candyfloss. There was something tough in her. Something angry, too.

'If you're going to steal my best lines from me, then this won't be much of a conversation,' he said.

'Your *best* lines? Jesus!'

And for a moment they both laughed.

After they'd been brought their coffee he tried again. 'But you wanted that picture? You were intrigued by it?'

She was tearing the empty envelope of sugar into little strips, littering the red and white checked tablecloth with them. 'I guess so.'

'Why?'

She gave the question some thought. Outside the swelling siren of an ambulance or a police car rose above the constantly querulous background of traffic, the low cacophony of impatience. 'It would take too long to go into all that,' she said at last.

'But I want to know.'

She shook her head. 'Suppose you tell me something,' she said. She was looking at him very intently suddenly. 'Why did you buy that picture?'

'Because I like it.'

'But are you going to hang it on your wall?'

'Certainly I am. Why do you ask?'

'It's just that I figured you might be some kind of art dealer. Buying it to turn it over for a quick buck.'

'Well, yes, I am an art dealer. But no, I don't intend to

sell it on. I like that picture, very much indeed. It's for me, for my own private collection. My name's Parnello Moran, by the way.'

He held out his hand to her and she shook it. A trifle reluctantly. 'Alexandra Hamilton,' she murmured.

They sat in silence for a while. Parnello reached for his packet of Ducados, shook one out and lit it. As an afterthought, he offered the packet in her direction. She shook her head, preoccupied.

'So why did you buy it?' It was as if she was trying to trap him, seeing if he changed his story.

'It's the sort of picture I like,' repeated Parnello.

'Why do you like it?'

'Because it's very romantic.'

'What does that mean?' He had the impression she did not ask the question out of ignorance; more to test him.

'It's a special style of landscape painting. Nature seen through a temperament. I like temperament.'

'You like temperament.' She repeated the words disbelievingly, as if he had just confessed to something sordid.

'You know what temperament is?' he challenged her.

'Sure, I know what temperament is. But I don't mind hearing what you think it is.'

He considered the question. 'In this context it's a specially tempestuous sort of imagination.'

She wasn't looking at him. She was looking out of the window into the traffic. ' "The lava of the imagination whose eruption prevents an earthquake",' she quoted suddenly.

It took him a few moments to register what she had said. Then the extraordinary truth hit him. 'My God! You've read Byron.'

'Is that a problem for you?'

'No, it's quite the reverse. I just . . .'

'You didn't think I looked the type, I suppose?'

'You like Byron?'

'I didn't say I liked him. I just like some of his poetry.'

She paused, frowning in the effort to disentangle the artist from his art. 'I reckon that as a character he was probably pretty intolerable.'

'In what way?'

'Arrogant. Self-indulgent. All that crap about man's love being a thing apart, but a woman's her whole existence. That's pretty damned patronising. But the guy was Olympic class at deluding himself, wasn't he?'

'You don't think men and women fall in love differently?'

She looked up at him out of long-lashed eyes. She seemed about to answer, but then she caught herself up. 'Look, I haven't got time to sit here discussing dumb questions like that, OK? Just tell me one more time: you're an art dealer, but you really don't intend to sell it on, this picture that you've bought? For a profit?'

'No, I said. I'm going to keep it myself.' The resolution had come to him back there in the saleroom, crystalising at the moment he found himself exceeding the original limit he had set on his bid. He wanted this picture. Not to trade. But to keep for his own collection. It was his trophy. A monument to his expertise, to his ability to read the handwriting. And more important because the picture itself had something to say to him, something about a certain way of looking at nature which struck a chord of sympathy across the centuries. Temperament. A special sort of tempestuous imagination. The lava from the eruption which prevents an earthquake.

She was talking again, in a tone that was strangely anxious and concerned. Almost tender. 'I had a close look at it, that painting, back there in the saleroom.'

'I know. I saw you. What did you make of it?'

'It seemed kind of dirty.'

'You're right, it is dirty. I don't think it's had any attention for forty or fifty years. It needs cleaning. I've got a friend with a gallery here and I'm going to show it to her restorer. He's meant to be good. I'll see what he advises.'

She nodded thoughtfully, then she shrugged and drained her coffee. 'I have to run. I've got to get back to work.'

'Can I drop you somewhere? Where have you got to go?'

'It's only three blocks away. I'll walk.'

'What do you do?'

'I'm in the fashion business.'

'A model?'

'No, not me. I sell clothes.' She paused, then added, as if she needed to explain herself: 'It pays some bills.'

He took a final drag and stubbed out his cigarette. 'Everyone always ends up doing what they're second best at,' he said.

'I guess you're right there.' There was a warmth to the way she said it that made him realise he'd caught her off guard. Touched something. He ventured:

'What is it you'd rather be doing?'

She shrugged, hopelessly.

Just occasionally these things came to him. As if he could read people, like he could read a painter's handwriting. 'Is it theatre?' he asked. 'Would you rather be an actress?'

'How did you know that?'

'Did you do acting school?'

'Four years.' She laughed ruefully. 'Now that really doesn't pay the bills.'

'Give it time. I can see it now, up in lights on Broadway: starring Alexandra Hamilton.'

'Dream on.' Her voice was harder, more distant. He'd got too close and she was pushing him away. She still didn't trust him.

She got up. He left a five dollar bill on the table for the coffee and stood up with her. He very much wanted her to trust him. He wished he could identify what it was that made her uneasy.

'If you're so interested in that picture, maybe you'd like to see it when it's cleaned,' he suggested. 'I'd be happy to show it to you.'

'Maybe,' she said. 'Thanks for the coffee.'

'Give me your number, anyway.'

For a moment he thought she was going to refuse. She frowned; but when he offered her his pen, she quickly scribbled it on a napkin. Perhaps simply to get rid of him. Perhaps because she saw it as the swiftest way of making her exit.

'When we meet again, I hope there'll be time for you to tell me what your interest really is in that picture,' he called after her.

She paused in the doorway and looked back at him. Tall, graceful. Elusive. Hiding something from him. 'Maybe,' she said, and hurried off into the street without looking back.

SEVEN

The waiting was terrible, like living with a cancer temporarily in remission but bound at any moment to flare up again. Each morning Alphonse Baugniet awoke heavy with a sense of doom. They had the photographs. When would they use them? Why were they so long in coming back to him, in extracting from him the 'small service' that would discharge his appalling obligation to them? Two and a half months now. Two and a half months of blighted family life, of being unable to contemplate his wife or his beautiful children without imagining them horror-struck by the images that he dreaded them ever seeing. The images of his shame.

Estelle noticed there was something wrong. How could she not? In order to placate her, in order to explain his preoccupation, he invented a series of mysterious headaches, substituting his secret spiritual malaise with a more acceptable physical one. He was packed off to the doctor who could find nothing wrong with him and diagnosed stress. He came home with a bottleful of pills that he religiously flushed down the lavatory, two a day, as prescribed on the label.

How could they have known it, he asked himself? How could his torturers have known to come for him the one evening his wife and family were away in Neuchatel, the one evening he was vulnerable to them? And he realised with a slow, aching horror how closely they must have been watching him, awaiting their moment. How deeply they had penetrated into the secret details of his life.

He no longer accompanied Ricki and Paul and Ernesto to the Antelope Bar on Friday evenings. He could not bring himself ever to enter that place again. It was where he had lost his moral equilibrium, the killing ground of his self-respect. Supposing he saw her in there? To meet her again would have been unbearable. To be reminded of her short skirt and wanton mouth. The ultimate horror was the fear that lurked in the murkiest recess of his imagination: the fear that, if he saw her again, he might find his lust for her returning. The first two or three Fridays he had manufactured excuses to his friends. Now they no longer bothered to ask him to go with them. He'd grown apart from them. But the one thing that did not suffer was his work. He went to it with renewed vigour, as if his application and diligence was some sort of advance expiation for what he might be asked to do in the future. For the betrayal that he knew in his heart was some time to be demanded of him.

That day he reached a decision. He was going to do something about it. To force the issue, to put an end to the waiting. He spent the morning relocating properties in the Free Port, and at lunchtime he retreated into the small office from which he organised the paperwork, and closed the door after him. Surrounded by files of dockets, he brought out his notebook with that number inscribed in it, the Geneva number he'd been told to telephone once he'd received the original set of photographs. Just a small service, the man's voice had said that first time, back in December. Then the negatives would be destroyed. What small service, Alphonse had demanded? Anything, his panicky tone had indicated. Just tell me what I have to do. But the man had not been forthcoming. You'll be given your instructions, he'd said. At the appropriate moment. All you have to do is wait.

He dialled the number again now.

'Could I speak to Mr Corbière?' he said when the call was answered.

'Who wants him?' It was a woman's voice.

'Baugniet. Alphonse Baugniet. From Bartsch.'

A man now: 'Corbière here. What is it?'

'I was wondering . . . wondering how we stood?'

'How we stood with what?' The words were sharp, clipped. Impatient.

'With our arrangement.'

'Listen, Baugniet. When you're needed, you'll be contacted. Not before, OK? Meanwhile, don't ring here again. Not unless you want those photographs plastered all over the front page of the *Tribune de Genève*. Got it?'

'Got it,' said Baugniet miserably, and replaced the receiver.

EIGHT

———◦◦◦◦◦———

'Hard times? Don't talk to me about hard times.' Shagger Parks nursed his vodka and tonic in the Polo Bar of the Westbury Hotel and stared back at Parnello with the look of nostalgic sentimentality that successful art dealers reserve for the contemplation of their own exigent beginnings. 'I can remember one month when I was so hard up I had to get amorous with an old age pensioner to sell a Russell Flint.'

Parnello considered this definition of a professional nadir. 'So what are you saying? That now business is booming you're a bit more hard to get?'

'Not half.' Parks dragged happily on his cigar. 'I suppose I might still offer myself to that Sharon Stone to shift a Canaletto. Nothing less.'

'I can't help feeling, my dear Shagger, that she'd be more likely to buy the Canaletto if your advances weren't part of the deal.'

'I can't think what you mean.'

'I mean she wouldn't want to be screwed twice.'

Parks cackled with unexpected laughter. 'You know your trouble, don't you my son?' he went on philosophically. 'You're not hungry enough.'

'Aren't I?'

'No, you're not. You've got a fabulous eye. You find smashing pictures. But you're a sodding dilettante. You're the sort of mad idealistic bugger who'd prefer not to sell

a picture than have it end up on the wall of someone who
doesn't understand it.'

Parnello shrugged and smiled. He could not entirely deny
it. Instead he reached for a Ducados and said, 'So what did
you make of the prices yesterday?'

It was the day after the sale: time for post-mortems.

'Too much money chasing too much crap,' pronounced
Shagger. 'As usual, the only people who win out are the
auction houses.'

'Buy anything?' Parnello asked him.

'A couple of things. For clients. What about yourself?'

Shagger knew perfectly well. He'd been in the auction
room. He'd seen him bidding on the Dahl.

'Nothing much,' said Parnello.

As he spoke he was aware of a man standing next to
them. Hovering discreetly; soliciting attention. They both
looked up at him. He had thick, grey-flecked hair and wore
a wellcut suit.

'Good to see you,' said the man. 'Do you mind if I
join you?'

He must have been addressing Shagger, because Parks
waved an arm of invitation, and the man drew up a chair.
When he spoke he did so deferentially, with a degree of
politeness which in an Englishman would have set Parnello
instantly on his guard. But he wasn't English, nor indeed
American. Parnello inspected him surreptitiously. He was
neat, almost precious in his movements. From his manner
and accent he could have been Middle-European, but it was
difficult to be specific. You never knew in sale weeks in
New York. All kinds of operators drifted into town: sellers,
collectors, speculators, hangers-on. All kinds of people with
fingers in the pie.

The newcomer was served with a scotch on the rocks.
He raised his glass. Then he sighed and said to Parnello:
'Interesting places, hotel bars, don't you think?'

'In what way?'

'To the student of humanity.'

'And you are a student of humanity?'

'I enjoy watching people, yes.'

'Who are you watching now?'

'I am watching that very beautiful dark woman at the table by the door. Maybe I have a weakness for feminine beauty. She is drinking mineral water. I mean, who is she fooling? She is waiting for someone, and I don't think it is her husband.'

'What makes you think she is married?'

'She's wearing a bleeding wedding ring, isn't she?' observed Shagger, standing up to go. 'Will you both excuse me? I've got dinner with a client.'

Parnello was uneasy at being left alone with the man. His manner craved an unwanted intimacy, made sly emotional demands, cloaked in a glibness that was constantly trying to prove something.

'Can you maybe guess what I do for a living?' persisted his companion.

Lounge lizard, Brenda would have said. That was her description for anyone who combined even faintly foreign looks with a tendency towards smoothness. But he resisted the temptation to pass it on. 'A gossip columnist?' he suggested. 'Or a private detective?'

'Neither,' he laughed. There was a pause.

'What are you, then, Mr . . .'

'I am so sorry. My name is Raven, Nicholas Raven.'

Parnello knew at once that this was not his real name. Fake signatures; fake names. Seeing through one was the complement of seeing through the other. Something did not feel right, did not carry conviction. Nonetheless he introduced himself in return and shook the so-called Mr Raven's hand. He was still inclined to put the man down as a harmless comedian.

'So what business are you in, if you're not a journalist or a detective?'

'I am a consultant.'

'That covers a multitude of sins. What sort of a consultant?'

'Parnello, listen: I find things for people, OK? Things they want very much.'

'Like what?'

'Precious things. Rare things.'

'What sort of rare things?'

'I mean excuse me, but like the things you deal in, Parnello. Like pictures, for instance.'

'How do you know I deal in pictures?'

'You must understand, I have good sources of information. When I need them.' He paused thoughtfully. 'I know something else about you, too, actually.'

'What is that?'

'You bought a picture yesterday at auction. Lot 147. You paid $90,000 for it.'

It was public enough knowledge. Anyone who had been present in the saleroom and kept his eyes open would have been aware of the buyer's identity. After all, it had been part of Parnello's latter strategy to bid aggressively. Conspicuously. 'More like $100,000 actually,' Parnello corrected him, 'with the auctioneers' premium. So?'

'Listen. Where is the picture now?'

There was a sudden urgency in his tone, a glimpse of unexpected steel, that made Parnello instantly wary. He'd collected it that morning and given it into the care of Marvel's gallery; Marvel was going to show it to her restorer tomorrow to get his opinion on cleaning it. But that was none of Raven's business. 'Why do you want to know all this?' he demanded.

Raven turned towards him and smiled, conciliatory again. 'OK, Parnello, I'm sorry if maybe I seem inquisitive. You see, there is a good reason for all these questions. Good news for you, Parnello, actually. I represent someone who would very much like to buy this picture from you.'

'It's not for sale,' said Parnello. He drew back a little. Suddenly Raven's face was rather close to his own, and he could smell his after-shave.

'My client would be generous. He will pay you 140,000 dollars for it. In cash. Immediately.'

'Why didn't he bid at the auction?'

'He's only just become aware that this particular picture was available for sale. The information reached him within the past twenty-four hours, just too late to take part. It's the source of considerable frustration to my client to have missed it. It's a painting that he has particularly set his heart on, actually.'

For a moment Parnello's professional curiosity was aroused. Who was this mysterious client? Did he know what Parnello knew? If so, how did he know it? What was his connection with the picture? But these weren't questions for Raven. All Parnello said now was: 'I see. Well, I'm sorry, but as I said it's not for sale.'

'Please! OK, Parnello, maybe I give you now a mathematics lesson. What I'm offering you means 40,000 dollars profit in your pocket just like that. I mean really, 40,000 dollars for barely lifting a finger.'

The man's tenacity depressed him; his insistence on the money struck him as sordid, an error of taste. 'I don't care if you're offering me 140,000 thousand dollars profit. I like that picture. I want to keep it.'

'Parnello, I mean really, these are shadows you are chasing. I thought you were a businessman.'

'I am. And I'm choosy about who I do business with. Look, it's not for sale. OK?'

'You're making a mistake if you do not accept my offer.' The man wasn't funny any more. No longer harmless, either. Suddenly there was a threat implicit in the way he spoke.

'I'm not selling,' Parnello repeated.

Raven shrugged. 'Listen, think about it.' He pulled a card out from his pocket. It was inscribed simply with his name. He scribbled a telephone number on it and pushed it over to Parnello. 'Give me a call later. I'm staying at the Plaza. There's my room number, OK?'

Parnello got up, eased his long body out from behind the table, and walked away. Saying nothing. Leaving the card untouched next to the empty glass. He didn't need men like

Raven. He was rich enough in his own right not to have to bother with them.

That was the trouble of course. Parnello wasn't a proper dealer, not in the hungry, profit-driven sense. He lacked enthusiasm for the quick buck. Almost anyone else would have taken the money and run. Shagger, for instance; he might have refused, too, at first, but only as a ploy. After playing Raven along, he would have come back with his own price. 180,000 dollars he would have said. But he would have settled for 150 in the end, and gone away happy. As would have Raven. No doubt Shagger had done similar deals with Mr Nicholas Raven often enough in the past.

But that wasn't how it worked out this time. Not once Parnello reacted badly to the man, took a dislike to his devious manner, set his face against doing business with him. He didn't trust him, all insidious charm one moment and veiled menace the next. Once Parnello decided something like that, he wouldn't budge. It became a matter of principle. He could be very obstinate indeed, when he put his mind to it. And of course there was another reason why Parnello could not possibly have accepted the offer, even if he'd been tempted by it, which he wasn't: how could he have explained it afterwards to Alexandra Hamilton? To Alexandra Hamilton, who'd had his assurance that he wasn't going to trade the picture. To Alexandra Hamilton, who worked in a fashion store, had read Byron, and tore up sugar packets into distracted shreds.

As Parnello passed the attractive woman at the bar she was embracing her date. 'Honestly, sweetheart,' she was saying to him, 'what kind of a man is late for his tenth wedding anniversary dinner?'

NINE

'Staying away much longer, are you?' demanded Brenda on the telephone the next morning.

Parnello yawned and rubbed his eyes. 'Another day or two. It depends. Look, do you know what time it is?'

'It's 12.15 in London. That makes it 7.15 in New York.' Brenda could be surprisingly well informed when she put her mind to it. 'Too early for you?'

'It is rather, yes.'

'Oh, I do beg your pardon. Are we not alone?'

'We're very much alone.'

'Shame. So did the foreign geezer get hold of you?'

'Which foreign geezer?'

'Fellow who rang here yesterday requesting your whereabouts. Wanted to know if you were still in New York.'

'Was he called Raven?'

'Wouldn't give his name, would he? Seemed to need you urgently, though. I told him what hotel you were in.'

'I think I met him last night. He's a rather ill-mannered friend of Mr Parks.'

'Do any business with him?'

'No. I didn't like the look of him. I turned his offer down.'

'Well, you know best,' said Brenda, without much conviction.

Parnello replaced the receiver. On the whole he felt optimistic. He was the new owner of a very beautiful romantic landscape by Dahl, which had been paid the highly reassuring compliment of another man's covetousness. Later in the day Marvel's restorer was coming in to look at it. Parnello anticipated that it was going to clean extraordinarily well. The sunset: that was going to be a revelation, once those fiery reds had been released from their deadening pall of dirty yellow varnish.

And later in the week he'd take a plane back to London. There was no hurry. No hurry at all.

He dressed, ordered breakfast, and ate it flicking idly through the channels on the hotel room TV. From the weather channel he learned that the maximum temperature in New York City today would be thirty-seven degrees. There were market reports from Tokyo and Hong Kong on CNN. The index was moving up. Further on, a well-developed girl called Colette in orange leotards was explaining to a muscle-bound youth named Brad the merits of something called a step-exerciser. In time to loud disco music she was treading on and off a simple rectangular block of wood about six inches high. 'Great for calf-toning,' she informed Brad. Brad grinned, sweating stylishly into his teeshirt. No under-arm perspiration; just chest. 'Order Now', said the subtitle on the screen. 'Only $139.95.'

It was 8.35 when the telephone rang again. He was surprised to hear Marvel's voice on the other end of the line; surprised because she said she was in the gallery, and even Marvel, driven though she was, did not normally get into work this early; and surprised because of her tone. She was upset, but not angry-upset. He knew that tone well enough and how to respond to it. No, this was different. This time there was something new in the volatile emotional cocktail of her state of mind. The element of fear.

'What is it, Marvel, what's happened?'

'The cops are here. They rang me at home. Could you get over here, do you think?'

'Of course. But what's happened? Is anyone hurt?'

'Just come over. Like now.' There was a hysterical edge to her voice that he'd not heard before.

'I'm on my way.'

He paused to pull on his overcoat. '. . . And this one is great for the abs . . .' Colette was intoning, contorted crablike over a huge beach-ball. He switched off the television.

It was a bright, cold winter's day, the temperature barely above freezing. The air had a glacial clarity, and the trees in Central Park traced sharp, spidery patterns against the sky. But even before the taxi turned into East 79th Street he felt uneasy. Then he caught sight of the patrolcar with the flashing blue lights drawn up in the street outside Marvel's gallery and the foreboding grew heavier.

He hurried in and there was Marvel, leaning against her desk, gesticulating to the pair of uniformed cops, berating them. Fear made her aggressive. She was kneading the beads round her neck with anxious, tormented fingers. She turned to greet him. 'Thank God you've come,' she said. 'Look what the bastards have done.'

She led the way through into the rear viewing room, then down the steps into the store-room at the back. There was broken glass all over the floor. Looking up, he saw that the skylight had been forced.

The heavily-built patrolmen had followed them in and stood there stolidly in their leather jackets. 'Guess there must have been two of them,' the first surmised, barely breaking the motion of his gum-chewing jaw as he spoke. 'Looks like one of the bastards climbed back out off of this filing cabinet. Handed the merchandise up to his buddy on the roof.'

His partner removed his dark glasses and nodded his head in agreement. 'Two of the bastards,' he repeated thoughtfully. 'Ain't possible to have got it out alone.'

'Didn't the alarm go off?' said Parnello.

'Sure the alarm went off,' Marvel answered him. Taut. On the edge. 'But you don't expect the cops to get here in time to catch anyone, do you? This is New York City, for Christ's sake.'

'Has much been taken?'

'Oh, shit, Parnello. Didn't I tell you on the phone? No, I guess I didn't.'

Still he didn't get it. 'What's this all about?'

'They only took one picture.'

'Only one?'

'It was your landscape. The one you bought in the auction on Tuesday.'

As it sank in, he thought of two people. Of Raven.

And of Alexandra Hamilton.

While Patrolman Murphy prowled round the store room one more time, bending to inspect shards of glass, reaching up to measure distances, Parnello sat down with Patrolman Schenk and provided him with the formalities. Like the value of the picture missing. Like its size and the name of the artist. Like the small photograph torn from the auction catalogue. But all the while his mind was racing.

Raven. Raven wanted that picture, for a client. Wanted it badly. But for some reason he'd been just too late to buy it at the auction. He'd located Parnello, made contact with him. In the Westbury bar he'd proposed a generous financial offer to buy it from him. But he'd been forced to the conclusion that the picture was not going to be winkled out from Parnello by money. So Raven had switched to the fall-back plan. The more extreme measure. Raven, with his excellent sources of information, had discovered where the picture was and sent someone to get it. Or two people, if you believed Murphy and Schenk. In the freezing small hours of the morning they had climbed on to this back roof, forced the skylight, and spirited it away.

But there was something else about all this, something more disturbing. Suddenly Raven was rather more than the lounge lizard playing stupid games. Raven was serious. Raven was someone who found things out and made things happen. True enough, it had taken no great feat of intelligence to establish who the buyer of lot 147 had been. And when that buyer had refused to do a deal with him, it had taken rather more resource to discover where the picture was. And to act so swiftly and ruthlessly upon that information.

What was going on here, anyway? Why did someone want that particular picture so badly? The fact that it had been catalogued only as 'German School, nineteenth century' but was actually by Johan Christian Clausen Dahl made it more interesting, of course. But it wasn't the only Dahl available on the world art market, he was quite sure of that. What made this one so special?

And what was Alexandra Hamilton's role in all this? What connected her so passionately to the picture? An aspirant actress making a living selling clothes in a fashion house with a thing about German Romantic painting? It didn't make sense. Even if she could quote Byron.

As he watched Patrolman Schenk laboriously writing out the last lines of his statement, Parnello was conscious of another emotion. He was angry. He'd identified the Dahl, he'd come all this way to buy the picture, he'd outfought all the competition fair and square in the auction, and now it had been stolen from him. It wasn't the money, the financial loss. It would be tiresome, but he could sort all that out with the insurers. No, it was being deprived of something whose ownership had given him pleasure. And the thought that he had in some way been defeated; that he'd lost the game at the very last gasp. That was what rankled. He wasn't going to lie down and let them walk over him. Whoever they were. He was going to fight back.

But on the other hand he was reasonably certain that Patrolmen Murphy and Schenk were not going to be the answer. Their report would be dutifully filed at the New York Police Department. And there it would stay, mouldering, one more minor incident of larceny to add to all the others, significant only as a statistic for the politicians and the socio-criminologists. No, if his picture was going to be retrieved, he was going to have to find it himself.

So when Schenk looked up at him and demanded: 'Is there anything else you have to tell us?' Parnello didn't mention

Raven. It suddenly seemed pointless. Raven's existence was information more valuable to him than to these two clowns. He watched as the two policemen left the gallery and climbed into the patrolcar. Murphy was still chewing gum; Schenk carefully replacing his dark glasses. And when the car drew away, he said to Marvel:

'Marvel, darling, I'm really sorry about all this. You must be sick of the sight of me now, after all the trouble I've caused you. But I'll make it up to you, I promise.'

She sipped a cup of coffee, her other hand still kneading the beads round her neck. She was still angry, but a little calmer; less inclined to rant. 'At least the bastards didn't take the Sisley,' she said.

'Any news from your buyer?'

'He's ringing me this afternoon.'

'Then we'll celebrate.'

'Not the way my day's gone so far.'

'Do you mind if I make a couple of telephone calls?' he asked gently.

'Help yourself.'

No, said the woman at the Plaza, there was no Mr Raven currently staying in the hotel. Last night? Hold the line a minute. Yes, there had been a Nicholas Raven last night, but he'd checked out very early this morning. No, she had no information about where he had gone, but guests checking out that early generally had flights to catch. Have a nice day.

Shagger was still in his room at the Westbury. After all, it was not yet ten.

'What bloke Raven?'

'He said his name was Raven. Come on, Shagger, you know each other. You invited him to join us, and the three of us had a drink in the bar. You remember, last night.'

'That tosser? I never set eyes on him before. I thought he was your friend.'

Parnello rang off and paced to the window. He looked out at the passers-by, well wrapped against the cold. Already the early morning sun was dulled, and a bank of threatening grey cloud was moving in from the west. Then he reached into his pocket and found the tattered napkin with her telephone number scribbled on it.

He met Alexandra Hamilton at six-thirty in a bar just round the corner from the shop on Madison Avenue where she sold very expensive French and Italian dresses to women like Nancy Onslow. The bar was full of office workers drinking beers. Parnello ordered one too, but she just asked for mineral water. She undid her coat, but did not take it off. Her presence here was provisional, she wished to imply. Liable to cancellation at short notice.

'It was a relief to get through to you this morning,' he told her. The cold of the evening made her cheeks glow.

She regarded him suspiciously. 'Why was it a relief?'

'Because just recently people who've given me their telephone numbers have shown an alarming tendency to abscond when I ring them back.'

'I'm not running anywhere.' She sighed, and shook her long blonde hair out so that it fell in cascades over her shoulders.

'I'm glad about that,' he said.

'So what was so urgent that it couldn't wait? What do you need from me?'

'It's that picture. The landscape.'

'Oh.' Her eyes dulled. At first sight it might have been boredom. But then again it might have been to hide some sort of pain. 'You've had it cleaned already, have you?'

'I wish I had. No. It's been stolen.'

'Stolen?' Even allowing for her four years at drama school, her surprise seemed genuine. But it wasn't just surprise. There was a glimmer of something else as well. Outrage, perhaps. And a hint of unease.

'Where from? When?' she demanded.

'It was taken last night. From the gallery on 79th Street where it was being stored.'

'That's bad,' she said. 'I'm sorry. What do the police say?'

'What do the police ever say? I don't imagine their clear-up rate for this sort of crime is ever very high.' He paused, looking hard at her.

'So?'

He took a sip of his beer. 'So I think the time has come for you to talk to me. Tell me what you know.'

'Wait a minute.' She was suddenly on the edge of fury. 'Are you saying what I think you're saying?'

'I'm just asking you to tell me what you know.'

'I don't believe what I'm hearing. Are you crazy? You actually imagine I had something to do with this, don't you?'

He wasn't going to tell her that by now he thought anything was possible. Instead he said, 'Look, I'm not accusing you of anything. But I'm turning to you because I need your help.'

'My help?'

'Yes. Your help.' He paused. 'You see, there's something very strange going on here. I don't understand it. And I don't like things happening to me that I don't understand. I think you know a lot more about this picture than you've told me so far. Perhaps I know things that you don't, too. What I'm proposing is a fair and honourable exchange of information. A pooling of resources. That way we may even get the picture back.'

'We?'

'Yes, we. For some reason that you won't explain to me, you feel strongly about that picture. I respect that, because I do too. There have been worse bases for co-operation.'

She still looked dubious. Troubled. 'Why should I trust you?' she asked.

'Because I'm on your side. Why won't you accept that? I mean, do I look like a con-man?'

She contemplated him. 'I guess not,' she said. 'Right now you're looking like some kind of tormented bloodhound.'

She giggled unexpectedly, and he laughed too. Then he saw her sliding her coat off her shoulders. It was her gesture of submission. 'OK,' she sighed. 'But you tell me what you know first. As a gesture of good faith.'

So he did. From the moment when he'd first seen the catalogue entry that wet morning in Jermyn Street. How the attribution to Johan Christian Clausen Dahl had all checked out in the Witt Library. How the picture had been in a sale in Weber in Berlin in 1931. How he'd come to New York to buy it in the auction and finally succeeded. How the mysterious Raven had approached him about reselling it. How he'd refused the offer and now the picture had been stolen.

'There's something going on,' he repeated. 'Something that I don't understand. I don't understand who's taken it, and I don't understand why. But it's not in my nature to leave it at that. I have to get to the bottom of it.'

She nodded, sighed again, and stood up. 'I don't understand it either,' she said, beginning to rebutton her coat. 'But what you told me figures as far as it goes. I think you'd better come with me.'

He stood up too. 'Where are we going?'

'We're going to pay a visit to my mother.'

It was her fingers he noticed as she clutched the photograph frame. She had long, thin, once elegant hands now withered by the years so that the diamond engagement ring that she wore on her second finger seemed too heavy for such a flimsy support, too loose, rattling like a bauble on a twig. But as he watched, her fingers tightened, gripped the frame with such a force of agonised contortion that for a moment he thought she might crack the glass. She was sitting there on the couch, staring very hard at the photograph. And Parnello was sitting next to her, perched gingerly, suddenly afraid for her in her frailty, suddenly fearful that his visit here was not merely an intrusion on her privacy but a source of unfathomable pain.

And behind them hovered Alexandra, simultaneously

anguished and expectant, her hands taut in the pockets of her jacket.

Alexandra's mother wrenched her gaze away from what she was holding and turned to him. He could sense the supreme effort of will she was making. To put her mind in order. To come to terms with the shock she had just sustained. When she spoke, she did so very deliberately, in a slow, precise tone, as if she was walking on the edge of a precipice and any step might plunge her into the void.

'And is this the picture that was in the auction here on Tuesday?'

Parnello looked once again. The photograph showed the interior of a room. An elegant, panelled room. A room from the past. You saw a pair of heavy chairs, a substantial mahogany desk, a large and rather ugly plant with spreading leaves. And a fireplace. Pictures hung in proliferation on the walls, pictures that had been caught with surprising clarity by the camera lens so that many of their images were identifiable. The landscape to the left was the one that he couldn't take his eyes off. It showed a river with a ferry, an elegant villa on the hillside above. If you looked very closely indeed you could even make out the bonfires burning in the distance. And imagine the clouds touched by the crimson sunset.

'I can't be absolutely sure from this photograph, but it certainly looks like it,' he conceded.

'I recognised the view immediately in the saleroom,' confirmed Alexandra. 'I couldn't believe it.'

Her mother nodded, perplexed. 'But why, Alex? Why didn't you tell me?'

'Oh, darling, I don't know. I didn't want to worry you. I couldn't quite be sure.'

'How can we be sure?'

Alexandra leant forward and stroked the side of her mother's face. It was a gesture of enormous tenderness. 'We could look in the album,' she murmured. 'The one in the bureau.'

For a moment her mother closed her eyes. Then she stood

up and without saying anything she walked over to the bureau, scrabbled for a key in an upper cabinet, and opened the drawer below. Parnello had also got to his feet, awkward; an intruder. He watched Alexandra. It was not possible to witness how moved she was by what was happening to her mother and remain unmoved himself. He barely knew these people. But he had the feeling that in the space of a few minutes he had been unwittingly propelled into the deepest intimacy with them. Not just with them individually; but – and this was the greater intrusion – he had become intimate with the relationship between the two of them as well.

Alexandra's mother bore the battered album back to the couch and sat down again. She leafed through the pages with enormous care, as if what she was holding was dangerous, as if she were nursing an untamed animal only not violent so long as it remained in her exclusive control. Only when she reached the photograph she was looking for did she turn the album round and show it to Alex and Parnello. 'There,' she said. 'Is that clearer?'

It was. What they were looking at was an ancient but professionally taken photograph of a painting. A photograph of the Dahl. Parnello's Dahl.

'This is the one,' he confirmed. He recognised the chance felicity of the brushwork in the sky. It was the same picture he had found in the green folder in the Witt Library that rainy afternoon last week in London. The same picture that he had bought here two days ago. There was no doubt. 'Whose pictures were these?' he asked.

'My father's. He put together this album.' She paused and looked away. Then she added in a softer voice, 'It . . . it was one of the few things I managed to retrieve.'

And then Parnello remembered what it was that had been niggling at the back of his memory. Of course: the writing on the back of the panel. The hanging instructions, in German. *Links neben dem Kamin.* That was exactly where this painting was hanging in the framed photograph of the room. To the left of the fireplace.

'Where was this room?' asked Parnello gently, picking up the framed photograph again. Recognising he was moving into sensitive territory. Not wanting to hurt her, because she seemed so frail with her thin, anguished fingers. 'Was this a family house?'

'Yes, Mr Moran.' Alex's mother spoke very softly, barely above a whisper. 'This was my family's house. A very long time ago.'

'Where was it?'

She paused, and took a deep breath, as if the information she was about to give him would finally project her over the edge of the precipice. 'In Berlin,' she said. 'In Berlin, beside a rather beautiful lake called Wannsee.'

'Were you brought up there?'

She nodded. 'There. And on my father's estate in Pomerania,' she told him. 'The last time I saw this house I was ten years old. That was in 1944.'

As she spoke, he realised what was distinctive about the delivery of her words. There was a dominant overlay of American to her accent; but something else kept rising to the surface. A matter of the merest inflexion. A hint of German. Only perceptible if you knew.

'And your father was a collector?'

'Yes. And my father's grandfather, too. He inherited pictures from him as well.'

'Was that the last time you saw the collection? In 1944?'

'Yes, that was the last time.'

He had to keep asking the questions. She needed their continual stimulus to speak at all of these matters. But he would not have kept pressing her if he hadn't felt that something in her needed to speak of them, that her replies were an obscure relief to her.

'What happened to the pictures?'

'I understood them to have been destroyed. The house certainly was. The Russians turned it to rubble when they took the city.'

It was only then that Parnello looked down once more at

the photograph of the room that he was holding, allowed his gaze to wander away from the Dahl, to other details. To other paintings hanging on the wall. It was only then that he saw it. Only then that he registered it. The picture hanging above the fireplace itself.

It couldn't be. Could it? It was a shock even greater than the recognition of the Dahl.

'And this one?' he kept his voice deliberately calm. As if he were merely inquiring which fruit was riper at the greengrocers. 'Do you remember this one?'

'I am not sure.' Her eyes narrowed at the effort of memory.

Alexandra leant over the back of the sofa again and asked, 'Why? Who do you think that's by?' As she peered at the photograph, she was suddenly very close to him. He caught a breath of her scent.

Parnello looked again at the wheatfield. At the distant line of trees. At the troubled sky. 'Van Gogh,' he said.

'Shit!' said Alexandra.

'You don't by any chance have a larger photograph of that one too, do you?' ventured Parnello. 'In the album?'

The older woman turned the pages once more. Still keeping the book close to her on her lap. Possessively. 'Here,' she said at last.

He did not have to look very long at the detailed image to know that there wasn't any doubt. He wondered if Alexandra caught it too. The uniqueness of the vision. The distinctiveness of the handling of paint. The flagrance of the human sensibility through which this landscape was refracted.

Later Alexandra's mother allowed him to look through the album himself. One side of it rested on his knee. The other side on hers. She controlled the turning of the pages. He noticed, too, that she kept her fingers firmly clamped inside at a certain point. There were pages beyond, he realised, that were forbidden, not for anyone else to see. Certainly not an interloper like himself. But from the twelve or so photographs of individual paintings that he did absorb, he realised that her family collection had been substantial and impressive. There were several outstandingly good Dutch seventeenth century pictures; there was the Dahl; there was a Max Liebermann. And that magnificent van Gogh.

'Can you think what might possibly have happened to these things since you last saw them in 1944?'

She shook her head. 'As far as I am concerned they were all destroyed at the end of the war.'

Except they hadn't been, had they? Not all of them, anyway. Because here was the Dahl resurfacing more than fifty years later. The Dahl that someone had wanted so badly that they had had it stolen from him in the early hours of today.

'When did you leave Germany?' he asked her.

'In January 1946.'

'And you came here?'

'That's right, to New York. I am American now. My husband was American. My daughter is American.' She reached out and took Alexandra's hand. As if that orientated her, anchored her more securely. Distanced her from things, too.

Parnello felt a terrible pity. 'So these photographs are all you have?'

'Not quite all. There was one painting which survived. It's nothing, not by comparison with the ones in these photographs, but I've always looked after it because it's my one link with . . . with the past.'

'Where is it?'

'It's that one over there, above the table.'

She pointed, and their eyes followed. It was a still life of a bunch of flowers lying spread out on a tablecloth. Everything about it was heavy: the paint, the colour, the tonality. Parnello got up and went to look more closely at it. It was signed by a minor German painter of the turn of the century, Emil Lindemann, and it was dated 'Berlin 1899'. After the photographs in the album, it was hard to find words tactfully to praise it.

'Interesting,' said Parnello feebly.

'I know it's not well painted, Mr Moran, and I know it's not worth more than a few hundred dollars. But it was painted by my grandmother's teacher. She was quite an accomplished artist herself, in fact.'

Parnello turned back to face them both. 'And this is the only painting left from your family's collection in Germany.'

The old woman nodded.

'What was your father's name?'

She took a deep breath again. 'Seitz,' she said. 'Gottfried von Seitz.'

Parnello paused. He knew the name from somewhere. It triggered a faint historical echo. He did not press the point. It was dangerous territory with any German of Alexandra's mother's age to probe too far into their father's activities. Pretty soon you came up against the stumbling block of what he might have done in the war, and you never knew what embarrassment might lie concealed under that particular stone. But she herself answered the question he had suppressed. She spoke with pride, but with an odd defensiveness, too.

'My father was a member of the 20th July plot,' she said. 'The conspiracy to assassinate Hitler.'

Alexandra saw him out, and they stood on the landing waiting for the elevator.

'Thank you,' he said. 'Thank you for bringing me here.'

She shrugged. 'It was important for us too, you know.'

'Is your mother going to be all right? I realise all this has been a shock to her.'

'I'll stay with her a little.' She paused, then asked him: 'What will you do now? About the Dahl, I mean.'

'I am going to find that picture. I'm going to get it back.' He was surprised by the elation in his own voice. He recognised suddenly that he had found what his life lacked for long periods, what he needed to kick-start himself out of stagnation. A cause.

'How?'

He thought for a moment. Raven was untraceable. He had no leads. The situation was not promising. 'If we can't go forwards, then perhaps we should go backwards,' he said.

'What do you mean?'

'I've got this feeling that the key to all this may be in something that happened to the Dahl since it left your grandfather's collection. So I'm going to work back over the past fifty years or so. Trace its history back step by step from when I bought it. See if that makes it clearer why somebody is so anxious to lay hands on it now.'

'But how do you do that?'

'The first step must be to get in touch with the person who consigned it for sale in the auction. Find out where he got it from.' He could hear the elevator approaching, so he reached out and touched her arm. 'Perhaps we could work together. After all, we've both got a vested interest now in laying hands on it again.'

'Maybe,' she murmured dubiously. 'But different vested interests.'

Was it that she still didn't trust him? Or was it something else that made her afraid? Something that it was beyond his understanding to identify. Something that she had deliberately concealed from him.

'You must be proud of your grandfather,' he said.

'Look, I'd rather not talk about him. OK?'

Her tone was suddenly sharp. Bitter. She turned on him the same resentful look that he remembered from the first occasion he'd seen her, that time in the saleroom three days earlier. The look that told him he was an unwelcome intruder in her life. The look that he'd hoped the last two hours might have banished from the repertoire of their relationship.

There was a brief period of silence between them, filled by the elevator doors clanking open. He was about to step inside, when she seemed to relent and kissed him quickly on the cheek. 'Of course I'll help you,' she said. 'If I can. Without hurting people.'

And before he could ask her what exactly she meant, she had turned back into the apartment and closed the door behind her.

TEN

As he heard his secretary come into the office, Heinrich Stahler looked up from his desk and removed his reading spectacles. He barely needed them, but wearing them was an act of calculated strategy, to add authority to his image, to achieve a measure of political gravitas. He was forty-five, but there were times when it was to his advantage to be considered older. To his political advantage. He was good at working these things out, at deciding when to emphasise the energy of his relative youth, and when to play on the extent of his experience, the accumulation of wisdom which he had acquired himself as opposed to the accumulation of family wealth which was his by inheritance. His opponents called him calculating. He preferred the word disciplined. He believed in leaving as little as possible to chance.

'Is that my schedule, Frau Müller?'

With her brisk but dainty little footsteps she crossed the luxuriously carpeted expanse which separated his desk from the doorway. She was a neat, blonde woman of enormous correctness. Although she had worked for him for nearly ten years, he knew very little about her. He believed she lived in Meerbusch, or Wuppertal; one of those suburbs, anyway. She had a husband, but he had never met him. She blushed easily, but that was the nearest she got to an expression of emotion.

'Here you are, Herr Doktor. There are one or two changes, as you will see.'

He put his spectacles back on to study the piece of paper.

'So I am still to address the EEC meeting in Strasbourg on Thursday? But at 2.30, not 12.'

'That is correct.'

'And is it the Special Commission on Immigration, or the Special Commission for Immigration? These distinctions are important.'

'I have checked it with Strasbourg this morning. It is "on Immigration".'

He nodded. 'And there will be adequate security arrangements?'

They both knew what he meant.

'Again I have checked with Strasbourg. There are contingency plans for access by a side door should it become necessary. The driver is fully briefed. But they do not anticipate many demonstrators.'

Heinrich Stahler shook his head and sighed. 'They are fools, these youths, with their placards and their whistles. They have not thought their position through. I suppose they wish for their streets to be overrun with Rumanian gypsies, they want all the riffraff of Eastern Europe camped in their back gardens. Because that's what they'll get unless they listen to me.'

Frau Müller stood up very straight and said, 'You are absolutely right, Herr Doktor. Here in Germany there is not room for all these people. We have already been accommodating enough.' She blinked, and blushed slightly.

'And after this meeting: there will be time to reach Cologne for the televised debate?'

'Albrecht will be ready at 4.15 to drive you direct to the studio. Strasbourg to Cologne should not be more than two hours forty minutes.'

Thoughtfully he ran his finger down the page. 'Then there is the rally in Frankfurt next day.'

'Again Albrecht will drive you.'

'And after the lunch on Friday, no more commitments.'

'I have kept the afternoon free.'

'Good.' He paused, as if calculating the impact of the revelation he was about to make. And savouring it a little. 'Because it is my little girl's birthday party. I have promised to be there, and she will be heartbroken if I miss it. For me there is nothing more important than the family.'

'Yes, Herr Doktor.'

'The family is the cornerstone of our society.'

Beyond everything he believed in its sanctity. All good motives sprang from the values which it engendered. He looked across at the Renoir hanging above the table to his left. His father had bought it in the late 1960s. It showed a mother gazing fondly at the young child on her knee. He thought of his wife Liselotte and his two girls Petra and Nina. For a moment the emotion threatened to overwhelm him. But then staring at the image on the wall reminded him of something else.

'Oh, and by the way, Frau Müller, have we heard from Tübingen yet about this picture?'

Her eyes followed his. 'The Renoir?'

'Yes. Do they or do they not want it for their exhibition?'

She smiled with relief. 'The fax came through half an hour ago from the director. They would be very honoured to accept the loan.'

'But on my terms?'

'They agree to illustrate it on the cover of the exhibition catalogue.'

He nodded with satisfaction. He was used to getting his way.

'On the subject of the Renoir,' continued Frau Müller, 'there is a further question from the director: how is it to be designated? With your name? Or just "from a private collection"?'

He considered the matter. Strictly speaking it was the property of a foundation which he had set up. A foundation with very substantial tax advantages. Then again, in many ways it

109

would be gratifying to see it recorded in the catalogue as 'from the collection of Dr Heinrich Stahler, Düsseldorf'. But in the final analysis he had to follow his political instinct, which told him that publicising his enormous family wealth in this way might be a mistake for a candidate for high office.

He said with regret: 'It must be recorded as simply "from a private collection". It is sad, you know, that there is still so much envy in our society.'

'You are right, this is much to be regretted,' she agreed.

'You know, Frau Müller, already at the end of the nineteenth century my grandfather was one of the leading collectors of works of art in Germany. I think his blood is still running in my veins.'

He gave a sharp little laugh, and Frau Müller blushed again at such a very personal revelation.

'Do you need me for anything else now?' she inquired.

'Not now.' Stahler glanced at his watch. 'But tell Albrecht to have the car ready in ten minutes.'

'Of course, Herr Doktor.'

As she left the room it crossed her mind to wonder where he might be going. Because for the next three hours there was absolutely nothing on the schedule. Nothing official, anyway. And it was not the first time that such a thing had happened. Not that these unexplained absences were a regular occurrence, but Frau Müller had a meticulous mind which registered all deviations from the norm. Over the past six months she could recall three other occasions when the Doctor had summoned his car and disappeared for an afternoon without there being anything in his diary.

She gave a little gasp of horror as a terrible thought came to her. She tried to suppress it, but it would not go away. What if Herr Doktor had a mistress? What if he was stealing away for romantic assignations in some secret boudoir? She wanted to run back into his office and remonstrate with him; warn him of the possible consequences of his actions, the hideous dangers. It would be a political disaster if such matters came to light. Great things were in store for Doktor

Heinrich Stahler, she was convinced of it. He was a man of destiny. A leading member of the Bundestag today . . . who knew what tomorrow? She could not bear the thought that the highest political power, which was waiting just round the corner for him, maybe attainable even at the next elections, might be snatched from him by scandal. It would be a tragedy. And all for the sake of some little painted trollop in some penthouse in Essen, some pampered tart utterly unworthy of the greatness of the Herr Doktor.

But no. She was getting herself unnecessarily worked up. It was her over-active imagination. Had he not on countless occasions extolled the virtues of the family? Was it not one of the cornerstones of his political philosophy? Was it likely that such a man of principle would lower himself to keep a mistress, would jeopardise his entire political achievement by such an involvement? She was being ridiculous.

Wasn't she?

He gave Albrecht instructions and the large Mercedes set off through the midday traffic. The interior temperature control eased efficiently into action, and Stahler sat back to take stock for a moment. Out of the window he contemplated the pedestrian population of Düsseldorf drifting up the Koenigsallee on what was the first sunny day of the year. On the whole he was pleased with what he saw: the elegant women; the affluent men; the group of Japanese, all clad in identical dark overcoats and blue scarves, bringing trade and prosperity to the city. Even the skinhead swathed in the colours of Fortuna Düsseldorf, the local football team, did not entirely displease him. He was a German, at least, expressing his support for a German entity. He was undoubtedly a patriot.

Stahler began to think out in a little more detail his speech to the Commission on Immigration. Inevitably he would face opposition to his views. It was all very well for British delegates to bleat on about individual liberty and the protection of the rights of political asylum seekers. How

111

many landborders did Britain have, how many easy points of access for the eastern hordes? Britain was secure because it was Germany who was absorbing these people. Germany was in the front line. Oh, yes, there would be the usual liberal squealings about human rights. What about the human rights of the hundreds of people who wrote to him every week complaining about the way Germany was being inundated by foreigners? Taking German jobs and usurping German benefits. That was one of the reasons why he had gone into politics, why he had decided to try to put something back into the society in which his family – and his father in particular – had flourished with such conspicuous commercial success. In order to give those ordinary Germans a voice, a voice they had lacked so far. Duty and Rights. There was a satisfying interplay here between the two concepts: ordinary German men and women were winning back their rights because of his own highly-developed sense of duty.

But then again, his family had a strong tradition of public duty. Maybe it was unfashionable to look at it like this, but his own father had been a patriot, doing no more than his duty as he saw it when he had served his country faithfully in the war. That war. So long ago, and yet still its memory was not yet eradicated from the world's consciousness, its long shadow casting an unfair taint on Germans even today.

He remembered bringing the question up once with his father, not long before he died in 1978. Normally his father had been voluble and assertive, a massively successful industrialist who in the two decades following 1945 had built the financial empire on which Heinrich's family fortunes now rested so securely. His father was used to expressing himself in forthright and categoric terms. But the war was the one subject upon which he had remained uncharacteristically reticent. Until Heinrich had forced the issue, by asking him point blank: 'There's an awful lot of self-righteous nonsense talked about that war, wouldn't you agree?' His father had looked troubled, and bought some time by lighting one of the interminable cigars in whose smoke he habitually wreathed himself, using it now like some sort of defensive screen. 'You had to have been there,' he muttered gruffly. 'You had to have been there. Otherwise it's not fair to make judgements.'

Judging fairly. Fairness mattered. Not just about the war. But with other things, too, with things that stretched even further back in time. More personal things. In a sense what Heinrich Stahler was doing this afternoon was an oblique attempt to right a historical wrong for his family. For his father and his grandfather before him. To redress an imbalance in the scales of justice.

There are still woods in the Ruhr valley where you can lose yourself on foot, despite their proximity to one of the biggest conurbations in Europe. Twenty minutes after they had drawn clear of fashionable Koenigsallee, they turned off into a deserted country road which ran through heavily forested land. After two kilometres, Stahler tapped Albrecht on the shoulder and told him to draw into the next layby on the right and wait for him. He would not be more than forty minutes. If by any chance he had not returned within an hour, then Albrecht was to ring the number on the attached card and ask for Otto. Otto would give him instructions which he must obey to the letter.

Albrecht nodded impassively, and sat back to wait. He was paid enough never to ask questions.

Stahler strode forward along a path between the trees. He drew his cashmere coat about him, but the air had a pleasant glimmer of warmth carrying the first promise of spring. The sun cast dappled light through the branches on to the bed of pine needles which softened his steps as he walked. A bird was singing. He began to feel a little sentimental about nature. About the changing seasons, each with its own special beauty. How many other politicians had his sensibilities, he wondered? Heinrich Stahler was no mere bureaucrat. He was a man of vision. An art collector. True enough, he yielded to no-one in his determination, in his political acumen and willpower. But he had his softer side as well. That was important. Important for voters to know, too.

Five minutes later he reached the clearing, and stood still for a moment. It was very quiet.

'Doktor Stahler.'

He didn't know where the men had come from. They must have been hiding behind a clump of trees. Waiting there for him. He recognised one of them, the balding, faintly dissipated figure with very small dark eyes in sallow, puffy skin, like currants set in dough. The one he knew as Mikhailowsky. But the second was a different proposition. He was short and thick-set, with dark, close-cropped hair. He had a battered, swarthy, pock-marked face. The sort of face that could not conceal its long familiarity with violence. For a moment Stahler wished he had brought Otto with him. Otto was at home in this sort of situation. Otto had a physical presence; he could counter aggression simply by the way he stood, or by a quick, minatory sway of his shoulders.

'You are alone?'

'As you instructed,' said Stahler. And then, putting on a show of mild impatience to cover his unease, he added: 'But I did not expect to be greeted by a deputation.'

Mikhailowsky disregarded his remark. 'So, Doktor Stahler,' he said. 'I have good news for you.' He spoke German with an accent, but it was still difficult to define.

'Yes?'

'Matters are now satisfactorily arranged. The deal may progress.'

'I am pleased to hear it.' Stahler paused. He was relieved, but he was irked by the man's attitude. Keen to assert himself over him. Over both of them. 'I was beginning to lose confidence in your people's ability to deliver under the terms of our agreement. What is your colleague's name, please?'

The second man smiled, and pushed his hands down further into the pockets of his belted raincoat. He waited sufficiently long for the pause to verge on insolence, then said, 'I am called Hoffmann.'

'Hoffmann? Right. Well, Herr Hoffmann, let one thing be understood. By both you and Herr Mikhailowsky. Let it be understood clearly. This is not the way I am accustomed to doing business. I don't like delays. I don't like people messing me around.' His political opponents knew that well enough. These two must be made to understand it, as well. So why was Hoffmann still standing there smiling at him with such insolence?

'There is no problem now.' Mikhailowsky spoke briskly, but he was not smiling. 'The technical difficulties have been sorted out. We can proceed.'

'Wait a minute.' These people still did not seem to have grasped it. Their stupidity was immense. 'It is perhaps not so easy as that. You take my compliance for granted, as if I were in some way dependent on you. But I must remind you that you are equally dependent upon me. So I need to be satisfied once more on certain points.'

Mikhailowsky shrugged his shoulders, but did not raise objections. He stood there expectantly. Out of the corner of his eye, Stahler observed Hoffmann turning away, flicking light to a cigarette.

'So,' continued Stahler. 'If we proceed, we shall do so on the terms acceptable to me. At the price agreed.'

'At the price agreed,' confirmed Mikhailowsky.

'I must emphasise again the conditions under which this transaction shall take place. One, I insist on receiving every single item from the list. There shall be no substitutions or deductions from it. And two, I demand absolute confidentiality. If either of these two conditions are not met, I shall call it all off. Everything. Our agreement will be null and void.' He paused, and took a few thoughtful paces across the pine needles. 'Oh. And I shall need to inspect the merchandise once more. To satisfy myself that it is still intact. After these so-called technical difficulties.' He tried to inject a measure of contempt into the phrase. Of disdain for an organisation so incompetent as to be susceptible to such setbacks.

'That is not impossible.' The man's tone was still gallingly assured. As if the people he represented were negotiating from a position of indefinable but unassailable strength. How many times did Stahler have to remind them they needed him just as much as he needed them? Their separate interests were held in mutual equipoise; it was the only basis on which to do business with such men. Kracht had said so. Kracht knew. As Kracht had engineered things, it must appear that neither side could expose the other without inflicting prohibitive damage on themselves.

'Good.' He narrowed his eyes meditatively, as if trying to conjure up before him one of Frau Müller's exemplary schedules. 'As it happens I will in all probability be there next week. On an official visit. It is possible that I could find an hour or two of leisure time for the purpose of this inspection on Tuesday afternoon.'

Mikhailowsky nodded. 'We will make the arrangements.'

'Discreet arrangements,' insisted Stahler.

'Of course. We would send a car to the hotel.'

'At 4 p.m., please. There will be two of us. My advisor will also be present.' He had no need for advisors, of course. He prided himself on his own judgement in these matters. No, he had resolved to bring Otto. Otto, with his physical presence, would be more use than any advisor.

Hoffmann kicked at a stone. Stahler looked at him again, furtively, trying to make up his mind. Wondering if he was perhaps Rumanian. Speculating as to whether his swarthiness betrayed gypsy blood.

Hoffmann drew on his cigarette and asked his first question. 'And the money?'

'What about it?'

'It's still in place?'

'Of course. Your people can check, if you have any doubts. It remains in the Swiss escrow account, as arranged. Only to be released upon our joint instructions.'

Hoffmann nodded. The two men seemed satisfied. The meeting was over. Mikhailowsky approached Stahler with hand outstretched. Stahler shook it, a little unwillingly.

Hoffmann's extended hand he barely touched. But these things were necessary. As a gesture of good faith.

As he walked back to Albrecht and the safety of the car, he wiped his palm clean with a tissue that he found in the pocket of his cashmere coat.

ELEVEN

'My dear chap,' Humphrey was saying, 'You have to understand that's quite impossible. We're bound by house rules, you know.'

He had emerged from his office somewhere behind the scenes at the auction house to greet Parnello, summoned by Parnello's request to discuss something urgent with him. To ask a favour.

Humphrey stood there jacketless in the well-heated interior of the saleroom, wearing a bow tie and a pair of calculatedly ostentatious braces. Such a sense of style, you could hear him wanting people to say. Only an Englishman could get away with it. What a peacock. And what a charmer.

'But surely,' said Parnello, 'there must be circumstances under which you would reveal such information.'

Humphrey leant gracefully against an eighteenth-century commode on view from the upcoming furniture sale and considered the matter. 'It would have to be a court order or similar,' he suggested. 'I'd have to consult the legal department.'

'It seems rather an extreme position.'

'My dear chap,' he said again, 'I'd love to help you. But please remember where we are: this is New York, for God's sake. Such damned litigious people, these Yanks. If we start giving away this sort of privileged information, we could be sued. And in this town, believe me, that can hurt. Look, I'm desperately sorry that the picture's been stolen. Rotten for you.'

'I still don't see what harm it can do for you to tell me who the seller was.'

'That's just how trouble starts.' His tone turned a trifle querulous. 'You dealers just don't understand, do you, with your constant corner-cutting? We give our sellers an undertaking of anonymity, if they request it. And they have in this case. We have to abide by it.'

'But Humphrey, these are special circumstances. The picture's been stolen, for God's sake.'

'I'll say it again. I'm very, very sorry that this has happened to you. But we can hardly be held responsible for someone else's negligence. It's not as if it was stolen from our premises.' He laughed urbanely at the very thought of such a possibility. 'And actually, now I come to think of it, I can't see what help it's going to be to you in getting your picture back to know who the seller was.'

Maybe you can't, thought Parnello. But the reason for his need to know the identity of the seller was not something he was going to explain to Humphrey now. He said:

'So there's absolutely nothing you can suggest, then?'

Humphrey rubbed the palms of his hands over his eyes and massaged his upper cheeks. 'Oh, dear,' he confided, 'such a late night last night. Now let me see. I'd love to help you, as I say. What about this, as a special favour? You write a letter, to the anonymous vendor, asking him or her the questions you need answers to, hand it to me, and I'll send it on to him. Or her. That way the vendor can decide whether or not to have contact with you.'

Parnello imagined the interminable wait before any answer came back. A week? Two weeks? And what was the likelihood that under these circumstances the seller would choose to reveal himself? Or herself? Pretty negligible.

'That's kind of you,' he said ironically. 'I'll think about it.'

'Do that, old chap.'

'I'll be in touch.'

'Coming this evening?' asked Humphrey encouragingly.

Perhaps he felt an oblique desire to make up for his lack of helpfulness. Or perhaps he was just feeling expansive. After all, there is nothing easier than issuing invitations when you're not personally picking up the tab. 'We've got a special view of pictures and furniture from the De Marne Collection. Oodles of champagne, it'll be fun. Bring a chum, why don't you?'

Parnello thought about it. An idea was germinating. 'I might do that, thanks,' he said. 'And thanks for your help.'

'No trouble, I assure you,' said Humphrey vaguely, but it was clear his attention had been caught by someone over Parnello's shoulder. 'Good heavens. Isn't that Ivana Trump? You must excuse me.'

He edged away, composing his features into a greeting which combined an appropriate degree of deference with a devilish English charm.

Parnello picked her up at the shop that evening. Its interior was bare and white and minimalist, its exclusivity indicated by the scarcity of actual clothes on view, and the absence of any hint of price on those that were.

'Welcome to the morgue,' said Alexandra.

'Thank you for coming with me tonight,' he said. 'You see, I've got this plan.'

They took a cab to the auction-house reception.

'You want me to do what?' she said as they crawled across town in the rush-hour traffic.

'It's our best chance now to get the information we need. Unless you have a better idea.'

'I'm to be the femme fatale?'

'I don't think you'll find it too difficult.' She had dressed up for the occasion, changed in the shop before he arrived. Beneath her coat she was wearing a short black dress under an elegant white jacket. With her blonde hair and soft brown skin, she looked sensational, irresistible in a way that made it hard to decide how long to allow your eyes to rest on her. Either you were conscious of lingering too long; or you were constantly looking away. 'Think of it as a drama school exercise, if you like,' he suggested. 'You know, role-playing.'

'And what role will you be playing in this little charade?'

'Oh, just the usual tormented bloodhound.'

'Uh-uh. I've seen that one. It's too easy for you with those eyes.'

'Innocent onlooker, then.'

'Not so innocent, I think.' She smiled at him momentarily, then it was she who looked away.

He guided her upstairs with his hand on her elbow. On the landing he paused to get her a glass from the waiter holding a tray.

'Champagne?'

'No thanks. Just water. I don't drink when I'm working.'

He raised an eyebrow of admiration. 'A true pro.'

'Stand by for the performance of a lifetime,' she promised.

They came across Humphrey ten minutes later, holding court to an admiring circle of New York dowagers. Snatches of his conversation could be heard at some distance away. 'One of the greatest Rembrandts in private hands ...' '... when I was skiing last year in St Moritz ...' '... so I said to Princess Margaret ...'

They approached closer. 'Is that him?' whispered Alexandra.

'I'm afraid so. Do you want that drink after all?'

Humphrey caught sight of them. His dissertation must have been losing its momentum, because he broke off almost abruptly and came forward to greet them.

'Parnello! Splendid that you could make it. And in such decorative company too.'

'Humphrey, can I introduce you to Alexandra Hamilton?'

'Enchanted,' said Humphrey, kissing her hand.

'Humphrey's a vice-president here,' explained Parnello.

'Senior vice president, actually,' murmured Humphrey discreetly.

'Oh, my God!' Alexandra exclaimed, suddenly wide-eyed with enthusiasm. 'You're a senior vice-president here?

Working in an auction house like this must be just about the most glamorous life I can imagine. What's your specialty?'

Humphrey smiled modestly. 'I look after the old masters, for my sins.'

'Did you say old masters? I do not believe this! I've always had this thing about the old masters, I've been hours in the Met studying the Dutch seventeenth century. What's it like to spend your life working with such beautiful objects?'

For a moment Parnello wondered if she was coming on a little too strong, but one look at Humphrey reassured him. The man was captivated. 'Let me show you one or two very beautiful French eighteenth century things in the De Marne sale,' he suggested eagerly, wrapping lingering fingers round her elbow. 'If you've got a moment, that is.'

'Humphrey, I'd just love that,' gushed Alexandra.

Parnello extricated himself and watched them walk off together. There was something simultaneously impressive and disturbing about her in the full flight of her theatricality. She did it well. But it was a dimension of her that he didn't know, that distanced her from him. If she could so easily slip into other personae, how could he be certain that the Alexandra Hamilton he thought he knew was the real one? One thing was for sure: if she went on like this much longer, the girl would deserve an Oscar. And very shortly Humphrey might need an ambulance.

Oh, well. He looked about him. In order to display the glories of the De Marne collection, the huge auction-house viewing room had been set up as a cross between a museum and the interior of a grand French chateau. Heavily ormulued eighteenth-century desks, bureaux and tables were arranged gracefully against the walls. Above them hung a variety of elegant mirrors and paintings nearly by Fragonard, Boucher and Watteau. Everywhere there were flowers, monuments to the endeavours of East Side's most fashionable florist. The clever thing was, this was more than a museum. It had a thrilling accessibility. You could walk amongst these objects and actually touch them; later, if you had the money, you could even acquire them. It was like wandering into a gathering of startlingly beautiful women and suddenly realising that any one of them would be ready to go to bed with you. At a price.

Now the room was seething with people. There was nothing Manhattan loved more than a big private view. Tired arbitrageurs with deep voices and permanent tans discussed high finance with the unctuous interior decorators who danced avaricious attendance upon them, while the wives of Wall Street moved amongst the exhibits with secret desire. Those Wall Street wives. Never had he seen such a tribute to the exercise, diet and cosmetics industries, so many women of so advanced an age crammed into so little, their figures held in check by diet plans and worked out by personal trainers until the tiny micro-dresses designed for girls twenty-five years their junior would hang convincingly about them.

'Quite a show, isn't it?' said a man at his side. Parnello turned and smiled in recognition.

'What, the collection or the guests? How are you, Ryder?'

'I'm well,' said Ryder.

'Are you here as a buyer? Have you seen something you fancy?'

'Me? God, no. Nancy drags me along. And I guess I quite enjoy watching the people.'

'What do you make of this bunch?'

'Some of them are genuine works of art in their own right, don't you think?'

Parnello laughed, but Ryder went on, 'No, I'm serious. It reminds me: do you know what the biggest boom industry in this country is?'

'What?'

'Plastic surgery.'

'Really?'

'Yep. A generation ago, plastic surgeons were purveyors of a service to the rich. Now they are the rich themselves.'

'There's quite a cross-section of clientele for plastic surgery here tonight. Past and future.'

'Don't you love it? Hey, look at that one. Over there by the floral arrangement. Every time she raises her eyebrows she has an orgasm.'

The waiter came and refilled their glasses. Parnello drank, thought a moment, and decided to risk it. 'Can I ask you something, Ryder? A professional question?'

'A professional question? Now this intrigues me.' Ryder's scrubbed red face beamed back at him.

'Yes. You're a German twentieth-century historian. I take it that means you know a little bit about the Second World War.'

Ryder considered the proposition. 'A smidgeon. What aspect of it?'

'Tell me about the Hitler Bomb plot in 1944.'

'What, the 20th July plot to assassinate the Fuehrer? The one that half the population of Germany was involved in?'

'How do you mean?'

'You know, I've noticed a very strange thing. How almost every German you meet today has an uncle or a grandfather who was crucially enmeshed in that conspiracy.'

Parnello laughed, but not as loudly as he might have done before he'd met Alexandra. Before he'd spent last night listening to her mother. Looking at her photographs.

'You begin to ask yourself,' went on Ryder, 'how did the plot fail, considering the huge number of people involved?'

'I think academic life has turned you into a bit of a cynic.'

'Well, you've got to admit, the 20th July conspiracy is a pretty desirable club to belong to if you're German. Most of them were aristocrats. So if you can establish a family connection with one of them, you're simultaneously asserting your credentials both as a Good German and as a toff.'

'A "toff",' repeated Parnello. 'That's a word I haven't heard for some time.'

'Toffs. Nobs. Aristos. What do you English call them? But

that's what most of those conspirators in the Bendlerstrasse were, weren't they? Toffs.'

'Yes, but you can't really hold that against them. Should their good breeding have disqualified them from standing up to Hitler?'

'No, of course not. What I'm really saying is that I don't think their motives were that heroic, in many cases. You've got to ask why they only started standing up to Hitler so late in proceedings. I mean how come it took till 1944 before they made a meaningful gesture of opposition?'

'What about von Trott? What about Bonhoeffer?'

'OK, there may have been a handful who opposed the Nazis from day one out of conscience or for ideological reasons. Hats off to them, it can't have been easy. But I think the majority only joined the plot when they saw the way the wind was blowing. They were perfectly content to wear their Nazi badges and strut up and down in their uniforms so long as Hitler seemed to be leading them to victory. It was only when he started losing that they turned against him.'

'But you can't take away the fact that they did turn against him.'

'Too little. Too late.'

'But these were men who risked their lives to oppose the regime. And paid the price. A lot of them ended up against a wall being shot in cold blood, didn't they? You can't ask more than that.'

There was a pause. The party was at its high tide; Parnello was aware of waves of human sound breaking and eddying about them. 'This isn't a subject I expected to find myself discussing in this place tonight,' mused Ryder. 'Why do you ask? About the Hitler bomb plot?'

Parnello considered his two-thirds empty champagne glass. 'Does the name von Seitz mean anything to you in that connection?' he said at last.

Ryder's forehead puckered in the effort to place him. 'Von Seitz? Wasn't he one of the plotters, an officer on

Stauffenberg's staff in Bendlerstrasse, at the War Office? A bit of a shadowy figure. I'd have to check, I can't immediately recall, but didn't something rather strange happen to him in the end?'

'I don't know. That's why I'm asking you.'

'Jesus,' he said, pointing at his drink. 'It's too much of this stuff. The memory's going. Maybe I'm mixed up. Maybe I'm thinking of the wrong guy.'

'Would it be a terrible imposition if I rang you in the morning to get the definitive version?'

'Of course you can. I'll look up the literature the moment I'm back in the apartment. But this intrigues me: what's so special about Seitz?'

'It's nothing serious. Call it a bit of idle art historical research if you like. But I'd be grateful for more information if you can find it without too much trouble.'

'Just cut me in for ten percent,' laughed Ryder. 'If it ever comes to anything.'

And Parnello wandered off casually, to check on the progress of von Seitz's American granddaughter.

He found Humphrey explaining the relationship of Fragonard to Watteau; and Alexandra giving him her most rapt attention. They were ensconced together on a sofa in an alcove behind a large vase of lilacs. He waited a moment around the corner, pretending to inspect a little school of Chardin still life. And he listened.

Humphrey was saying, 'I've got a suggestion to make: what about a spot of dinner a little later in the evening? We could scoot off to a rather delightful Italian place I know. The longer we talk, the more I feel that you and I have got in common.'

'I'd love that,' said Alexandra breathlessly. 'But we don't have to rush off yet, do we? I find this place just so fascinating. Everything about it.'

'Let me see, then. What else can I show you here?'

'I'd love to catch a glimpse behind the scenes. What really

goes on in a place like this? Where do you work, Humphrey? Where's your office?'

'You want to see my office?' Now Humphrey's voice was a little thick with pent-up emotion.

'Oh, is that not possible?'

'My dear girl, nothing is impossible. If that's what you'd like.'

They rose, Humphrey a trifle unsteadily, and Parnello followed at a discreet distance. He heard Alexandra murmur: 'And you really sold a Canaletto for eleven million dollars last year? That's incredible!'

'I've got the photograph of the picture back in the office. It may amuse you to cast an eye over it.'

Humphrey held open a door marked 'Private, Staff Only' which led off the main saleroom where the crowd of guests still milled. She walked through, giggling, and the door closed after them. Ten seconds later Parnello followed, and stood for a moment in a stairwell, the ebb and flow of the party suddenly dimmed and distant. He heard Alexandra giggle again, some way above, and he climbed noiselessly up two flights of stairs in time to see another door closing ahead of him. He reached it just in time to catch it before it clicked shut, and thanked God that he had when he found that it was only to be re-opened by tapping in a security code.

He walked softly along a corridor lined with bound auction catalogues, then stopped abruptly when he came to the door marked 'Humphrey Gardener, Department Head'. It was ajar, and he could hear their voices again.

'That's amazing,' she was effusing. 'I guess Venice must be just about the most beautiful city in the world.'

'But you must have been there?' Humphrey's voice was increasingly thick; the champagne and the passion in combination were making it difficult for him to get the words out.

'No, I haven't. But I hope to visit Italy some day.'

'I adore Venice. I practically lived there when I was a student. I know it like the back of my hand. But it's criminal that you haven't been there, Alexandra. The city was made for you. It would be the perfect backdrop for your beauty.'

'What a sweet thing to say.'

There was a pause. Parnello did not dare look through the glass panel of the door, but he could imagine Humphrey moving closer to her; stroking her hair, perhaps, or reaching feverishly for her hand. He was aware of an unexpectedly acute shaft of jealousy. Then he heard her voice again:

'Wow! Is your computer terminal? I bet you got an incredibly sophisticated system here.'

'I believe we have.' From his tone of voice, computer technology was not one of Humphrey's strong points. Or perhaps it was not high on his list of priorities at this moment.

'Won't you switch it on for me? Show me how it works?'

'Are you sure it really interests you?'

'C'mon Humphrey. You promised I could get to see a bit behind the scenes. Hey, wait a minute. Don't tell me you don't know how to work the darned thing. Is that it?' There was a hint of scorn in her playfulness, an implied sleight on his manhood in her suggestion that he was not up to the challenge of operating a complicated piece of machinery.

He laughed urbanely. 'My dear Alexandra, I use this toy every day of my working life. Just move over a little and I'll show you.'

There was the sound of a keyboard being tapped, and the clicking and whirring of the system gathering speed. Humphrey provided a brief commentary. 'There you are, you see, I'm logging on to the system, so . . . I'm putting in my name and specialist department, here . . . Now, please avert your eyes while I enter my personal password . . .'

'Oh, let me see. I love secrets.'

'Naughty girl. Don't peek.'

She giggled. Parnello had to admit she giggled well. Convincingly. Disturbingly.

'Now what?'

PHILIP HOOK

'Now you can choose various options,' said Humphrey. 'What's it to be? Cataloguing, Sale planning, Property system . . .'

'That one there. Property system.' Good girl, thought Parnello. She'd remembered it right.

'There we are, then. Property system.'

'Hey, you know something? This is really neat . . .'

'And you are very beautiful.'

'Whoa there, Humphrey. You're tickling my ear. Look at the pretty designs here on the screen. What can we do next?'

'Well, we could key in a client's name and see what he's sold recently . . .' There was a pause. A brief sequence of fumbling. '. . . Or we could key in a sale date and lot number and find out who the owner was.'

Parnello held his breath. Steady, Alex. So near now. Keep your nerve. Don't blow it at this last, delicate stage.

'Hey, you're tickling me again,' he heard her say. She giggled once more. 'That's really nice.'

A further interminable pause, and then she spoke again. In a new tone: seductive, intimate. 'You know what I'd really like now? More than anything in the world?'

'What's that, sweety?' Humphrey's voice had risen an octave.

'A glass of champagne.' He heard her sigh. 'Hey, how about just you and me having a glass together? Up here? In private?'

'It's a lovely idea, but . . . I could nip back down to the saleroom and get us some, I suppose.'

'Great!'

'What do you think? A bottle and two glasses?'

'Go for it!'

'I won't be long. Just wait here and don't move. OK?'

'Hurry, hurry!'

Parnello just had time to hide himself behind a rack of catalogues before Humphrey blundered out past him. Then he in turn slipped into the office.

130

'Oh, God!' she said as he came in. 'Were you out there long? Did you catch all that?'

She was still sitting in front of the screen. Breathless; a little dishevelled.

'I certainly did.' He reached out and touched the top of her head in a gesture of admiration. Her hair felt soft. 'It was Academy award stuff. Now I estimate we've got about ninety seconds before he's back.'

He leant over her and tapped quickly at the keyboard. Three times back came the response 'Incorrect Command'.

'Bugger!' he exclaimed, increasingly desperate.

'Here, let me,' she said, reaching over. The screen flickered, and then, miraculously, the required option appeared.

'Yes!' she breathed triumphantly.

He read on, following the instructions: 'Insert sale date: now what was Tuesday? 25 February, wasn't it? And we put the lot number in here. 147. Now press "enter" . . .'

And then there it was, up on the screen in front of them. Just like that. One framed oil painting, landscape, German School nineteenth century. Owner's name: Lars Persson, Storvejen 34, 11125 Stockholm, Sweden. And a telephone number.

'You brilliant girl,' said Parnello and kissed her quickly on the cheek.

They met Humphrey just inside the main saleroom, scampering back clutching a bottle and two glasses. He was perspiring freely and there was a wild look in his eye.

'But where are you going?' he demanded a little pathetically as he caught sight of Alexandra.

'Miss Hamilton has suddenly remembered a previous engagement,' said Parnello, taking her arm. 'But it looks as though you've got something rather cosy planned with that champagne. We won't hold you up. Have a good evening.'

'What time is it in Stockholm?' Alexandra demanded. Her eyes were shining. They had ended up in an Italian restaurant, perhaps out of oblique deference to Humphrey's original intentions for the evening.

He looked at his own watch. 'Ten to four in the morning.'

'Too early to ring, I guess.'

He laughed. 'He might not appreciate the wake-up call.'

'Yes,' she mused. 'It's probably not the best way to get Mr Persson on our side.'

On our side. He felt her closer to him, sensed that the success of the evening's operation had loosened whatever it was which restrained her in his presence.

'So what will you do?' she demanded. 'Try in the morning?'

'First thing.'

'And then what?'

'That depends on what I hear. I might even go to Sweden myself. If the leads look promising.' Byron again. A man must travel and turmoil, or there is no existence.

'You're really serious about this, aren't you?' It was as if she was regarding him for the first time, seeing him clearly.

'You know I am.'

'I suppose I do. Now.'

'It's the way I'm made. I get an idea in my head, and suddenly it engages all my emotional energy. It sends me into a sort of overdrive.'

'That's it, an overdrive.' She nodded, contemplating the word. 'It's kind of scary.'

'I suppose it must be. I'm sorry.'

'Scary. But exciting, too.'

She had a way of looking at him from beneath long lashes which was unsettling. It made him want to reach out and touch her face, run his hand through her hair. To stop himself, he shook out a Ducados from his packet.

'Of course my mother's totally won over by you,' she went on ruefully. 'She says you've got wonderful eyes.'

'And you're not so sure?'

'Can I be honest with you? You give me this uneasy feeling. I like being with you, and yet I'm worried that you may be trouble.'

'Trouble?' He inhaled deeply. 'How do you mean, trouble?'

'I'm worried that you could end up doing my mother and me harm.'

'How?'

'It's difficult for me to explain, but through the Dahl for one thing. You're so passionate. In pursuing the Dahl like you are, you may be unintentionally opening up things that are better kept hidden. Digging up the past.'

'Listen, the last thing I want is to do you or your mother harm.'

'I know. And don't get me wrong, I'm curious about the picture too. I want to know the truth. But be careful, Parnello. For all our sakes, be careful.'

He was staring into his glass and watched as the waiter filled it. 'And then apart from the Dahl,' he went on slowly, 'there's something else as well. Something incomparably more valuable.'

'What's that?'

'There's the van Gogh.'

There was a sudden stillness between them. 'The van Gogh,' she repeated softly. She pronounced it 'Van Go', in the American way.

'You must have thought it. What I thought when I first saw the photograph of that picture last night.'

'What was that?'

'That if the Dahl has survived, then maybe, miraculously, so has the van Gogh. Somewhere.'

She nodded. They both sat there, silent. Awed by the dream being given expression in words.

She said at last, in a low voice: 'What's your take on that van Gogh? Is it a good one?'

'I've done a little checking today,' confessed Parnello. 'Rung a friend in the impressionist department in Sotheby's in London. Asked him about that picture. In a general sort of way. Completely off the record. He says it's in

the books, in the catalogue raisonné, as last known in
Berlin in 1928. It was in an exhibition at the big dealer
of the time, Paul Cassirer. Since then it's untraced, assumed
destroyed in the war. He confirmed my reaction to it.
As one of the last series of wheatfields, it's incredibly
desirable.'

'So what's it worth today?'

'You must bear in mind that this guy's estimates are
notoriously conservative. Even so, he said between 25 and
35 million dollars.'

'Jesus!'

'And if the van Gogh did resurface, your grandfather's
heirs would have a claim on that, too.'

'Jesus!' she said again.

'Are there any other heirs? I mean, does your mother have
any brothers or sisters still alive?'

'No,' she said softly. 'She's alone. Her brother died. He
was thirteen. She doesn't like to talk about it.'

'I understand.' Like the way Alexandra didn't want to talk
about her grandfather, either. For some reason that went as
yet too deep for words. For some reason that lay between
them niggling and unresolved, an unspoken obstacle to their
fullest intimacy.

'So she's the sole heir,' he went on. They sat in silence
again, contemplating the implications. Fantasising.

'But perhaps we shouldn't be getting too excited about
it all,' he said finally. 'Because I also asked my friend at
Sotheby's what he reckoned was the likelihood of this picture
resurfacing, if he'd heard any rumours at all about it over the
past year or two. He said no, he'd heard nothing. You see, they
get to hear about most major pictures becoming available,
even the ones that don't get to auction. And frankly the
chances were pretty negligible of it reappearing suddenly,
at this stage. He'd be prepared to bet against it. It's too
long ago.'

She shrugged. 'I guess you're right,' she said. 'It's too
long ago.'

There was regret in her tone. But perhaps he detected a tinge of relief, too.

'When I was very young,' said Parnello as the waiter filled their glasses again, 'we used to go on holiday to Greece. I can't have been more than six or so. There was this rock, about fifteen feet up from the sea. My older cousins used to dive off it. I couldn't get it out of my head. I dreamed about it. I could hardly bear to look at it. I didn't tell anyone, but I knew I was going to have to jump off it myself. I spent a whole morning willing myself to do it, preparing. And then, when no-one was watching, I scrambled up there. I remember it so vividly, standing there looking down this incredible distance to the water. Realising that to jump was the last thing that I wanted to do. But knowing that if I didn't it wouldn't be possible for life to continue with me as me. I would become someone else. And I didn't want that.'

'So you jumped?'

'Yes. The jump was fine. But I resurfaced a bit too close to the rocks and cut my head open. Still, even though I had to go to hospital to have stitches, I was happy. I'd done it. I was still me.'

'So getting the Dahl back is a bit like jumping off that rock?'

He nodded, impressed by the way she'd seen the point of the story, had realised why he was telling it almost before he'd realised it himself. 'I've got to do it, because the challenge is there. And if I don't meet challenges when I perceive them, I diminish myself.' He paused, to take a drag on his cigarette. He watched her through hangdog eyes, rheumy with the smoke. 'And of course there are other reasons now.'

'Other reasons?'

'Since I met you and your mother.'

'What does that change?' She was looking at him very intently. With a sudden rediscovered mistrust.

'I know now that this was your family's picture, this Dahl,' he said carefully. 'Your mother, as your grandfather's heir,

135

could well have some claim on it. I am keen to sort that out.'

She closed her eyes for a moment. 'You owe us nothing.'

'Perhaps I don't owe you anything. But I still feel the need to sort it all out, untangle it, make it fair again.'

'Why?'

'I suppose there's something in me that just can't bear injustice. Can you understand that? But I think I'm different from other people: with me my need for justice is – how can I describe it? – tied up with my need for romance. It's as much a matter of aesthetics as morality.' He paused, drank from his glass, then peered into it. 'Have you got any idea what I'm talking about? I'm not sure I have.'

She laughed, relaxed again. 'I blame it all on Byron,' she said.

'You once began to tell me why you disapproved of Byron,' he reminded her.

'I did, didn't I?'

'So why do you?'

'Because he's a selfish bum. Because he wants to have it both ways the whole time. He wrote that really stupid line "And after all, what is a lie? 'Tis but the truth in masquerade . . ." I mean, is that crap or what? It's insulting to the intelligence. Anyone who can seriously maintain that point of view is a menace, to themselves and other people. Very long in charm and very short in reliability.'

'Not the sort of man to get involved with?'

'Do me a favour.' She paused, then giggled without warning. Giggled like she had with Humphrey earlier that evening. 'OK, I guess the guy had something. You probably had to be pretty careful if you went out to dinner with him.'

He called a taxi and gave the address of her apartment.

'I'll drop you off,' he said.

'My God,' she said, 'I've had a lot to drink. And I've got this audition tomorrow.'

'What for?'

'An off-Broadway production. Something very experimental. *Two Gentlemen of Verona* set in Las Vegas. Or is it *Two Gentlemen of Las Vegas* set in Verona? I guess I'll be going in with cucumbers over my eyes.'

Parnello had had a lot to drink, too. 'You'll knock 'em dead,' he assured her. 'Anyway, you deserved to celebrate tonight, after that unforgettable performance starring opposite Humphrey Gardener. "How about you and me scooting off to a rather delightful little Italian place I know?"'

' "Oh, Humphrey, I'd just love that",' she giggled.

The cab drew up at her apartment. 'Want a nightcap?' she asked. 'Jesus! Did I just invite you in? Now I know I must be drunk.'

' "The best of life is but intoxication",' Parnello quoted. Byron again. Sometimes he couldn't help himself. He followed her up the stairs.

There were two bedrooms, he noticed. She told him she shared the place with a guy who worked in films. A guy called Tony who was away a lot. Like tonight.

'Is he your boyfriend?' asked Parnello.

She shook her head.

'Good.' He sat down next to her on the sofa and watched her eyelashes from very close to. He remembered that the bird with the longest eyelashes was the toucan. He was about to tell her, then decided against it. Instead he kissed her.

'You're dangerous,' she said.

'Dangerous? To who?'

'To anyone who gets close to you. And probably to yourself, as well.'

'Why do you think that?'

'Because you're easily bored.'

'I'm not bored now. With you.'

'And in the end you live for sensation.'

'Sensation. Mmm, that's nice.'

'Being with you is like driving very fast in a car that's almost out of control.'

'The overdrive again?'

'I guess so.'

'Don't worry. I've got both hands on the steering wheel.'

'No, you haven't,' she breathed. 'It's only my willpower that's keeping it on the road at all.'

The question still would not be suppressed. It kept resurfacing in his mind, niggling him even as he kissed her, and finally he asked it, even though his face was buried in her hair. Even though the way she was lying in his arms made it easier for him just to say nothing and go on kissing her. But he wanted to know. To remove that final barrier between them.

'So why don't you want to talk about your grandfather?' he murmured in her ear.

It was as if he'd touched the switch that short-circuited the system. She sighed, unwound herself from him and sat up dishevelled on the edge of the sofa.

'That's enough for one night,' she said, her long back arching as she slipped the strap of her dress over her shoulder again. 'Going home time.'

'Sure,' said Ryder on the telephone next morning. 'Sure I've had a chance to check. I didn't need to, in fact. When I woke up it all came back to me. I guess I was fuddled by the champagne last night. You know something? I've got to lay off that stuff.'

Parnello's head was none too clear itself. 'And what did you find?' he asked, feeling the roughness in his throat, the smarting in his eyes.

'It's as I suspected. If the guys in that conspiracy against Hitler were divided between the idealists and the opportunists, I'd have to mark your friend von Seitz down as one of the latter.'

'What makes you say that?'

'You have to look at how he ended up.'

'How?'

'He was executed.'

'Oh, come on, Ryder. They were all executed, weren't

they? Taken by the Gestapo, tortured, given show trials, hung from butcher's hooks?'

'No, no. You don't understand. You don't understand who executed him. It wasn't the Germans.'

'Wasn't the Germans? Who, then?'

'It was our side. The Russians, actually. Three days after they liberated Berlin. He'd been held in gaol by the Gestapo up till the end, but they hadn't finally got round to carrying out the death sentence they'd imposed on him. No, it was the Russians who sought him out and put him up in front of the firing squad.'

'The Russians? But why?'

'Something pretty tacky somewhere south of Kharkov in the Ukraine in 1942. On the Eastern Front. Seitz was responsible for the cold-blooded shooting of seventeen Russian prisoners. All civilians, apparently.'

'Oh, God,' breathed Parnello.

'So he may have been a toff, but he wasn't a very good German after all.'

'Flawed, certainly.'

'More black than white.'

'No,' said Parnello. 'Grey, more likely. Grey, like most of us.'

PART THREE

———◦◦◦◦———

South of Kharkov

TWELVE

———∞———

Gottfried von Seitz came to a halt where the pine trees ended and the wheatfield began. He waited for the drone of a passing aircraft to wax, wane, and fade into the distance. Then everything was still. He had not expected Russia to be so hot. Nor so beautiful, so moving. The silence was intoxicating: he loosened his tunic and leant back against the tree behind him, feeling himself gradually absorbed into the landscape as if his long thin body had become some sinuous adjunct to the trunk itself. It was a dangerous sedition, this solitude. It was a dangerous sedition to subvert the discipline of his daily life and allow thought to triumph over action in this way. But there were times when it was essential, when he clutched its comfort as others sought it in a bottle of Schnaps.

He ran his eye across the field of deepening yellow, luxuriating in its colour, delighting in its expanse. '*Ce sont des champs qui s'étendent à l'infini.*' The line would not go away. It played on the edge of his consciousness like some sweet, dimly-remembered passage of music. It was the first week of August 1942: the wheat was turning gold, ready for harvesting. It stretched across to a column of birch trees a quarter of a mile away, spreading itself in a profusion of ripening perfection. He was suddenly disturbed by the richness of the crop before him. There was a time for reaping, a climactic moment when the harvest must be gathered in. If you missed that moment, decay would follow; decay and corruption. But who would bring this harvest in? He was torn by the agony of the missed moment. The potential for waste gave him pain.

He thought of home. He thought of Morwald. What if this were his Pomerania, what if these abandoned fields were his family's own estates? What if those were his own tenants' farmsteads whose burning ruins decorated the horizon with wisps of blackened smoke?

It was strange that something like this wheatfield had the capacity to move him, caught him unawares with the poignancy of its dereliction. It was strange because far more terrible things no longer touched him. He was anaesthetised to the bloodshed now, inured to it. He had felt more shock before the war at the wild boar felled by a clean shot through its coarse-furred skull than by the fresh-faced lieutenant next to him whose shoulder he had seen blown away two days ago, or the young artilleryman who had sunk in slow motion at his feet with one side of his head missing. But even so he felt compelled to test the anaesthesia now and then, to make sure that it was up to strength. Without it he would fall apart.

Falling apart. He needed to be alone with himself because it was as if he were two people, and each side of him needed the periodic full and private attention of the other if they were to continue the bonded coexistence which defined his own survival. The side of him that predominated was, of course, the soldier. It could not be otherwise. He was the bearer of a torch of tradition, a tradition of duty and service whose flame had burned as strongly in his family in the eighteenth century as it did today. He was the servant of the Fatherland in its hour of greatest extremity. That was his prime duty, the answering of a call that would have been as familiar and irresistible to his great-grandfather as it was to him. You were nothing without tradition. You were nothing without family. You were nothing without love of country.

And then there was that other side to him, the side that found sadness in a field of wheat. Why did he find this view so beautiful? Why was it at once so moving and so true? *'Ce sont des champs qui s'étendent à l'infini sous un çiel nuageux et il ne m'est pas difficile d'y exprimer toute ma tristesse, cette infinie solitude.'* The man who had written those words had died more than half a century ago. And yet Seitz felt linked to him as he stood here. Linked to him by bonds that the soldier in him could not countenance or understand. Linked to him through this wheatfield.

The soldier in him would legitimately have pointed out that this was alien, enemy country. These trees were the backdrop to terrible but necessary brutalities. This crop was growing in soil irrigated by rivers of blood. Every acre of Soviet territory had been won at terrible cost. The advance whose speed and facility had been predicted so blithely as they set out in June last year had slowed at times to a laborious crawl. The Russians were not conventional opponents. They did not know how to lie down and die. Or rather they knew how to die, but they did not know how to lie down. They did not surrender. You cut through them with the might of a Panzer Division, you inflicted huge losses, you ground them into the dust. But even then they rose again behind you, grimy relics of humanity barely still living and yet regrouped to wage guerrilla warfare at your rear. These diehard bands of partisans would lurk in shadows, emerging silent from the woods to threaten your supply lines, to gun down your reserves, making you wary of advance without the assurance of untrammelled support. Yes, this enemy was composed of Bolshevik criminals whose eradication from the face of the earth would be a service to mankind. But part of you still admired their resilience, marvelled at their resource. And shivered at the threat behind your back.

He leant against the treetrunk, flailing an angry hand through the storm of gnats encircling him. He reached inside his tunic pocket for a cigarette to light in order to disperse them. The gnats were like the Russians. They kept coming at you because it was their nature, they knew no other way. When was a gnat ever prepared to surrender, to

145

give himself over to the enemy as a prisoner of war? They might be temporarily driven back by cigarette smoke, but they would not give in.

For a moment there was peace. Peace of a sort, snatched on the edge of a field fifty miles south of Kharkov in the eastern Ukraine. Peace, after seventy-two hours of lacerating action, of total absorption in the maelstrom of noise and flame, of terror and elation, which was the front line. Three days of ceaseless artillery fire, three days of painfully slow tank advance. The artillery behind showered molten rain on to the enemy; then the tanks moved forward like ponderous caterpillars over the ground the artillery had prepared for them. Exhausted, his company had come down from the battle line last night and struck camp in the clearing on the other side of the woods. In the deserted farmbuilding where he had pitched his own camp bed, he had fallen immediately into a fathomless sleep; a sleep from which he had awoken, shaking and fearful, four hours later, quite unable to reattain oblivion.

Moving amongst his men the next morning he had noticed that he was not alone: others were shaking too, as if in delayed response to the cataclysmic reverberations of the past three days. He saw brown, muscular forearms quivering in the sun. He saw battle-hardened hands shaking so violently that they could barely hold metal cups to their mouths, scarcely guide savage cigarettes to their chattering lips. Hollow-eyed they sat around bemused at this lack of command over their own bodies, like machines suddenly rendered impotent by the malfunctioning of a single part. And soon, in a matter of days, they must return up the line to the front. Soon. It was dangerous to think too far ahead. Or to look too far into the past, either. He must lean back here against this treetrunk, aware only of the pleasure of the cigarette between his lips. And the harrowing beauty of the wheatfield.

The wheatfield. A gentle breeze, sensed first in the trees behind him, rose and fell, sending undulations over its surface like the wind on the sea. In his imagination there was another wheatfield now, a wheatfield of sharp yellow slabs of paint where the outlines of the heavily-laden brushstrokes simultaneously built images and formed patterns, each touch charged with an edge of feeling whose power was almost intolerable. It was the wildness which entranced him. A measureless yellow plain beneath an azure sky shot through with emerald. The tortured clouds chased each other across the heavens. A wild intelligence had brought this image into creation. A wild man had taken this scene and animated it with the expression of his own feeling. A wild man who spoke to him. Not to Seitz the soldier; not to von Seitz the Pomeranian landowner; but to that other person within him. To that other person who knew that even the most lovely landscapes are nothing if not in some way refracted through the human spirit.

He heard the rustling of footsteps in the trees behind him and turned quickly, suddenly alert. The soldier in him tensed. He was separated from his company, an easy target for an enterprising band of enemy partisans. It would be a gross irresponsibility to allow himself to be killed or captured here. A dereliction of duty.

Then, at the far side of the semi-circular indentation into the woods formed by the clearing at whose edge he stood, he caught sight of the familiar figure of Lieutenant Ebers and relaxed.

'Captain von Seitz?' Ebers always reminded him of a dog; a gundog, maybe a spaniel. He moved with the same singleness of purpose. You sensed his eagerness to please, his simple satisfaction in tasks achieved. His need for approbation.

'What is it, Ebers?' Seitz dropped his cigarette end and ground it with his heel into the earth. The turf was surprisingly yielding here. There must have been rain not long ago.

'I think you had better come, sir. Major Seidler is waiting for you.'

Annoyed by the intrusion, Seitz demanded: 'Who is Major Seidler?'

'He has arrived with a lorry.'

'I don't care if he has arrived with five tanks and the Vienna Boys' Choir. Who is he?'

'He is arrived from HQ, sir.' Ebers paused, perplexed and a little uneasy. 'I think you had better come.'

Seitz cursed once, then walked wordlessly into the woods in the direction of the camp. Ebers trotted anxiously at his heels. In the forest thickets it was almost dark; the mass of foliage gave out a pungent, tarry scent. After the sunlight, the gloom was disheartening, ominous, as if they had descended into some joyless nether world.

In a larger clearing they skirted the charred remains of a farmstead. A smoke-blackened stove pipe jutted out of the debris. Seitz ran his eye dispassionately over the heaps of bricks, the fragments of broken dishes, the child's bed with the spring mattress warped by flames.

'Soviet bastards,' muttered Ebers.

'What do you mean, Ebers?'

'Well, they're burning their own houses, aren't they, sir? They'd rather see their property destroyed than have it falling into our hands.'

Seitz nodded thoughtfully. The wilful destruction angered him, too. He was wondering if this was the dwelling of the family who should by now have been harvesting the wheatfield.

The first thing he saw was the lorry, drawn up in the middle of the encampment. An armed soldier stood next to it, on guard. This was an unfamiliar soldier, not one of his own men. His own men sat about in the sun smoking and, if they noticed the intruder at all, regarded him with an exhausted indifference. The officer, who had himself been sitting in the cab smoking, jumped down when he saw Seitz and Ebers approaching.

'Captain von Seitz? I am Major Seidler. I have instructions to deliver you the contents of this lorry.' He spoke abruptly, but even then Seitz could sense his unease; noted the strange, impersonal use of the term 'contents'.

'I must hand over also to you this order,' continued Seidler. His eyes did not meet Seitz's. They seemed to be looking towards the pine trees behind him. 'I suggest you read it now.'

Seitz took the paper without comment. He was aware of Seidler's unspoken desire to move on, to be out of here. He didn't know why the man was impatient, but Seitz was not going to be hurried. The order was from Colonel Franz Diederich at HQ. It concerned arrangements for the unexpectedly large numbers of Soviet prisoners of war that had been taken by the regiment in the past week in the drive towards Stalingrad. He read it once. Then he read it a second time.

'No,' he said simply to Major Seidler.

They began to walk away from the lorry, till they were on their own in the shadow of the trees. The midges were out again. It was five o'clock and the sun was still hot. 'No,' he repeated. 'This cannot be right.'

'I am sorry,' said Seidler. He looked embarrassed. 'But these are orders. You are not the only unit to which it has been necessary to issue them.'

'These seventeen men you have in the lorry. They are all Soviet commissars?'

'I understand so. Commissars.' Seidler nodded, as if taking comfort from the word.

'But what these orders require me to do is not the duty of a Wehrmacht officer.'

Seidler shrugged. He looked very tired. 'Nonetheless, I am instructed to give you these orders.'

'I am sorry, but under the circumstances I have to speak to the senior officer who issued them.' Seitz looked at the paper again. 'To Colonel Diederich at HQ. Please excuse me. I must use the field telephone.'

'These are orders, Captain.' Diederich had finally been traced. From his tone of voice he had clearly come to the telephone reluctantly, angry at the distraction. 'Are you querying orders?'

'What these orders require me to do is not the job of a Wehrmacht officer,' Seitz repeated, with an increasing desperation. He remembered Diederich now, by reputation at least. A hard man. A zealot. A convinced Nazi.

'There, Captain, you are totally incorrect.'

'What do you mean, incorrect?'

'You are familiar with the Commissars' Order?'

Seitz frowned. 'Broadly.' He knew that commissars were the officials attached to every division of the Red Army and every civilian community to police their political indoctrination. He knew too that they were the men identified by the Fuehrer as the focus of rottenness in the Soviet system.

'In that case may I remind you that under the terms of the order it is mandatory for the army to execute all Russian civilian and military commissars who fall into its hands. These are unequivocal instructions. To disobey could be a court-martial offence.'

'And these men you have sent me in the lorry are commissars?'

'To all intents and purposes. Look, I will tell you something, Captain. So that you will understand once and for all. We are dealing with exceptional circumstances here. We are dealing with unexpectedly large numbers of enemy prisoners. The result is that everyone, even front line troops, must do their share in processing them. And I do not need to remind you also that we are dealing with an enemy who is not civilised. An enemy who needs treatment with exceptional measures. Therefore the Fuehrer himself has dictated this order in relation to commissars.'

'Surely these men have some rights, as prisoners of war?'

'They have no rights, beyond the right to die by firing squad. The army's orders are clear. These are the orders given by the Fuehrer himself, to whom you have sworn an oath of allegiance. As a soldier. And as a man of honour.'

'My God.' To hear himself lectured on his duties as a man of honour by Diederich suddenly made him feel sick. Sick, and angry.

'These men are for execution, Captain,' continued Diederich. 'There is no room for misplaced sentiment. These men are Russians. Vermin. If you do not carry out the order, the SS most certainly will. Einsatzgruppe commandos are in the area, and will shortly be joining us in mopping-up operations.'

Misplaced sentiment. Seitz walked slowly back to rejoin Seidler by the lorry. Trying to control his anger. Trying to come to terms with the enormity of what he had been instructed to do.

'Are matters clear now, Captain?' asked Seidler.

'I wish to satisfy myself that these men are commissars.'

'You can take that as already decided. By others more competent to judge.' Everything about Seidler's movements spoke of his desire to be shot of the problem. To wash his hands of it. To move on.

But Seitz was already at the back of the lorry, tearing open the canvas flap. He was not prepared for what he saw. Or smelt. Seventeen pairs of hostile, nervous eyes were turned upon him. Eyes blinking in the sudden sunlight. Eyes belonging to men whose bodies were wedged upright, their limbs contorted in the compressed space. The heat was like an oven, and the stench of human bodies was unleashed at him like a heavy, foetid cloud farting out into the daylight. A foetid cloud which incorporated a more subtle, insidious scent. Perhaps the scent of fear.

'You! Yes, you. Are you a commissar?' Seitz spoke the words slowly, in German because he had no Russian.

'He will not understand you,' said Seidler.

'What is your name?' persisted Seitz.

The man stared back at him mutely, but with a certain defiance. He had close-cropped, gingerish hair and many days' grime and stubble on his face. He wore a filthy dark green shirt in which he had sweated profusely.

'You are wasting your time,' said Seidler.

'Name,' repeated Seitz.

The man still stared back uncomprehending. But then a balding, older colleague leant across to him and muttered a few words The ginger man nodded, and the bald one addressed Seitz in broken German:

'He is called Vladimir Grigorovich. My name is Nikolai Serov.'

'And he is a commissar?'

They both looked blank.

'Commissar. You and he, commissars?'

Both shook their heads vigorously.

'Farmer,' said Serov simply. 'He is farmer. I am postman.'

'Of course they will deny it,' said Seidler as they walked away. 'I tell you, Captain, it is easier if you just accept your orders. Easier for all concerned. This is a war, for God's sake.'

And the words came back to Seitz. The words of the oath he had taken: 'I swear by God this sacred oath, that I shall be unreservedly obedient to the leader of the German Reich and People, Adolf Hitler, Supreme Commander of the Wehrmacht, and prepared as a brave soldier to risk my life for this oath at any time.' And as he remembered them, he sensed their macabre and unsuspected power of entrapment.

'So,' Seidler was saying. 'I hand these men over to your care.' And he turned away, aware perhaps of the hideous irony of the term he had just used.

Like a man borne off on a current against which he cannot swim, Seitz listened to his own voice deploying a dozen men from his exhausted troops to stand guard over the prisoners. To chivy them from their lorry like animals. To marshal them into a group drawn up by the clump of birch trees.

He was a man of honour. And he had sworn an oath.

Now it was not difficult to smell the fear in the prisoners. Some kicked truculently at the dusty ground; others shrugged in bemusement. But it was not far from the surface. Momentarily you caught that look in their eyes; a hint of despair; an unwillingness to see further ahead than the next five minutes.

As Seitz contemplated this ragged flotsam of warfare, he glimpsed the workings of the mechanism, understood how men might be persuaded almost unwittingly into ruthlessness. These forlorn elements of humanity before him were not to be considered as people; they were simply a classification. A classification which by definition demanded a certain military response. An obedience to orders. Once you had convinced yourself of this group's inanimate existence as a category, you were all but there. Then, as he watched, one prisoner separated himself from the rest, started trudging doggedly away in the direction of a clump of trees. He stood for a moment in their shade, as if deciding whether to run for it, to make a break for freedom. Out of the corner of his eye, Seitz was aware of the sentry to his right cocking his rifle, and training it on the renegade. Seitz held up his hand in a gesture of restraint. And then slowly, with a weary resignation, the prisoner fumbled with his fly, sagged his shoulders, and began to relieve himself against a treetrunk. Seitz turned away. There was something degrading about the spectacle. Doubly degrading: it humiliated both perpetrator and spectator alike.

Seitz watched as the guard with Seidler reached into the back of the lorry and spilled out on to the ground a collection of implements which he saw were spades. As the lorry disappeared down the farm track, its wheels grinding a cloud of dust and exhaust in its wake, the spades lay there, fallen haphazardly in a pile across each other. Like the game that his children sometimes played, when sticks were dropped in a heap and you had to pull one out without making the others move. His children. His children, Curt and Ella, safe in Pomerania. Swimming in the lake, playing in the forests. Forests of pine, like these woods here.

For a moment Seitz stood there transfixed, paralysed by memories. First his children; and then his wife. His Waltraud, turning away from him the last time he had seen her, her face set in a mask of blandness. A mask assumed not because she had no feeling, but because she had too much. Repression: that was what wartime existence had become. He who repressed the most would win. Feeling was a luxury which no-one could afford.

He shook his head to clear it. He was aware of the hiatus, aware of the tension amongst the prisoners, aware of the furtive curiosity of the sentries, aware of the questioning look on the face of Ebers at his side; Ebers, charged with a boundless energy, a seething, unchanneled desire to do the right thing. Like a man suddenly finding the key to his handcuffs, he broke the enthralment with the slightest of nods at Ebers, a movement whose enormous significance was in inverse proportion to its brevity, to his consciousness of even having made it.

In that tiny gesture it was as if a switch to a momentous piece of machinery had been triggered. Ebers moved instantly into action, communicating quickly and efficiently the order to the sentries to pick up the spades and distribute them amongst the prisoners. They were lined up, herded together, prepared to move off, surrounded by their guard, when Ebers clicked his heels next to Seitz. Clicked expectant heels. Eager, like a dog waiting to be taken for a walk.

Seitz was a man of honour. And he had sworn an oath.

What did they think, these men, this detritus of Russian peasantry gathered together on the edge of this wood south of Kharkov, what did they think when the spades were thrust into their hands? Did they understand these spades to be the guarantees of their own mortality, the means of disposal of their own remains? Or did they perhaps cling to the illusion that they were off to perform some menial act of forced labour, that they constituted some prisoner-of-war work party detailed to dig cabbages? Or did they think nothing? Were they too brutal for these ironies?

He gave the order for them to move off in the direction of the forest. Along the path which he had himself taken earlier that afternoon. Along the path towards the wheatfield.

They passed the clearing where the debris of the farmstead lay. As they marched, his eye was caught by a quick movement in amongst the charred ruins. From behind the bricks darted a ginger cat. Its energy was suddenly exhilarating amid the desolation, its affirmation of life refreshing. The cat paused for a moment, regarding over its shoulder the intrusive assembly of humanity straggling its way through the forest. Then it sped off into the trees. Within seconds it was invisible. It might never have been there.

They reached the edge of the wheatfield, and in the grassy indentation which bit into the trees, on that semi-circular margin between crop and forest, he told the men to halt. The ground was softer here, he remembered. Easier to dig. Oh, God. How easily those spades would sink into the turf. How swiftly that trench would be banked with freshly exhumed soil. How simply could men be compelled into the digging of their own graves. He cast his eyes once more out across the wheatfield.

It was like the sea. Only you couldn't drown in it.

'Lieutenant Ebers,' he said slowly. 'Please walk over here with me a moment. I wish to discuss arrangements.'

He was a man of honour, and he had sworn an oath.

At 8.30 that evening, as dusk fell, Seitz sat smoking numbly in the deserted farmbuilding where he had pitched his camp bed. And for the second time that day he heard Ebers' voice calling him, intruding into his solitude.

'What is it now, for God's sake?'

'Captain, there is Sturmbannfuehrer Borg who wishes to see you.'

'Sturmbannfuehrer Borg?'

'He is SS. From the Einsatzgruppe. He has six guards with him.'

In the tiny mirror in which he had shaved that morning with a hand still shaking from the reverberations of the front line, he now caught sight of his own reflection, fourteen hours on. He recognised himself in the sense that his features were unchanged. Still the same thin face and the same long aquiline nose. The same grey-blue eyes stared back at him, bloodshot with sleeplessness. But was he the same person any more? Slowly he stubbed out his cigarette and refastened the buttons on his tunic.

'Sturmbannfuehrer.' Seitz saluted.

'Heil Hitler.' At first Seitz thought the man was laughing at him, but then he realised that the man's mouth curved up naturally into a smile, even in repose, even when he was serious. As he was now.

'I understand there may be prisoners for our attention still held here. Under the Commissars' Order. I have come to take delivery of them.' Again the line of his mouth created the illusion that he found some secret amusement in the situation.

'There's no need.' Seitz spoke quietly. In a dead voice.

'No need? I was given to understand that there might be some problem in this instance ... Some problem needing our attention.'

'I am sorry. Your journey has been in vain. Matters have already been expedited.'

'Expedited.' There was a pause while Borg considered the word. Took in the information. It was possible to detect even a tinge of passing regret in its assimilation. 'I see. In that case, Captain Seitz, I compliment you on your diligence. If only all your fellow front-line officers shared your lack of squeamishness. It makes our job that much easier.'

What has this war become? wondered Seitz. How can it be that I am standing here having this conversation with this man? How has the honour of the German army reached this point of degradation? The events of this afternoon and evening had unfolded like a succession of scenes from a waking nightmare. He wondered if perhaps after all he was hallucinating, if he was not in fact in some advanced state of shell-shock brought on by so many days and nights in action. He did not trust himself to speak for the moment, so he merely shrugged his shoulders.

Borg sighed. He seemed to relax a notch. 'In that case, Captain, as you have saved me one extra assignment this evening, perhaps you will join me for a moment in a glass of

Schnaps.' Without waiting for Seitz's agreement, Borg stood his small guard of waiting SS men down, told them to wait, and led the way back into Seitz's quarters.

Once inside the ruined farmbuilding, Seitz realised that his companion's camaraderie was even more objectionable than his contempt. Borg leant back against the wall and uncorked a hip-flask. He passed it to Seitz who managed to reach for his own battered metal mug and pour a measure into it. To have drunk direct from the same vessel as this man would have been intolerable. Would have made him vomit.

That night, as he lay down to sleep, he was certain only of one thing: the return to front-line action could not come quickly enough now. The battlefield would be a purification, military engagement a welcome expiation of the demand that had just been made on him. And if next week a Russian shell were to take half his head away, then it seemed to matter less than it had yesterday. His hold on the fundamental moral principles which gave ballast to life had weakened. There had been a massive act of betrayal today. What he could not work out was to what extent he had been its perpetrator, to what extent its victim. Either way, because that betrayal had happened it now mattered less whether he lived or died.

He dreamed of the wheatfield. The painted one. The one in the picture which he owned back in Berlin, which hung in his study where he could enjoy its violent colours and its wild distortions in private. And not for the first time its exaggerations were a comfort to him, the anguish of its creator touched a chord of sympathy. He sensed in it a document of a different sort of life, one in which human feeling was allowed to assert itself over unthinking action, an existence in which duty did not always suppress emotion.

And he saw the ginger cat darting off into invisibility in the sea of wheatstalks, as if in flight from a bestiality all the more shocking for being human; and then it wasn't the cat running away any more but the ginger-headed man, the Russian called Vladimir Grigorovich, his green shirt matted to his torso with the sweat of fear, bolting off like an animal into the oblivion of the field of infinite yellow.

THIRTEEN

'Your garden is looking well, Gottfried.'

Christoph Ahlenburg rose from the sofa and led the way to the French windows of Seitz's study. He was a rotund, almost portly figure with thinning blond hair; faintly absurd next to the willowy Seitz. Faintly absurd as a soldier, too, with such an ungainly shape; but Seitz knew that you underestimated his physical strength at your peril, that his endurance and determination were belied by his appearance. He remembered the ten-year-old Ahlenburg lifting and bridging a small stream with a length of timber that he himself had despaired of ever moving; he remembered him a year later refusing to give up the search when a favourite dog had gone missing, and coming home triumphant carrying the injured animal at eleven at night; he remembered many things about those days, thought about them often now. As some sort of solace. As some sort of barrier against the present.

Together the two of them stood on the threshold of the garden, in the uniform of their regiment, contemplating the sun setting across the lake beyond. They looked out at the lawn that led down to the water's edge, admiring the profusion of flowers: heliotropes and begonias in neat beds cut in rigidly symmetrical shapes.

Seitz nodded. He was thinking how much he disliked those flower beds. How their orderliness depressed him. How if he ever spent any length of time here again, beyond the odd days snatched on leave as now, he would work to create something less regimented. Something wilder. 'It's hard to believe,' he said quietly.

With the familiarity born of a lifetime's friendship, Ahlenburg followed his train of thought. 'Yes. At moments like this the Russian front seems a long way away.'

'Even though it's getting closer all the time.'

Ahlenburg looked at him. Curiously. Seitz was obscurely aware of his companion's heightened interest. Well, it was true: there was no point in denying it. Ever since Stalingrad had finally fallen, in February, the army had been in retreat in the east. Slowly but inexorably the Soviets were advancing. These were the military realities.

They walked out into the sweet-smelling garden in silence, pacing slowly between the flower beds towards the little landing stage at the water's edge. Seitz followed the progress of a distant sailing boat on Wannsee, tacking for home in the breeze. It was August 1943. Would it still be like this next summer? Would people still be able to go pleasure cruising on the lake in twelve months' time? What inroads into the Reich would the enemy have achieved by then?

They paused by the ornament which stood two thirds of the way to the water and halfway between the curving flower beds, the focus of the garden's design. It was an elegant, eighteenth-century sundial, its stem formed by two entwined putti supporting the small, flat clock turned full-face to the heavens.

'My earliest memories of this house revolve round this sundial,' said Seitz. 'My grandfather offered me two marks if I could run to it and back to the house in under fifteen seconds by his stop-watch.'

'And did you?'

'I think I only succeeded once. Peter did it several times, even though he was two years younger than me.'

'Who, your Stahler cousin Peter?'

Seitz nodded. 'He was always competitive.'

'Rather tiresomely over-endowed in that department, I

seem to recall. But it's a splendid sundial. Where did he get it, old Herr Stahler?'

'My grandfather? The family legend is that he saw it once at some Schloss in Schleswig-Holstein and set his heart on it. Finally he prevailed upon the owners to sell it to him, and he had it installed here soon after the house was built at the turn of the century. You know what persistence and energy he could bring to bear when he wanted something.'

Ahlenburg laughed. 'Quite a family, those Stahlers. I have told you before, Gottfried: it's very good for you to have that healthy Stahler blood coursing through your decrepit old von Seitz veins.'

Seitz laughed, too. He and Ahlenburg were cousins, but on his father's side, not through his mother's Stahler family. He detected in Ahlenburg's tone the old landed ambivalence to Berlin merchant success; what Ahlenburg meant was not so much healthy Stahler blood reinvigorating decrepit von Seitz veins as healthy Stahler Reichsmarks replenishing empty von Seitz coffers. And that, after all, was what had happened, wasn't it? When old Friedrich Stahler had died in 1931, he had left his Berlin house and its contents to his daughter Hedda, Seitz's mother, and his country house and most of his business interests to his son Max, Peter's father. Thus it was that when Hedda had died of pneumonia a mere two years later, Seitz had found himself, as the main beneficiary of his widowed mother's will, the owner of Friedrich Stahler's Wannsee villa and an outstandingly good collection of seventeenth, eighteenth and nineteenth century works of art. He had become the recipient of something else, too, something rather less desirable: the rarely spoken but often sensed enmity of his uncle Max and cousin Peter, who resented his possession of what they considered Stahler patrimony.

Seitz was sensitive enough to be worried by this ill-feeling but resilient enough to withstand it. After all, there was no element of dishonour in his position. His grandfather had made a clear and independent decision to divide his property between his two children in the way that he had. It was hardly up to him to hand the house and its collection back. Seitz suspected, however, that there was another dimension to his own Stahler inheritance, perhaps a more subtle, less definable one. At certain moments he was aware of the twin pulls of his character, the two sometimes contradictory impulses which defined him as a sentient being. He was tempted to label that side of himself which responded to the call of duty, service and tradition as his von Seitz identity. Could it therefore be that this other element, the one that craved wildness, the one that found sadness in a field of wheat, the one that had to be suppressed in order for him to function as a soldier, was in some way a Stahler streak? Could it be that the Stahler seed, which had manifested itself in old Friedrich Stahler in the urge to acquire works of art, and in his mother in the desire to paint them, had flowered in him in a more sublimated, exotic form?

His mother had been an artist, a painter in oil and water-colour. She had been to art school in Berlin in her youth, and she was talented, Seitz could recognise that. Painting, to her, had been an absorbing and probably therapeutic hobby, an exercise which must presumably have come to constitute its own reward in that she never exhibited publicly after her marriage. His father simply did not understand what all the fuss was about, could not comprehend how his wife could sit for hours on end faced only by an easel and a view. Such apparent inactivity disturbed him. But as a child Seitz had watched her at work in this very garden, marvelling at her ability to reproduce so accurately what she saw with her eyes using only a brush and coloured pigment on a canvas for this act of magic. Surreptitiously he had watched her face, too, as she worked; these were the times when he had seen her truly serene, fulfilled. He had tried from an early age to imitate her skill. But none of her talent had passed into his hands; only perhaps into his mind.

'You're very thoughtful this evening,' observed Ahlenburg.

'I am sorry. I was remembering my mother painting here

in the old days. Actually, she painted this sundial once or twice.'

Ahlenburg rested his hands on its surface and peered closely at it, frowning. 'Look, there's an inscription on the dial here. Translate it for me, Gottfried: you were always the Latin scholar.'

' "Horas non numero nisi serenas",' read Seitz slowly. 'It means "I only register the sunny hours".'

Both men were silent. It had turned suddenly colder; there was the first breath of autumn in the air. Finally Ahlenburg said softly, 'You know, I think that sundial may be rather underemployed for the next few years as far as our country is concerned.'

'What do you mean?' asked Seitz. But he knew perfectly well.

The two friends began to walk back towards the French windows before Ahlenburg replied. 'It's all going wrong, Gottfried. Badly wrong. You know that, don't you?'

The words hung there. Challenging. Too challenging to assimilate immediately.

When they were once more inside the study, Seitz went to a cupboard and uncorked a bottle. 'Would you like cognac?' he asked. 'Peter has sent it to me. From Paris. It's rather good.'

'Thank you. But since when has Peter Stahler been sending you peace offerings?'

Seitz shrugged. 'He's always unpredictable. Maybe Paris is mellowing him. You know how well the SS make a point of doing themselves wherever they are.'

'Perhaps he's finally forgiven you?'

'What, for taking this house and all the pictures away from his family? I don't think he'll ever quite do that.' Seitz paused, recalling the constant dissatisfactions of his cousin, the suppressed energy, the way he could never sit still. Peter Stahler, SS Sturmbannfuehrer. Brother officer to men like Borg. 'You know he once told me that, as far as he was concerned, our grandfather died two years too early; which

163

was a polite way of saying that my mother died two years too late. Either way his father, Uncle Max, would then have inherited the house and collection as well, and everything would have been all right.'

As Seitz went to pour two glasses at the table in the corner, Ahlenburg walked over to the fireplace. Looking up he said: 'I see you've still got this extraordinary picture hanging.'

Seitz smiled and nodded. 'Yes. That's one of my own purchases.'

'Got to be honest. Never could understand what you see in this man's work.'

'I suppose you prefer my Stahler grandfather's taste, don't you? Less modern painting.'

'Now you mention it, I suppose I do. I like a landscape that I can believe in. Like the pictures here, either side of this monstrosity. Or like the ones in the dining room, your grandfather's seventeenth-century pictures, they transport me back. I know that's how Holland looked then. They give me an insight into the past.'

This was what Seitz valued most in Ahlenburg. His stolidity. His dependability. His predictability. Of course he was going to prefer Dutch old masters. Anything else would have been unthinkable. Still, Seitz felt compelled to justify himself in the eyes of his friend.

'I agree. But this picture gives me an insight too.' Seitz paused, suddenly embarrassed. This sort of personal revelation of feeling was not part of the normal repertoire of their relationship. In flight from one unmentionable in the garden, it was as if they had strayed unwittingly into another dangerous conversational area. He finished pouring the cognac and handed a glass to his friend.

Ahlenburg stared into it thoughtfully. Then he looked up again at the picture above the fireplace. Next to the more sober views either side of it and against the heavy wooden panelling of the room, it leapt out like something untamed, a flame flaring in the night. He said slowly: 'But it's all distorted. How can that give you insight?'

'It's a different sort of insight.'

'What are those shapes meant to be? Are they clouds? They look like lumps of disintegrating rock.'

'It's a wheatfield. With a troubled sky.'

A wheatfield. And for a moment he was back there last summer, on the edge of that wood. The dusty heat and the sweating bodies of the Russians. The clearing where the ground was softer, more yielding. The ginger cat darting off into the trees.

Ahlenburg shook his head. 'The man who painted this was clearly unstable.' He drank from the brandy glass as if the act conferred an imprimatur of truth upon his verdict.

'Your diagnosis is correct. He was an inmate in an asylum for a time not long before he did it. A little later he took his own life.'

Ahlenburg gave a brief, mirthless laugh. 'There you are, then.' He sat down slowly, lowering his bulk tentatively into the cushions. Once settled, he reached for a cigar. There were several beads of sweat on his forehead. He reached to undo the top two buttons of his tunic. 'Sometimes I think the whole world's going mad, anyway.'

'There's madness and madness,' said Seitz quietly. 'I prefer this man's version.' He gestured to the picture.

'As opposed to who else's?'

Once again the question hung there, too delicate to answer, too pregnant with implications. Seitz shrugged. To dismiss it was the reaction of the soldier in him. But that other part of him reflected how easy it was to pass off cowardice as discretion.

Nonetheless a change had come over Ahlenburg. Seitz recognised that expression, the determination in his eye. At that moment Ahlenburg had made a decision, had resolved on a course of action from which he was not to be deterred. 'Can we speak frankly?' he said.

Seitz's mouth was suddenly dry, despite the cognac. 'If you and I cannot speak frankly with each other, Christoph, who can?'

Outside the evening was darkening unto twilight. As the shadows lengthened across the lawn and the sun finally disappeared over the lake, the shapes of the garden were shrouded in an ominous melancholy. Darkness meant danger in Berlin. Night time brought a shroud of anxiety. How long would the charade of repose endure? How long before the mocking semblance of peace was sundered by the whine of the air raid sirens?

Ahlenburg drew on his cigar and said: 'You see, it is as a friend that I want to speak to you. Not as a Wehrmacht officer, not as a servant of the Fatherland. How old were we when we first became friends, do you remember?'

'Six or seven.' Seitz suddenly felt shy. These shared memories were too intimate; should be felt, not articulated. And yet his embarrassment was not simply for himself. It was also for Ahlenburg. For the solid, reliable Ahlenburg, being drawn into treacherous, unfamiliar ground. For Ahlenburg, having to speak of his own emotions.

'Six or seven,' Ahlenburg repeated meditatively. 'Yes, we used to play in the stream at Morwald. The one that led to the lake, the lake where our families' estates met.' He paused, as if trying to visualise the soft expanse of water from which the ducks rose in flight, over which the wind could whip in cruel gusts in winter. 'Our families are pretty much interlocked over the past two centuries, wouldn't you say?'

'Pretty much.'

'So on the basis that we are cousins, almost brothers, I have to speak to you, Gottfried. I want to talk about things that should go no further than this room.'

'You know we can speak in total confidence.' Even as he said it, Seitz recognised that he was taking a significant step towards something dangerous. That he was acknowledging the existence of other, possibly stronger ties than those which had disciplined his life for the past four years. Ties like those of family and friendship; ties that bound him closer to his class than to his country.

'You see, I feel there have been terrible misjudgements made. Terrible misjudgements in our conduct of the war.'

'Go on.'

'Excellent military opportunities have been squandered by flawed decisions. Flawed decisions at the top.'

'And good men have been forced into bad actions,' murmured Seitz, his voice barely more than a whisper.

'You agree with my analysis?' Through the cigar smoke Ahlenburg was gazing at him with an unprecedented intensity.

Seitz nodded. The images were surging back now, like the pain of wounds that would not heal. The smell of that evening south of Kharkov. The halt in the forest clearing by the charred ruins of the farmstead. The sweat-sodden shirt of the ginger-headed man. The sickening fear in his eyes. The expectant way his sentries fingered their machine guns, too stupefied with battle to question the enormity of the act they were about to be asked to perform. And later that evening, the look of amusement on Borg's face every time he spoke. In order to banish the procession of memories, Seitz began talking, taking comfort from the measured flow of his own words.

'Looking back,' he said, 'I am now convinced that our whole policy on the advance into Russia was wrongly conceived. The hostility with which we treated the Russian peasantry was utterly counter-productive. Here were a down-trodden, afflicted people for whom our invasion might have been a source of joy rather than oppression. If we had presented ourselves as sympathetic liberators rather than implacable enemies, who knows how many of them might not have flocked to us in support of our advance. As it was, they impeded our every step forward. Because we believed that no Bolshevik was worthy of our alliance, they had every reason to hate us, every reason to oppose us. But were these people even Bolsheviks at heart? Is anyone ever anything political, at heart? Before they are Communists, or Anarchists, or even National Socialists, men are first human beings, with finer feelings to which, if right is on your side, you can appeal.

'No wonder progress became slower and slower, when we were alienating the very people who might have helped us. No wonder we were bogged down. No wonder that appalling winter took its toll on us. If things had been only slightly different, we would be in Moscow now.'

'And who do you blame for this misconceived policy?' Ahlenburg spoke slowly, as if directing a child over stepping stones.

'I cannot blame the army for the way it has conducted itself in the field. I still believe that the German fighting man is the finest soldier in the world. There were moments out there when I was unspeakably proud of them, when they achieved things no other army could achieve. And there were moments when I wept for them.'

'Why did you weep for them, Gottfried?'

'Because they were asked to do things that should have been demanded of no honourable soldier.'

There. It was out in the open. It had been said. 'What things?' demanded Ahlenburg.

'I do not want to speak of them. But I think you know. I don't believe that anyone who has fought on the Russian front cannot have been aware of them.'

Ahlenburg closed his eyes for a moment. Perhaps it was the smoke from his cigar. When he opened them again he asked simply: 'Tell me this, then: who made these unacceptable demands upon honourable soldiers?'

Seitz shifted in his seat and stared into his cognac. 'You could lay some blame with the generals, I suppose. With High Command. They were responsible for the day-to-day waging of the campaign.' But they both knew he was avoiding the issue.

'They had sworn oaths of allegiance,' Ahlenburg reminded him softly. 'Binding oaths of allegiance.'

'We have all done that.'

He had sworn the oath. And he was a man of honour.

As Colonel Diederich had reminded him over the field telephone. Standing there listening in the cloud of midges that hot August afternoon.

'So answer me something, Gottfried.' Ahlenburg leant forward in his chair, and there was a new urgency in his voice. 'Answer me this: is there a point at which an army, through doing no more and no less than obeying orders, can thereby be deemed to have lost its honour?'

Seitz thought for a moment. 'I suppose there is such a point, yes,' he admitted.

'And by the same token, would you not also say that there comes a point when a leader, by making unacceptable, even dishonourable demands upon his men, loses his right to their oath of allegiance? When that oath must be broken?'

Seitz closed his eyes. 'This is high treason,' he murmured.

'That's not how I see it.'

'How do you see it, then?'

'There are times when by not committing high treason you are guilty of an even higher betrayal.'

'So you could put aside the oath that you have sworn? The oath we both swore as soldiers? As men of honour?' The questions came not as accusations, but as genuine inquiries. As the gropings of a man lost in a dark cave who sees a glimmer of light above him.

'The oath to the Fuehrer, you mean?' Ahlenburg lowered his voice, even though they were alone in the room. 'To a madman?'

At that moment, there broke across the great city the slowly-rising wail of the air-raid siren, cranking implacably from a low dirge to a plaintively insistent alarm. Both men started involuntarily; immune to fear but afflicted suddenly by the novelty of a shared guilt. Avoiding each other's eyes, they gathered together glasses and cigars. Seitz walked slowly to the French windows and adjusted the black-out.

'Come,' he said, picking up the cognac bottle, 'if the RAF is to wipe us out tonight, we can at least go happy.'

They stepped out into the shadowy hall where Clara, the

elderly housekeeper, was locking the front door. She moved with a perpetual stoop, a small, wiry figure bent forward not so much with age as eagerness. Her energy was prodigious. She ran this entire house now single-handed, took pleasure in its solitude.

'The black-outs are all in place, Clara?'

'I have checked them myself, Herr von Seitz.' She paused, tucking a stray wisp of grey hair back into her bun. 'Shall I make coffee? It could be a long night again.'

'No, you go on down to the cellar. Get some rest.'

She paused with her hand on the door that led to the domestic quarters. 'You will ring if you need anything?'

'Of course. You go on down.'

The siren surged on.

When the door closed behind her, the two men stood in silence for a moment. It was as if the communal menace from the skies was a barrier to their previous conversation, rendered it inappropriate when the whole country was under threat from the enemy. Ahlenburg waved a hand at the pictures hanging in profusion and said awkwardly: 'You know, Gottfried, you should perhaps take steps to protect these things. They are I suppose in danger like everything else. Flying glass . . . Well, unnecessary damage could be avoided.'

Such practicalities were a refuge to them both. 'You are right, of course,' agreed Seitz gratefully. 'I have been putting it off. Somehow it seemed too much like an admission of defeat.'

'No. Mere common sense.'

'I will see to it. They will be wrapped and stored below stairs.'

Ahlenburg gave a little laugh. 'What would old man Stahler have said about such measures?'

'My grandfather?' Von Seitz paused, recalling the opulent, greying figure with the rubicund face. 'I suppose he would have been outraged.'

'He would have been outraged by many things in the past five years if he'd lived to see them.'

'Come on. Bring your glass. We'll go down. The cellar is reasonably comfortable these days.'

Ahlenburg followed him. 'And at least down there I won't have to stare at that horrible picture any longer.'

The villa cellars were extensive, divided into several rooms and furnished in basic fashion with items retrieved from the attic under Clara's direction. A strange little subterranean womb of security had been created. An illusion, of course. They were more like hunted animals, tunnelling underground for refuge in their darkened warrens; lurking, waiting to be flushed out. How could these things be happening here, in Berlin, at the very centre of the Reich? The Reich that was to last a thousand years?

Seitz switched on lamps and gestured to Ahlenburg to sit on the sofa. The sofa with the floral pattern that his wife Waltraud had had brought all the way over from Morwald and then found she didn't like in the drawing room in the villa. At least now it was getting some use. 'I can offer you a camp bed down here, too,' he said. 'If it goes on all night, that is. And we needn't even resurface for refreshment. The wine cellar is directly through that door.'

'You have things admirably arranged.' Ahlenburg laughed, but he was preoccupied. He poured himself more brandy and lit another cigar. He drew on it and stared ahead of him in silence, brooding.

Seitz drummed fingers on the armrest of his chair. He was thinking about Waltraud now. About Kurt and Ella, with her in Pomerania. What future would the Fatherland hold for his children? Where was all this leading? Where would they be in ten years' time? Finally he turned to Ahlenburg and demanded: 'So you think he's mad, do you?'

'I think he's not fit to lead us any longer.' Ahlenburg spoke decisively, as if this conclusion had suddenly become clear to him.

'And you feel that the oath we swore is therefore no longer binding?'

The oath. That oath. Like a million other soldiers he

171

had taken it, swearing unreserved obedience to the will of Adolf Hitler, Supreme Commander of the Wehrmacht. The words resonated through his memory. Ensnaring him. Mocking him.

'No. No longer binding. Not now.' Ahlenburg shook his head firmly, as much to reassure himself as his friend. 'Not now that we have been led to the brink of military disaster by this man. Look, an oath is a reciprocal undertaking, is it not? Hitler has broken his a thousand times and so often lied to and deceived his people that an oath to him has no further validity.'

'I see what you mean.'

'These things cannot be described as treason when they are dictated by the interests of our country. We would say that we have reached a point where it becomes our duty to take action against this madman.'

'We, Christoph? Who do you mean by "we"?'

He paused, and drew the palms of his hands down the full length of his cheeks. It was difficult to tell if the gesture was one of exhaustion or regeneration. 'You must understand that you and I are not the only people in Germany who feel like this,' he said at last. 'There are others, many others like ourselves. Good men, disturbed by the direction things have taken. Good men increasingly prepared for drastic action. Do you understand what I mean?'

'I think so.'

'And Gottfried – this is a difficult question, but it's got to be asked – do you agree that the time is approaching for drastic action? Are you with us? Would your conscience be clear?'

His conscience.

And for a moment he was back there again. At the camp on the edge of the wood. Giving the order for the Russians to be marched off into the trees. These, of course, were men who had to be eradicated from the face of the earth, men who by their national, racial and political status had forfeited the right to civilised treatment. They stood in the way of the glorious expansion of the Reich. They might claim to be postmen, farmers, or whatever, but officially they were commissars. Therefore these men did not deserve to live. These men constituted a category. These men had to die.

'My conscience would be as clear as that of any other soldier who has had orders to obey in this God-forsaken war,' he said at last.

'Orders.' Ahlenburg spoke the word thoughtfully. 'Do you remember what Frederick the Great told his commanders about orders?'

Seitz shook his head.

'He said, "Gentlemen, I did not make you officers only in order to know when to obey, but also in order to know when not to obey."'

Seitz closed his eyes. There was nothing more now. The issue was decided, beyond doubt. There could be no further argument, no hiding behind moral dilemmas. A clear choice had emerged. A choice between action and cowardice. A choice between expiating the evil demand that had been made of him and letting it fester.

A little later Ahlenburg said gently: 'I think you should come with me soon to meet a very exceptional friend of mine. To meet Claus.'

Inexplicably, Seitz found that his heart was beating faster, that his blood was pounding. 'Claus?' he asked.

The other man drew on his cigar. A distant explosion caused the lampshade to sway gently. 'Count Stauffenberg,' he said.

FOURTEEN

'Are all our soldiers very brave, Papa?'

Gottfried von Seitz looked down at his twelve-year-old son Kurt and considered the question. They were standing at the edge of the lake at Morwald on a cool April afternoon in 1944, watching the duck rise raggedly off the water and head out west in the direction of the evening sun. Seitz preferred this lake to Wannsee. It was wilder, less decorous than the manicured banks of that other, more docile expanse of water in Berlin.

'Yes,' he said. 'All our men are incredibly brave.'

'And you are the bravest.' It was a statement rather than an inquiry. Kurt was still of an age to retain unquestioning confidence in his father, to proceed on the assumption that the rest of the world would always fall short of his own father's achievement. They stood there, father and son, Seitz tall like a tree bending in the wind, and Kurt, barely up to his elbow, holding himself as high as he could as if in tribute to the heroism of the German army. And Seitz reflected on the nature of courage. It was a curious thing, this campaign on the Eastern Front: in a sense it had made him brave. If, as he had once read, you defined cowardice as having too much time to think, a lack of the ability to suspend the functioning of the imagination, then that for Seitz was no longer a danger. He had learned what was in many ways the greatest gift a soldier could acquire, the knack of suspending your imagination and living completely in the very second of the present minute. The Russian campaign was an exhausting and utterly absorbing passage of military retreat, punctuated with incidents of extended horror and brief, illusory hope. But in its complete absorption it became tolerable. By an extraordinary irony, that absorption even became some sort of solace.

What was much more difficult to bear were these short hours of leave snatched at home in Pomerania with Waltraud and the children. He had arrived late last night, the smell of the front line still impregnated on his uniform, that blend of cordite and antiseptic, of cigarette smoke and the adrenalin of fear. He had bathed, succeeding in washing the grime of the battlefront from his body if not the barrage of the guns from his ears. Then he had taken a drink, and settled down to talk for half an hour with his wife. There was an unbreakable convention between them on these occasions: they never touched on any subject which might demand an emotional response from either of them. So they conversed formally, about problems on the estate, about Waltraud's cousin Helga who was getting married in the summer, about the children's progress at school. The list of things they did not talk about was rather longer. That included the Russian advance, the criminal purblindness of the Fuehrer's direction of the military campaign, and the men Seitz had seen die in the past three days; the way men met violent death, the look in their eyes, the expression of surprise and incomprehension, as if some mainspring deep within them had snapped. Nor did it include the bad dreams Waltraud had whenever she slept, the way she would wake up crying in the night; the certainty she felt at each parting from him that this would be the last time she would set eyes on him. That was the nature of the compact between them, the only way they could get through these twenty-four hours. Without it they would fall apart. Emotion kills. He who represses survives. And at seven o'clock tonight he would depart prepared, as he had been last time and the time before that, for the strong possibility that her anxieties were justified. That they would never see each other again.

So he stood now on the edge of the lake with Kurt, clenching his fists in his pockets at the agony of his son's proximity, hardly able to rest his eyes on this boy who was growing a step closer to manhood every time he saw him. And it was now that the cowardice manifested itself, that he could no longer rein in his imagination. He found himself yearning to be away from this poignancy, to be back insensate amid the artillery fire. Life was simpler and more manageable, lost in the ceaseless barrage of noise. It numbed feeling, pushed thought to the very margins. For the first time in his existence, he had discovered a salvation in not thinking. In not thinking about Ahlenburg and Stauffenberg. In not thinking about the forest clearing south of Kharkov. In not thinking about the madness of the Fatherland's leadership. But in devoting himself simply to that Fatherland. Working mindlessly towards the single aim of saving his country by holding back the Russians. Losing himself in the pursuit of arms.

'What's a defeatist, Papa?' Kurt had turned to him again.

Seitz considered the question. 'A defeatist is someone who looks only at the discouraging events, who has no confidence in his side's ability to win the victory. Why do you ask?'

'I think Odo is a defeatist, then.'

'Odo, a defeatist?' The man had been in his family's service here at Morwald for the best part of forty years, punctuated only by a period of fighting in the trenches, in the Kaiser's war. 'Why do you say that?'

'Odo told me that the Russians have been pushing our men back. That they are winning the war. How can that be, Papa, when all our soldiers are so brave?'

'Sometimes brave soldiers lose battles. Sometimes bravery is not enough.'

'Why isn't it enough?'

'It's not enough when they are badly led, when the generals make bad decisions. Do you understand that, Kurt?'

The boy frowned. 'But it will come right in the end, won't it?'

Seitz glanced at his watch. Two hours till he must leave. How could it be that he wanted the time to pass quicker? 'I hope so,' he said, 'I truly hope so.'

They turned back towards the house. The wind was blowing in from somewhere in the direction of the Baltic. Seitz put his hand momentarily on the boy's shoulder, then withdrew it. Any show of affection made it worse.

It was Odo who met them at the doorway. Seitz looked at him afresh, in the light of his son's assessment of him. He was thinner than he had been before the war; no-one got quite enough to eat now. But his face was still ruddy with the innate good health of the countryman. He proffered an envelope.

'Telegram for you, sir. The postman's boy brought it out on a bicycle because he thought it looked official.'

Seitz tore it open. He read it, then sighed.

That was that, then. He was being relieved of his active command. He was not to return to the front. He was being promoted, posted to Berlin, to Bendlerstrasse. To the Headquarters of the Reserve Army.

Ella had joined them now in the hall, her long blonde hair as ever immaculately brushed. 'What's Papa reading?' he heard her demand of her elder brother.

'Be quiet. It's a telegram.'

For Ella that meant one thing. 'Is it bad news?' she demanded, not without relish.

'No, it's not bad news,' replied Seitz.

But in a sense it was. Contemplating the prospect of his new appointment, he felt only an enormous unease. He was going to have to start thinking again. Using his imagination. Opening himself up to the past and the future in a way that had not been demanded of him amid the artillery fire.

Afterwards he reflected that Ahlenburg, already ensconced in the War Office, was probably behind his call to Bendlerstrasse. And behind Ahlenburg was Stauffenberg, anxious to build round him a group of men whom he could trust. A group of men who thought like him. A group of men who could distinguish between treasons.

So he returned to bomb-ravaged Berlin in spring. He returned to his house in Wannsee just as the lilac was beginning to blossom. And he began to think again. He began to feel. He rediscovered the torment of his conscience. He became a victim of extremes, alternating between bouts of deep despair and occasional shafts of ridiculous optimism. As if to fill the vacuum left by the removal from his life of the constant physical challenge of military action, he became aware of an unprecedented intensity within himself, a conviction that as the war his country was fighting entered its last most crucial phase, so he too was entering the last act in his own personal drama. That before too long there would be resolutions. One way or another.

The villa with its lawns running down to the lake was still watched over by the solitary and vigilant Clara. The gardener who up till last autumn had still found time to come in three afternoons a week was now fighting in France. To Clara's impotent fury, the grass had grown unkempt and there were weeds in the flowerbeds; sometimes she was to be seen outside, her wiry frame bent nearly double in the wind, hacking away ineffectually at the bindweed. But to Seitz this overgrowth was a source of secret pleasure. In it he saw the beginnings of the wildness which he craved.

The house itself played an increasingly important role in his life that summer. Not just because he was living there again, going in each day to his work in Bendlerstrasse; but also because it became a secret meeting place, a refuge where certain people gathered in the evenings to discuss things too sensitive to dwell on at length during the day. Ahlenburg was one of them, of course. He brought others with him. One grey June evening Stauffenberg himself came for an hour. He was a tall, energetic figure with a mangled hand and an eyepatch; it was hard to tell whether this disability, the result of a serious wound sustained in North Africa, was a constriction to his dynamism or actually its impetus. Either way, his energy teetered constantly on the edge of impatience.

The fourth man there that night was Garbrecht. Major Garbrecht was a silent and thoughtful, almost ascetic soldier. If a monk had shed his habit for military uniform, he would have looked like this, reflected Seitz. Garbrecht was clever, no-one doubted that. His contributions to debate were generally brief but invariably cogent and perceptive. He was a difficult man to read, still less to get to know. Yet Seitz felt reassured that a man like this was on their side, believed in their cause enough to compromise himself by consorting with them. Garbrecht sat there now, looking a little uneasy in the heavily-upholstered luxury of Seitz's study, listening to Ahlenburg.

'The news from France is not good,' he was saying. 'According to this evening's teleprinter messages, the enemy have consolidated their positions. There is no denying they have gained a permanent foothold. The landings in Normandy have not been repulsed.'

Stauffenberg stood up and walked to the fireplace. Momentarily his eye fell upon the picture above it, the one remaining picture hanging in the room. The wheatfield. Almost everything else had been carefully taken down and stored in the basement next to the wine cellar. The image of a tormented sky above the swirling crops was a strangely appropriate backdrop to the stiff, upright figure with the eyepatch who turned to address them. 'I disagree that these developments are necessarily bad news,' he announced. 'They may be our salvation.'

'Why do you say that?'

'The time for fantasy is past. We must be brutally realistic. Despite what Dr Goebbels tells us, we all know what is really happening on the Eastern front. Most of us have personal experience of it. We will not hold out forever there. The Soviets will gradually come in for us, it is only a matter of time before the Red Army is fighting on German soil. Under those circumstances, it is legitimate to take the view that the allies' advance in the west cannot come quickly enough for us.'

There was a pause while the point of view was assimilated. Seitz said: 'But you cannot be advocating surrender in the west?'

'Not surrender. But a negotiated peace with the western powers as soon as possible.'

'That would make sense if it protected Europe from being overrun by Russia,' added Ahlenburg. 'Even to the British.'

'The allies will never negotiate with Hitler,' said Seitz.

And then it came. Stauffenberg banged the top of the fireplace with the palm of his good hand, and said in a voice of icy venom: 'That's why Hitler must go.'

Here, spoken out loud, was the most dangerous sedition of all.

'Who would take over?'

'In the first stages the army must fill the vacuum.' Stauffenberg spoke decisively. 'Colonel-General Beck has indicated his willingness to assume the role of temporary head of state, once the Fuehrer is removed. A legitimate civilian government will follow. But meanwhile Beck is a figure to command respect. He is not tainted.'

'But even then,' persisted Seitz, 'would the western powers be prepared to negotiate, even with Beck? We know the terms of the Casablanca agreement between Britain, Russia and America: under those terms, Germany cannot end the war by any means other than unconditional surrender.'

Stauffenberg paused. An expression of anguish passed over his features. Seitz was inclined to interpret it as impatience or frustration; but then it occurred to him that perhaps it was simply physical pain. The man's body had been damaged almost beyond repair in North Africa. The blast would have killed someone of less prodigious natural strength and resolve. For a moment he sensed that the man standing before him was held together only by a superhuman effort of will.

The moment passed and Stauffenberg continued: 'Last

week I was discussing this exact point with General Beck. He is very fond of the riding analogy: he says you will not get over the next fence unless you first throw your heart over it. And that is what we must do now: make a jump of faith. We have to believe that once Hitler is gone, and once we Germans have been seen by the outside world to be purging ourselves of our tainted leadership, then we will be perceived as people with whom business can be done. We have to have faith that the western powers will come to realise that their interests are best served by negotiating with us, rather than destroying us.'

Garbrecht slowly removed his spectacles and wiped them on his handkerchief. Without them his eyes seemed hollow, his face emaciated, curiously incomplete. He looked up at Stauffenberg and said: 'How? How is Hitler to go?'

'I cannot tell you how exactly. But the attempt will be made. In such a way as to ensure success.'

'Assassination?'

'There is no other way.'

'And who will do it?'

There was rain in the air. A gust of wind blew through the bindweed in the garden and rippled the water on the lake. Seitz shivered. It was unseasonably cold for June.

'I will do it,' said Stauffenberg simply.

'You? You will do it yourself?'

Stauffenberg turned away from them and looked out of the French windows towards the lake. As he spoke, he seemed to be contemplating the distant shore. 'You see, the more I think about it, the more I realise it is my destiny. When that bomb exploded beneath me in Tunisia, I had no right to survive. I believe I was spared for a purpose.'

'You can get close enough to the Fuehrer to make the attempt?' asked Garbrecht. He was leaning forward now, his whole intelligence engaged.

Stauffenberg gave a brief, mirthless laugh, and turned back to face the other three. 'That will not be a problem. I have recently been so close to that man as to be sickened by the proximity. Let me, to reassure you on this point, inform you of my movements three days ago. On the night of 7th June I took the train from Bamberg to Berchtesgaden. There, the following afternoon, between 4 and 5 o'clock, I accompanied General Fromm to a special briefing with Hitler. Fromm was there as Commander of the Reserve Army, and I as a member of his staff. There were just four others present: Keitel, Goering, Himmler, and Speer.

'The Fuehrer came towards me and took my good left hand with both his own hands. His touch was clammy and weak. I looked at him, and he would not meet my gaze: in a curious way, his eyes were veiled. I cannot describe to you how it was in that room. Close to, I saw that Goering was clearly wearing make-up. With the possible exception of Speer, they were all psychopaths. The atmosphere was mouldering and rotten, making it hard to breathe. As I looked across at Hitler, he began to shuffle situation maps with a shaking hand, and I saw how it would not be impossible to shoot him. To turn a gun on the lot of them. Or better a bomb. It would be like cleaning out an infected place.'

Garbrecht asked: 'When? When will it be done?'

'I cannot say exactly when, but soon. Perhaps sooner than you may think.'

Stauffenberg had an appointment that evening which meant he had to leave soon afterwards. Ahlenburg went with him to drive him to his destination. Seitz and Garbrecht were left standing in the hall, a little awkward. A little deflated.

'I must go too,' said Garbrecht, reaching for his cap which lay on the table.

At that moment Clara appeared and asked Seitz when he would be requiring dinner.

'Shall we say in half an hour, Clara? At eight-fifteen?'

'Will that be for one or for two?'

There was an uneasy pause. Seitz murmured mechanically, 'Won't you stay, Garbrecht? I'd welcome the company.'

Garbrecht shrugged, as if food was not high on his list of

priorities for the evening. But then he replaced his cap on the table and nodded. 'Thank you,' he said gruffly.

To his surprise, Seitz found himself rather pleased by the other man's acceptance.

'We are having duck,' announced Seitz when they were sitting at dinner in the large empty dining room. 'Duck from Morwald.'

'Where or what is Morwald?'

'Morwald is my family's estate. In Pomerania.'

'Ah.' Garbrecht nodded, and stared at his plate. There was a period of silence.

'Do you shoot, Garbrecht?'

Garbrecht looked up at him, apparently amused. 'Do I shoot?'

'Yes, you know, do you shoot game ... Are you a hunter?'

'No, Major von Seitz. My background, I fear, is somewhat different from yours. Somewhat different from most of my colleagues in Bendlerstrasse, I suppose. I was born with neither a shotgun in my hand nor a silver spoon in my mouth.'

Seitz laughed to cover his embarrassment. He could not decide whether there was bitterness or just mockery in Garbrecht's tone. 'None the worse for that, I imagine,' he observed. 'Forgive me: I don't know what you did in civilian life. I'm reasonably sure you're not a career soldier.'

'No. You're right. I was an academic. A lecturer at Leipzig University.'

'In what subject?'

'In Economics.'

'Not my strong point,' said Seitz with a smile.

Garbrecht smiled too, but did not seem prepared to expatiate on his field of academic expertise. A further silence ensued. Garbrecht was not a builder of bridges between conversations, not an oiler of social wheels. And yet Seitz was not inclined to put his reticence down to shyness. Perhaps he simply did not find it necessary to turn those social wheels. Or perhaps it was something else, something subtler. He sensed Garbrecht watching him. Assessing him. Manipulating him, even, by his refusal to yield to small talk. Silence is not necessarily an indication of insecurity. Sometimes silence is an assertion of power.

Clara brought in the soup, a very thin watercress comprised mostly of hot water. Seitz began to eat, grateful for the activity.

Finally Seitz said, 'And is that where you come from? Leipzig, I mean.'

Garbrecht laid down his spoon, removed his spectacles and rubbed his eyes. He shook his head and said wearily: 'Not precisely. I was brought up in a little place nearer Weimar. My mother was the village schoolmistress. My father was a postman.' He gave a short, rueful laugh. 'Rather different from your upbringing, I suspect. You probably did not consort much with postmen.'

It happened like that now and then for Seitz. A single word could trigger the memory. And at once he was back there with the gnats, flinging open the canvas flap of the lorry, unleashing the foetid cloud of human sweat and fear. The ginger-headed peasant; no, not him. The older man, next to him, that was the one. The man with a few words of German.

'I met a postman once,' said Seitz slowly.

'You did?'

'He was a Russian postman.'

Garbrecht replaced his spectacles and stared at him. He was suddenly alert. 'Do you want to tell me about it?' he asked with unexpected gentleness.

To his amazement, Seitz found that he did, that with this monk-like man whom he had hardly known until this evening he could unburden himself; he could speak of the unspeakable. Granted it was a time of unparalleled emotional tension, but why with this man at this juncture he sensed a potential release he could never afterwards quite define satisfactorily. And so he began the narrative of what had happened to him two years before in Russia. Of the seventeen so-called commissars that had been entrusted to him on that afternoon of shimmering heat. Of what he had been asked to do to them in that indentation where the forest met the wheatfield fifty miles south of Kharkov. To other people at other times since he had put forward other versions of events, doctored according to the demands of the occasion. But now he told the truth. Exactly as it had occurred. Without additions or glosses or subtractions. As some sort of expiation.

Garbrecht listened intently, saying nothing until Seitz had drawn to a close.

'Under the circumstances,' he said simply, 'you could have done nothing else.' There was a finality about his judgement. And Seitz felt oddly comforted.

After dinner, Garbrecht leant back in his chair and looked up at the turgid still life hanging opposite him, the only picture left in the dining room. Following his gaze, Seitz gave a little laugh and said: 'That's by the Berlin still-life painter, Emil Lindemann. My mother studied under him briefly in the nineties. It's not very good, I'm afraid.'

Garbrecht rose from his chair and went over to look at it more closely. 'No, it's not,' he said at last.

'I left it there because it's not valuable,' explained Seitz.

'I see.'

'Are you interested in art?'

Garbrecht considered the question. 'I don't collect it, if that's what you mean. But I like painting, yes. I like looking at it very much indeed.'

'May I show you some of the better things in my collection? They are in the cellar for safekeeping.'

Garbrecht shrugged, with the gesture Seitz now recognised as indicating compliance, and Seitz led him out of the dining room, with its vitrine now empty of the Meissen, through the hall, bereft of the Dutch landscapes. Once downstairs he switched on the lights. There were his pictures, leaning in stacks against the wall, separated by the large sheets of cardboard that Clara had inserted carefully between each one to protect them from damage. There was something forlorn about them here, face in, like animals in hibernation. The sense of waste they induced was like watching a beautiful woman in a coma. Seitz reached down to lift a small van Goyen from the stack and passed it to his guest. Garbrecht inspected it, nodding. Then Seitz propped back three smaller pictures against his leg in order to expose to Garbrecht a large Salomon Ruysdael, a beach scene. 'I like the light in this picture,' said Seitz. 'It is extraordinarily well handled.'

But Garbrecht was not looking. He was pulling out another picture, and holding it to the light, entranced. It was vibrant with colour, a swathe of golden yellow cutting across the central area of the composition.

'Now this is good,' he said. 'This is the original, of course.'

Surprised and impressed by its incisiveness, Seitz confirmed Garbrecht's judgement. 'You are right. The version in my study is just a copy. I did not want to be without the image on my wall when I had to hide this down here for safe-keeping, so I found the copy my mother had made some years ago and hung it up there. Although my mother was an accomplished artist, her copy is nothing by comparison with the real thing.'

'My God, but this one is outstanding.' Garbrecht searched for the words to express the impact it made on him. 'The painter has not just looked at this landscape. He has felt it.'

He has felt it. '*Ce sont des champs qui s'étendent à l'infini sous un çiel nuageux et il ne m'est pas difficile d'y exprimer toute ma tristesse, cette infinie solitude.*' He has felt his sadness in the unending fields, the wheatfields rolling on to infinity. They both stood contemplating the landscape, the way the brushstrokes dipped and whorled across the surface of the canvas. The way the colour attacked you, shrill and restless and uncompromising. After the competently prosaic version upstairs, this was a revelation, like an electric charge. Seitz's gaze was caught by Garbrecht's hands as they clutched the frame. They were graceful, sensitive fingers, not like Ahlenburg's, which were stubby and worn by a lifetime's outdoor pursuits; and not maimed, like Stauffenberg's. Garbrecht's hands had been moulded by pens rather than guns, by reading books rather than skinning elk.

'I know this artist,' went on Garbrecht. 'He is a Dutchman, isn't he? His name is van Gogh. I have seen his work before.'

Seitz nodded. 'Vincent van Gogh.'

'This is a very powerful painting. You are lucky to own it.'

Garbrecht had a curiously direct way of expressing himself. Yes, I am lucky, thought Seitz. Lucky in this picture beyond anything. It is what makes me different, what defines me. He said, 'You know, if this house were hit by the RAF tonight and I could save just one object, it would be this picture.'

'I can understand that. You have had it for a long time?'

'It was my own purchase. One of my first. I bought it from a dealer here in Berlin in 1928.'

Garbrecht nodded thoughtfully. 'You must have bought it from Cassirer.'

Seitz looked at him, startled. 'Yes, Paul Cassirer. How did you know?'

'I saw the exhibition which Cassirer put on that year. That major one of van Gogh's works. For many people, including myself, it was their introduction to the artist. His work made a strong impression upon me.'

'Upon me, too.'

'Yes. Well.' Garbrecht seemed to catch himself up. It was almost as if his guard had slipped, that in his enthusiasm he had exposed too much of himself, rendered himself vulnerable. 'The difference between us is that whereas I only stood and admired, you had the financial resources actually to buy one.'

Seitz paused awkwardly. Finally he said: 'Of course there are plenty of people who do not share our appreciation of the artist. No doubt you are aware that the guardians of our culture have declared his work degenerate. One of our leading

National Socialist critics speaks of "the pictorial infantilism of a syphilitic spirit". And perhaps you have heard the Fuehrer's opinion of van Gogh?'

'Not favourable, I imagine.'

'No. I once read that he disapproves of his style as being "unfinished".'

' "Unfinished",' mused Garbrecht. 'A curiously inadequate criticism.'

'One more instance of the Fuehrer's abject failure of judgement, I am afraid.'

'Yes, one more instance,' agreed Garbrecht. 'The Fuehrer has singularly missed the point. The right reason for being wary of van Gogh is because he is dangerous.'

'Dangerous?'

'Yes. His passion is infectious. It is too communicable.'

'Is passion a disease?'

Garbrecht gave the question considerable thought before answering. 'I think so, don't you?' he said at last. 'If it is not rightly channeled.'

'Nonetheless, I think he must have been an extraordinary character, this van Gogh. Troubled, but oddly sympathetic.'

'Not easy in his mind, perhaps.'

'No. Not easy in his mind.' Seitz paused, then remembered the quotation he had been searching for. 'The dealer from whom I bought the picture showed me a letter van Gogh once wrote to his brother. I have never forgotten one sentence from it. He said, "Many a man has a bonfire in his heart and nobody comes to warm himself at it. The passers-by notice only a little smoke coming from the chimney and go away." I think that was sad in the case of this artist. And I think it is also true in many other cases.'

Garbrecht turned his head in Seitz's direction, but from the way the light suddenly fell against his glasses it was impossible to see his eyes. 'Sometimes you can get too close to men with bonfires in their hearts, you know,' he said. 'Then you get burned.'

*　　*　　*

In the hall, on the way out, Garbrecht turned to him and said:

'I have to tell you something: I do not entirely agree with Colonel von Stauffenberg's analysis of the military and political situation facing us.'

'In what way?'

'I am not necessarily so eager as he to rush headlong into the embrace of the west.'

'The embrace of any enemy is not particularly pleasant to contemplate. But it is perhaps the lesser of two evils. A means to an end.'

'A means to an end.' He played with the words, as if they had suddenly caught his imagination, as if they possessed an ulterior significance, a coded meaning beyond the grasp of Seitz. 'A means to an end. Perhaps.'

'But you do believe in the importance of taking action against Hitler? In the importance of Germans taking action against him?'

Garbrecht's gaze drifted slowly back to Seitz; but behind the spectacles his eyes were suddenly galvanised, intent. 'I believe that the Fuehrer is one of the most evil human beings who ever lived,' he said simply. 'If I were asked to pull the trigger, I would not hesitate.'

'And what do you make of Colonel von Stauffenberg?'

Garbrecht paused, and frowned. He had picked up his cap and was poised on the doorstep. 'He is truly an exceptional man; the sort of man who can indeed change destinies. I admire his resolve enormously. But listening to Colonel von Stauffenberg, I realise that there is something else there. Something upon which I could not at first put my finger, but a quality with which I am not entirely in sympathy.'

There was a scholarly quality to his analysis, a precision to the way he expressed himself. Intrigued, Seitz encouraged him to be more specific.

'How can I put it?' Garbrecht rotated his cap in his hands, searching for the words. 'Perhaps there is always an element of arrogance in courage. Perhaps that element is particularly pronounced in the case of our friend.'

And he strode out down the path to the gate, not looking back, but raising his hand in a wordless gesture of farewell.

FIFTEEN

On the morning of 20th July 1944, Gottfried von Seitz awoke at 5.45 a.m. He got out of bed immediately because he knew already that this was a day when action must suppress thought. He had taken unbroken all but fifteen minutes of the four hours' sleep which he habitually allowed himself. Indeed, his service on the Russian front had seen to it that he was now incapable of more, even when circumstances permitted it. He reflected gratefully that last night had been miraculously free of enemy air raids, and read into that a positive omen. It was as if the air forces of the western allies, sensing today's significance, had decided to grant Germany's capital a brief respite from external attack. Here is your moment of opportunity, they were saying. Take it now, or bid farewell to your last chance of salvation. Your last chance of honour. Galvanised by an enormous sense of purpose, he shaved quickly, pausing briefly to register that even at this hour there was the promise of another day of intense and airless heat; the rising sun, shrouded in a haze of cloud, was bathing the pockmarked city of Berlin in an oppressive film of steamy grey light.

He who represses survives. But for a moment he lapsed. He allowed his memory to stray back to a holiday on the Friesian coast when the heat had been unrelenting like this, when the sun had shone hot to the skin, day upon day. Were they dreams, those times? He saw his own children playing in the sand at St Peter-Ording that last summer before the war.

Kurt had been seven and Ella five, and all that year they had
been pleading to be taken to the seaside, just once, instead of
spending all the summer in Pomerania. And, perhaps sensing
a last chance, he had acquiesced, renting a house there for
the month of July, installing wife, nanny and cook. Dear
God, it was another world. He stifled the recollection with
all the strength of will he could bring to bear.

All he need know about his children was that they were
safe. Safe with Waltraud at Morwald. Then he must shut them
from his mind. Berlin was no place for children. Particularly
not today.

Today. As he walked slowly downstairs, buttoning his
tunic, he felt a sudden unaccountable elation, a wild surge
of hope. This was the most momentous day of his life. This
was the beginning of the expiation, the day when his country
might start to retrieve some small part of its self-respect.

Clara brought him coffee in the dining room. Although
her body was bent, her arms were still strong and she carried
the tray with a determination that bordered on the aggressive.
'So,' she said as she placed the cup and the pot in front of
him. He knew what she was really saying to him: that she
hadn't forgotten what he had suggested to her in January,
and that she remained as implacably opposed to the idea
as ever. 'What? Leave the house?' she had exclaimed in
a rare display of emotion. 'Just lock it up and leave it
uncared for?'

'The bombing's getting worse every day. Surely you want
some respite from it all? At your age, Clara?'

'At my age I am indifferent to my own safety.' She had
spoken with absolute conviction. 'If I die tomorrow, I have
had a good run. What does matter is the house, the porcelain,
the pictures. Someone should look after them.'

'They are as safe as they can be, locked up in the cellar.'

'No, this is not right. Old Herr Stahler would turn in his
grave. With your permission, Herr von Seitz, I will remain.
We cannot have the enemy winning such unchallenged
victories.'

Such unchallenged victories. He set his cup down in the saucer and ran his eye round the room, taking in the cabinet where once the Meissen had been displayed, taking in the walls once hung with the Dutch seventeenth century landscapes and still lives so beloved of his grandfather. Everything was bare now, the dereliction relieved by the solitary late nineteenth century flower picture, the Lindemann about which Garbrecht had been so dismissive. Garbrecht was right, of course: Seitz had kept it hanging here partly in order to have something on which to rest his eye as he ate, and partly because it was a work of such little merit that he felt its destruction would at least be some compensation for a direct hit on the house. This picture, and to a lesser extent his mother's copy of the wheatfield still hanging in his study, were the two sops he offered to the enemy. If one of their bombs found this target, those two canvases could be their unchallenged victories. So long as the specially strengthened cellar held firm, with its infinitely more precious contents.

What he wanted to explain to Clara was that there were other victories that it was even more important not to leave unchallenged than those which might be yielded to the RAF. That at some point a stand had to be made against dishonour. Even if it was on your own side. Particularly if it was on your own side. How could he explain that to her, he wondered? How could he explain it to himself, that such a situation should have come about here in the Fatherland, in the country which he loved?

The car was waiting for him outside. Clara hovered momentarily in the hall as he picked up his cap and briefcase. Then he did something quite uncharacteristic: he turned to the old woman and shook her by the hand.

'Thank you, Clara,' he said quietly. 'Thank you very much.'

She said nothing. Perhaps she was too surprised. But she must have realised then that this was to be no ordinary day.

As he walked through the garden to the road, he heard a

bee droning. A bee, in a garden of flowers in this ravaged, battered city. Its innocence was almost unbearable.

There was another officer already sitting in the back seat of the car. It was only as he opened the door to get in that he recognised Garbrecht. The hollowed eyes in the drawn, grey features stared out at him from behind the spectacles; there was a flicker of recognition, a greeting expressed not by anything as much as a smile, but by a tensing of muscles about the mouth and a quick lifting of the hand. The driver had obviously picked Garbrecht up first, then come on for Seitz. It made sense, after all. Petrol shortages were now acute, even for the High Command of the Bendlerstrasse.

They drove on in silence. Seitz kept his eyes on the passing townscape outside. Even now the tension was rising.

Rubble. Berlin had become a city of rubble. In some streets every other building was damaged: churches, factories, schools, houses. Here and there bricks and masonry had spilled into the roadway like an unchecked avalanche. Most shop windows were boarded up, their glass panes long since shattered, the continual effort to replace them no longer worthwhile. The car turned a corner past an air raid shelter out of which straggled the procession of dejected humanity that had spent the night there: anxious mothers leading exhausted children; gaunt-faced men with hunted eyes blinking in the unexpectedly strong light. There was a numbness to these people, a leaden paralysis born of too many nights of interrupted sleep and the close proximity to too much destruction.

It was Garbrecht who broke the silence. 'So,' he murmured softly, glancing down at his wristwatch, 'our friend will by now be on his way to Rangsdorf airfield.'

Seitz nodded. It was 6.18 a.m. He suddenly realised that this waiting was worse than the waiting on the front line. His throat was dry.

Garbrecht reached forward to close the glass partition that separated them from the driver, to ensure their privacy. 'This time it will really happen?' He still spoke quietly, barely above a whisper.

'This time it has got to happen.'

'Meaning we cannot afford a repetition of last week.'

Last week had been an unintentional dress rehearsal, heart-stopping in its uncertainty. They had waited in suspense all day at Bendlerstrasse, knowing that Stauffenberg had flown out to Fuehrer HQ in East Prussia for a meeting with Hitler, carrying a bomb in his briefcase. And nothing had happened. The attempt had been aborted because Himmler had not been present. Late in the afternoon they had stood down from their secret state of readiness. In a way the standing down had been a relief; the temporary release from tension had promoted an absurd euphoria. And a shortlived euphoria, as the realisation impinged that it was only an agony deferred.

'Apart from anything else,' said Seitz quietly, 'I don't think that certain people's nerves could stand it.'

'Olbricht?'

'Yes, General Olbricht for one. The pressure on him last week must have been intense. Don't forget he'd issued the Valkyrie order at 11 in the morning in anticipation of . . . of a successful attempt by Stauffenberg. When it didn't happen, retracting the order was really touch and go for him. For us all.'

The Valkyrie order triggered a state of emergency and gave the army exceptional powers. Over the civilian population. Over the political processes. And over the SS. It was a legitimate operation, endorsed by Hitler himself for use in an extremity, such as an internal uprising of foreign workers. But the beauty of it was the ease with which it could be adapted into the first step in the coup that was to follow the assassination. It gave instant and over-riding power to the army to fill the vacuum of power left by the Fuehrer, to take any measures deemed essential for the security of the state. Those obeying the order need not necessarily be on the side of the plotters; but simply by doing their duty they would unwittingly be facilitating the coup. Thus the power to orchestrate its progress could be concentrated in the hands of a few committed conspirators. Committed conspirators like

General Olbricht and Colonel Mertz von Quirnheim. Like von Seitz and Ahlenburg and Garbrecht. And above all like the man shortly setting off from Berlin's Rangsdorf airport on the flight to Fuehrer HQ in East Prussia. Like Colonel von Stauffenberg.

Last week's false start had come dangerously close to disaster. General Olbricht had succeeded in persuading those unit commanders who had received the prematurely-given Valkyrie signal that it had been a false alarm, merely an exercise. Clearly it was not the sort of exercise that could be repeated a week later. The next time the order went out it would have to be the real thing.

Garbrecht nodded, remembering the sequence of events of five days earlier. 'Fromm was apoplectic, was he not?'

General Fromm, commander of the Reserve Army and Olbricht's superior, had been away from Bendlerstrasse that day. He had flown with Stauffenberg to the Wolf's Lair. He had returned to Berlin to discover the Valkyrie debacle; shortly afterwards he had received a severe reprimand from Field Marshal Keitel at Fuehrer HQ.

'Furious,' agreed Seitz. 'But you never quite know where you stand with Fromm, do you? Was he angry because the military incompetence endangered the success of the coup, or because it endangered the safety of the Reich?'

'What do you think?'

'I suspect he would like to have it both ways. To keep his options open.'

'I think there will be many like that today. Keeping their options open, until they see the way the wind is blowing.' Garbrecht spoke slowly, almost as if he were talking to himself rather than to Seitz.

'And then there's our friend,' continued Seitz.

'What about him?'

'I don't think it's humanly possible for someone to go through what he's got to do another time after today. Priming the bomb, getting the briefcase close enough to the Fuehrer, timing his exit from the meeting . . . No, it's got to happen now, this morning. He is resolved upon it. Can you imagine what his feelings are each time he sets out on this mission?'

Garbrecht was silent for a while. Perhaps he was indeed envisaging himself in the assassin's role. After all, he had assured Seitz that he would not hesitate to pull the trigger personally in the face of such evil. But once again Seitz found it difficult to read what was going on behind those glasses. After their solitary dinner together last month at the villa, certain barriers between them had been broken down, it was true. But the barriers were those which Garbrecht had chosen to dismantle. Seitz still had no insight into the heart of the man, no inkling as to how his imagination really worked. He had not breached that citadel of intimacy. He suspected that few people had.

'At what time do we expect news?' murmured Garbrecht at last.

Seitz had run through the sequence of events a hundred times. He frowned and said: 'He should be landing about ten or so. Then there is the drive to the Wolf's Lair. Half an hour, perhaps a little more. The meeting is scheduled for midday. Of course, you can never be sure, these timings change. But with luck there should be some . . . some outcome by lunchtime.'

'Some outcome by lunchtime,' repeated Garbrecht slowly. 'And then?'

'And then it all depends on us.'

'Of course. On us.'

For a moment their eyes met, there in the back of the car. Afterwards Seitz never quite forgot the look Garbrecht gave him. There was a certainty of purpose that at the time he found reassuring. And that day you grasped reassurance wherever you thought you could find it.

'What do you give for our chances?' asked Garbrecht a little later.

'It's impossible to predict.' Seitz frowned again, confronting the series of operational questions that had absorbed them constantly over the past few weeks, in secret planning sessions, in surreptitious testings of the water, in ultimate leaps of faith. 'It's not as if there is any precedent for our situation. At the moment there is a spider's web of potential sympathisers fanning out from Bendlerstrasse. That's our centre, Bendlerstrasse. But as you yourself implied just now, we can't count on everyone's support by any means, even at High Command. In my judgement, the first few hours will be crucial. If people react positively to the news of the assassination, if they rally to us in numbers at once, then we may stand a chance. But it must happen immediately, while those close to the Fuehrer are still in a state of disarray at the Wolf's Lair. And we won't get enough people reacting positively unless the Valkyrie order goes out immediately and everyone it reaches understands why it's gone out and follows the order without delay.'

'What do you think will be decisive in persuading people to follow the order?' Garbrecht spoke the question with a singular urgency, as if Seitz's answer might itself decide the outcome of the enterprise.

'Most will obey, I think, if they are convinced that they are acting in defence of the state. That means they must believe the order has been legally given, following correct chains of command.'

Garbrecht gave a short exhalation of breath; not so much a laugh as a sigh. 'We Germans are curiously enamoured of legality, are we not? As a nation we look always for the railway lines that must be laid out for us to travel along.'

'Those railway lines are both our strength and our weakness,' said Seitz. Then he added thoughtfully: 'But in extremity it is the people who don't need railway lines who make the difference.' He paused. He could not go into it now with Garbrecht, but he meant the people who respond to the wildness of life, the people for whom action was the product of their imagination rather than its suppressant. The sort of man which part of him yearned to be, the sort of man who found sadness in an overripe cornfield, who could put his hand on his son's shoulder without retracting it in horror.

Garbrecht was talking again, staring meditatively out of the window. 'And where will they be found,' he asked quietly, 'these people who do not need railway lines?'

'Let us hope they come forward. They will certainly be needed today.'

'Yes. The ones with bonfires in their hearts.'

Seitz looked sharply across at him, but Garbrecht's gaze was still absorbed by the passing streets outside.

'I'll tell you something else about today,' continued Seitz. He felt a sudden need to return to the practical, to address the logistical dynamic of what lay ahead. 'Communications are going to be absolutely vital. Our signals bunker is going to have to perform heroics.'

Garbrecht thought before he spoke. The car had turned south out of the Tiergarten into Bendlerstrasse, and was approaching the clumsy, box-shaped administrative block which was their destination. They were pulling into the Bendlerblock courtyard when he finally muttered: 'I think we're all going to be called upon to perform heroics in the next few hours, my friend. Each in his own separate way.'

Each in his own separate way. As Seitz gathered his briefcase and papers and opened the door to get out, he reflected on the variety of men who formed the resistance to Hitler that had its secret epicentre here in the War Office. Ahlenburg, the traditional Prussian aristocrat, whose sense of honour had been outraged. Garbrecht, the postman's son, the intellectual whose hatred for his country's leadership sprang from less definable sources but was equally implacable. Stauffenberg, the hero with the mangled body in whom physical courage and natural leadership blended with a curious mysticism. And Seitz himself. Two sensibilities in one. The soldier on the edge of the wheatfield.

About eleven Ahlenburg came into his office, closed the door and sat down. 'Dear God,' he said, wiping the perspiration from his forehead with a white handkerchief. 'I could stand the heat. Or I could stand the waiting. But the two together: it's too much.'

A fan turned slowly in the corner of the room, the monotony of its movement exacerbating rather than relieving the oppression. Against a pane of the window a fly buzzed insistently.

Seitz sighed. He knew how Ahlenburg felt. There was too much time this morning. Too much time in which to think. Suspension of the imagination was no longer possible. He got up, and with the file he held in his hand attempted unsuccessfully to guide the fly to the open section of the window. Looking out, his eye lighted on a church in the distance that he had not noticed before: with a shock he identified it as the Matthiaskirche half a mile away, yet one more strange new vista of Berlin blasted open by the bombing.

He pointed out the distinctive, fortress-like tower to his cousin. Ahlenburg looked briefly in the direction of Seitz's gaze, then waved a distracted hand to indicate the incapacity of his mind to engage with anything other than the immediate concern that was eating at them all.

'Where is he now, do you think?' he demanded. His voice had an unfamiliar timbre to it. An urgency. A momentary need for reassurance.

Seitz looked wearily at his watch. 'He will have landed some time ago,' he said.

'Who is with him?'

'Von Haeften, I believe. At this moment, if all has gone to plan, they will be driving together to the Wolf's Lair. Maybe they will even have arrived.'

'Von Haeften will help him prepare the mechanism in the briefcase.'

'That is the plan. But Stauffenberg wants to be certain. He wants to do it himself. He has had a special pair of pliers made that he can operate with his three remaining fingers. To set the timing device.'

'Dear God,' said Ahlenburg softly. 'He's a brave man. There will be a time in the future, Gottfried, when you and I will be proud to tell our grandchildren that we knew him.'

Seitz looked down at his old friend, at the familiar receding line of blond hair, at the burgeoning jowls of his jaw. At least there was no doubt where Ahlenburg's sympathies lay. He was not a fence-sitter. He was a man to be counted upon. Seitz drew a bottle from his desk drawer. 'It's a bit early, I know. But today is different. Can I offer you something? Schnaps, perhaps?'

Ahlenburg shook his head. 'No. I don't need that, not now. Not yet.' He got up and paced towards the window. He had a matchstick in his hands which he was twisting distractedly between his fingers. 'You see, I've been doing a lot of thinking. Going over things.' He paused, anxious, uncertain how to go on. Then he said quickly, urgently: 'Apart from anything else, the military situation is such a damned disaster. Every day brings bad news. You get to dread those wires coming in on the teleprinter, don't you? The enemy's advancing at such a sickening rate, in the west, in the east. And every time that bloody man's making the wrong decision. Sacrificing whole divisions unnecessarily. It makes your heart bleed. Those are good men who are dying out there. Good soldiers. Good Germans.

'Look at this, for instance. Have you seen it?' Ahlenburg pointed to the sheaf of papers he had brought into the room with him and deposited on Seitz's desk. 'This shows the current deployment of our divisions in Courland. It's clear that they are almost cut off by the Red Army. They have got to withdraw. But Hitler won't give the order. Yet again he can't bear to see German troops withdraw. He'd rather lose them. The man's insane.

'Have you studied the figures on this page? Look, there it is in black and white. The Red Army offensive against Army Group Centre between 22 June and 8 July annihilated twenty-eight divisions. Twenty-eight, for God's sake! Many of those men could have been saved. But he won't listen, will he? That's why he's got to go.'

Seitz raised his gaze from the papers and looked up at him. 'There's no doubt, is there, Christoph? We're doing the right thing.'

'No.' He was emphatic, his earlier need for reassurance gone. 'There is no doubt in my mind at all. Do you know what Stauffenberg said to me two days ago?'

'What?'

'It was as we were walking towards his flat in the evening. He stopped suddenly in the street and he said, "Christoph, I know that he who acts will go down in German history as a traitor; but he who can and does not will be a traitor to his conscience. If I did not act to stop this senseless killing, I should never be able to face the war's widows and orphans . . .".'

'He's right. Of course he's right.'

'And he reminded me once more about the oath we'd sworn. As soldiers.'

'As men of honour,' murmured Seitz.

'It is precisely because we swore it as men of honour that this oath is null and void. No longer binding. The dishonour into which we have been compelled collectively through obeying it invalidates it.'

'Collectively,' repeated Seitz.

'Yes. I believe we must take some collective responsibility for the dishonourable things that have been done in our country's name. Even if there is no individual blame.'

Collective responsibility. No individual blame. The two ideas beat about his brain like moths trapped in a jar. The heat of this office in Berlin; the warmth of the Russian summer sun.

And he was back there again. In the clearing fifty miles south of Kharkov. The field telephone clamped to his ear.

'No,' he was saying to Colonel Diederich. 'This cannot be right. What these orders require me to do is not the duty of a Wehrmacht officer.'

'May I remind you that under the terms of the order it is mandatory for the army to execute all Russian civilian and military commissars who come into its hands. These are unequivocal instructions. To disobey would be a court-martial offence.'

'And these men you have sent me in the lorry are commissars?'

'To all intents and purposes.'

Since then he'd had the time to think. To analyse the likelihood. Seventeen commissars in a single lorry? When a single commissar was responsible for a whole division of the Red Army? His instinctive doubt had been confirmed when he swept open the flap and met their frightened eyes. These men were simple peasants. Farmers. Country postmen. Troublemakers, no doubt. Easier, therefore, to classify them as commissars and have done with it.

'Surely these men have some rights, as prisoners of war?'

Diederich, inflexible again: 'They have no rights, beyond the right to die by firing squad ... There is no room for misplaced sentiment. If you do not carry out the order, the SS most certainly will.'

'My God.'

'My God,' he said again now. And Ahlenburg, who could not possibly have followed the direction of his thoughts, said gruffly:

'It gets to you, doesn't it?'

If you do not carry out the order, the SS most certainly will.

'It's the tension,' said Seitz. 'It's just the tension.'

Ahlenburg nodded thoughtfully and wiped his forehead and neck with a handkerchief. 'You're right, of course. That's what it is. I just wish something would happen.'

'Not much longer now. We should hear within an hour or so. Two at most.'

'The message will come through to General Olbricht?'

'As I understand it. Once we've got that one positive

communication from the Wolf's Lair, the place will be isolated. A signals black-out. They won't know what's going on.'

'And then we move?'

'And then we move at once. Valkyrie, this time the real thing, the order going out across the Reich. The army takes over. The first few hours will be crucial.'

There was a comfort in action; or at least a comfort in its contemplation. Ahlenburg smiled back at him. The wild hope surged once more.

SIXTEEN

One o'clock passed, then one thirty. Seitz could feel the tension in his stomach, the rising panic familiar from the waiting moments just prior to action on the front line. Physical engagement was the distraction needed to master this panic. But now nothing came, no release. And so the panic mounted. It was lunchtime, but he knew he was incapable of eating. His office was like a prison: it seemed that he had been enclosed within these walls for weeks rather than hours. Others passed in and out, but something kept him here, loath to separate himself from its confinement, as if leaving would be a desertion of his post. As if he might miss something crucial by being away, even for a minute. He sat at his desk shuffling files, staring at the telephone, listening to the fly that was still buzzing incessantly against the window pane. Finally he got up, rolled a newspaper, and prepared to dispose of the fly once and for all. He drew back his arm and, with a quick hard movement, brought the newspaper down on the glass. He missed. But the fly, galvanised, soared and at last found the right trajectory to propel itself up and out through the open section of the window.

Simultaneously the door burst open and Ahlenburg was in the room again. His cheeks were flushed; he seemed to have been running.

'Has it happened?' demanded Seitz.

'I was in there, in Olbricht's office,' he spoke breathlessly. The collar of his tunic was soaked in perspiration. 'It's come through: they've had a message from General Fellgiebel in Rastenburg. But it's ambiguous . . .'

'Is the Fuehrer dead?'

'That's what no-one's sure of. There certainly seems to have been some sort of explosion. A pretty massive one. But the message from the Wolf's Lair suggested the Fuehrer might still be alive. There are conflicting reports.'

'So what happens here?'

'That's just it. No-one's sure what to do.'

Suddenly Seitz saw the whole situation with such clarity that the way forward seemed indisputable. 'Oh, God: think about it, Christoph. Aren't the people at Fuehrer HQ bound to try to muddy the waters? The Fuehrer dies in a bomb explosion. Wouldn't their first reaction be to deny it had happened, to buy themselves a bit of time? We've got to set things in motion here. Now.'

Ahlenburg shook his head. 'That's not how Olbricht sees it.'

'Don't tell me – he's terrified of activating another false alarm?'

'That may be part of it. On the other hand Mertz von Quirnheim takes your view. He wants to get going at once, activate Operation Valkyrie, military action to secure the state. But Olbricht's unsure. I think the consensus is they're going to wait for Stauffenberg to get back. After all, he can confirm the truth. He was there.'

'But this is appalling: we're losing precious time. When's Stauffenberg due back here in Berlin?'

'Four o'clock, they think.'

'Four o'clock! And meanwhile what do we do? Sit and sweat for two hours? It's madness. This is the crucial opportunity, the time when we should be getting troops on to the streets, disarming the SS, taking over broadcasting stations . . . Let's go in a deputation to Olbricht, force him to push ahead. This is our chance.'

'You may be right, but there's no point at the moment: Olbricht's gone.'

'Gone where?'

'He's gone to lunch. To think things over.'

Seitz stood up, speechless with frustration. The momentousness of the opportunity was utterly clear to him. He had a vivid sense of witnessing history in the balance. Whether Hitler was alive or dead, the explosion must be the spark to light the uprising. Now, if ever, the men with bonfires in their hearts must let them burn. There would be no second chance. They could sit here immobile, and perish, for perish they would now that the bomb had ignited. Or they could push ahead and hope. Hope that the fire would spread, that all those disaffected with their country's leadership would rally to the cause.

There was a soft knock on Seitz's door. Both men looked up guiltily. By no means everyone in the Bendlerblock that day was part of the conspiracy. Seitz composed himself and called, 'Come in.'

It was Garbrecht. They relaxed again.

'I apologise for this interruption,' he said quietly. 'May I join you for a moment?'

Seitz gestured him in and told him to shut the door.

'I understand there is news,' continued Garbrecht. His drawn, ascetic face was curiously unemotional.

'Yes, news,' said Seitz. 'An explosion, certainly. But we're not sure if Hitler's dead. It's not conclusive.'

Ahlenburg nodded, and made an impotent little gesture with his hands.

Seitz could bear the indecision no longer. His whole physical being cried out for action. 'I'm with Mertz. We should push ahead now, at once. By delaying longer we'll be losing the one advantage we may get today. What do you think?'

Garbrecht didn't answer at once. The two other men both looked up at him, expectant. Seitz registered again that he carried a certain authority about him. That what he said mattered. Finally he spoke: 'What if the Fuehrer is not dead?' He paused, allowing his words to sink in. 'Then we are in difficulties. As things stand, only a limited number of men will be implicated in the plot and lost. By moving too soon we could be sacrificing a much larger number of good men needlessly. I think it would be a mistake to act precipitately before that question is clarified. It will be hard, but if that is what General Olbricht has decided, then I can understand the logic of that decision. We must wait for Stauffenberg's return.'

Seitz opened his mouth to object, but caught Ahlenburg's eye. He could see that his friend was wavering. Garbrecht's strategy was seductive, clothed in the same allure that had rendered last week's postponement of the issue momentarily euphoric. Ahlenburg said: 'Perhaps it would be irresponsible to push ahead at once. As Garbrecht says, it could endanger a lot of people unnecessarily. If the worst comes to the worst, and Hitler's not dead, there's the chance to regroup and fight another day. Perhaps we should wait after all. Just until Stauffenberg gets back. Then he can confirm the truth, one way or the other.'

Seitz shrugged impotently. In his heart he knew his own strategy was the right one. He knew that even if Hitler weren't dead – and he still felt convinced that he was – their best chance was to push ahead now. There would never be another opportunity like this. But Christoph was a significant indicator of the wider mood amongst the conspirators. If even he was against proceeding immediately, then not enough people would be carried on the wave and the outcome was doomed anyway. They would all just have to wait.

Garbrecht stood there for a moment, as if about to speak again. But he decided against it; the muscle flickered about his mouth, he raised his hand slightly in that distinctive gesture of silent farewell, and left the room.

Ahlenburg sighed. 'He's an odd fish, that one,' he observed. 'Sometimes I feel I can't get the measure of him. But one thing I'll tell you, Gottfried: he's a very, very clever fellow. Probably got more up here than you and I have put together.'

'You trust his judgement?'

'Certainly I do. I think he talks a lot of sense.'

So did Seitz. But something told him that this was one of those very rare instances when Garbrecht had got it wrong. And afterwards, when he looked back, he wondered whether people as intelligent as Garbrecht ever got things that wrong. And he concluded that they didn't. Not by accident, anyway.

The next two hours brought a surreal suspension of activity, a time of turmoil for Seitz, when all he could do was pace his office contemplating opportunities missed, feverishly speculating what possibilities might still remain. Once he went down to the canteen in the basement and drank a cup of coffee that he did not want, marvelling at the normality of it all, the way the business of the day was proceeding as if nothing out of the ordinary had occurred. Part of him was willing Stauffenberg back as quickly as possible; and part of him was dreading his return, and his discovery of the Bendlerblock's tragic inactivity.

At about 3.45 Seitz could bear his confinement no longer and went for a brief walk about the courtyard in order to clear his head. It was hotter than ever outside. He stared up at the vast firmament of the sky above, now a thick, hazy blue, and wondered at nature's indifference to the extremes of human drama being enacted below. The same impartial sun was beating down on him here in the centre of Berlin as was illuminating the enemy's advance in France, and the army group's increasingly desperate plight in Courland; not so far east, at the Wolf's Lair, in its beams the dust was settling on a momentous explosion; and out of that sun even now a plane was descending towards Berlin carrying the man who could point the way forward. The man who could confirm whether he had assassinated the Fuehrer three hours ago.

Then he heard his name being called by an orderly from the doorway; he must come in at once because Mertz had summoned a meeting of the senior officers of the Army Office. An urgent meeting. Seitz hurried upstairs, suddenly disproportionately encouraged. Even as he climbed he felt his gloom dispersing, his purpose returning. The drift was over.

The room was full. Seitz looked about him at the stressed and sweating faces of his colleagues: Ahlenburg, his brow furrowed in concentration; Garbrecht standing at the back, gaunt and unreadable. The anticipation was intense: but while everyone sensed that something extraordinary was happening today, not every man in this room could be counted upon as a sympathiser. Whatever Mertz said now, he must choose his words with care.

'Gentlemen, I have an announcement to make,' began Mertz. He was a small, balding figure with spectacles; at first sight his breeches and boots looked incongruous, as if a bank clerk had been drafted into the cavalry. But his tone of voice commanded respect. He spoke with authority. There was iron in this man, thought Seitz. 'We have received confirmation that at just after 12.45 this afternoon the Fuehrer was assassinated.'

A surge of adrenalin passed through the gathering like a charge of electricity. There was a simultaneous murmuring of incredulity, elation and fear. 'This confirmation,' went on Mertz, 'has come in both from Fuehrer HQ and from Major von Haeften who has just arrived in Berlin by air and was an eyewitness to the explosion. I have to tell you that General Beck has taken over as head of state, and Field Marshal von Witzleben has assumed all executive functions of the commander-in-chief of the Wehrmacht. Accordingly the Valkyrie order has been issued to all military districts. The army is in control now. I won't waste your time further. You all have jobs to do. The safety of the Fatherland depends on your doing them promptly and well.'

A copy of the teleprinter message that was going out to all area commanders across the Reich lay on Seitz's desk when he got back into the office. As he read it, he realised that there was no going back now. Orders were given not only to secure all important buildings and facilities, but also that all gauleiters, government ministers, prefects of police, senior

SS and police officials, and heads of propaganda offices be arrested and that the concentration camps be seized without delay. The most telling phrase came last: 'The population must be made aware that we intend to desist from the arbitrary methods of the previous rulers.' There could be no equivocation: this was a coup d'état. It must succeed, or everyone involved in it was doomed.

Then he heard the noise of a vehicle entering the gates outside. He went to the window and saw the staff car pulling up. Stauffenberg's staff car.

The familiar figure flung open the door, eased his long, damaged body out of the car, ran stiffly across the courtyard, then inside. Seitz paused for a moment, then ran out of his own office towards the stairway up which he knew Stauffenberg must come. He arrived just in time to see him pass: he was hurrying in the direction of Olbricht's office. Irresistibly drawn on, Seitz followed behind. He had caught a glimpse of the expression on Stauffenberg's face. The expression of anguish. Of frustration. Of determination. He knew that they were all now at crisis point. That whatever procrastination there had been before, something would happen now.

Seitz stood in the ante-room to Olbricht's office. Through the open door he could hear Stauffenberg's voice raised in anger:

'When, Olbricht? When did the Valkyrie order go out?'

'Mertz finally issued it about fifteen minutes ago.'

'But this is madness! You have done nothing for three hours!'

'The reports were confused. We weren't sure . . .'

'Hitler is dead! Can none of you understand that? I cannot believe that nothing has happened all this time. Pray God it's not all too late. Right, let's go to Fromm . . .'

Stauffenberg led the way. His hair was wet with perspiration. He hurried past Seitz, closely followed by Olbricht. The whole entourage seemed galvanised by his energy. Seitz thought, My God, that's the man who's just assassinated the Fuehrer. I can reach out and touch him.

Without really thinking, Seitz followed on, running along the corridor after them. He had to be there. He had to know what was going on. He found himself in the map room adjacent to Colonel-General Fromm's office. He positioned himself in the doorway and listened.

Stauffenberg again, shouting: 'He's dead! This morning!'

'It is impossible,' Fromm countered. 'Keitel assured me that it was not so. On the telephone, just now.'

'Field Marshal Keitel is lying as usual. I myself saw Hitler being carried out dead.'

Olbricht came in now. 'In view of the situation we have issued the codeword "Valkyrie" for internal unrest to the commanding generals.'

Fromm rose to his feet and beat his fist on the desk. 'That is sheer disobedience!' he shouted. 'What do you mean by "we"? Who gave the order?'

'My chief of staff,' said Olbricht, 'Colonel Mertz von Quirnheim.'

'Send Colonel Mertz in here at once.'

Mertz was already in the map room behind Seitz and pushed past him into Fromm's office. 'Colonel Mertz,' Fromm demanded, 'did you issue the Valkyrie order?'

'I did, sir.'

'You did so without my permission. You are under arrest.'

Stauffenberg stood up and confronted Fromm. He spoke slowly, with an icy clarity. 'General Fromm, I myself detonated the bomb during the conference in Hitler's head-quarters. There was an explosion like that of a fifteen centimetre shell. No-one who was in that room can still be living.'

Fromm flinched and swallowed. 'Count Stauffenberg,' he said quietly, 'the assassination failed. You must shoot yourself at once.'

'I shall do nothing of the kind.'

Olbricht broke in again: 'General Fromm, the moment for action has come. If we do not strike now, our country will be ruined for ever.'

Fromm rounded on him. 'Does this mean that you, too, are taking part in this coup d'état, Olbricht?'

'Yes, sir.'

'I hereby declare all three of you arrested.'

'You cannot arrest us,' said Olbricht firmly. 'You do not realise who holds the power. We arrest you!'

Seitz heard a chair fall over, and the noise of a brief scuffle. He ran into the room with several other officers and separated Fromm and Olbricht. Haeften and Lieutenant von Kleist drew their pistols; von Kleist actually pointed his into Fromm's stomach. Fromm's eyes, betraying fear, scoured the room for allies. Seeing none, he said in a deflated voice: 'Under the circumstances I regard myself as under constraint.' He was rapidly bundled into the adjoining room and the door was locked.

For a moment Stauffenberg stood there with an expression of pure anguish on his face. The anguish of the man who by a superhuman effort has held back the sea and then found his followers have not taken advantage of the free passage he has temporarily created for them.

'So,' he said, looking out of the window across the courtyard. 'The Valkyrie order has at least gone out now. If the commanders respond quickly and positively, we may yet carry the day.'

Olbricht said: 'Troops are moving into Berlin as we speak to seal off the Government area. Once the Wachbattalion "Grossdeutschland" is in place we can isolate Goebbels and the Propaganda Ministry, and make our own broadcast.'

'Who is commanding the Wachbattalion "Grossdeutschland"?' demanded Stauffenberg.

'Major Remer.'

'Major Remer.' Stauffenberg frowned. 'How reliable is he?'

'Provided he believes in the authority of his orders, he will follow them to the letter.'

Stauffenberg nodded. 'Let us hope that nothing occurs in the next few hours to undermine that belief.'

The group of conspirators began to disperse. Seitz was not sure when Garbrecht had joined them, but he was there now. He followed him out of Fromm's office. There was work to be done; more to the point, now that Stauffenberg was back, there was a focus to the operation. They had thrown away some of their advantage by the delay, but Stauffenberg's presence renewed the conviction that the situation could still be retrieved.

Even then, Seitz felt the wild hope surge once more.

Over the next two frenetic hours Seitz ran back and forth repeatedly to the signals traffic centre, the room in the basement which was handling the stream of messages emanating from Bendlerstrasse to the various military districts across the Reich. All Waffen-SS units were immediately to be incorporated into the army and rendered subject to military control. All party officials were in the same way subordinated to the Wehrmacht. The SD, the security service, was dissolved. The order had gone out all over the continent: to Vienna, to Prague, to Munich. To Paris.

To Paris. As that one went, Seitz thought of his cousin Peter, still stationed there. Still in the SS. Peter, his boy's face straining to be first in the race to the sundial. Peter, all ambition and envy, implacably set in the pursuit of his own will. How would Peter greet subordination to the Wehrmacht? Would he resist? As these messages reverberated out into the ether, as Operation Valkyrie was triggered throughout the Reich, nothing would ever be the same again. Would it?

But first the battle must be won here in the capital of the Reich. By now, thought Seitz, the Wachbattalion 'Grossdeutschland' must have moved into position, and central Berlin must be under their control. That meant the broadcasting stations were secured. That meant Goebbels and the Propaganda Ministry were isolated and rendered harmless. That meant the SS could not offer any resistance. With luck, the balance might be swinging in their favour.

If only enough men stayed resolute.

And then some time not long after 5.30, it happened.

Afterwards, when he looked back on the ebb and flow of events in those agonising hours, he realised that this was the knife-edge moment, the juncture in the day when the issue was most delicately poised in the balance. If there was ever a time when the outcome could have gone either way, it was now, in these minutes. If certain things had taken place now, if certain nerves had held, if certain people could have been denied access to certain information a little longer, then the unthinkable might just have been within reach and the conspiracy, against all odds, might have succeeded. The bonfires might have been lit in enough men's hearts for a full-scale conflagration. For a conflagration that could have caught, swirled and surged irresistibly, till it finally swept them all away: the concentration camps; the Gestapo; Goebbels, Himmler, Hitler himself; the sickness at the heart of the Reich.

That was what made what happened now all the more extraordinary, its full enormity all the more difficult to comprehend. Until later. Until there was time to reflect.

And later there was, of course, an eternity in which to reflect.

Seitz was making yet one more of his visits to the Signals Traffic Centre. The basement rooms were filled with the incessant chatter of the teleprinter, and the harried voices of the female telephone operators. The muted switchboard bells never stopped ringing. Here was the engine room of the conspiracy, churning out to the world its coded message of insurrection. Seitz grabbed another thick sheaf of teleprinter messages and hurried back in the direction of his own desk. He passed the door of Garbrecht's office, and, in search of something – perhaps a brief respite with a secret ally in this moment of supreme crisis, perhaps some reassurance from a judgement as rigorous as Garbrecht's – stopped to look in. He didn't knock. At a time like this such a time-consuming courtesy would have been superfluous.

The handle opened noiselessly. Garbrecht, with his back to him, was on the telephone. He hadn't heard him come in. He was in the act of speaking to someone, his head with its short thinning hair bent forward in concentration, his shoulders hunched into that attitude which some people adopt in prayer. But his tone of voice was neither devotional nor supplicatory. He spoke in short, sharp, urgent sentences. Seitz, frozen suddenly into shocked immobility, stood there in silence listening while Garbrecht continued for perhaps a minute and a half. At last, thoughtfully, he laid down the receiver, and for a moment ran slow fingers along the full extent of its smooth surface. Then he shook his head, turned round and caught sight of Seitz.

Their eyes met. For a split second both men's faces registered a horrified uncertainty.

And then the shouts and the running footsteps in the passage outside created an irresistible diversion, and there was no time to pursue it. No time to investigate the full implications of what Garbrecht had said and Seitz had heard.

The two men hurried out. The noise which had drawn them was of people running into Ahlenburg's office where there was a radio. A statement from Fuehrer HQ had just been promised. No-one could afford to miss it. It was beginning just as Seitz put his head round the door.

'. . . an attempt on the Fuehrer's life was made with explosives this afternoon. The Fuehrer himself has escaped with minor injuries. A number of the Fuehrer's entourage have been seriously wounded . . .'

What did it mean, for God's sake?

'Of course he's dead,' said Stauffenberg a few minutes later. There were eight or ten of them in the room, all conspirators, all seeking reassurance. 'They're lying. The communiqué's a sham. What we've all suspected is true . . . Hitler has a double, and they'll be making use of him from now on.' There was a terrible pause, while you sensed that even Stauffenberg's conviction might be waning. Then he caught himself up, and said in a louder, much more determined voice: 'Anyway, all that's irrelevant. There's still everything to play for. Even if he isn't dead, the machine's running. The assassination, successful or not, is the catalyst for change. Goebbels and the Propaganda Ministry are sealed off by now, and it's imperative that we make our own broadcast very shortly. We can still do it.'

Seitz looked round the room. At Olbricht; at Mertz; at Hoeppner, who had assumed Fromm's role; General Beck he had seen in the next office, anxiously pacing the carpet, the head of state in waiting. Except he wasn't now, was he? Not if Hitler was still alive. And Garbrecht. What in the name of God had Garbrecht been doing? Suddenly the situation in all its confusion seemed hopeless. Suddenly what they were up against seemed catastrophically too big for them. It was like trying to light a bonfire with too many wet leaves. The flame might flicker briefly, but it would never ultimately take. It would smoke a little, then die.

But for Seitz there was a difference between sensing the hopelessness of the situation and giving up. He still continued to work furiously, fielding calls from military district commanders requiring clarification in the chaos, reasserting the validity of the Valkyrie order, repeating to them like some sort of mantra, 'Yes, the Fuehrer is dead. Other stories are false.' But as the shadows lengthened outside, and evening drew in, there was no denying that things were falling apart. No broadcasts went out over the airwaves from the insurgents. No news came through of Goebbels' arrest.

At eight, Field Marshal von Witzleben appeared at Bendlerstrasse. By chance Seitz was in the passage near the stairwell and witnessed his arrival. He watched as Stauffenberg approached his senior officer to offer a report, and flinched as Witzleben brushed him aside with the furious exclamation, 'What a mess!'

Witzleben stayed for forty-five minutes closeted with Beck and emerged, red-faced with anger. He stalked through

219

the throng of officers waiting outside, Seitz among them, descended the stairs and drove off. There was no mistaking that he was turning his back on them. That he had made his final contribution to the coup.

Half an hour later Ahlenburg came to him. It was not quite dark, and the summer night was still warm, the atmosphere close. Outside there were ominous sounds of men running and, further away, of tanks manoeuvring into position.

'It's all over,' said Ahlenburg simply. He stood in the doorway, swaying. 'I've just been talking to Kleist. He's just come back from the City Commandant's Headquarters.'

'What did Kleist say?'

'The Wachbattalion "Grossdeutschland" has defected.'

'Defected? Oh, my God.'

'We can no longer count on any troops loyal to us. We can give orders, but there's no-one left to obey them.' Ahlenburg shrugged in a gesture of despair. He went on: 'What I can't understand is why nothing actually came off . . . why haven't we succeeded in making broadcasts? Why wasn't the Propaganda Ministry properly silenced? Why wasn't Goebbels arrested?'

'Who was meant to arrest Goebbels?'

'It should have been Major Remer.'

'What happened to Remer?' But Seitz knew the answer already.

'Apparently something happened to change his mind. He was persuaded to take orders from Goebbels rather than arrest him. Up to that point everything seemed to be going according to plan.'

'What? Remer changed his mind at the last moment?'

'It seems so,' said Ahlenburg dully.

'Dear God.' Seitz paused. 'Where's Garbrecht?'

'What's Garbrecht got to do with it?'

'Garbrecht . . .' He started, then he couldn't go on. 'Oh, it doesn't matter any more. Not now.'

Seitz held his head in his hands. There was nothing more to

say. The stream of messages flowing into the Bendlerstrasse from all over the Reich for the past hour or so had told a common story: Operation Valkyrie had come and gone. Under a deluge of counter orders from Fuehrer HQ, from Goebbels' Propaganda Ministry, the flame of rebellion had withered and was all but extinguished. Seitz's efforts to staunch the flow of doubt, to stiffen the resolve of wavering area commanders as they telephoned in for guidance, had finally foundered. And now here he sat, exposed, as the last flames in the bonfire died, as even the lingering wisps of smoke began to melt away.

'I can't stand it in this place any longer,' said Ahlenburg in a voice from which you could hear the life dying. 'There's nothing more I can do.'

Here was something in its way more shocking than anything yet today: Ahlenburg giving up. His despair was terrible to see, an utterly unfamiliar emotion in the man. There was no word of comfort that Seitz could think to offer. 'Where will you go?' he asked.

'Two streets away I have a car with a full tank of petrol. I am going to drive all night, to Pomerania. I want to see my home again. Just once more, before . . . Come with me, Gottfried.'

Morwald. Curt and Ella. To put his hand on his son's shoulder one last time. One last time before they took him away.

'No, there's no point,' said Seitz. 'You'll never get through.'

Ahlenburg shrugged. 'You may be right. But I'm going to give it a go.'

'Good luck, Christoph.'

'And you? What will you do?'

'I want to stay here in Berlin. But I think I shall go home soon. To Wannsee.'

'They'll come for you there, too, you know. The SS. We're all marked men now.'

'I know that, Christoph. But at least we tried. That's the important thing. At least we tried to do something.'

221

Ahlenburg turned to go. It was 9.45. Seitz went over to him and embraced him quickly, then watched him disappear down the corridor. It was the last time he ever saw him.

SEVENTEEN

At some indeterminate length of time later – perhaps it was approaching eleven – Seitz also caved in. He had just fielded his final telephone call, from Hamburg. A sharp nasal voice from the Gauleiter's office confirmed that there too Operation Valkyrie had been aborted, the order countermanded by the Wolf's Lair. He swept a hopeless arm through the festoons of teleprinter messages which enveloped his desk, and stood up. Outside in the passage he could hear the sounds of volatility, of energy conjoined with fear: running footsteps, raised voices, imminent brutalities. Wearily he eased open the door, and was immediately accosted by a group of pistol-toting General Staff officers who demanded where his allegiance lay. Was he for the Fuehrer, or against? Was he a loyalist, or was he one of the filthy swine who had plotted to stab the Fatherland in the back? Seitz found himself temporarily incapable of speech. His spirit had capsized. He felt physically sick at this spectacle of opportunistic self-righteousness, this late rallying to the swastika, now that people could see which way the day had gone, now they could tell without doubt the way the wind was blowing. Men were in danger of being trampled in the precipitate rush to clear themselves of association with the plot.

So Seitz merely raised his hands in a silent gesture of despair, and the loyalists, who were after bigger prey, interpreted his response favourably and surged on down the passage shouting Stauffenberg's name. Seitz, left alone, reached the central stairwell and stumbled down blindly in search of relief from the oppression. He slipped out through the doorway into the darkness of the blacked-out courtyard and leant for a moment with his back against the wall, breathing the night air. He thought suddenly of the wheatfield in Eastern Ukraine where he'd propped himself against a tree two years before. That was the beginning of all this. Wasn't it? That, or some other wheatfield. The sound of raised voices drifted down to him. But it was too late. He felt that irresistible need to be alone with himself. There was nothing more he could contribute here.

As he stood in his dark corner of the courtyard, he closed his eyes in a forlorn attempt to blot out what was going on. His spirit was in turmoil; he was aware of men running back and forth, of constant movement about him. And then he opened his eyes again and suddenly he registered a familiar figure slipping by quite close to him, moving swiftly, surreptitiously through the shadows.

The shock of recognition brought back Seitz's power of speech.

'Garbrecht!' he called out.

Garbrecht turned back and caught sight of him. He was in a hurry, carrying a small suitcase. He seemed at first inclined not to stop. But he did. A slow half-smile spread over his face.

'Oh, it's you,' he said.

Then Seitz could not restrain the question. He had to know. Even now he had to know, even though it didn't matter any more.

'Why?' he demanded.

'So you were there long enough.' Garbrecht spoke slowly. Assimilating. 'You heard what I was saying.'

'I heard what you were saying. I want to know why.'

Garbrecht's deep-set eyes were unusually animated. He regarded him with such uncharacteristic vigour that for a moment Seitz wondered if he was drunk. But when he spoke the words came out with a cold incisiveness: 'I suppose I should shoot you, Seitz, knowing what you do about me. But perhaps there is no need. I think I can leave the SS to do that job for me. They won't be long in coming for you now.'

'I still don't understand,' Seitz persisted.

It came out suddenly then, with a rush of deep-suppressed antagonism. 'Of course you don't understand, Seitz. You're not built to understand. The truth is, people like you have had your day, you've got no more relevance for Germany. You're dinosaurs, you aristocrats with your duck shooting and your absurd, exclusive codes of behaviour.' He paused, then went on a little more calmly: 'But despite all that, I recognise that you acted from motives that were honourable. And because of that, I will explain one thing to you, one thing that you deserve to know before you die . . .'

Garbrecht spoke on for perhaps a minute. At the end Seitz was silent. He felt dizzy, dislocated. The world was changing too fast for him. It would never be the same again.

All he could find to ask Garbrecht was, 'Where are you going now?'

'Far from here.'

'Where?'

'I have a pass to join my old unit in Norway. From there it will not be too difficult to slip across the border into Sweden.'

'And then?'

'And then there are arrangements which do not concern you.' He paused, and smiled. Properly. For the first time. 'So. I will say goodbye to you now.' He held out his hand, and Seitz, like an animal blinded by a terrible light, reached for it. Not so much to shake it as to prevent himself falling.

Then Garbrecht was gone, vanishing out of the gate past the remaining guards and into the shadows.

Seitz could not move. He stayed in the darkness of the courtyard trying to order his thoughts, trying to make sense of what he had just heard. Then voices were raised

225

even louder from within, and shots followed. He ran to the doorway which led back into the offices but his way was barred. Then he ran to the entrance to the courtyard itself where he found to his horror that sentry duties were now in the hands of the SS. He was not allowed to pass. No-one, he was told, was allowed to pass. Everyone in this building was deemed guilty until proved innocent. Guilty of the most heinous crime against the Fatherland. Guilty of the most heinous crime against the Fuehrer.

He was about to remonstrate when he was forced to step back to permit three armoured trucks to speed in through the entrance of the courtyard. More heavily-armed soldiers poured out. The trucks themselves were parked to face in a semi-circle to the right of the doorway leading to General Staff HQ. There was an ominous purpose to their arrangement, a macabrely suggestive focusing of intent. Seitz lurked in the farthest darkest corner of the quadrangle, trapped. Unable to get away. Unable to look away.

So it was that he witnessed the unfolding of the horror. From his hidden vantage point in the shadows he watched the prelude to the monstrous pageant about to be enacted: the throwing up of the sandbags against the wall, the switching on of the hooded headlights of the trucks for illumination, the deployment of a squad of marksmen between the trucks. And then they came, clattering down the stairs, jostled by armed guards, the four of them, the bravest men that Seitz had ever seen: Mertz, von Haeften, Olbricht; and last, shackled but unbowed, walked Stauffenberg. But this was a different Stauffenberg. For a moment Seitz could not identify why he didn't look the same, and then he realised. Stauffenberg had abandoned his eyepatch. He stood there, erect in the eerie light of the headlamps, both eyes exposed, his mangled hand behind his back, seemingly restored for one brief last instant to his pristine wholeness. And the craven loyalists shoved them, abused them, lined them up, tried vainly to expunge by physical intimidation the moral inferiority that these men's very existence imposed upon them.

There was no doubt what horror this was leading up to. And in that realisation Seitz wanted simultaneously to weep and laugh out loud.

It all happened very quickly then. The four of them stood against the sandbags. The crackle of gunfire rang out. It seemed that Mertz fell first, that he had somehow managed to throw his body in front of Stauffenberg in the vain attempt to protect him. Someone cried out. It could have been Stauffenberg himself. Seitz thought the words were 'Long live holy Germany', but he could not be sure.

Then none of them were standing any more.

Garbrecht, he thought, you should have been here now. Here is your answer. Here is the ultimate justification for the code of behaviour that you deem absurd.

And now, as the bodies were heaped ignominiously into the back of a truck, Seitz took counsel to save himself. He must get out of this place, this quadrangle of horror, this infernal killing ground. He knew that Garbrecht was right in one respect: that they would come for him before too long, that as a member of the conspiracy he was now a marked man, that he could not elude them forever. But if he could buy a few more hours' freedom, if he perhaps could get back to Wannsee to think a bit, to set his affairs in order, then he would be ready for them.

He sensed there were even more men milling about in the dimly-lit courtyard, many of them in SS uniform. The exit through the archway to the Bendlerstrasse and temporary freedom was firmly secured against him, but still he walked in that direction because there was nowhere else to go.

Only SS has leave to pass, he had been told. Only SS. All others are tainted. All others are guilty.

And then he saw Borg. Unmistakably. Five metres away, also heading in the direction of the gateway to the street, in his SS Standartenfuehrer's uniform, barking out an order to a subordinate. He had not set eyes on him for three years, not since that one evening south of Kharkov, but he recognised at

PHILIP HOOK

once the way the man's mouth still curved up naturally into a mocking smile. Even now. Even here in this place.

Even stranger, Borg recognised him.

'Major von Seitz, isn't it?'

'Standartenfuehrer Borg.'

'A despicable business here tonight.'

'Terrible.'

'You are leaving now?' Borg asked him the question politely as they approached the gate, and Seitz thought, My God! For some reason he doesn't suspect me. For some reason he makes no association between me and the 'despicable business' in the Bendlerblock today.

'Yes,' murmured Seitz. 'My duty is over.'

'May I offer you a lift?'

'I'm sorry?' For a moment Seitz thought he had misheard; or perhaps that Borg was mocking him.

'I have my car outside.' There was impatience in Borg's tone. Nothing more.

Why doesn't he suspect me?

And then it came to him. Almighty God! He thinks I'm one of them. He thinks that because three years ago he came from Einsatzgruppe Headquarters to collect seventeen so-called commissars from me and I told him that their execution order had already been expedited, he thinks because of that I'm loyal. Because of my lack of squeamishness that I'm to be trusted. That I am above suspicion.

He fell into step with his unlikely saviour, watched as he saluted the SS guard on the gate, passed with him out into Bendlerstrasse.

Once more he did not know whether to laugh or cry.

Borg drove west.

'My quarters are in Charlottenburg,' he said. 'Is it any good to you if I drop you near the S-Bahn station?'

'I can walk from there. Thank you. I'd be glad of the fresh air.'

Seitz was pleased to get out of the car. There was something

228

revolting about being driven by this man, as if sharing his journey was an admission of sharing his convictions, too, a final betrayal of everything he had striven for today. 'Despicable business,' Borg had declared, complacently assuming that Seitz was no more likely to dissent from the opinion than he had been to disobey the Commissars' Order.

And as Seitz wheeled away and set off on foot in the direction of Wannsee, he heard Borg call from the window, 'Heil Hitler!'

He didn't look back.

He walked the rest of the way home. All the way to the villa, along fractured pavements, picking his way through the suburbs of the broken city lit by the flickering moon. He was unmolested by either the Gestapo or the allied airforce. Once a lone armoured car did draw up beside him, its commander pushing his head out in a nervous show of aggression. But Seitz's languid salute deflated him, and the vehicle drove on.

When he reached the gate to the garden, he felt a surge of massive relief. Not that he expected the house to be a refuge for more than a few hours, but he was grateful to see it again, to walk through the garden to the front door. A soft breeze moved through the foliage, and he could hear a dog barking in the distance. There was an exquisite scent of mimosa just before he let himself into the silence of the hall.

Here were the ghosts. The ghost of his grandfather, the huge man he remembered from his youth, rolling about the house in a frock-coat, fingering his pocket-watch. The ghost of his mother, with her soft, almost diffident manner, walking out into the garden to set up her easel. And soon he would join the ghosts himself, too. Would Kurt one day stand here and remember the man his father had been? Would he remember him with pride, as a man of honour who had been led as far as possible by his conscience, had done his best to expiate dishonour? Or perhaps he would remember him merely as a dinosaur. A man who had tried but was doomed to fail.

His mind raced back. The Russian who kicked against

the sandy soil, then shuffled over to the treetrunk to relieve himself. The spades, insouciantly thrown out from the back of the lorry. Catching the eye of one of the Russian prisoners and seeing the fear. The naked fear. Stauffenberg, shackled, sweating; but erect and unbowed. The shots crackling in the furtive gleam of the trucks' headlights. All the men in whose hearts the bonfires never quite caught light.

And Garbrecht. Garbrecht, standing there in the night, his eyes exultant. Garbrecht, the greatest enigma of all.

Suddenly there were so many things he must do before they came for him. It was 2.30 in the morning, but there was no question of sleep now. He walked quickly into his study, switched on the light at his desk, and settled himself to write. It was imperative that he set it all down, that he recorded it for future generations. The world should not remain in ignorance of these things, of what had driven his friends and colleagues to stand up to evil; even to sacrifice their lives in the unsuccessful attempt.

And Garbrecht.

He must write all that down, too. Accurately, because he was the only one who knew, the only one who could pass it on. The full significance of what Garbrecht had done was only now registering. Both the overheard telephone call, and his subsequent highly-charged conversation with Garbrecht in the courtyard had taken place at times of such bewildering activity that there had been no opportunity for analysis. But as Seitz sat there in the cool of his study, listening to the distant water of the lake lapping beyond the sundial, the full implications of what he had witnessed were finally borne in on him.

He was powerless to do anything about what he had discovered. All he knew was that he must write it down. So that if he died, the momentous knowledge would not die with him.

From the act of writing, he derived an easing of the spirit. He was conscious of the shedding of a burden. Since his personal survival was no longer an issue, then neither was the emotional repression that had been its precondition. As the words flowed from him, unchecked, undammed, he discovered a miraculous and unfamiliar freedom. And some time after four o'clock, when he laid aside his pen, he was suffused with an unexpected emotion. It would not last, of course, but he savoured it: a sense of expiation; of satisfaction in having, for once, given utterly honest expression to his feelings. After months, even years, of lies and self-deceptions, of repressions and concealments, he had finally told the truth. The pure untrammelled truth.

He poured himself some cognac and walked with it back across the hall and into the dining room. There his eyes fell once again upon the poor feeble flower piece by Lindemann which he'd last seen at breakfast that morning. The meal seemed a lifetime ago. He stifled a quick shaft of pain at the memory of that breakfast's innocent optimism. It was like looking at a photograph of a laughing child who was now dead. To distract himself, he took the painting down and peered at it for a moment, holding it out in front of him. Then he suddenly knew what he had got to do.

He moved urgently through the shadows of the hall, almost breaking into a run as he took the stairs down to the cellar. He had to see it again once more. The van Gogh. It might be his last chance. The picture lay against the wall in a stack under a blanket, and he pulled it out, the right one first time. He marvelled once more at the vitality of the paint, at the thickness of the impasto, at the whorls of the brush-strokes imprinting mad circular footprints across the canvas. The brutality of the colour exhilarated him. He felt the old elation, the delight in the possession of something so magnificent; for a moment he had found a refuge, lost in this endless wheatfield.

It was just before 5 a.m. when he knocked on Clara's door. He called her name softly, and she came out in her dressing gown, one stray wisp of white hair falling down her cheek.

'I have something I want to give you, Clara,' he said. 'It is important.'

She looked up at him, her old eyes blinking. 'What is that, Herr von Seitz?'

'The letter in this envelope. I want you to make sure Frau von Seitz gets it.'

'Of course.'

'And then there is something more. I want you to have this. Accept it, as a present. Look after it.'

He handed the picture over to her. Was he mad doing this, he wondered? But it seemed the right thing now. The only thing. The gesture was appropriate: it needed making.

He suddenly felt very tired.

Solemnly she took the picture, clutching the frame in her bony hand.

'I will make coffee,' she said.

But he never drank it. Before the water had boiled two big black cars had drawn up at the garden gate. Five SS men came for him, smashing open the front door and clattering across the hall.

He didn't resist. There was no point. But he did notice that it was refreshingly cool in the garden as they led him away.

PART FOUR

———❦———

March

EIGHTEEN

The 747 lurched, a sudden reminder of its massive unwieldiness, then set itself for the final approach to Arlanda airport, Stockholm. Parnello stretched his long legs awkwardly and rubbed wakefulness back into his eyes, watching as the ground surged closer. Spread out beneath him were wide acres of forest and lake, patterns of trees and land and water in a discoloured carpet of ancient, deep-frozen snow. Under the grey sky this landscape had a primaeval quality: he could imagine it extending northwards almost infinitely, to the Arctic circle and beyond. He shivered, daunted and yet faintly exhilarated.

Still somnolent, he asked himself once more what he was doing here, why he had left her behind, deliberately torn himself away, separated himself from her?

Ostensibly the reason was Persson. Lars Persson, and the key he might hold to the Dahl that had been stolen from him. It was the adrenalin of injustice that had driven Parnello on to this aeroplane, sustained him through an abbreviated night of broken sleep and strange, half-conscious dreams. Yesterday morning he had called four times from New York to Persson's Stockholm number. Four times he had met only the answerphone, infuriating in its bland obstruction, in its meaningless assurances that he would be rung back as soon as possible. No, he had decided. I will not wait. I am going there to find out for myself. Throughout his life he had always found comfort in action.

So he had rung the airline and booked a ticket to Stockholm. On an impulse. An impulse like the one that had carried him from Los Angeles to Paris all those years ago, at the very beginning of his art-dealing career. Then he had left Marvel behind: and now he was doing so again, this time to pick up the shards of glass from her violated store-room. But Marvel wasn't the problem. She might be neurotic, but she was tough. She could cope. She was covered by insurance. No, it wasn't Marvel he was thinking about now.

It was Alexandra Hamilton.

'You're really going? To Sweden? Tonight already?' She had sounded distracted the previous afternoon on the telephone. Distant.

'Tonight. Listen, can you talk?'

'It's difficult. There's a customer waiting for me. I'm on my own here this afternoon.' He imagined her, nursing the receiver at the counter of the shop. Awkward. Too public. They gave no privacy, the wide open spaces of those exclusive fashion stores.

'I'm leaving for JFK at six. I'll call you tomorrow, when I'm there. In Stockholm.'

'Do that. Please.'

'Alex . . .'

'Yes?'

What had he wanted to tell her? That he hated the telephone? That he had fallen in love with her? That because of that, he had to go away?

'When's the audition?'

'Oh, God. Tonight.'

'Don't forget the cucumbers.'

'I sure as hell need them. Listen to me, Parnello: look after yourself, OK?'

He'd drawn comfort from that last tenderness. But even as he put down the telephone he'd been aware of the underlying constraint between them once more. It was a constraint nourished by shadows from the obscurer past. The shadows of seventeen so-called Russian commissars, drawn up on the edge of a wood somewhere south of Kharkov. It was a constraint animated by the voice of her mother's father, echoing across the generations, giving the order for them to die.

So he came to this northern edge of the world. In very early March. When it was hard to believe in anything but an endless winter in this bruised and strangely colourless landscape.

Arlanda airport lies nearly fifty kilometres from Stockholm, a metaphor for the struggle between efficiency and social conscience that burns slowly in the Swedish soul. Its uneasy resolution banishes far from the city the pollutions of an airport, and in so doing inflicts upon travellers the inconvenience of an expensive and time-consuming taxi drive to get there.

'You are American?' asked his driver.

'British,' said Parnello. Conversation passed the time on the interminable journey, at least offered some relief from the nagging click of the meter.

'And this is your first visit to Stockholm?' He spoke English with the faintly absurd, sing-song intonation common to most Swedes.

'My first visit to Scandinavia.'

'You are here on business? Or pleasure?'

Parnello reflected. 'On business,' he said.

'And what is your business, sir?'

The inquiry was innocent enough, but Parnello suddenly felt obscurely threatened, defensive. He gave the reply calculated to put an effective end to conversation: 'I'm a banker,' he lied.

He watched as the car negotiated the outer suburbs of the city, then penetrated towards its centre, past a sex-shop clinically juxtaposed next to a grocer, no line of demarcation drawn between cauliflowers and cunnilingus. Gradually the streets took on a greater sense of purpose, then all at once opened up to reveal that Stockholm is built on water, its long facades reflected in the grey surface of the Baltic. He began to understand how this city was constructed on meeting points: between land and sea; between Europe and the Arctic; between provincialism and empire; between the straightforward stolidity of the Anglo-Saxon world and the less penetrable complexities of countries further east.

The taxi drove along Strandvagen, then swung round to deposit him at the Diplomat Hotel. As he paid the driver, the man pushed a brochure into his hand. It was decorated with the long, naked body of a dancing girl. 'You like nightlife?' he asked earnestly. 'Show this card and you will get reduction.'

Parnello smiled, and pocketed it.

'You will want the nightlife while you are here in Stockholm. Girls. Excitement. After business.'

'Thank you,' said Parnello, reflecting that the impersonation of bankers brought unexpected dividends. The wind was cold. He hurried up the steps into the hotel.

It was noon by the time Parnello had settled into his room. He paced to the window and glanced out across the water to the islands. In the distance he could trace the intricate rigging of an ocean-going sailing vessel, etched against the unremitting grey of the sky. Perhaps it would snow soon. For a moment he wondered what Alexandra would be doing now. Still asleep, probably, in her lower east side apartment. Of course it was only 6 a.m. in New York. The sun would not yet be rising across Central Park. He wondered what she was wearing in bed, if she were lying there naked; if her hair fell across her cheek as she slept. For a moment he felt the desolation that always accompanies arrival in an anonymous hotel room in an unfamiliar city. Then he reached out for the telephone and dialled Persson's Stockholm number.

Once again he got only the answering machine. First came the message in Swedish, then in English: 'This is Persson Import/Export AB. There is no-one in the office to take your call, but if you leave your name and number we will get back to you soon. Please speak after the bleep.' It was a male voice. Parnello assumed it was Persson himself; if so, there was a strange overlay to Persson's Swedish accent. The lilt was suppressed by something heavier, more guttural. Something Slavic or Germanic, perhaps. 'Hallo, Mr Persson, this is Parnello Moran again. It's Thursday noon. I'm in Stockholm now and I'd very much like to see you. To talk about a business matter, about a picture you sold in New York last week. Could you call me at the Diplomat? Thank you.'

He replaced the receiver. He stood up and stretched, then went into the bathroom and splashed cold water over his face. He felt gritty-eyed from his night on the plane. His neck muscles ached. He came back into the bedroom and took a beer from the Minibar. Drinking it made him feel sleepy, and he lay back on his bed for a moment's relaxation.

The next thing he knew he was being awakened by the urgent ring of the telephone. He sat up, momentarily disorientated, under the impression that he was still in New York. He glanced at the clock to check the time. It was twenty to four.

'Hallo,' he said, a degree too loudly, as people always do to disguise the fact that they have just been asleep.

'Mr Moran?' It was a woman's voice.

'That's me.'

'This is the secretary of . . .' she hesitated, '. . . of Mr Persson. We have received your message. I am sorry but Mr Persson left last week on a long business trip. He will not be back for at least a month.'

Parnello was sitting on the edge of his bed now, running a hand round the back of his head. His mouth felt dry and uncomfortable. 'That's exceedingly inconvenient,' he said. 'Can I get a message to him, do you think? Will you be speaking to him?'

'I regret that to contact him is impossible.'

'But doesn't he ring in to you?'

'No. Only if there is an emergency.'

'But where is he?'

'I believe he is travelling in the Far East. I do not know in what country exactly.'

Parnello paused. 'What's your name?' he asked her.

'My name?' She sounded suddenly nonplussed, as if his inquiry were not part of the script.

He laughed. 'Yes. You must have a name.'

'It's . . . it's Marianne.'

'So, Marianne, you're Mr Persson's secretary?'

'That is correct.' She spoke with more confidence. 'I am Mr Persson's secretary.'

'Listen, Marianne. Then perhaps you can help me. Do you know about the painting that Mr Persson sold in New York last week?'

'Mr Persson sells and buys many paintings.'

'This was a landscape by . . . well, it was German, anyway, and it showed a river with a ferry, painted on panel. It was lot 147 in the old master sale last week. Do you know anything about its history? Where Mr Persson may have got it?'

'I regret I have no information about these things. And Mr Persson will not be returning until next month.'

'But someone there must be able to tell me what I need to know.'

'Mr Moran, please understand, there is nothing for you here. You are wasting your time. Only Mr Persson can answer your question and he is away for several weeks. I am sorry. I must finish now. I have other calls to make.'

She was gone. Parnello rubbed his eyes and cursed her for her obstructiveness. But perhaps it wasn't her fault. Operators like Persson probably did lead secretive, unpredictable lives, punctuated by lengthy buying trips abroad. Lengthy buying trips on which it was all but impossible to contact them. But that did not get him very far: certainly no closer to the recent history of the Dahl.

He felt very hungry. He went down to the hotel cafe and ordered an open sandwich and another beer. After that he had a glass of Aquavit. The drink revived him, warming his whole upper body as he sipped it, making him pleasurably light-headed. He had another one, and lit a Ducados. He felt better. A choice was opening up for him this evening. He could stay here and get pleasurably plastered. Or he could go out and continue his quest for Persson.

As the waiter stood there, Parnello hesitated. Then he said, 'Bill, please', paid it, and ordered a taxi at the reception. When it came he gave the driver Persson's address in the old town.

He could hardly give up now, could he? What would he tell Alexandra, if he went home now?

The taxi took him into the saccharine quarter of the city, where the streets were narrow and the houses huddled together in a picturesque proximity that reminded him of Switzerland, of the old towns in Geneva or Zurich. He was left at a tall white building with green shutters. He peered up at it, and his head swam in momentary vertigo as he saw how close its roof seemed to lurch towards the gable of the house opposite, arching over and almost touching in the night. It was vertigo, mixed suddenly with a whiff of claustrophobia. He was hemmed in here. And yet the facade seemed innocent enough as he gazed up at it. Innocent. Or deliberately bland. Giving nothing away.

There were three bells by the front door. The middle one said simply Persson. He rang it, long and hard, three times. There was no reply. Then he rang the other two bells. The top one, Larsson, also went unanswered. The bottom one, Schwarz, finally brought forth a quavering woman's voice on the entryphone. She spoke only a mystified Swedish which Parnello did not understand. He thanked her politely in English, and stepped back to look up at the building once more. Its blank windows stared down sightlessly at him. It was still giving nothing away.

The snow that had been threatening all day began to fall now, a damp, watery snow, caught in the streetlights of this narrow alley. Two houses further on was a bar called Green Crocodile. He made for its sanctuary, hurrying down the four steps to the door. Inside it was empty, except for a single figure with a long blond pony tail polishing glasses behind the counter. From the rear view Parnello thought it was a woman, but when the figure turned round it transpired he was a man of forty-five, with an earring and eyes that focused none too rapidly. He wore a white teeshirt with the single word 'Love' emblazoned across it.

'I'm sorry,' said Parnello, 'are you open?'

'Yeah, man. We're open,' said the barman. 'What can I get you?' His accent revealed that he was Swedish, but perhaps he'd spent some time in the United States. Or else he'd watched a lot of American television.

'A beer, Carlsberg.' He needed a chaser for the aquavit.

The barman frowned. 'Beer,' he repeated, and stood there motionless.

'Is that a problem?'

He leant forward with his elbows on the top of the bar, cupping his chin in his hands and staring hard at Parnello. 'You are what you eat, man. And what you drink.'

'So?'

'Carrot juice. Think carrot juice. I got it right here, just made it. It's fresh. And it's organic. One hundred per cent.'

The significance of the colour in the name of this bar suddenly dawned on Parnello. 'I think I'd rather be a glass of beer than a carrot,' he said. 'Even an organic carrot.'

The barman shrugged, then let out an unexpected cackle of laughter. 'Hey, that's good, man, I like that. Beer it is, then. Whatever turns you on.' The whole exchange seemed to put him into a much better mood, and he hummed tunelessly as he opened the bottle and poured it into Parnello's glass. He handed it over and said, 'Thirty kroner. Name's Johnny, by the way.'

Parnello shook his proferred hand. 'Ed,' he said briefly. He had become wary. He felt the need to keep part of himself secret, disguised. He took a seat at the bar and sipped the beer. As far as inquisitive taxi-drivers and elderly hippies were concerned, he was a banker called Ed. 'Do you know this neighbourhood well, Johnny?' he asked.

Johnny fingered his earring meditatively. 'Depends what you mean by well.'

'Have you worked here long?'

'Couple of years.'

'Do you know a man who lives two doors down the road at number 34? Lars Persson?'

'Persson? You mean the big guy, comes in here for cigarettes sometimes?'

'Could be. I've never met him myself, but he's a businessman. Import-export, that sort of thing.'

'Yes, I know this guy.' Johnny spoke cautiously.

'What's he like?'

'Far-out.'

'Far-out? In what way?'

'Like, he's got this black leather jacket that he always wears. Never seen him without it.'

'And that makes him far-out?'

'That. And other things.' Johnny began polishing the same glass again, as some sort of comfort device.

Parnello sensed Johnny's reluctance to elaborate on these other things. 'I need to talk to Persson,' he said. 'Do you know where I might find him?'

Johnny gave a laid-back kind of laugh which couldn't quite conceal his unease. 'He owe you bread, man?'

'No. Why do you ask?'

'No reason.'

'You mean it's happened before? People have been round here looking for him when he owed them money?'

Johnny raised his hands in a gesture of unctuous innocence. 'Hey, cool it man, I'm not party to this guy's business affairs, OK? He just comes in here sometimes to buy cigarettes.'

'Any idea where he is now?' persisted Parnello.

The barman shook his head. 'He's on the road a lot.'

'Is he married? Got a girlfriend?'

Johnny nodded.

'Which?'

'Both, I guess.'

Johnny shrugged. He was edgy. It was difficult to tell whether it was questions in general which made him nervous, or these particular questions. He reached behind him for a tobacco tin, opened it, and began to roll a cigarette. Although he did it with dexterity, his hands were shaking slightly. Only when he had finally lighted it and drawn deeply did he murmur:

'Look, Ed. I like you, OK? That's why I'm going to give you some advice. Be careful of this guy Persson. I don't dig his friends, they're kinda strange. It's a bad scene, OK?'

'What do you mean, kind of strange?'

'Just believe me, man. You don't want to have too much to do with those guys.'

A young man and a woman came in and sat at a table in the corner. Johnny gratefully accepted the opportunity to edge away from the bar to serve them, clattering over the stone floor in an exotically decorated pair of boots. Parnello heard him urging on the couple the merits of the carrot juice.

He reflected on what Johnny had told him. Persson Import/Export no doubt dealt in a wide variety of merchandise. He'd be prepared to bet that the business involved the handling of many more things than pictures, some of them a lot less respectable. But if he could just get hold of the proprietor, he would make it clear to him that he had no intention of interfering in his other activities. He simply wanted to know where the Dahl had come from, so that he could take one step further back in tracing its history. Then he'd leave Persson in peace, to do the things he wanted to do: parading in leather jackets, evading his creditors, chasing girls.

Parnello left the Green Crocodile and walked out into the damp evening. There were still spots of snow in the air, and a wind was beginning to whip up from the sea. He drew his overcoat closer round him and glanced back up towards the doorway of the white house with the green shutters. His interest quickened: at that moment an old lady with a bag of shopping was negotiating her way in. Mrs Schwarz, he guessed. Instinctively he ran towards her and arrived just in time to hold the door for her as she heaved the plastic bag inside.

She looked uncertainly at him as he shut the door behind them. They were standing in a small communal hallway out of which led a steep stairway with ornate ironwork banisters. He smiled back at her reassuringly. 'Mr Persson,' he said, indicating the floor above. 'Friend.'

She nodded and turned away from him to the entrance to her apartment, reaching into her bag for the key. He trotted nonchalantly on up the stairs.

At the top of the second flight, he found the bell with the name 'Persson' next to it. He paused, listening to Mrs Schwarz closing her front door below and drawing a bolt across it. Then he rang Persson's bell. Hard. Twice.

Well, it was possible that the intercom to the apartment was out of order, wasn't it? Maybe there was someone in there who would hear this time. Someone in there who could help him. Like a wife. Or a girlfriend.

There was silence. In the far distance he heard the hooting of a ship. But from within Persson's flat, nothing. He sighed. It was a thick, oak-panelled door, discouragingly solid. As a formality, he reached for the handle and turned it.

Unexpectedly, the door opened.

He pushed inside, through a hallway, and found himself at the entrance to a large reception room, lit dimly by the streetlamp outside.

'Hallo?' he called. 'Is there anyone there?'

Silence. He reached for the switch and flooded the room with light. Persson, it appeared, ran his office from his flat. There were two low-slung sofas, covered in box-files, some of which were spilled open. On a table by the window was a personal computer, its screen saver display flickering like a television left on after the end of transmission time. It was hard to tell whether the chaos was the result of untidiness or of someone having been looking for something in a hurry. Parnello walked slowly over to the fax. No recent messages had come through. Next to it was the telephone: he recognised its number, the one which he had already dialled that day. The telephone, too, was flashing. It was switched to 'Answerphone' but there was no cassette in the mechanism.

Of course: it had been taken by the secretary. By Marianne. She'd returned his call earlier that afternoon. So she must have been in to get the tape between his leaving the message at lunchtime and her ringing him back at twenty to four. Remiss of her not to replace it. Still more remiss of her to forget to lock the door as she left. She must have been in a hurry, had her mind on other things.

There was something curious about this sequence of events. Something disturbing, on which Parnello could not quite put his finger. He stared a little longer at the telephone, trying to work it out. Then he remembered an old trick. Experimentally, he pressed the redial button. A number showed up at once on the LCD display: the last number Persson, or perhaps his secretary, would have called. There was a succession of clicks, and finally the engaged signal. Parnello took out his pen and made a note of the number that had appeared on the screen, before replacing the receiver. He was like a beachcomber, gathering random pieces of evidence. In the faint and increasingly desperate hope that one of them would come in useful later.

He opened the window gently and peered out. Below him, to the right, he could see three men going into Green Crocodile. A girl on a bicycle pedalled by. He turned back into the room and picked up one of the files. It contained airline bills of lading, detailing consignments of goods. One was for leisurewear, port of origin Taipei; another, from Seoul airport, was for gentlemen's neckties. A third was for electrical appliances from Budapest. He cleared a space on the sofa and sat down, working his way through them all on the slight chance that one might record the port of origin of a painting. A nineteenth-century landscape. A German landscape showing a river with a ferry.

But the information wasn't there.

What was there, in the final file, was a more curious discovery. Two Swedish passports. He opened one and found it was Persson's. He studied the photograph of the man. He had longish, straw-coloured hair, rugged features, and gazed aggressively back at the camera. It was a look that asked you questions rather than gave you answers. The question that occurred most insistently to Parnello as he stared at it was what this passport was doing here if its owner was travelling in the Far East?

He picked up the second passport. It was in the name of someone called Erik Sorensen. But when he turned the page, he got a shock. The photograph showed Persson again. It wasn't the identical shot, but there were the same rugged features. The same aggressive look in the eyes. Unmistakably him. And tucked neatly into this passport was something else. A Russian visa in Sorensen's name. The same photograph of Persson was attached to it. It was valid for travel on 5 March. Tomorrow.

A man with two passports. A man with something to hide.

And of course a man with two passports might well have three or four, thought Parnello. In that case the presence of two of them here did not preclude the possibility of his travelling abroad in the Far East on another. Under what name this time, he wondered? But the Russian visa was strange; here was something else that did not quite add up. The Russian visa for tomorrow. Why this visa for tomorrow if the only person equipped to use it was away in Singapore or Tokyo or wherever? He held it in his hands, peering at it, speculating. Then he slipped this second passport into his pocket. He was the beachcomber again. What he had stumbled across here was more promising. It was evidence of something. Of some wrong-doing. Maybe at some point in the future it could be bartered for information about the Dahl. If Persson became difficult, that was.

As he shifted on the sofa, he reached down and felt

something small and hard wedged behind him in the cushions. He groped for it and his fingers tightened around a small cylindrical object. A camera film. Rewound, ready for developing. Persson's film, presumably. Mislaid, or maybe just forgotten on his departure for the Far East.

Parnello frowned, then slipped this film too into his jacket pocket. He had come on a legitimate quest for information, he told himself. If Persson could not be there to provide that information for him, then he must help himself to it wherever he could find it. Anything not immediately relevant to the history of the Dahl he would return later.

He got up and tried a second door which led off the main room. He discovered a bathroom and a kitchen, neither of them very clean, both showing signs of recent use. In the kitchen he found a vodka bottle, empty, with three unwashed glasses; in the bathroom a slowly dripping shower, a towel lying on the floor. He came back into the big white room and approached the last door leading out of it. He paused for a moment, his hand on the knob, listening. Had he heard someone on the stairs? He suddenly remembered what he was doing. That he was in another man's apartment. Prying through another man's possessions. If someone came in now, it would take a little explaining.

He waited, tense. There was silence again. Then he pushed open the door and went in.

For a brief instant he thought the bulky figure on the floor by the bed was asleep, perhaps drunk. And then all at once he knew he wasn't. As he ran his eyes up the torso to his head, he saw the cord wrenched round the neck. He saw the neck lying at an unnatural angle. He saw the face, purple and contorted. The eyes bulging. Bulging, but still aggressive, just as they had been in the passport photographs.

And what he registered last, tearing his sickened gaze away from the neck and back down the body, was that the man was wearing a leather jacket. A black leather jacket. Far-out. Even in death Persson had not been separated from it.

*   *   *

He backed out of the bedroom and sank down once more on the sofa, trying to master his shivering, trying to think clearly. Trying to stop his world from spiralling off into total and horrific unreason. He'd bought a picture at auction. It had been stolen from him. He'd gone looking for the man who could help him trace that picture. But he'd found that man dead. Lying there strangled in his own bedroom with the door to his apartment unlocked. The man shouldn't have been there at all. He should have left last week for the Far East on business. That's what his secretary had said. But he hadn't gone. He'd been in Stockholm all the time.

There must be some pattern to all this, some explanatory principle behind it, something that made it all add up. But he couldn't see it. Not sitting here shivering on this sofa. All he could see was the horror of his own immediate position. And the danger, too.

He'd inveigled himself into this building under false pretences. He'd walked in uninvited to the dead man's quarters. He'd rifled through his property. His fingerprints would be everywhere. Who would believe him when he said he hadn't killed him? Even if he ran out now, down into the Green Crocodile bar, galvanised Johnny into raising the alarm, acted in the way his civilised instincts told him he should, there would still be highly awkward questions to answer at Stockholm police headquarters. It wouldn't look too good that he'd given a false name at the bar when inquiring after the whereabouts of the dead man. He hadn't checked by touching the body, but it couldn't have been there that long, could it? Not if the secretary had been in earlier that afternoon and not found it. It would be difficult to prove that the killing had taken place long enough before he'd entered the apartment to lift suspicion from himself.

Then he heard the footsteps coming up the stairs. Slowly, insistently. Getting closer all the time. He froze, listening to the fumbling at the door to the apartment, the turning of its handle. A woman's voice. The wife? The girlfriend? Marianne? Whoever it was, she'd apparently paused in the hallway. Perhaps she was taking off her coat.

'Lars?' he heard the woman call. 'Lars, är det Du?'

He'd hardly slept on the plane. He was jet-lagged. He was confused, in an alien city, having drunk two aquavits. He suddenly felt that anything was preferable to being found by this woman in this burgled apartment with the strangled body of Lars Persson lying in the next room.

Swiftly and silently he ran out past the kitchen and into the bathroom. He eased up the window and climbed out so that he was poised precariously on the sill. A flat roof lay perhaps ten foot below him. He turned and swung himself down so that he was hanging full length, his long legs flapping in the bitter cold. He dropped the last three feet and landed intact, a little breathless. It was as he lowered himself the same way from the flat roof to ground level that he heard the woman's scream. Horrific in its clarity, lacerating the wet night air, resonating down the alleys and across the rooftops of the old town.

He found himself in a yard, saw a gate open leading to a street and ran off through it. The street was not the one by which he'd entered the building, but he set off through the snow-flurries purposefully, not running now but walking fast, intent only on putting distance between himself and the house he had just left. He zigzagged through the warren of alleys, past chic clothes shops and restaurants now beginning to fill up with customers for dinner. At one point he looked up and saw the magnificent spire of the German Church arrowing up into the mist. At the next junction he turned the corner and miraculously came upon an empty taxi. He got in and said, 'Diplomat Hotel.'

He was amazed by how normal his own voice sounded.

Back in the hotel, he tore off his clothes as if they were tainted, as if they constituted evidence against him. Then he had a long hot shower. Finally he drank three more glasses of aquavit and smoked two cigarettes. He lay down to rest. He was very, very tired.

NINETEEN

The woman was screaming again. Her voice was echoing from the upstairs window, cutting over the rooftops of the old town, pursuing him across the city. He sat up in bed, tense, frightened. Suddenly convinced that he might run, but he would never get away from that scream. Then he heard the sound again and relaxed. It was only the brakes of a lorry on Strandvagen.

Ten to eight. Outside it was still dark, the streets shrouded in the long night of the Swedish winter. He tested himself methodically, going back slowly over yesterday's events, forcing himself to confront them: the old town, the facade of the house, the bar. Johnny, with his pony-tail and his tee-shirt saying 'Love'. The apartment, with its spilled box-files. And the body. That face, with its distended eyes. The unnatural angle of the neck.

He remembered that night in Caracas. He was twenty-one, driving a taxi with only two working gears and periodically non-functioning brakes; he remembered the two passengers with knives who'd set upon him, demanding his evening's takings, the foolish resistance he'd put up, and the oddly painless sensation of the blade plunging into his shoulder; he remembered the flow of the blood, the local hospital, and the fainting; the strange unreality of it all. And he remembered waking up the next morning shaking. In shock. Barely able to suppress the tears.

It was the memory of those tears which galvanised him

now. He must not give into them a second time. He was forearmed to oppose them. For better or worse, he had taken a decision last night which propelled him inevitably now along a certain course. He had fled Persson's apartment when it might have been wiser to have gone to the police. But the fact remained that he'd done nothing wrong. He had merely indulged his curiosity about the activities of a man who'd been the previous owner of a picture that had been stolen from him. He couldn't have raised the alarm about the death of that man any quicker than the woman had obviously done with her screaming. Persson's killer could be found without his own involvement. It was probably some sneak-thief who'd panicked, some disreputable business associate taking debt-collecting a step too far. The police could handle all that. Leaving him free to concentrate on the provenance of the Dahl. On tracing its recent history in the hope that it might shed some light on its present whereabouts. In the hope that it might conceivably shed some light on the other, more valuable pictures in the von Seitz collection.

That's what he told himself then, anyway, as he lay in bed, with the taste of Ducados and stale aquavit still lingering on his palate, trying to master the panic. Trying to see the way forward. And in the cold blue light of the dawning Stockholm day, it seemed to work for him.

He ordered breakfast, and as he ate it in his room the determination strengthened in him to go forward. What he'd subjected himself to last night would be pointless if it didn't lead on to something positive. His curiosity was roused. He couldn't leave things now. He had to know more.

He analysed what he'd learned from the extraordinary events of the past twenty-four hours, what new facts had emerged. He was the beachcomber, the gatherer of trifles at random on the shore. Only when he got them home and re-examined them could he try to form them into a pattern. He started to do so now. He had at his disposal certain pieces of evidence that might be useful if he could only gauge their significance. One was Persson's passport, in the name of Erik Sorensen. And another was the telephone number. The one he had jotted down from Persson's telephone. He looked at it again. He registered that it was a number in a foreign country: it started 0097. He didn't immediately recognise the international code, and reached for the hotel phone book.

He flicked through the pages to the international section. And then there it was: 97 was Russia. Promising. The next digits were 812. He ran his eye down the list of city codes. He found it quite quickly. 812 was St Petersburg.

Parnello sat there thinking for a minute. Weighing possibilities. Remembering the visa in the name of Sorensen. The visa for travel to Russia today. Then, like a shipwrecked sailor clinging to the only piece of available wreckage, he reached for his telephone and dialled the full number.

He heard the ringing tone; then, miraculously, a man's voice. A man's voice in Russian.

'Do you speak English?' asked Parnello.

'Yes, OK, English. Who is this please?'

'I am a friend of . . . of Erik Sorensen.' It was a wild shot. But it hit some part of the target.

'Where is he?' There was a belligerence in the man's tone; but a belligerence laced with unease.

The visa. 'He's coming today,' lied Parnello. 'Coming to Russia.'

'Of course he comes.' The man's tone was impatient now. 'You tell him from me we are waiting for him this evening in St Petersburg.'

'Where's he to meet you?'

'At Pulkovo of course. Pulkovo airport. We send a driver to meet the plane, as usual.'

'The SAS flight?' hazarded Parnello.

'Of course the SAS flight.'

Parnello decided to push his luck. 'What have you got to offer him this time?'

'Like before. Only top quality merchandise. He knows.'

Now the big gamble. 'Like paintings, perhaps?'

'What are you, a crazy man, talking these things on the open line? Didn't you hear what happened to Kuslov?'

'What happened to Kuslov?'

'Where's Sorensen?' His anger had turned to suspicion. 'Who are you, anyway?'

'I'm a friend. A business colleague. I told you.'

'What's the matter with Sorensen? Make him speak, put him on the line. Why are you talking for him?'

'Don't worry. He'll be there.'

His heart was pumping as he replaced the receiver, then picked it up again and dialled SAS.

'The afternoon flight to St Petersburg is the 13.20,' said the woman. 'Arrival 17.10.'

'Just calling to confirm I have a reservation. My name is Sorensen.'

'Please wait a minute.' The pause was tense. Parnello stared hard at the floral design on the wallpaper, concentrating on analysing its pattern as a means of calming his racing brain. 'Yes, Mr Sorensen. You're booked into economy class.'

'Thank you,' he said. 'Thank you very much.'

It was madness, of course. But he was better off out of Stockholm now. And sooner rather than later.

The walls were suddenly very close, hemming him in, constricting his movement. He paced to the window and peered out across the city, as if searching for a route of escape. He opened the window a few inches and the fresh cold air was a shock, but simultaneously a relief from the oppression of the bedroom. He watched two girls and a man strolling along the quayside in the morning sun; further off a flock of seabirds lazily took wing and drifted across the water. And then as his eye travelled on to the road on the other side he caught sight of the police car, snaking urgently through the traffic, its blue light flashing.

And he remembered the secretary.

Of course: the secretary. What was her name? Marianne. How long before the police got to Marianne? How long

before she gave them the list of yesterday's telephone callers
to Persson's number? 'There was a Mr Moran. He was staying
at the Diplomat. Room 214. Look. I returned his call . . .'
How long before the police sped round to the hotel, with
their blue lights flashing? How long before they came for
him, to question this mysterious English visitor, the man
who'd had business with Persson, the man who'd needed
to see him urgently the day he'd died? Purely routine, of
course. Just to eliminate him from their inquiries. But would
he mind giving them his finger prints?

Then he'd be caught. Impaled on the skewer of his own
rashness.

Unless he'd already checked out. Unless he'd taken a taxi
to Arlanda. Unless he was on a flight out of the country.

But not a flight back to London. Not now. That would be
too dangerous. By the time it left, the gate would be watched
by vigilant men. Men set on the capture of a suspect named
Moran, a British passport holder who had been staying in
the Diplomat hotel.

No, it would be the 13.20 SAS flight to St Petersburg.

He walked quickly into the bathroom and stood in front
of the mirror, contemplating his own reflection, considering
the mystery of physiognomy. He observed his face at different
angles, under different plays of light, animated by different
expressions. If a camera had caught him at those various
separate moments, would you necessarily conclude that the
photographs were all of the same man? Then again, how
many people were there in the world? Several billion. How
could there exist several billion discernible variations on
the same basic pattern of hair, two eyes, a nose and a
mouth? If you lined up all the people in the world, then
you would surely encounter millions of individuals whose
facial differences were too small to register, who looked to all
intents and purposes the same as each other. Maybe his own
hair was a shade darker than Lars Persson's, for instance, a
shade longer too. Maybe his look was less aggressive, his
eyes more morose; but the shape of his face was much the

same, the alignment of his features. It was not beyond the bounds of possibility that someone looking at Persson's photograph could be persuaded that it showed Parnello Moran. Particularly if that photograph had been taken a few years ago.

And if that was so, then Parnello might equally pass himself off as Erik Sorensen, too.

He hurried back to the wardrobe, found his jacket and felt around in the pocket. His hand tightened reassuringly round Erik Sorensen's passport. Back in front of the bathroom mirror, he opened it up to check. To compare. He wavered, then snapped it shut decisively. Sometimes you just had to trust to luck.

He dressed quickly, packed, and let himself out of his room. As he took the lift to Reception, he told himself that it was reasonable enough for him to be leaving now. After all, Marianne had told him categorically that Persson was not here in Stockholm to see him. If the police arrived and found he had already departed, that would not in itself arouse suspicion. It would even appear more logical.

He paid the bill and ordered a taxi. When it came and he sank into the back seat, he felt a surge of relief, an irrational euphoria. He was mobile now. A moving target rather than a stationary one.

It was 10.30. He had nearly three hours to kill before the flight to St Petersburg. He gave the driver instructions to head out to Arlanda. He had one priority: to put as much distance as possible between himself and Stockholm as quickly as he could. The fifty kilometres separating city and airport, so absurd upon arrival, was a comfort now. Every so often he glanced back over his shoulder as the taxi sped along the dual carriageway. He wasn't quite sure what he was looking for. But he was relieved each time he didn't see it.

The gate was not even open for check-in when he got to the airport. He paced the departures hall, leafed through the magazines in the bookstall with unseeing eyes. Drank a cup of coffee and smoked a cigarette. Watching all the time. Surreptitiously alert.

Just before noon he approached the SAS desk. The flight was now open. He handed over his ticket and checked in his bag.

The girl said something in Swedish that he didn't understand. He kept smiling and presented his passport and visa. A good guess. She reached out and took them, and he held his breath.

Mechanically she flicked through them. Her eyes barely rested on the photographs. Perhaps she was thinking of her lunch break. She closed the red booklet with the visa folded neatly inside and handed it back. She said something more which he assumed was Swedish for 'Have a nice flight.' He smiled at her again and walked on.

At passport control the official glanced at his papers, saw they were Swedish, and did not even bother to inspect them. Parnello was waved through with a quick gesture of the hand. He felt suddenly excited, as though he was winning a game. Then the flash of elation passed. He reminded himself how different the reaction could have been if he'd shown his own passport. For all he knew, the alert had gone out now. Detain Moran. British, mid-thirties, probably travelling to London. Wanted for questioning in connection with a serious crime last night in the old town. Get him. Don't let him through.

Even as he waited at the gate to board the aircraft, he kept the ground-staff desk under constant surveillance. Every call answered could be a last-minute alert from the police. The steward's sudden questing look around the assembled passengers might be in search of him. But boarding was announced and he was allowed to pass like everyone else. He took his seat, attached his safety belt. The engines of the DC-9 slowly wound into life. A few minutes later the wheels of the aircraft left the tarmac. He relaxed. It had worked. He was free.

The snowy forests below, on arrival faintly disturbing, now receded into miniature until they disappeared entirely

beneath a light covering of cloud, and he was up there in
the clear blue ether. Out of it. Beyond the jurisdiction of
the Swedish police. He had done it.

But even now, as he savoured the illusion of escape,
concentrated on it, tried not to think too far into the future
or the past, he knew there was something not quite right. He
could not immediately identify it, but it was there, nagging
at him, something that did not quite fit in. And finally he
yielded, set himself once more to run over the events of
the past twenty-four hours. Methodically. To try to pin
it down.

It all came back to one question. Why would Persson
have told his secretary that he was going to the Far East
on business last week when all the time he was actually in
Stockholm? What was she doing coming regularly into his
flat to get his messages and not noticing the evidence of its
continuing occupation by its owner? Or had Persson in fact
only just returned – unexpectedly – from his travels? Was
it possible that Marianne could have come in late enough
yesterday afternoon to have got Parnello's message on the
answerphone, but early enough to have missed both her
employer's unannounced return and the killer's visit which
followed? And a small but nagging question – why would
a secretary efficient enough to call back all those who had
left messages on her boss's answerphone not bother to
replace with a fresh cassette the one that she took away
with her?

The more he examined the evidence, the more unlikely
the story that he had been fed by Marianne appeared.
And gradually another explanation came to him. Seeped
into his consciousness, bit by bit. Insidiously. An explanation that was more and more plausible. And even more
frightening.

Maybe Persson didn't have a secretary called Marianne at
all.

Maybe the woman who'd rung Parnello at 3.40 yesterday
afternoon had been an imposter, an imposter who had had

access to the cassette of Persson's telephone messages. The cassette that she had been given by Persson's murderer, with whom she was in collusion. The cassette that the murderer had snatched from the machine as he'd made his escape from the apartment.

This scenario opened up a whole sequence of even more disturbing questions for Parnello. Why, he asked himself now, why had they bothered to ring him afterwards, to feed him with false information about Persson's absence abroad? Would it not have been easier simply to ignore his messages and leave it at that? The explanation could only be that there was some special urgency about keeping him away. Some reason why he must be positively persuaded to go home quietly, deterred from the purpose of his visit to Stockholm. Prevented from asking any more questions about the Dahl.

The Dahl. Maybe it all came back to that picture. Could there be some connection between the theft of the Dahl in New York and the killing of Persson in Sweden? Could it be that ownership of the Dahl carried with it some unfathomable danger?

But why? What was it about that picture?

There had been two owners of it in the recent past, Persson and himself. And Persson was dead. Maybe that made Parnello lucky to have got away with being the victim of a mere burglary in New York. It certainly suggested that the deeper he delved into the picture's history, the more he was putting his own life on the line.

And something else occurred to him, too. Something which at first brought reassurance, and then, the more he thought about it, a growing apprehension. If Marianne, the secretary of Lars Persson, did not actually exist, then the cassette was unlikely ever to find its way into the hands of the Stockholm police. In that case it would have been no problem for him to have taken the London flight this afternoon as Parnello Moran. To have gone home unscathed.

Instead here he was as Erik Sorensen flying on to St Petersburg. Flying on to St Petersburg to meet an as yet undefined but potentially even greater danger than anything he had encountered in Stockholm.

TWENTY

Leaning back in the aircraft seat, Parnello closed his eyes, and concentrated very hard. In the background, the engines died a little, and the descent into St Petersburg began. He combed through his mental store of acquaintances, of chance encounters remembered over fifteen years' racketing across the world in the quest of good pictures. He was searching for one name. And at last it came to him.

Dobiachowsky. That was it. Alexei Dobiachowsky.

It must have been in the summer of 1985. On his only previous trip to Russia.

'Going to the Soviet Union?' someone had said to him at a party the week before he'd left. 'If you're going to Leningrad, you must go and see Dobiachowsky.'

'Who's Dobiachowsky?' Parnello had asked with a guarded courtesy. In his experience people offered such recommendations as a means of showing off their prior knowledge of unusual or exotic places rather than with any serious intention of introducing like-minded spirits. Actually to take up such an introduction was all too often a recipe for an evening of unmitigated boredom.

'An art historian. Teaches at the university. The remarkable thing about him is that he's not like the typical Eastern Bloc academic. You know the way they all tend to be a bit cowed and furtive. But not Dobiachowsky. No, Dobiachowsky's an original.'

Parnello had joined a tour to visit Moscow and Leningrad.

To look at the Pushkin and the Tretyakov Museums, and then on to the Hermitage. It had all been highly supervised, controlled. By the time he'd reached Leningrad he felt an overwhelming need to escape from his shackles. So he had decided to risk Dobiachowsky. Anything was better than the bland platitudes of the Intourist guide.

It was the last afternoon of his three-day visit to the city and Parnello had finally triumphed over the Leningrad telephone system and managed to make an appointment with the voice that answered his call. Dobiachowsky turned out to be a big man, with a huge moustache. It was difficult to say which was more extravagantly luxuriant, his moustache or his belly. He lived in a tiny two-room flat off Nevsky Prospekt, a flat whose every wall groaned under the weight of books and files. Before their conversation had got beyond the formal exchange of politenesses, he had plied Parnello with two glasses of neat vodka.

'Life's easier since my wife moved out,' he confided. 'I can express myself. Of course I'm quite impossible to live with. I don't blame her for leaving in the least. She went off with a ballet dancer from the Kirov. Surprising, that. Normally they're all homosexual.'

'What are you working on at the moment?' Parnello inquired. It was the sort of safe, serious-minded question he asked in those days.

'Constructivism, Dr Parnello. Constructivism has always been my speciality. I know more about the early work of Malevich than I do about my own ass-hole,' said Dobiachowsky; but even as he was speaking he rose from his seat and crossed the room to the transistor radio on the table. Winking at Parnello, he switched it on. 'About this time in the afternoon there's generally an exceptionally good programme of Russian folk music. I like to listen to it. Rather loud.'

As music flooded the room he sat down again, closer to Parnello, speaking in a lower voice. 'That's the official version, anyway,' he said. 'I have to go through this pantomime for the benefit of any unwanted eavesdroppers.'

'You mean your flat is bugged?'

'I have found it safer to act on the assumption that anywhere I talk is bugged.' He poured himself another glass of vodka. 'Even in these enlightened days of glasnost, the presence in my apartment of a westerner such as yourself, although on the most innocent of pretexts, may excite certain people's interest.'

Parnello sat there fascinated. After nine days of anodyne visits to museums and palaces under the all-seeing supervision of the Soviet-approved guide, he had suddenly broken free from the artificiality, the careful control. This was real. This was life on the edge.

Russian folk music. He particularly liked that touch.

Even afterwards, when he was back in London and an informed acquaintance at the Foreign Office assured him that switching on a radio, however loud, was no protection against bugging, he still enjoyed it. It showed a sense of theatre on Dobiachowsky's part, a feeling for the dramatic to which Parnello instinctively responded.

'Things are changing here, you know,' Dobiachowsky continued. 'In the most extraordinary ways. Therefore it is a very precarious time. In the not too distant future, life in the Soviet Union may get very much better. Or it may get very much worse.'

'Which do you think it will be?'

'I do not know. It's in the balance. But one thing's for sure: if restrictions continue to loosen up, it'll soon be a great time to be a historian here. There are so many secrets in this country. Whole hidden archives which no-one is allowed to see yet. Once they start to be unlocked, there won't be enough historians to cope with the deluge of material. It'll be unbelievably exciting.'

'Exciting for art historians too?'

'Especially for art historians. I have colleagues in Moscow who are already working on the most amazing material. Come back and see me in a year or two's time, Dr Parnello, and I'll show you things you wouldn't dream of.'

Things you would not dream of. But Parnello had not come back. Until now. Under rather different circumstances from those he might have anticipated for his second visit to Russia.

The plane touched down at Pulkovo airport and taxied to its stand. It was snowing gently. In the distance, like huge insects, bulldozers crawled back and forth clearing the runways. As the engines were stilled and everyone stood up, stretching their limbs and reaching for handbaggage in the lockers above, Parnello looked about him, surveying his fellow passengers. They were an unremarkable enough group, mostly blond Swedes in fur boots and earnest spectacles, laying aside copies of the Stockholm business daily as they eased themselves into overcoats and hats. Here and there was a face that might have been Russian, but these faces too wore the uniform, mildly concerned expressions of European business travellers, preoccupied with next month's sales figures, anxious as to how quickly they could grab a taxi to the hotel or home. These days, Parnello told himself, the passage from Stockholm to St Petersburg was a flight as innocuous as the one between London and Frankfurt.

Except that from here on, things were not quite so simple. From here on he was no longer Parnello Moran, art dealer. He was Erik Sorensen, Swedish entrepreneur with interests in the import-export business. He was in St Petersburg to set up deals with Russian contacts. Russian contacts whose driver would be waiting for him in the arrivals hall. Before that he had to negotiate Russian immigration control. And he had to do so using the passport of a man who did not exist, using a passport bearing the photograph of someone who had twenty-four hours earlier been strangled in a Stockholm apartment.

One thing was clear: if he was going to carry it off, he must think himself totally into the role, suspend his existence as Parnello Moran and convince himself that he was Erik Sorensen. If he showed the slightest uncertainty he would be lost. His best chance of persuading Russian passport officials to believe that he was the man shown in the photograph in Sorensen's passport was to believe it himself. To have no doubt about it. To walk through with absolute confidence, without giving it a second thought.

He felt a shaft of naked fear; and simultaneously a charge of pure adrenalin. He was alive. Alive, in Byron's sense. The great object of life, after all, was sensation.

The airport terminal building was comfortless and functional. Parnello followed his fellow passengers past the signs indicating passport control and baggage reclaim. His expression registered nothing beyond a certain impatience with the formalities: he had made this journey many times before. His eye rested briefly on the advertisements for American Express and Macdonalds, for a shop offering the best quality fur coats in Russia. And he passed on. Every step bringing him closer to the next crisis. Every step bringing him closer to Immigration.

There were three people ahead of him in the queue. He stood there nonchalantly, watching as an elderly man and his wife laboriously reclaimed their papers and moved on through. The man in front of him moved up to the window. Now Parnello was next in line.

It had been easy at Arlanda. They had barely looked, any of them. Not the girl at the desk. Not the man at passport control.

But here at Pulkovo it was different. The man behind the window was taking longer with each passport, studying it exhaustively. Making comparisons. Checking against lists. Tapping numbers into computer terminals. Now he was leaning forward, asking questions of the owner, demanding information. His face was alert, unyielding. Whereas in Stockholm the official had been dressed in a jacket and tie, this man seemed to belong to some branch of the military. Didn't Parnello remember reading once that border controls

in the old Soviet Union had been in the hands of a branch
of the KGB? Was that still so? Behind the official checking
passports, in the shadows, it was possible to catch a glimpse
of his colleague. This man was also in uniform. In his hands
he held a medium-sized machine gun. He was fingering it
purposefully. It was not just decoration. You were left in
no doubt that he would use it.

At that moment Parnello heard a woman's voice immediately behind him in the queue saying something in Russian.
Saying something to him. He turned and found himself face
to face with a girl in her early twenties. She was exceptionally
tall, only an inch or two shorter than he was, and wore very
long boots and very tight trousers. She had long dark hair
and wild emerald eyes.

'I'm sorry,' he said, smiling at her. 'Do you speak
English?'

He was Sorensen. Sorensen, with a Swedish passport.
Maybe he should have addressed her in Swedish, but he
knew none. It couldn't be helped.

'Oh, English,' she laughed delightedly. 'Sure. I know
English. I am saying this man is an ass-hole.'

'Which man?'

'This one.' She gestured to the passport official. 'He sits
there all day in his little cage fucking people up.'

'He's not exactly fast, is he?'

'I am Irena,' she said, extending her hand to him.

'Erik,' he said, shaking it. 'Erik Sorensen.'

'You are English? American?'

'Swedish,' he said firmly.

She shrugged, then laughed again. 'London, New York,
Stockholm. I love to be in all those places. Only when I come
back to Russia it makes me depressed.'

'You've been to all those places?'

She concentrated, ticking them off on her fingers. 'Stockholm, three times. London once. New York, never.'

'And why are you depressed when you come back home?'

'Because of ass-holes like this man who sits behind his

little window and thinks he is a king. Because Russia is a country of ass-holes. Men who think they know everything when in fact they know nothing. Nothing.'

'Every country has got people like that.'

'None as many as Russia. See, he is calling you now. The ass-hole.'

He moved forward slowly and placed the passport and visa meticulously on the ledge. Then he put his hand back into his pocket. To hide the fact that it was shaking slightly.

The man frowned and picked up the slim red book. He opened it and stared at it mistrustfully. Parnello tried to relax, idly examining a notice about duty-free allowances attached to the glass. He was aware of the official's eyes narrowing, of the fact that he was looking at him. With an enormous effort at control, he slowly moved his own eyes away from the notice and returned the man's stare. Not aggressively. Just casually. After a moment the official looked down and flicked the page over.

And then, ominously, flicked it back again. Back again to the photograph.

Keeping one hand on the outspread passport, he reached down with the other and keyed data into the terminal. Then he sat up abruptly and leant over to a second colleague sitting in the adjoining booth, showing him something in Sorensen's papers and pointing to the screen. They exchanged inaudible words. The next thing Parnello knew he was being addressed in Russian from behind the window.

'English,' he murmured dry-mouthed. 'Do you speak English?'

'You must go with him,' said the official slowly. 'Answer questions.'

'Go with who?'

The official said nothing but gestured to the armed guard behind him. The soldier with the machine gun was already moving out of the booth and beckoning him to follow. There was nothing he could do but comply.

He was led to a small room with a desk and told to sit down opposite a fat, balding man. The door was shut and the guard handed the papers to the balding man, then stood aside. But he remained in the room with them. Remained there, fingering his gun, yearning for him to make his day by running for it. For a moment Parnello stared into the abyss of panic, saw his life spiralling away once more into unreason. The bald man asked him something, first in Russian, and then in another language, probably Swedish. Uncomprehending, he sat there nodding, as if thinking carefully before framing his reply. His interrogator spoke again, more sharply. It seemed like the same question. But what the man was saying and how to reply was beyond him.

'English?' he murmured helplessly.

Then without warning there was a commotion outside, and a loud knock. The door swung open abruptly, and there stood Irena. Irena, very angry indeed. She shouted at the bald man in Russian. Then she shouted at the armed guard. Both looked bemused, even a little sheepish. The bald man began to remonstrate with her, in a whining, querulous voice, but it made no impression. Every time he spoke she shouted him down. She launched into a further tirade, gesturing occasionally to Parnello.

Finally the bald man shrugged, took up a stamp, applied it to the visa, and snapped the passport shut. He handed it back to its owner, with an ill grace, a little like a naughty child who has been found out in some misdemeanour.

'My God,' said Parnello when they were outside. 'Thank you for that. I think you just saved my life.'

Irena laughed, pleased with herself. 'Those men are ass-holes, like I told you. They try to throw their weight around.'

'They certainly didn't know how to handle you.'

'Not many people do. My friends, they call me crazy woman. But if something makes me angry, I have to do something. I have – what you call it? – impulse.'

'But what was the problem with my papers?'

'You have short memory, then, Mr Sorensen?' She regarded him, bright-eyed, with her head on one side.

'Short memory? For what?'

'You see, Russian authorities think you are dangerous criminal.' She was giggling.

'A dangerous criminal?'

'There. You have forgotten.' She shook her head in mock censure. 'Last month. On the Moscow highway. You drove your car much too fast, Mr Sorensen. You have an unpaid traffic fine outstanding. You do not remember?'

'Oh,' he laughed. 'That.'

'These ass-holes were hoping to get the fine out of you now. On the spot. They would have just pocketed the money of a gullible foreigner. I told them you would only pay the authorities in the approved way. I told them they could go screw themselves.'

'I probably would have paid it to them,' he admitted. 'I'm the original gullible foreigner.' He felt better, almost light-headed. The relief was flooding through him. So Persson, alias Sorensen, besides sporting leather jackets and chasing women, had also liked driving rather fast.

They stopped to wait at the baggage carousel and Parnello realised that she was regarding him with a mixture of interest and amusement. 'There was also another thing that made them curious,' she said.

'What was that?'

'They wanted to know why a man with a Swedish passport spoke no Swedish.'

'So what did you say?'

'I told them you'd lived most of your life in America.'

'That was imaginative of you. But why did they think you knew so much about me?'

'Easy,' she laughed. 'I told them you were my lover.'

Magically she had procured one of the few luggage trolleys in Pulkovo airport. She had a lot of luggage, which Parnello helped her pile on to it.

'It looks as though you've been away a long time,' he observed.

'Not long enough.' She regarded his own single suitcase. 'And you, you do not plan to stay here very long?'

'It depends,' he said. 'Here, let me push that for you.'

'No,' she said firmly. 'I push.'

'OK. You push.'

She paused. She stood facing him for a moment. 'So. Now I say goodbye. You may kiss me if you like.'

He leant forward and kissed her on each cheek. She wore an expensive scent. But through it he could smell her, too. It was suddenly exciting. 'Thank you for what you did,' he said softly.

'Goodbye, Erik.' The slight hesitation before she spoke his name was intentional. Faintly mocking.

'Goodbye, Irena.'

She began to move off with her trolley, then looked back at him and said: 'There is good reason, you see. Through those doors there is waiting for me my boyfriend. He is very jealous man.' She laughed at the absurdity of it all and walked on.

Parnello nodded. He remembered there was someone waiting for him, too.

He stood still for a few minutes, then followed her through the doors to the Arrivals hall.

His eyes surveyed the circle of people waiting there, in all the usual attitudes that you find in people meeting flights the world over. Their expressions ranged from expectancy to boredom: a few families with children; a group of soldiers on leave; various drivers holding up placards with names. Jones from Sony; Bukowski from IBM. And then suddenly there it was: Sorensen. Just the single name.

Once more the relief flooded through him. The fact that the driver held up a placard meant that he didn't know Sorensen, that he didn't expect to recognise him as he came through the doors. That one more crisis had been negotiated. That he was safe for the time being.

The driver was a burly man wearing a fur hat and sunglasses. Parnello approached him and identified himself. The driver took Parnello's bag wordlessly and led the way out through the swing doors into the bitter cold air of the winter's evening. Parnello followed him through the car park where a few desultory flakes of snow continued to fall. As he looked about that car park, he recognised it as a microcosm of contemporary Russia: most of the vehicles were ready for the breakers' yard, decrepit buses and outmoded lorries, barely functional saloon cars of antiquated design blackened with exhaust. And here and there, interspersed amongst this debris like ridiculously rich relations at some humble family gathering, were the sleek German cars, the gleaming top-of-the-range BMWs and Mercedes, shockingly opulent in these surroundings. The two Russias. The parallel realities. His driver stopped at one of the Mercedes and held the door open for him.

As he got in he glanced back momentarily and saw her, about a hundred yards away, leaning statuesquely against another large limousine while a faceless man stowed her luggage into the boot.

They drove into St Petersburg along a relentless dual carriageway whose margins were banked with blackened snow. Gradually the straggling fields gave way to urbanisation, to agglomerations of post-war concrete blocks providing storey upon storey of workers' homes. Gaunt and depressing, these discoloured slabs constituted architecture only in the sense that a rubbish tip could be described as landscape. They were monuments to the uniformity of the regime that had spawned them; and as that regime's epitaph they were eloquent beyond words. Here and there, as he was driven back in time through the rings of urban development that marked the progressive limits of the city's different historical expansions, Parnello noticed other monuments to the Soviet years. Statues of Lenin, for instance: now mere historic relics shorn of their political significance, dinosaurs cast in bronze and stripped of their power to rule lives.

PHILIP HOOK

He watched the queues of people waiting patiently for trams in the shadow of these disregarded colossi. As the car paused briefly at traffic lights, he caught a glimpse of their faces. Hard-featured men and women. Reconciled to queuing. Lifting their eyes neither to the statues nor to register the passing of a car which it would cost them more than a lifetime's wages to acquire. No comfort for them in either limousines or Lenin. They had simpler priorities. Like keeping warm. And getting enough to eat.

Now the car rattled over the potholes approaching the centre of the original city, its beautiful eighteenth-century kernel. They swung down the side of a canal against which elegant ochre palaces were drawn up, in varying states of patrician decay. Then at traffic lights they turned left into Nevsky Prospect, the grandest shopping street of pre-communist Russia. It was six-thirty in the evening, and the pavements milled with people. Wrapped against the cold, they shuffled grimly onwards, as if propelled by some atavistic, pre-revolutionary instinct to parade themselves on this once glamorous thoroughfare.

They came to a halt in a nameless street within sight of the Neva. The driver opened his door and Parnello emerged, turning his collar up against the cold, letting his eye run surreptitiously up and down the roadway. Admiring the ornate ironwork of the lamps. Measuring the angles of possible escape. Then he was directed through a door, and told to follow up the stairs. They passed into a simply furnished apartment on the first floor. The driver indicated an inner door that Parenello was to enter, and withdrew. Parnello closed his eyes for a moment, then reached for the handle.

The room he came into was sparsely furnished. Its walls, illuminated by an unforgiving fluorescent light, were a dirty mustard colour. They were hung with trade calendars, decorated with coloured photographs of Russian landscapes, country dancers, and naked girls. At a window behind the desk stood a short, thick-set man in a crumpled suit peering

272

out at the street through a gap in the curtains. He turned round as Parnello entered. He had thin, close-cropped hair and the sort of bulging neck round which no shirt collar could ever be persuaded to fasten, so that his expensive Italian tie hung permanently askew. He had a tough, coarse, pockmarked ugliness, as if the mould in which his face had been set had been filled with some defective compound of discoloured concrete. He took two steps towards his visitor but kept the desk between them; as if he needed it as a means of asserting himself over him.

'You are not Sorensen,' he said.

Parnello had been prepared for this moment. It had been inevitable, sooner or later. But still he felt suddenly exposed, unprotected. What happened now was unpredictable. Now he was starting a journey without maps.

'No, I am not Sorensen,' he said slowly. 'I am his colleague, his business associate. I think that you and I spoke on the telephone earlier today.'

'Why do you come instead of him? Where is he?' He leant forward with his hands resting on the desk-top, swaying slightly. Parnello noticed the beads of sweat on his forehead. Watching him, Parnello sensed his anger, the menace implicit in his movements. But they couldn't entirely mask another, more volatile element. An underlying panic. As if this man was on the edge. That if he were pushed, he might do something crazy.

'Sorensen suggested I should come. In case we could do business, you and I, directly together.'

'Who are you?'

Parnello paused. 'My name is Moran.'

'Moran.' The other man regarded him dubiously. 'Sorensen, he never spoke of you.'

Parnello shrugged. 'He often spoke of you.' This was a risk. He had no idea of the man's name. 'He said you were the best. The best in St Petersburg. That if I came here, I should come to you and you would find me the sort of merchandise I am looking for.'

The flattery worked, to the extent that the Russian now reached forward and extended his hand. 'Sergei Constantinowich Aronsky,' he said quickly, as if not wanting to be overheard. He stretched for a cigarette from a box on the desk. He lit it with a silver lighter in the shape of a handgrenade, then sat down and gestured to a black leather sofa opposite. 'You will drink vodka, Mr Moran?'

Parnello wanted to drink vodka very much indeed. 'Thank you,' he said.

Aronsky reached into a drawer and brought out a bottle with two glasses. He filled them both. As he passed one over to Parnello he said: 'Remember this, Mr Moran: I don't deal with time-wasters. I run big business here. Successful business. OK?'

'That's the sort of business I like too.'

'So first I ring Sorensen to check on you.'

'Go ahead.'

Frowning, Aronsky picked up a mobile telephone, flipped open a notebook, and tapped in a sequence. Peering across surreptitiously, Parnello recognised most of the digits from Persson's number. In the Stockholm apartment. In the apartment where yesterday he had been lying dead.

God knew who would answer. If Parnello were lucky, no-one. If he were unlucky, the Stockholm police department. 'You won't get a reply,' he said. 'I can tell you that now. Sorensen's away.'

'Away?' Aronsky looked back at him but kept the receiver to his ear.

'Yes. He's travelling.'

Aronsky kept it to his ear for perhaps thirty seconds. It seemed like thirty minutes. At last he flipped the mobile telephone shut. 'He's not answering,' he muttered.

'Like I told you. He's been away a week. In the Far East, on a buying trip.'

Aronsky rounded on him. Suspicious, aggressive again. 'Why do you give me this garbage, Mr Moran? You think I'm stupid? Sorensen's not in the Far East. I spoke to him yesterday. He was in Stockholm yesterday. He told me he was coming here to St Petersburg today.'

Parnello was suddenly frightened himself. 'What time did you speak to him?'

'He rang me. Around one, at lunchtime.'

'Are you sure it was him? Calling from Stockholm?'

'What are you? Dumb or something? Of course I'm sure. I know the guy's voice. And my machine tells me the numbers of my callers.' He gestured with momentary pride to his state-of-the-art telephone. 'I look before I answer. In case they're undesirables.'

Parnello nodded. Then he added, as much to himself as Aronsky, 'One o'clock. That would be eleven in Stockholm.' With a slightly sick feeling in his stomach, he realised that he had identified the time of Persson's last outgoing call on his office telephone. And confirmed the implausibility of everything to do with Marianne. There had never been any question of Persson going to the Far East. No chance that he had returned unexpectedly last night to be killed after she had removed the cassette from the answerphone. Persson had been in Stockholm all the time. He just hadn't been taking incoming calls. And the hands that had ripped the cassette from his answerphone had been those of his killer.

'Why do you ask me all these stupid questions?' demanded Aronsky.

'It's just a . . . a misunderstanding. I'm sorry. It's not important. The important thing is, I'm here to do business with you.'

Aronsky regarded him dubiously, then drained his glass and put it down on the desk. He picked up a pack of cards and began to play with them, splitting and shuffling them with the caressing dexterity of the practised gambler, as if the handling of them brought not merely comfort but the possibility of guidance, of inspiration. 'So perhaps you should tell me what sort of business you wish to discuss, Mr Moran?'

Parnello raised his glass and took a drink too. He felt he

needed it. 'I am interested in paintings. Western European paintings. You see, I was the buyer from Mr Sorensen of a landscape which I think he may have acquired from Russia. Maybe he acquired it through you. A German landscape of a river and a ferry, painted on panel. I liked that painting. I liked it very much. And I want to know if it is possible to buy more paintings from the same source.'

Aronsky snapped the cards together abruptly and looked at him hard. There it was, that expression in his eyes once more. Clearer than ever. The aggression which could not quite hide the panic.

'No more paintings,' he said. 'I do not handle paintings.'

'So Sorensen didn't acquire that landscape through you?'

'Look, I have no more to do with this business. I don't need it, OK? You talk to me about other merchandise, I find it for you. Women's dresses, all the best labels, Russian vodka, Iranian caviar. You want any of those things, no problem. Even guns. You want guns, I get them for you too. It costs you more, but I get them, no questions asked. But I don't deal with paintings any more, OK?'

'Do you at least know where that landscape of Sorensen's came from?'

Aronsky looked at him, sizing him up, as if debating whether to treat the question seriously. 'It came from Kuslov, didn't it? Look, I had nothing to do with it. I just put Sorensen in touch with him. They did the deal together, I wasn't in on it.'

'Can I meet Kuslov, then?'

'What are you, crazy? Didn't Sorensen tell you what happened to Kuslov?'

'No. What happened to Kuslov?'

Aronsky laid aside the cards and took a final, desperate drag on his cigarette. Then he stubbed it out. He spoke quietly, with a sort of resignation. 'He was strangled. Two days ago, in his apartment. He's dead.'

Then Parnello felt the panic himself, too. Drifting across

from Aronsky. Insinuating itself into his nostrils with the cigarette smoke.

'Who killed him?' he asked.

'Who killed him? I don't know. Go and ask the police department.' Aronsky laughed mirthlessly and refilled his vodka glass.

Parnello took a decision. He wasn't giving up now. Not having come this far. 'OK,' he said. 'Do me one favour. Give me Kuslov's address.'

'His address? Look, I told you: he's dead.'

'I understand that. But I still want his address. Where did he live?'

'What's the matter with you? Why do you want to go poking around at his address when the man's dead? Look, I'll give you a piece of advice for free. Keep away. They're dangerous people.' Parnello heard the echo of Johnny, the elderly hippy, hardly more than twenty-four hours ago. What had he said about Persson? 'Be careful of his friends. I don't dig those guys. It's a bad scene, man.'

'Who are dangerous people?' persisted Parnello.

'You don't understand the way things work in this country, do you? The people who killed Kuslov, they are dangerous.'

'I thought you said you didn't know who they were.'

'I don't. But I know enough about them to recognise they're dangerous.' He sighed, shook his head, and tore a page from his notebook. On it he wrote something down, scribbled quickly, as if speed exonerated him from any responsibility for what he wrote. 'So, OK: if you want to get killed too, I'll give you Kuslov's address. Here, take it. But don't bring me into this, OK?'

Parnello put the piece of paper into his notebook and stood up. 'Thank you,' he said. 'Thank you, I appreciate that.'

Aronsky shrugged. 'When you speak to Sorensen, tell him I'm waiting for his call. Tell him, where is the money he owes me? And tell him to stop sending me lunatics like you.'

'I will.' He paused. 'I think my suitcase is still in your driver's car.'

'It's OK. He'll drop you off. Where are you staying?'

'I don't have a reservation. Can you recommend somewhere?'

'I'll tell him to take you to the Grand Hotel Europe. It's the most expensive place in town, but I guess you won't live long enough to have to settle the bill.'

Parnello laughed. But as he turned to go he noticed Sergei Aronsky wasn't joining in.

They found him a room at the Hotel and he checked in under his own name. There didn't seem much point in prolonging his existence as Sorensen now. And he felt safer as himself. God only knew what unidentified enemies lurked here awaiting Sorensen, alias Persson. And he felt safer in this big, opulent hotel with its high-ceilinged rooms and its hermetically sealed atmosphere of international luxury. He could be in Frankfurt. Or London. Or New York. But he also knew that wherever he was, 'safer' was only a relative term. When he remembered what had happened to Persson. And now to the unknown Kuslov.

He felt very tired, but he needed to make one call before he slept. He calculated that it would be early afternoon in New York now. He lifted the receiver and dialled Alexandra's work number.

'I'm in St Petersburg,' he told her.

'You're where?'

'In St Petersburg. Russia.'

'I guessed it wasn't the one in Florida.' She giggled. Suddenly he could visualise her very vividly, standing in the shop. Leaning forward over the telephone at that counter which gave so little privacy. Fingering back behind her ear a strand of long blonde hair.

'So what are you doing there?' she asked.

'It's a long story.'

'And you can't tell it on the telephone, right?'

'Not in detail. But I think I'm making progress. Getting a little closer to what we're looking for.'

'Do you reckon it's in Russia? What ... what we're looking for?'

'I think it could be.'

'Parnello.' She spoke softly, but her tone was suddenly urgent, on a different level of intensity.

'What is it?'

'Will you tell me something? Honestly?'

'If I can.'

'Are you doing this for us? For my mother and me, I mean?'

'No,' he said. 'I'm doing it for me. But if it helps you both, I'd be very happy. Very happy indeed.'

It was as if she had not heard him. 'Because if you are doing it for me,' she went on, 'there's no need. I wish you wouldn't. Go home, why don't you? Don't put yourself in danger for ... for something we might not even want to know any more about.'

'Don't worry,' he lied. 'There's no danger.'

He heard her sigh. 'Take care, Parnello. I'd like to see you again, OK?'

As he lay down to sleep he considered the tangled strands into the past which defined Alexandra's ambivalence towards her own family background. And he reflected that it was a bit late for him to start taking care now.

TWENTY ONE

———⟨⊙⟩———

Most of last night's snow had been cleared from the city's streets, piled into miniature mountain ranges in the gutters. Parnello set out from the hotel into Nevsky Prospekt, seeking security in the sheer numbers of people who surged ceaselessly up and down its wide icy pavements, an army of shoppers with neither the goods to buy nor the money to pay for them. There was still something volatile, something provisional about this place, as if it were held together only by a series of uneasy compromises. As if at any moment, like the patched-up truck that spluttered past him choking exhaust, it might explode or fall apart.

'Sure I remember you, Dr Parnello,' Dobiachowsky had declared on the telephone an hour before. 'Still here? Of course I'm still here. You thought I might have moved on? What, become Minister of Culture, maybe, under this new enlightened regime? More like been carried up to heaven by choirs of heavenly angels. No, the Dobiachowskys of this world stay put. We don't budge. Come on over, why don't you?'

As he walked, his long thin frame set against the cold, Parnello drew his scarf tighter about his neck and thrust his fists deeper into his coat pockets. There he made an unexpected discovery. His hand closed over a small cylindrical object. He had completely forgotten about it: Persson's film. And so it was only now, in St Petersburg, that he found a camera shop and took it in to be developed. Out of curiosity. Because he was still the beachcomber. Because he needed all the help he could get.

'Welcome, Dr Parnello,' declared Dobiachowsky as he opened the door. 'It is always a pleasure to greet visitors from the Great British Empire.' He was still the same substantial figure, generously-built rather than gross, ample rather than bloated. His physique would not have worked if it had been thinner. He looked right as he was, in proportion: his splendid belly gave the impression of opulent upholstery, like some voluminously cushioned armchair. His memorable moustache, however, was now flecked with grey, and perhaps he'd lost a little of his insouciance. He seemed older, less vigorous.

'How are you?' said Parnello.

'Well enough.' He laughed ruefully. 'Well enough, all things considered.'

'A lot of changes here in Russia since we last met.'

He shook his head. 'In some directions, yes, Dr Parnello. In others very few. I am afraid my country has not taken easily to the capitalist dream. We seem to have established few of its advantages and most of its drawbacks. We have become a nation of poverty-stricken doctors and very rich criminals.'

'But you have survived well enough, I hope, yourself?'

'There have been good times. There have been bad times,' said Dobiachowsky. 'One of the worst was five years ago when my wife came back to me. The dancer at the Kirov turned out to be homosexual after all.'

'I am sorry to hear that.'

'But she moved out again after two months.' The big man brightened. 'She said there was not room for both her and my work.'

He led the way through into the living room. The flat was no bigger, but even more chaotic than Parnello remembered it. The books, journals and files now spilled out of the shelves and straggled in piles on the floor, over the bed, even on to the worktop next to the sink in the tiny kitchen.

'So this is the deluge,' said Parnello, looking about him.

'The deluge?' Dobiachowsky spoke from the kitchen where he was preparing coffee.

'When we last met you told me that if reforms continued there would soon be a deluge of archival material unleashed on historians. I assumed I was looking at part of it here.'

Dobiachowsky laughed as he came back in with the pot and two cups. 'That's not far off the truth.'

'So are all the secrets now revealed?'

'Of course not. This is Russia, Dr Parnello. It is in the Russian soul to love secrets. Even if there were none, we would have to invent them.'

'Still, a lot must have come to light about the past eighty years of Russian history. Now that communism is dead.'

Dobiachowsky put his head on one side. 'Dead?' he said. 'Maybe the corpse twitches now and then.' He paused thoughtfully, then went on: 'But yes, much has come to light.'

'And professionally things are better? For you as an art historian?'

He nodded as he poured out the thick black coffee. 'As an art historian, I have to say yes, definitely better. There is much more access to material. The chance to travel abroad, too. If you can pay the ticket.'

'And what happened to your colleagues in Moscow? The ones who were beginning some research that it was too dangerous to talk about when we last met?'

Dobiachowsky pushed a cup over to Parnello and drank from his own. 'Ah, that was something. That was the start of it all.' He spoke with relish, wiping the coffee from the ends of his moustache. 'Did you see the exhibition in the Hermitage two years ago? The one of the missing impressionist masterpieces that magically resurfaced after years of being hidden by the Soviets?'

'No, I wish I had. I read about it.'

'It's not too late. Most of the pictures are still on view. You must look at them while you are here. But the point is, that exhibition would never have seen the light of day if it hadn't been for the research that was starting in Moscow then. "Hidden Treasures Revealed", that's what the exhibition was called in English. They were all pictures that had been looted by Soviet Trophy Brigades from German private collections at the end of the war. They had been lying mouldering in storerooms at museums like the Pushkin and the Hermitage for the best part of fifty years. Under the Soviet regime, very few people knew about them, and those that did weren't allowed to admit their existence.'

'How did your friends find out about these secret pictures?'

'It was the most extraordinary story, even by Russian standards.' Dobiachowsky leant forward in his chair. Eager. Animated. 'It all started in 1987 when a curator of a branch of the Pushkin Museum in Moscow went looking for a photocopier.'

'A photocopier?'

'Precisely. They were like gold at that time, Dr Parnello, you had to go miles to find one that worked. This fellow thought there might be one he could use at the Ministry of Culture. By coincidence the Ministry were having a clean-out that day, and in the basement he stumbled across a batch of old files on their way to the shredder. But the shredder was not working that well either that day, so there was a bit of a pile-up. The usual chaos.' Dobiachowsky wheezed with amusement and reached for a Ducados from Parnello's open packet. He lit it and continued. Apparently his friend had decided to take a look through these old files, stacked up on the floor awaiting destruction. And he made the most astounding discovery. They were all about works of art removed from Germany at the end of the war. One handwritten document was entitled 'List of the Most Important Works of Art Kept in the Special Depository of the Pushkin Museum'. Apart from detailing a staggering array of pictures held in secret, the file also provided proof that the famous Trojan Treasure excavated by Heinrich Schliemann in 1873, which had mysteriously disappeared from Berlin in 1945, had not been destroyed but had been hidden in the Soviet Union for over forty years.

'And this curator literally just stumbled across these files when he went looking for a photocopier?'

Dobiachowsky laughed. 'That's it. That was Soviet bureaucracy for you. They were burying themselves under mountains of paper. Photocopying away. When the machine worked. Shredding away. When the machine worked. No-one knew what to do with the stuff any more. You know what the official term is now for the Soviet regime? "The years of stagnation". A happy little euphemism. But it's true in many ways. Certainly the system was stagnating under its own paperwork.'

'So what did your friend do with the information he'd found?' persisted Parnello. And Dobiachowsky told him how, armed with this initial data, various inquisitive art historians had got together and dug a little deeper. 'As a result they had built up systematised and extensive archives on the subject of secret "trophy art". Gradually rumours had spread about the Hermitage holdings, and finally all the outstanding impressionist and post-impressionist masterpieces were uncovered. But it had taken time before the authorities had gone public on the issue. As late as 1991 Suslov, the then Director of the Hermitage, had still been denying their existence.'

Parnello listened, absorbed. 'These were the pictures that included that marvellous Degas of the Place de la Concorde, didn't they?' he said. 'The one that's recorded in the reference books as "presumed destroyed in World War II".'

'That's right. And you know what? I was one of the first people to see that picture, when it came out of secret storage.' Dobiachowsky's eyes gleamed through the cigarette smoke at the memory. 'I was there, Dr Parnello. A friend on the curatorial staff of the Hermitage allowed me to come along; it must have been in 1992. We were escorted through into a room at the back of the Museum. An ancient porter with a very large key unlocked a very unpromising-looking cupboard. And there inside were all these extraordinary masterpieces, stacked together, unframed, canvas against canvas. In an incredibly fresh state of preservation, because in some cases they'd spent more than half their lives in that cupboard. But holding the Degas in my hands was the highlight. It was like a resurrection. I'll never forget that moment, never.'

Parnello nodded, trying to imagine the experience. But even as he was listening, the germ of a further possibility was forming itself in his mind. A possibility so extraordinary that he needed time to assimilate it. To decide how to approach it. He asked: 'And was there much opposition to the proposal to hold a public exhibition of this war loot?'

'Certainly there was. But at least it was debated reasonably openly. Some people feared that no good could come from such revelations, and argued that the pictures should remain unexposed. That revealing them would only lead to unjustified demands for their return. Others declared that there was nothing for Russia to be ashamed about: the pictures weren't so much war loot as genuine war reparations, legitimately extracted by the Soviet Union from conquered Germany as compensation for the destruction the Nazis wrought in the Great Patriotic War. They should be put on view and gloried in. Then again, still others argued that this was private property: that legitimate war reparations should only have been taken from German museums and public collections; that these private pictures should immediately be restored to their original owners or their heirs, without public exhibition in Russia. In the end a more moderate view prevailed, the one expressed by Piotrowski, the present Director of the Hermitage. He said, and I think he was right, that the main thing was for these pictures to be exhibited again, so that the public could have the benefit of them. Questions of ownership were secondary. Those questions could be decided in due course by the lawyers and the politicians.'

'And have they been decided, those questions of ownership?'

'No, of course not. They're still arguing. They go very

deep, these matters. They touch on the only thing that many people here have got left: their patriotism. No-one who fought in the Great Patriotic War wants to see these things given back to the Germans just like that. They would view it as a betrayal, as an admission that what was fought for then was in some way wrong after all. And there's no shortage of politicians here prepared to wrap themselves in the Russian flag on this issue. It's a vote-winner. But these matters also touch on the delicate question of present-day Russian-German relations. The Germans are important allies to us now. We need their Deutschmarks. We cannot afford to alienate the most important economy in Europe.'

'And are there many more pictures we don't know about,' Parnello asked, 'still languishing in Russian museum vaults? More pictures that were looted from private collections in Germany in 1945?'

Dobiachowsky scratched his ample belly. Considering his answer. 'It's always possible. But I think that most of them have been uncovered now, one way or another. Even Madame Antonova in the Pushkin was steamrollered into exhibiting some of their holdings of Trophy art. Admitting that it existed.'

'Madame Antonova being a traditionalist?'

'The Pope being catholic. Madame Antonova is a traditionalist who believes that nothing that was done by the Soviet Trophy Brigades in 1945 should ever be questioned. After all, she was herself a member of them.'

Parnello decided to risk it. 'I wonder if I could ask your advice?' he murmured. 'In confidence.'

Dobiachowsky drained the last of his coffee, wiped the bottom of his moustache with the back of his hand in a gesture that Parnello now recognised as characteristic, and smiled. 'Ah!' he said with delight. 'More secrets.'

'Yes, more secrets.'

'Of course I will give you my advice, if it is worth anything to you.' He looked at his watch. 'But first I must insist on one thing: it is late enough in the day for us to take a drink

PHILIP HOOK

together. A proper drink. I have here some exceptional apricot vodka.'

Parnello accepted the glass, and began an account of the events of the past two weeks. An edited account. He described how he had bought the Dahl in a sale in New York. How it had been stolen from him a day later. How he had established certain facts about the picture's provenance: that it had been bought at auction in Berlin in 1931, that it had last been recorded there in 1945 as part of the collection of a man called von Seitz, that it had been assumed destroyed at that time. And he mentioned what the von Seitz collection had also included: some good Dutch seventeenth-century pictures. And a van Gogh, of a wheatfield. A van Gogh recorded in the literature as 'presumed destroyed in World War II'. A van Gogh with a likely open market value of in excess of 30 million dollars.

There were other things, of course, that he did not tell Dobiachowsky. He did not dwell on von Seitz's grand-daughter in New York; and he did not mention what had happened to Persson in Stockholm or Kuslov here in St Petersburg. And he didn't bring up what Aronsky had told him about the dangers of investigating Kuslov further. There was no point in complicating the issue.

When Parnello had finished, Dobiachowsky levered his massive frame up from his chair and walked to the grimy window which looked out over the courtyard below. He paused there, as if trying to memorise the details of the view. 'So what exactly is it you wish to ask me?' he said.

'I want to know if you can help me establish where the Dahl came from, and in so doing find out if other pictures from the original von Seitz collection are still there too. Like the van Gogh. I mean, do you think that the van Gogh could still be held in some official vault here?'

'That,' said Dobiachowsky without taking his eyes from the window, 'is a very interesting question.'

'Is it a question to which we could ever find an answer?'

There was a barely perceptible shrug of the massive

shoulders. 'In Russia all things have become possible. And all things have become impossible, too. I can make inquiries. The archives on the subject may be able to help. Through friends I can gain access to them. But on the face of it, I think that it is unlikely that a work such as the van Gogh would still be held in a Russian museum vault. The recent exhibition here at the Hermitage would have been the ideal opportunity to show it again. It would have fitted perfectly the criteria for that exhibition: a great post-impressionist picture from a German private collection, not seen since 1945. If it had been known about, it would have been included. Unless . . .'

'Unless what?'

'Unless there was something sensitive about it.'

'What do you mean, sensitive?'

'Unless there was some reason why it was still not deemed politically convenient to admit its existence.'

'What sort of reason could that be?'

Dobiachowsky turned to face him. 'I am just speculating. I do not know. But as I said, these days in Russia all things are possible.'

'And impossible,' Parnello reminded him.

Dobiachowsky smiled as he walked back to his chair. 'Let's see what exists in the Archive, anyway,' he said. 'I can make some telephone calls this evening for the information. You see, Dr Parnello, I am not without influence.' There was a glint of self-mockery in his eye. For a moment Parnello understood how, for men like Dobiachowsky, life in Russia would always have been intolerable without a highly-developed sense of irony. On bad days the only refuge was cynicism. On better ones you could at least laugh.

'Meanwhile,' Dobiachowsky went on, 'I insist that you have another drink. And let me tell you a little story from Russian history.'

Parnello passed his glass over gratefully. 'What's your little story?'

Dobiachowsky poured a generous measure. 'You have heard perhaps of our famous Empress Catherine?' he asked.

'Catherine the Great?' The lines came back to him instantly, and he quoted them out loud:

> *She could repay each amatory look you lent*
> *With interest, and, in turn, was wont with rigour*
> *To exact of Cupid's bills the full amount*
> *At sight, nor would permit you to discount . . .*

'Who wrote this?'

'Byron.'

'Ah! The great Lord Byron. Well, he was correct: she was a very demanding woman. And from the Empress Catherine downwards, Russians have generally been difficult to do business with. We are a demanding people. And a proud people. We like to have the final word. So there is the story of Catherine entertaining in her boudoir the King of Poland. When he had finished making love to her, he announced in triumph: "Madam, Russia has just been invaded by Poland!" She replied, "On the contrary, sir: a tiny piece of Poland has just been absorbed by Russia".'

They both laughed. 'A warning to men who boast of their sexual conquests,' said Parnello.

'And a warning to invaders of Russia,' said Dobiachowsky. 'The plunderers tend to end up as the plundered.'

Parnello left him soon after, pleasantly light-headed with apricot vodka. He paused for a moment at the window on the communal stairs outside Dobiachowsky's top-floor apartment. In the courtyard below two mothers laden with shopping bags guided children in pushchairs through the snow. A man in a blue cap and red check lumber jacket was leaning over a car windscreen chipping ice away. It had turned into a beautiful winter's morning, and raising his eyes Parnello saw the sky stretched in a panoply of blue across the city, the sun glinting on its golden domes and spires. The sheer size of the place struck him; and beyond the city, the unimaginable extent of Russia itself, rolling on from here south and east, to the Black Sea and the Pacific

Ocean. You could hide things in this country so that they would never be found. But if you personally were suddenly the object of pursuit, could you hide yourself as securely?

He set off back to the hotel. The anonymity of the streets was a continuing reassurance to him. On foot he was just another figure in the townscape, just another tourist. He thought over what Dobiachowsky had told him, trying to marry it up with what he had learned in Stockholm, with the information he had gleaned last night from Aronsky. A sequence was emerging, the vestiges of a trail with some sort of coherence. Parnello had bought a picture in New York that had been consigned there for sale by Persson in Stockholm. Persson himself had acquired it from Russia, from St Petersburg, from a trader called Kuslov. Such a transaction would necessarily have been discreet and surreptitious: Russian law did not permit the official export of any work of art of the age of the Dahl.

But equally the acquisition of this picture by Persson would not have been considered by either party as any big deal. The artist had not been identified. It was just a nineteenth-century landscape. The fact that Persson had allowed it to go into the sale in New York with an estimate of eight to twelve thousand dollars was proof of that. With such an estimate the reserve could not have been more than eight thousand dollars, which meant that Persson would not have paid much more than about four thousand for it when he bought it from Kuslov. That was the art market for you, reflected Parnello. Nothing had any objective value. Works of art were worth different things to different people in different places. He had himself anticipated being able to sell the Dahl for as much as $100,000, and had ended up parting with that amount to buy it. Persson had gambled on paying $4,000 for it in the hope that it would be worth more on the international market.

Kuslov, in that case, must have acquired it for very little money indeed. So what made it so valuable now? What suddenly made it worth killing for in order to get possession of it? No: he caught himself up. Not just to get possession of it. That had been achieved in New York, by breaking into Marvel's gallery. Now he analysed them, he realised that the killings had a different logic. It was almost as if they had been undertaken in order to destroy a trail. In order to obliterate all evidence of the Dahl's passage from St Petersburg to New York, via Stockholm.

He walked on, perplexed. Perplexed, but a little elated. He felt like a man cutting his way through a jungle, who suddenly catches a fleeting glimpse through the mass of trees and undergrowth of what may be a clear path ahead. And as he walked, he heard the murmur of many voices, of people gathered in numbers not far off; he drew closer, and caught the sound of a single voice amplified above the others through a loud-speaker. He was approaching the domed cathedral of our Lady of Khazan. As he reached its grandiosely curving colonnade, he peered through and discovered the source of the commotion. Drawn up in front of a line of speakers on the cathedral steps was a crowd of three or four hundred people, decked out in red flags and banners. Everywhere was the emblem of the hammer and sickle. The sight was a shock, like a bad dream revisited. The voice of the man at the microphone reached a crescendo, and a desultory cheer swept through the audience. Parnello looked more closely at them: there was something at once sinister and yet pathetic about this ragged gathering, this bedraggled assembly of humanity afflicted either with too much hope or too little. Here they were: the men who craved the comfort of repression. Some were zealots, no doubt, ideologues who had never abandoned the party line; some were old men and women with suffering in their eyes, hankering after the security of the system; and some were more difficult to place. Opportunists, perhaps. Or just men who loved secrets.

He surveyed it, drawn up before him. Communism. The twitching of the corpse.

He glanced behind him, and then he saw the man again. The man in the blue cap and the red check lumber jacket.

The man who had been chipping ice from the windscreen of the car outside Dobiachowsky's apartment.

Parnello edged into the Cathedral itself, stepping over a beggar snoring noisily in the doorway. It was very dark after the sunlight outside. As he blinked to accustom his eyes to the shadows he became aware of the heavy scent of incense, thickening the air, impregnated deep into the very stone of the walls. The depleted residue of the Soviet regime left behind outside represented merely one era of recent Russian history. Here he had stepped into another much older time, passed from the ephemeral to the eternal. There were people of all ages here: old men and women shrouded in black holding up crucifixes to bearded priests for dousing in holy water; young families in cheap anoraks kneeling for impromptu blessings. Everywhere he saw features animated by expressions of such intense piety that it was hard to believe they belonged to the twentieth century, let alone stood on the brink of the twenty-first.

In a side-chapel his eye was caught by a series of antique pennants displayed triumphantly across each other on either side of the altar. Approaching closer he discovered that this chapel was dedicated to the sacred memory of the divisions of Russian cavalry who had first held back then finally overcome Napoleon's army in the bitter winter of 1813. Von Seitz and his men had not been the first invading force to find the combination of fanatical Russian resistance and intolerable cold too much for them. These pennants had been claimed from the French cavalry as they, too, retreated through the snow. These pennants were Trophies of War.

The plunderers plundered: trophies of war, just like the paintings the Soviet Brigades had carried home from Germany in 1945. Just like the Dahl, maybe. Just like the van Gogh.

When he came out, stepping over the same sleeping beggar, he found the Communist rally was beginning to disperse. Banners were being rolled up, microphones folded away. Dispassionately a group of policemen stood on the margin, surveying the scene. Amused. Ambivalent.

293

Parnello looked about him, then walked on, melding once more into the teeming crowd surging down the pavement of the Nevsky Prospekt. He crossed at the traffic lights, then ducked into the camera shop where he collected his developed film. He slid the wallet of photographs into his pocket and emerging into the street again turned left away from the hotel rather than right back towards it. He walked quickly to the pedestrian underpass, hurried through the tunnel, then spent fifteen minutes doubling in and out of a huge arcaded department store, roving at random among the paltry displays of consumer goods and the crowds of people who moved yearningly amongst them. Finally he retraced his steps through the underpass and, re-surfacing at ground level, strode quickly to the turning to his hotel. As he reached the corner he glanced back. The man in the blue cap and red check lumber jacket was about thirty yards behind, staring with absorption into the window of a shop selling videos.

Once inside the hotel, Parnello hurried up to his room and double-locked the door, pulling the chain across on the inside. He sat down to gather his thoughts. Calming himself. And then, there on the bed, he spread out the photographs. Persson's photographs. Messages from beyond the grave.

The first six were dull enough. They showed what Parnello assumed to be items from Persson's stock of antiques. There were shots of a pair of ormulu candlesticks. There was an undistinguished nineteenth-century table. They seemed to have been taken in what looked like a warehouse, because in the background you could see other objects lying around: a stack of boxes containing computer equipment; two nineteenth-century bronzes of horsemen; a sign saying 'Rökning Förbjuden': 'No Smoking' in Swedish. And then there, in the seventh photograph, he saw it. In the background, behind another undistinguished table, but its image was unmistakable. An unframed picture leaning against a filing cabinet. An unframed picture showing a wheatfield with a distant line of trees swaying in the breeze.

Here it was: unassailable evidence of the van Gogh's survival. And proof of Persson's recent possession of it. Parnello held the photo up and stared at it, mesmerised. There was only one likely explanation: Persson must have acquired it from Kuslov at the same time as the Dahl. And Kuslov had got them from where? From some secret store here in Russia, perhaps? That would make sense. Persson had sent the Dahl off to New York for disposal. It had not been important. Not by comparison with this far greater prize.

Parnello stopped for a moment, suddenly overwhelmed by the full implications of the discovery he had just made. Men were not killed for the sake of a Dahl, no matter how romantic its sunset. Not in the systematic way Kuslov and Persson seemed to have been eliminated. But for the sake of a 30 million dollar van Gogh, there would be a far greater compulsion to the taking of life. Not just, it seemed, to lay hands on the picture. But also in order to obliterate the trail.

Had the people who strangled Persson got to the van Gogh and spirited it away? In that case, where was it now?

And assuming that the same people who had killed Kuslov and Persson were also responsible for stealing the Dahl from him in New York, why had it been necessary to go to those lengths to get hold of that picture too? Surely, by comparison with the prize of the van Gogh, the Dahl was an irrelevance?

He lit a cigarette and lay back on his bed, surrounded by Persson's photographs, considering a number of more personal concerns. Why was he being followed? Who did the people following him think he was? Sorensen? Or Parnello Moran himself? And finally he came to grips with the most frightening question of all about his own position, the one he'd tried to put off confronting for as long as possible: given what had happened to Persson and Kuslov, why was he still alive at all?

TWENTY TWO

They had taken her rings off for the operation. Not just the engagement ring, but the wedding ring, too. Absurdly, that was what worried Alex most. She sat there, helpless, fearful, uninformed, staring at her mother's thin pale hand lying outstretched on the sheet as she slept. It was an uneasy sleep. She breathed irregularly, twitching now and then; occasionally she would let out a low sigh, as though troubled by dreams. She was in a place where Alex could not reach her. The hand looked pathetically frail. Round the wrist was fastened a plastic label which Alex leaned forward to read. On one side was her mother's name; and on the other her hospital account and credit card number. They were smart, these hospitals; they weren't going to let anyone die on them without paying the bill. And a further unease stirred within Alex, the one that had lurked not far below the surface as long as she could remember, ever since the move to East 29th Street, the old one about money. Could her mother afford a long illness? How far would the medical insurance stretch?

She couldn't remember ever having seen her mother's fingers bare like this, stripped of the precious symbols of her marital union. There was something defenceless about them, something naked. This was her mother bereft of the emblems of the one thing that had defined her life, her marriage to Joe Hamilton. Those rings. Alex's anxiety found a focus in them. She began to rummage through the drawers of her mother's

bedside table, her handbag, her toothmug. Looking for them
gave her something to do. To contribute.

She had seen the surgeon half an hour earlier. She had
insisted. The guy had met her in the corridor, busy, distracted,
fresh from the operating room and another patient, still
wearing the green short-sleeved operating tunic. He had very
hairy arms and very pink, scrubbed hands. His chest hair was
visible at his throat, too. And yet, as if in compensation for
such plenitude elsewhere, his head was nearly bald, its dome
shining under the artificial light. He had mumbled a few tech-
nicalities to her, awkward, reluctant, barely comprehensible.
His eyes were not so much evasive as indifferent.

'So what are you saying?' she had insisted, trying to master
her panic, trying to prevent it exploding into anger. 'What
are these complications?'

'She's being kept in for observation.'

Answer my question, you schmuck. But she didn't say it.
Instead she asked, 'How long?'

'Until we get the results of the tests.'

Jesus, just tell me how long, can't you? She wondered if
these guys were trained in obstructiveness, or just naturals
at it. Whatever happened to beside manner? 'What tests?'

'Pretty much routine.'

'Should I be worried?' she had said in desperation. Offering
him a little female frailty to assert his masculinity over, as a
last resort.

Even that hadn't interested him. All he had given her
had been a non-commital 'Not unduly', before making his
excuses and hurrying on. Too busy for beside manner. Too
busy to work on that side of his game.

'Your mom's sleeping,' the nurse had told her. 'She needs
her rest now.'

'How's she doing?'

'Just fine.' The reassurance was formulaic and therefore
worthless.

'I'll sit with her for a while, then.'

*   *   *

When her mother murmured in her sleep, Alex did not recognise the word at first. It was barely more than two quick exhalations of breath, but it was definitely meant to signify something because it was accompanied by a distraught movement of the head.

'It's all right, Mom,' Alex reached out her hand to hold her mother's. And then she heard it again, more clearly this time.

'Papa!'

The name was a novelty to Alex. Her own father had been 'Dad'. Good old American 'Dad'. Who was Papa?

Then her mother murmured again: 'Papa . . . they took Papa away . . .'

'It's all right, darling,' repeated Alex. She was suddenly frightened herself. At this unexpected descent into the past. Into the depths. Into the unknown. Gently she stroked her mother's hand.

'And Kurt, Kurt was ill. Never . . .' there was a pause, 'never saw them again . . .'

Kurt would have been saved today. With modern medicine. With antibiotics. That's what her mother had told her. The uncle Alex had never met, her mother's brother who had died in that last terrible winter of the war. Just thirteen, he had been. And mom had been eleven. She tried to calm her now, standing up and stroking her forehead where the lines wrinkled. She looked pinched, and suddenly very old.

What had her mother said, two nights ago, on the eve of her hospitalisation?

'Your friend Mr Parnello Moran. The Englishman, with the eyes . . .'

'What about him, Mom?'

'Where is he? Did he leave New York?'

'That's right, Mom. I told you, he went to Sweden. He's trying to get the picture back.'

'Don't let him do it, Alex. He's a decent guy, he means well, but don't let him.'

'Don't let him do what?'

'Don't let him open it all up again. By going after those pictures. I couldn't bear to have it all out again.'

Having it out again.

They'd only ever had it out once, mother and daughter. Three years after the incident with the album.

Alex is eighteen, all but through with high school. It's a hot, airless July afternoon. The windows of the apartment on 29th Street are wide open, but still the heat permeates the room, impregnating the fabric of the sofas, steaming the musty curtains with the humid odours of the launderette and the Bangladeshi delicatessen. Alex is irritable. Eighteen-year-old irritable. Her mother's been needling her all year; there has been continual friction between the two of them. The point at issue is Alex's future. Her mother wants her to go on to a good college. 'You're a smart girl, honey. You could get into one of the best universities. It would be a crime to waste it.' Alex is set on drama school. 'It's what I want, Mom. It's what I'm good at.'

'Your father would have reckoned it a waste.'

This is unfair, this pronouncement from beyond the grave. There is no answer to it. Alex bites back the reply that would have led to tears and recrimination. She sits there, surly and unforgiving.

Finally she says. 'Look: I'm eighteen, OK? Stop treating me like a child.'

'I'm not treating you like a child.'

'You are so. You just can't accept that I'm an adult now, can you? You want me to go on being ten years old all my life. You want to make all my decisions for me. You want to control me. Control what I eat. Control what I study. Control what I know.'

Her mother looks at her now. Suddenly alarmed. She's caught the allusion. The allusion to something that, although they never talk about it, is always there, not far from the surface, like a guilty, constantly suppressed desire. 'What do you mean, I control what you know?'

Alex pauses, then goes for it. She's only eighteen after all. She's curious. And she wants to cause pain. Get back at her mother. 'For a start, you've never told me the truth about my grandfather. About your dad.'

Alex has got her wish. A look of pure pain crosses her mother's eyes. She closes them for a moment. She sits up very straight and says: 'What exactly do you want to know?'

Alex wants to know if it's true. What she read in the school library last year, when her class was studying the Second World War. Her teacher mentioned the 20th July bomb plot on Hitler's life. Alex felt a reflected glory. She knew her grandfather had been involved. So she went to look up more details. At last she came across a book on the German Resistance, and flicked through the index for the name von Seitz. She checked the last reference first, and there it was: Major Gottfried von Seitz was executed by firing squad on 8th May 1945. He survived Gestapo prison only for the liberators of Berlin to shoot him dead. As a war criminal. She said nothing at the time, not to her friends. Not to her teacher. Not to her mother. She was lost in a sort of awe. This guy's my mum's dad. And he's a criminal. A murderer. Jesus, my Grandpa.

'What exactly did he do, your dad?' she says now. 'Did he murder Russian civilians? I have to know. The Russians must have had a good reason for shooting him?'

There is a silence. Alex wonders if it will ever end. Finally her mother murmurs: 'He was a good father, Alex. That was the most important thing. I loved him very much.' Her mother is sitting very still, unnaturally upright. Her only movement is with her hands, which clutch a handkerchief on her lap. She is twining it round her fingers in an ecstasy of anguish. 'And he was very brave in 1944. He stood up to Hitler; no-one can take that away from him. But the other thing? Look, there was never a proper trial. The facts never came out. I just don't know. I was eleven years old, honey.'

Alex is implacable. 'What about your Mom? Didn't he ever tell her? Didn't you ever ask her?'

She shook her head. 'No, Alex. I never asked her about it. I told you, she was pretty much an invalid after we came to America, and she died in 1952.' She sighed and added, 'But I truly don't think he ever spoke about it to her. He kept all that side of his life separate from her. To protect her.'

Alex knows about that. In her experience men don't talk to their wives about the most important things. After all, look at her own father. Look at Joe Hamilton and his secret financial disasters from which he so sedulously shielded his wife right up till the very end. But she doesn't say it. She senses she has done enough damage now. There is a pause, then her mother goes on:

'I guess no-one can know what it's like in a war. No-one can know how they're going to react. We've all done crazy things under pressure. It would be wrong to judge him.' So that's how she's rationalised it to herself, Alex thinks. That's how she's survived as the daughter of Gottfried von Seitz. As the daughter of a war criminal.

'So what are you saying here, Mom? We should just sweep it under the carpet and it'll go away?'

'If that's how you want to put it, yes. I guess I'm saying that it's not worth opening these things up again unnecessarily, it's better to let them rest. There's too much pain. It's easier for you to go through life as Alexandra Hamilton than as the granddaughter of Gottfried von Seitz. People talk. People don't understand.'

Alex begins to see something. How the only way her mother has survived and built a new life on the wreckage of the old has been by embracing America wholeheartedly. By turning herself American. By subjugating herself totally to her American husband. By eradicating from her vocabulary all the little *liebchens* and O *Himmels* that might have lingered on. Not because she wanted to deny to herself her past, or the father whom she had loved. But because people would talk. Because people wouldn't understand. And that would be more painful than she could bear.

Then her mother rises. Very slowly. And walks through

the intolerable afternoon heat out of the room. She is still clutching the handkerchief. Alex half rises, perhaps to follow her. But the shutting of her mother's bedroom door behind her signals the end of the conversation. For now. Possibly for ever.

Alex got her way. She went to drama school.

With the result that here she was, ten years on, still earning peanuts. Selling dresses; chasing off-Broadway auditions; and having to admit that her only piece of paid work in front of the cameras this year had been a commercial for a carpet cleaner.

OK, it was fine to suffer for your art. Fine, until you found yourself at your mother's hospital bedside wondering how the hell the medical bills were going to be paid.

Her mother was calm at last. No more murmuring. Alex stroked her hand one last time and leaned over to kiss her forehead. A poor feeble gesture of contrition for all the pain she'd caused in her eighteen-year-old anger. She glanced at her watch and remembered that she'd promised to be back in the shop in twenty minutes' time. Nadia had to go to lunch.

As she walked briskly through the cold to Madison Avenue, she took a long, critical look at herself. She was perplexed by what she saw. Just lately she'd lost the plot. That wasn't like her. Normally she was positive, clear-sighted, in control. Obstinate at times, maybe, but with a lightness of touch that won people round by making them laugh. Somewhere along the line, it had all eluded her. And now she was the one who needed lightening up, she found she couldn't make herself laugh.

Why? It wasn't just the growing anxiety about her mother. It was wider than that. Wherever she looked, her life was circumscribed by dissatisfaction.

She'd had it with selling dresses. That big white showroom was like a desert. And the customers: talk about fashion victims. Those women were the walking wounded from the front line of fire. A while ago she'd begun to imagine a comedy set in an haute-couture store. Funny, sharp, satirical. For a time writing it had been her revenge, an outlet for her frustration. Now even that didn't work any more, and the screenplay lay abandoned in a drawer.

She'd had it with experimental off-Broadway productions, the self-indulgent brain-children of crazed young directors with monumental egos and minimal talent. *Two Gentlemen of Las Vegas*. Jesus! A couple of motorcycles revving on stage throughout, not to mention a ritual disembowelment. Her role would have involved simulating sex with a fruit machine. She no longer needed parts like that.

She'd had it with Barry, too. His departure for California two months ago had released her from a two-year relationship that was going nowhere. The irregular contact that she maintained with him now was increasingly irksome. That was another one to draw a line under.

And then there was the other unease, an underlying apprehension, nagging at her. Tied up with her concern about her mother. It was the unease about the past; an insecurity; a fear of disinterments.

And of course there was Byron. Byron made her uneasy, too.

The telephone was ringing as she came in through the shop door. Nadia picked it up.

'Hi, Alex. It's for you.'

'Don't tell me: it's Bob de Niro, and I've got the part.'

'It's a guy, anyway. Says it's personal.'

She had a premonition as she took the receiver, one arm already out of her coat. Her heart was beating faster with the dread and the excitement of it. 'Parnello?' she said.

'Hey, kid. It's Barry. All the way from LA. How are you doing today?'

TWENTY THREE

He was still being followed. No longer by the man in the blue cap and the red check lumber jacket, but by others more adept. Less conspicuous. As Parnello walked the streets of St Petersburg on his second morning in Russia, he glanced behind him now and then; there was never anyone he could positively identify as his shadow, but he could sense his own surveillance. He was uneasily aware of being someone's prey, of being tracked, toyed with. For how long? At some point the game would end. At some point the predator would pounce.

He had a rendez-vous. It was sunny again today, but the wind cut in off the frozen Neva as he loped up the steps of the Hermitage Museum, and he was grateful for the warmth that he found through its doors. Once inside, he kept moving, through labyrinthine chambers sparkling with Fabergé, up sudden magnificent staircases topped with porcelain urns taller than a man. He passed groups of laughing schoolchildren, knots of students, and twice he came across the same young soldier embracing his giggling girlfriend in the shadows. The guardians of the treasures, the babushkas, sat immobile on their chairs, radiating eternal disapproval. It was huge, this place: you could wander for hours lost in its measureless halls. What had the Intourist guide told them ten years ago, with that meticulous reverence for statistics deployed as a substitute for humour? If you spent ten seconds looking at each of

the works of art housed here, it would take you more than
thirty years.

Occasionally he caught glimpses of the lyrical view from
the long windows across the Neva, to the spire of the fortress
church of St Peter and St Paul glinting in the sun. But he
did not stop to savour it. He hurried on urgently, searching
for the particular rooms he wanted. The pictures he had
come to see.

He reached them suddenly, half concealed in a side
gallery. There they were, the Hidden Treasures Revealed.
Pictures from German Private Collections seized by the
Soviet Union at the end of the war. Revealed; but not
trumpeted. Not triumphant like the Napoleonic pennants.
There was something equivocal about their exposure here,
something unresolved about their status. They hung there
suspended in a legal limbo, like defendants accused of serious
offences waiting while the jury argued.

The Absinthe Drinker. She was one of the defendants.

He was drawn at once to her. Early Picasso; he stood in
front of the pastel marvelling at its power, at the confidence
of its execution. And he marvelled at its condition, too. What
had it been through since confiscation from its original owner
in Berlin more than fifty years ago? Pulled from ruins, packed
on to lorries, loaded on to trains, manhandled by soldiers
more used to machine guns than works of art; rattled across
the fractured rail tracks of eastern Europe on a journey that
took weeks rather than hours; and then at the Soviet border
reloaded on to another train, a train that ran on a different
gauge, that inevitable rite of passage for all freight entering
Russia by rail. Finally unpacked and sorted and numbered,
then stashed away in the bowels of the museum here in
Leningrad. Put to sleep for half a century. Hidden in a
cupboard. It was a pastel, the most fugitive and unstable
of media. By some miracle it had come through its travails
intact. And now it hung here, a refulgent image of Parisian
lowlife. A survivor.

Perhaps she was a survivor, too, this absinthe drinker.

She stared out into nothingness, sitting cradling her drink at a cafe table while behind her, lit by an eerie yellow glow, figures coupled in some manic dance. There was a wild and bedraggled beauty to her. How old had Picasso been when he'd drawn her? Barely twenty. And yet he had an instinctive understanding of these women of the night. He had captured both her toughness and her desperation. She was a woman on the edge. Or perhaps she had already tipped over into the abyss. He could not quite define what it was about her which reminded him fleetingly of the Russian girl. Of the one he'd met two days ago at Pulkovo. Of Irena.

'Not my type,' said a voice next to him. 'I prefer my women with a bit more meat on them.'

Parnello turned to find Dobiachowsky at his side.

'You're very punctual,' he said.

'I thought it was appropriate for us to meet here. Appropriate, and perhaps safer.'

Safer. So Dobiachowsky sensed it too. The need for care. The possibility that they might be watched; that Parnello was somebody's prey.

'So what do you think?' demanded Dobiachowsky. 'Of the exhibition?'

'I haven't seen it yet,' said Parnello. 'Let's walk round.'

He felt it again: the need to keep moving. To provide a pretext for their conversation. To offer a moving target rather than a stationary one.

'Do you have news for me?' he asked Dobiachowsky, an indifferent Monet and a delicate Pissarro later.

'News, yes,' said Dobiachowsky softly. 'I can confirm that the von Seitz pictures are not on any official lists of current holdings. I had the Trophy Art archive checked last night. That means that if they exist at all here, they are not in any public museum, or being held at official depots like the Monastery of Zagorsk.'

Parnello paused in front of a Renoir flower piece. It was a late, arthritic painting, coarsely and broadly executed. This was one that might better have stayed in the cupboard. He sighed. 'I suppose it was too much to hope that they would be recorded.'

'I didn't say that they weren't recorded.'

'What do you mean?'

'I didn't say that they weren't recorded at all. Only that there is no record of their present whereabouts. In fact the archive turned up something rather interesting. There is a reference to the pictures of Gottfried von Seitz of Wannsee on a bill of lading dated 13th June 1945 in Berlin.'

'Does it list them?'

'Apparently. They're all on there. Twelve of them. The Dutch seventeenth century pictures. The Dahl. The van Gogh.'

'My God! Bound for where?'

'Bound for here. For Leningrad.'

'Then they would have come to the Museum, wouldn't they?'

'No, Dr Parnello. It seems their destination wasn't the Hermitage. There was an unusual reference on the file. The shipment was separate from the normal ones. It was made under other auspices.'

'Other auspices? What do you mean?'

'This shipment was under the specific control of the NKVD.'

'The NKVD?'

'That's the KGB as they were then. So there is no record of who precisely unloaded them. Or where.'

They stood still again, this time in front of a Gauguin. They stared into the exotic colours of Tahiti. Here, in frozen St Petersburg, momentarily transported to the South Seas. Parnello said, 'What about KGB files?'

'Access to them is very difficult. Restricted.'

'What, even now? In the west it seems that hardly a day goes by without some new revelation from KGB files. It's a growth industry.'

'That's true, Dr Parnello. But it's an industry manipulated by the KGB themselves. They decide what is actually revealed and to whom. They're selective about what comes out, and often cash changes hands. Discreetly. It's one of the ways the KGB fund themselves today. They need money like everyone else.'

'Money for what? They must be running down their own operations, surely?'

Dobiachowsky shook his head with silent emphasis. 'Don't you believe it. Just because the Communists have gone, it doesn't mean the KGB have disappeared too. Every country needs a security service, after all.' He laughed ironically. 'I believe such things are considered necessary, even in the enlightened west.'

'So the KGB are still active?'

'Certainly. What is it they have been called in the past? A state within a state. Even now they retain a certain independence.'

The two men walked on into the final room. There it hung, the climax of the exhibition, Degas's Place de la Concorde. The greatest resurrection of all. It was a picture whose sense of space both thrilled and astounded you. A languidly aristocratic Parisian gentleman was taking his two children and a dog for a Sunday morning stroll in 1875. The figures were oddly positioned on the canvas, caught on the margins rather than at the centre with an apparent arbitrariness that was actually the product of inspired contrivance. The father walked one way, almost off the right hand edge of the picture space, and his daughters, with timeless disregard for parental authority, were coming in another, towards the spectator. They stood in silence in front of it for a few minutes. Then Parnello murmured: 'But why von Seitz? Why did the KGB take control of the von Seitz pictures particularly?'

'That's the interesting question, Dr Parnello. Maybe there's more to this man Seitz than meets the eye.'

Suddenly Parnello had a confused and tormented vision. Suddenly, there in the middle of the picture, in all that space in the Place de la Concorde, he saw the seventeen Russian civilians lined up before a firing squad. It was no longer the

Vicomte Lepic on the right hand side, but Gottfried von Seitz standing there, savouring the moment. Now there was reason for his children to move off in the opposite direction: they were running away. Running away from Alexandra's grandfather as he gave the order to open fire.

And then he shared it. Understood it. Her fear of digging just a bit too deep.

They finished their circuit of the pictures. Dobiachowsky excused himself reluctantly. He had to give a lecture at the University at midday. On the inevitable Malevich.

'For me this is busy time,' he said. 'In Moscow too I have to give this lecture later in the week.'

'You're in demand.'

Dobiachowsky shrugged modestly, unable to conceal his pleasure in Parnello's observation. 'And you, what will you do now, Dr Parnello?' he asked.

Parnello smiled. It was the question that had been preoccupying him, too. 'I'll probably spend the rest of the morning here in the Hermitage,' he said. 'Catch up on some of the things I missed ten years ago.'

He needed time to think. To ponder the information Dobiachowsky had given him.

'You have my telephone number. Call me if you require the further assistance of a humble academic.'

'I will. Thank you for everything you've done.'

'Always at your service,' said Dobiachowsky solemnly. 'God save the Queen.'

Parnello watched the bear-like figure disappear through the far doorway. Then he himself walked on slowly. Trying to look like any other tourist. Wondering which pair of unknown eyes was trained on him and not the works of art.

In amongst the Rembrandts he came across her. She was standing there tall and glamorous, wearing a short scarlet skirt, black wollen stockings and high boots. At first he thought she was gazing particularly intently at the brushwork of the Prodigal Son. Then he saw her hand go up surreptitiously to arrange her hair, and he realised that she was merely looking at her own reflection in the glass.

'Irena,' he said.

She turned to him and smiled. 'Erik! What a nice surprise. I did not know that you were art lover too.'

He caught sight of her wild emerald eyes and heard himself offering to buy her a drink, which she happily accepted. When he asked where she'd like to go, she suggested his hotel, so they took a taxi back. The wind had dropped, but it was still cold beneath the cerulean blue sky.

They were shown to seats in the bar; her long and shapely legs spilled out gracefully from under the table. He sat down opposite her, suddenly awkward, feeling that there was not room for both himself and her legs in such a confined space.

'I like this place,' she said. 'I come here sometimes at lunchtime. I like the ambience.' Something about the word struck her as funny. Parnello laughed too.

'So being back in Russia has not made you too depressed this time?' he said.

'I think you are teasing me,' she murmured. She frowned, and for a moment her sophistication was undermined and she looked suddenly young; almost vulnerable.

'I'm not teasing you at all. Let me get you a drink. What is it to be?'

'Thank you, champagne.' She lit a cigarette and her poise returned. 'So, your stay in St Petersburg is profitable, I hope?'

'Up to a point.'

'You are here on business? Or you make holidays? You come to see the sights?'

'A bit of both.'

The waiter came with their drinks, and a sandwich for Parnello. She raised her glass to him and he lifted his too. 'To your stay in St Petersburg,' she said.

'To you,' he added. 'For making it possible.'

She smiled at that. But it was a guarded smile, less transparent, more difficult to read.

'So,' he said. 'Tell me about your life here. Do you come from St Petersburg?'

She leant across and extinguished her cigarette, considering the question. 'I was student here. In the music conservatory.'

'You are a musician?'

For a moment she looked embarrassed, as if she had admitted to something compromising, disreputable. 'I did not finish my studies. There was always the need of money. I had to take up other work.'

'What other work?'

With a long, thin, red-nailed finger she drew two parallel lines across the top of the table. 'My life was in two,' she said. 'There was my life at the conservatory,' – she ran her finger down one line – 'and there was my other life.' She indicated the second. 'See: these two lines must never cross. Otherwise personal catastrophe.'

'And did they cross?'

She nodded. 'Once or twice. So I gave up.'

'What, your other life?'

'No. My studies.'

'So what do you do now?' Even as he spoke, he realised the futility of the question. That the answer would be unrevealing. That perhaps he did not want to hear the truth anyway.

'I have business interests,' she said vaguely.

She was a beautiful young woman. She was incapable of making any movement that did not subtly draw attention to the desirability of her body.

'Flourishing business interests, I'm sure,' he said.

She lit another cigarette. 'This afternoon for me is free. If you wish, I could show you something of the city.'

'Won't your boyfriend object?'

He could see her debating whether to take offence. 'You are teasing me again. Actually, he is out of town.'

Parnello nodded, thinking. Why not? He had no other leads, could see no other way of making progress. Perhaps she could be helpful. 'You are very kind. I would enjoy spending the afternoon with you. But I have something particular I want to do today and I would appreciate your coming too. As an interpreter.'

She shrugged and smiled back at him. 'I know that languages are not your strong point, Mr Erik Sorensen.'

'So will you help me?'

'I will help you if I can.'

A quarter of an hour later they were getting into another taxi together and Parnello was giving the driver Kuslov's address.

It was Irena who suggested they should have a drink in the small bar opposite. Parnello agreed in frustration. The granite block where Kuslov lived had yielded nothing. Yes, there had been his name beside one bell. But no, there had been no reply when he had rung it. No guarantee that it even worked. He had stood back from the building staring up. Remembering the old town in Stockholm. Shivering slightly, although the afternoon was rather warmer than the morning.

'It seems your friend is not at home,' observed Irena.

'I did not really expect he would be.' What had he been hoping for? A wife? A business associate? Someone who had known him?

'Then why do you ring his bell?'

'Just to be sure he's not there.'

'You are strange man, Mr Erik Sorensen. You are Swedish, but you do not speak your own language. And you go and call on your friends when you think they are out.'

'OK,' he said. 'Let's go in here and get a drink.'

It was a small, cramped space with grimy tables, more of a workman's cafe rather than a bar. Behind the counter a radio played Russian rock music. She looked out of place here, carrying an Italian bag and wearing expensive sunglasses.

It took him a few moments to register what else was strange about the dimly-lit interior. Another noise was coming from a corner of the room. The sound of a woman weeping. He looked across and saw her, crouched against the wall, her head in her hands. She was a large woman, of that indeterminate age that covers most women of the Russian working class once they are past twenty-five. The age when it doesn't matter any more. She had messy peroxided hair and large limbs. Her eyes and nose were reddened from tears. Her grief was disconcerting in the proximity of this confined space. There was something abandoned about it. Shameless.

Irena shrugged. A thin unshaven man in a filthy shirt and dilapidated trainers clumped out from the back room to serve them. He disappeared to bring them the tea that they requested.

'When he comes back,' murmured Parnello, 'ask him if he knows Kuslov.'

The woman in the corner had stopped crying now, seemed to be making a belated attempt at composing herself. She reached down to her feet and brought up to the table a large plastic bag filled with little boxes. She took two of them out and placed them on the table in front of her. Staring at them. Parnello felt a sudden shaft of pity for her.

The man came back with their tea, and Irena began to talk to him in Russian. Parnello heard her speak the name Kuslov, and noticed the man's reaction. Surprise; but a certain relish, too. He began to answer Irena's question in short little bursts of excited narrative. Parnello knew before she translated for him that Kuslov was dead: that his death had excited a local focus of voyeuristic awe and curiosity.

'How did he die?' Parnello asked Irena.

She put the question to the waiter, then translated his answer. 'He was murdered last Thursday, in his apartment just round the corner. He was found in his bedroom. Strangled. Unfortunately these incidents are not so rare in our city these days.'

Parnello felt the naked terror once again, the spiralling off into unreason. For a moment he could envisage it with a shocking clarity: the purple face; the protruding eyes. And heard the small, insidious voice within his own brain telling him: next time it's you.

The waiter withdrew. Irena regarded Parnello quizzically.

'I am sorry about your friend,' she said. 'But something makes me suspect that you knew this already.'

'He wasn't my friend. I never met him. But yes, I had heard that he was dead. I wanted to confirm it.'

'So what is your interest in this Kuslov?'

'I suppose we had something in common. At various times we both owned the same property. I wanted to ask him about it. Where it came from.'

They looked up because the woman who had been weeping was now standing beside them, placing two of her boxes on their table. The boxes contained cheaply-packaged torches, made in Korea. Parnello caught a glimpse of about thirty more of them in her plastic bag. She started speaking. Urgently. Pleadingly.

She paused, red-eyed, quivering. Irena contemplated her with distaste, as if demeaned by their shared nationality. The contrast between the two women was the contrast between the new and the old Russia: the one cool, glamorous, desirable; the other flabby, outmoded, derelict. The sleek Mercedes and the exhaust-belching home-market brand. Finally Irena translated: 'She says her name is Ludmilla. She has come looking for Kuslov too. She wanted to sell him this merchandise. It seems that Kuslov had bought things from her husband in the past. Now she wonders if you would be interested in the torches as she thinks you were a business partner of Kuslov.'

'What sort of things has her husband sold Kuslov in the past?'

The woman gabbled excitedly, increasingly breathless.

'She says that Kuslov bought from him some personal stereos. Sony Walkmen. And also once two icons. Except that I don't think she means icons. I think they were what you call – paintings.'

'Paintings?' Parnello's interest was instantly engaged. 'Where is her husband now? Can I talk to him?'

Irena asked the question. For a moment the woman was silent. Then she began to weep again. She sank down at the neighbouring table and buried her head in her hands. Huge sobs wracked her body. Parnello looked away, embarrassed, wanting to offer comfort but unable to begin to. At last she pulled herself together sufficiently to speak again, the words spilling out between her tears.

'She says you cannot talk to him.'

'Why not?'

'Because two days ago his body was found frozen in the canal.'

Parnello closed his eyes. The spiral was beginning again. The vertigo of terror. 'Does she remember the paintings he sold to Kuslov? What she calls the icons?'

Irena put the question, and the woman spoke again.

'She says he came home with them about three months ago. She can't remember them very clearly, but she thinks that one may have shown the image of a field. A field with corn. She says she didn't like it very much, it wasn't very good.'

It wasn't very good. Perhaps it hadn't been, to a man looking for icons. Perhaps it hadn't been to a man whose eye, in so far as it had been conditioned at all, was primed for devotional renderings of Our Lady of Zagorsk or the Virgin of the Burning Bush.

But what this woman's husband had somehow laid hands on were pictures from the collection of Gottfried von Seitz. He had supplied Kuslov with both the van Gogh and the Dahl. He'd stolen them, like he'd stolen the Sony Walkmen. Like he'd stolen this pathetic bundle of torches. The fact that he was now dead too was almost the guarantee that he'd handled the pictures.

He asked: 'She's no idea where he got them, I suppose? These paintings?'

The woman shook her head and spoke again. 'No idea,' confirmed Irena. 'She says she is now widow and has no money. She wants to know, will you buy the torches?'

Parnello reached into his pocket for his wallet. 'How much does she want for them?' he said wearily.

*　　　*　　　*

Soon after he called for the bill.

She reached into her bag and brought out a mobile telephone. 'I must go outside,' she said. 'To make a call. This does not work in here.'

'OK,' he said. 'I'll join you in a moment.'

As he waited for the man to bring his change, he wondered idly who she was speaking to. Maybe the boyfriend, out of town. Maybe one of her business contacts.

Then she was in the doorway again, beckoning to him urgently. 'Come,' she called, 'it is open now.'

'What's open?'

'The door to your friend's apartment block.'

He hurried out into the afternoon sunlight, clutching the bag of unwanted torches. There were still so many more questions than answers, still no clear way ahead. And then it was like a nightmare re-run of the snowy evening in Stockholm old town. He saw that the communal door to Kuslov's block was indeed ajar.

'Come on!' she called. She was already half way there. Instinctively he sprinted after her.

He had no clear idea what he hoped to find. But there must be something. Anything.

In the hall he looked about him. The door to the ancient lift was open. He went in, checked for Kuslov's flat number, and pressed the button for the fifth floor. Just as the doors clanked shut, she followed him in.

It was between the third and the fourth floor that the machinery abruptly died and the cabin stopped moving. It hung there, swaying barely perceptibly; otherwise immobile. Suspended, forty feet above ground level, held only by unknown tensions of steel wire. Then all the lights went out and there was a terrible silence.

She swore quietly in Russian.

In the semi-darkness he felt for the control panel and stabbed at the line of buttons. Nothing.

He stood still for a moment, trying to calm himself. And all at once he was aware of being very close to her, aware of how narrow the space between them was. He could not see her clearly, but with his every other sense he perceived her. They were facing each other. Their bodies were practically touching. As he inclined his head forward, he could imagine the open buttons of her silk shirt. He could imagine the gap between her breasts. He smelt that expensive scent again. And he smelt her.

Her cheek was against his. Her arms entwined about his neck. He felt her body move against him, and her lips come searching for his mouth.

Then he heard the footsteps on the stairway. Measured, controlled. Implacable.

He pulled away from her, instantly sensing danger, subliminally registering the terrifying vulnerability of the act of love. He grasped for the emergency telephone which he knew was there on the side of the wall. His fingers closed round the receiver, and as he pulled he felt it come away in his hand, unwired and unconnected.

The footsteps continued. He knew with absolute certainty that they were coming for him.

There were two sets of them now. One from above, one from below. He punched the buttons again, feverish, desperate. Nothing happened. He began feeling the panels of the cabin, wrenching at the ceiling, trying to force the grill. Anything to get out. Anything to get away from those footsteps.

Then he heard the men's voices calling out.

And, most shocking of all, he heard her answering them. In Russian. Immediately he sensed the betrayal. From her tone he recognised at once that she was complicit with them. That she was delivering him to them.

And all at once the lights went on again, the machinery above re-engaged, and the elevator clanked up to the next floor. When the doors opened they were there, waiting for him, one taller man and one stockier, both hefty and unsmiling. They took him by the arm and ushered him out. It was almost a courtesy, a parody of politeness. Except that once he was standing out there on the landing, they didn't relax their grip. She followed, running her hand through her hair. Smoothing the skirt back over her thighs.

'Who are you?' he said.

They did not answer. He tried to catch her eye as they led him back down the stairs. But she was looking away. Reaching for her lipstick in her expensive Italian bag.

TWENTY FOUR

Russia made Stahler nervous. As a city, St Petersburg struck him as hostile, the landscape alien. The people were wayward and untamed, their squat ungainly cars spat noxious exhaust fumes into the polluted air; even the snow was filthy. In his heart he was convinced of one thing: that it was perilous to think of Russians as anything but enemies. Today they might make a show of deference, of respect, because they needed Germany in general, and people like Stahler in particular. They wanted something out of them. But their deference was devious, antipathy in disguise. They were not to be trusted. You must be continually on your guard in dealing with them.

Lunch over, he was ushered through with his Bundestag colleagues to the press conference. He had already spent two days of this official visit listening to the honeyed words of his Russian hosts, the soft blandishments of reassurance about prospects for German investment, the economic miracle that was just around the corner, the way that the battle against organised crime was being won. He had not believed a word of it. The evidence of his own eyes gave the lie to their assertions. The drunks lying in the gutter at night. The paucity of the goods in the shops. The opulent entrepreneurs who moved nowhere without their bodyguards. And then there was the other matter. The private business which he had come to settle. Was this not itself the clearest possible indication of the corruption endemic to this place?

He was surprised by the number of journalists who had put in an appearance. As he took his place at the table facing them, he calculated that there must be at least forty, and behind them the cameras of five or six television stations. It was right, of course, that the Russian media should take intelligent interest in the visit to their country of such a substantial team of German politicians. Glancing quickly to left and right at his own colleagues, he concluded that the turn-out was something of a tribute to himself, that his substance was unquestionably the most weighty of the German delegation. Very well. He held himself up straighter in his chair. That being the case, it would do them all no harm to hear some plain speaking from Dr Heinrich Stahler.

The conference was conducted by the Russian deputy minister for foreign trade, an earnest-looking civil servant whose breast pocket sagged under the weight of ball-point pens. He dealt with a number of questions about the delegation's visits to local factories that had benefited from German financial investment, passing them on to members of the Bundestag team for comment. Then they moved on to the more general issue of German investment in Russia. Stahler shifted impatiently in his chair at the anodyne answers furnished by his colleagues, their patent unwillingness to touch on any point that might give offence to their hosts. They were cowards, all of them.

Then a short, rat-like man with a wheedling voice stood up in the second row to put a question.

'Gregor Antonovich, Moscow Press Agency,' he introduced himself. 'I would like to ask our distinguished visitors what their views are about the art works removed from Germany at the end of the last war by the Soviet Trophy Brigades. Do they see these as a serious obstacle to Russian-German relations?'

The deputy minister coughed awkwardly. He clearly felt the question inappropriate, an embarrassment. Several of Stahler's colleagues also looked away, fearful of catching the deputy minister's eye and being asked to deal with it. But Stahler was not daunted. He leant forward, arm half-raised, to attract his host's attention.

'May I say a few words on this matter, Deputy Minister?'

'Please.' There was a mixture of relief and apprehension in the movement of the Russian official's hands.

'I should make one thing absolutely plain at the start,' began Stahler. 'The art treasures we are discussing were illegally looted from German soil in 1945. We in Germany know it. In their hearts, most reasonable people in Russia know it too. These works should be restituted forthwith to the owners' legitimate heirs. I have made my views clear on numerous previous occasions. To claim that such objects were "war reparations" is patently nonsense. It would be morally wrong for the German government or German individuals to enter into negotiations with the Russian authorities for the return of these items if those negotiations involve any sort of compensation, financial or otherwise, being paid to Russian institutions. That is quite unacceptable. I look forward in the near future to the Russian Parliament reversing its intransigeant position and enacting legislation to facilitate the return of this private German property.'

'So would you be in favour of withholding German investment in this country until this matter is resolved?' The rat-like journalist seemed to be enjoying himself. His colleagues were writing fast, cassettes whirred, and simultaneously three of the TV camera lights were illuminated. At last, everyone sensed hard news.

'I would say this.' Stahler spoke slowly. Portentously. 'So long as this question remains unsettled, it cannot correctly be claimed that the Second World War has yet finally ended.'

There was a moment's silence, broken by an elderly man in the back row shouting, 'Shame!' There was a murmur of excited speculation from the press. Stahler's colleagues pretended to scribble important annotations to the papers in front of them, or frowned anxiously into the middle distance. None looked at him. Cowards, thought Stahler again.

'Thank you,' said the Deputy Minister, nodding desperately in Stahler's direction. 'Who has the next question, please?'

TWENTY FIVE

⸺◦∞◦⸺

The two men led Parnello back down the stairs of Kuslov's apartment block. When they reached ground level they did not leave by the front door. He was guided round to a smaller door at the back, a sort of tradesman's entrance that gave on to a deserted courtyard. Here a large grey car was drawn up adjacent to the exit, so that he stepped out of the building almost directly into the back seat.

'This is ridiculous,' protested Parnello. It wasn't that they actually used violence to persuade him in; but the threat of it was implicit in their every movement as the rear door was held open, and the taller of his two guards loomed over him, supervising his embarkation, then following him attentively into the back. The shorter, stockier man hurried round to the place next to the driver, and they accelerated away, heading out towards the Moscow Prospekt.

'This is ridiculous,' Parnello repeated. 'What is this, some sort of a kidnap? Because if it is, you've got completely the wrong man.'

It was surprisingly cramped in the back, given the size of the car. The man next to him sat hunched up, regarding him warily. But he didn't speak.

Parnello wondered if he should make a run for it when the car next slowed down at traffic lights; he wondered if he could swing the door open, leap out and sprint for cover. But he noticed the central locking was engaged. And he did not relish discovering in such a confined space whether either of his companions were armed. There was something else, too. A faint realisation in the back of his mind that this journey was his only lead, his only chance of progress. If he bailed out now, he would lose that chance. Maybe he would never be as close as this again to the answers he was seeking.

'Where are you taking me?' Parnello looked from one to the other of his captors. The man in front kept his gaze firmly on the road ahead. The man next to him deliberately avoided his eyes. If they understood English, they certainly weren't going to admit it.

Parnello stayed silent as they drove on. With the back of his hand he wiped the last remnants of her lipstick from his mouth.

They left the Moscow Prospekt and took the highway towards Peterhof, the summer palace of the Tsars. A few miles further on they veered off this main road down a lane whose surface was treacherous with impacted ice. They slithered round narrow corners, past summer dachas with green wooden walls and shuttered windows, their roofs now coated with frozen snow. The road deteriorated further, and then all but petered out. The car drew to a halt in a small turning space dug out of the drifting snow. They ushered him out into the late afternoon sunshine. A little way ahead he could see a huge expanse of white which he suddenly recognised was the frozen sea, and the three of them began to tramp slowly through the snow in the direction of the shore. No-one spoke. But there was a purpose about this brief walk. Parnello sensed that he was reaching the end of a long journey.

From a fair distance away he caught a first glimpse of the man at the water's edge silhouetted against the horizon. He stood there with his back to them, staring out to sea, tall and gaunt and solitary. The unending expanse of the white-frozen waters of the Gulf of Finland dwarfed him in a backdrop of infinite melancholy. Once more Parnello glimpsed the vastness of Russia; sensed how in the end the landscape might always have a greater power over its inhabitants than they over the landscape.

The man did not turn round until Parnello and the other two had drawn very close to him. When he did so, he moved with unexpected grace. He was tall and muscular, with a mane of greying, almost shoulder-length hair swept back off his face. The puffiness under his eyes and at his jowls could not mask the underlying perfection of his bone-structure, the vividness of the draughtsmanship of his features. There was a theatrical quality to him: in other circumstances he might have been an ageing pop star, a matinee idol run slightly to seed.

'Mr Moran,' he said. 'I have been looking forward to meeting you.'

'Who are you?'

'My name does not signify. But I think we have business to discuss.'

'I don't do business with people whose names I do not know.'

He smiled and shrugged. 'Very well. Call me Vladimir Ivanovich.'

Vladimir Ivanovich. Nicholas Raven. It was irrelevant in the end what names they gave themselves. But what counted was that they needed him for something. Otherwise they would not have gone to the trouble of bringing him here. As long as he had not delivered it, he had some power over them.

'I hope you will forgive this choice of meeting place. Sometimes I prefer the freedom of the open air for delicate discussions.'

Parnello remembered the Russian folk music turned up loud. Some things in Russia did not change. The need to protect secrets. The need for secrets themselves.

Vladimir drew a crumpled packet of cigarettes from his pocket, shook it, and extracted one directly with his lips in an action both practised and sensual. He lit it and said:

'If it were not for me you would be dead by now. You know that, don't you?'

An icy breeze blew in from the frozen sea. A bitter, cutting wind. They were unprotected here, exposed. Parnello forced his gloved hands deep into the pockets of his overcoat, and said nothing.

'It was rather more difficult to keep you alive than to have you killed. Can you understand that, Mr Moran?'

Parnello remembered the purple face in the apartment in Stockholm old town. He thought of Kuslov. And the woman's husband whose frozen body had been pulled out of the canal. He nodded.

'I've gone out on a limb to give you this chance,' persisted Vladimir, as if craving some acknowledgement of his humanity.

'Why?' asked Parnello. 'Who are you?'

Vladimir took a lengthy drag on his cigarette. He had a way of smoking that was extraordinarily physical. He tore at the cigarette, attacked it with his lips as if it were an enemy. Or a lover. 'I've been watching you, Mr Moran,' he said softly. 'I've noticed things about you.'

'Like what?'

'Like the way you paid 100,000 dollars for a piece of property in New York. A piece of property that was rightfully ours, a piece of property that had been stolen from us.'

'I didn't know that. And who is "us", anyway?'

'An organisation here in Russia. A legitimate organisation. An organisation integral to the functioning of this country.'

'By what right had you come by this property?'

'Do you want a history lesson, Mr Moran? We had authority to take possession of it, many years ago. As reparation. On behalf of the Russian state.'

What had Dobiachowsky said about the KGB, thought Parnello? A state within a state?

'So you stole the picture from me in New York?'

'No. It had been stolen from us. We merely restored it to its legitimate ownership. But not before you had been offered generous financial compensation for it, which you were unwise enough to refuse.' Vladimir paused, and turned away to the sea, narrowing his eyes as if trying to glimpse some illusory coastline across the water. 'But myself, I was intrigued by you. 100,000 dollars was a sum that interested me: it was more than our own valuation of that item. Then I watched you chasing half-way round the world in pursuit of it, and I admired your persistence. I suspected that you might also be on the track of some other merchandise which was stolen from us at the same time. Some rather more expensive merchandise.'

'What happened to that other merchandise?'

'I am happy to be able to tell you that we have recovered that piece too.'

'From Sweden?'

Vladimir nodded. 'Fortunately, unlike the picture you acquired, it had not reached the point of appearing at a public auction.'

'So what do you want from me?'

Vladimir took a final impassioned drag on his cigarette, then ground the stub into the snow with the sole of his boot. 'I will speak frankly with you. We are in the process of finalising a deal for the sale of both pieces, to someone who wants to acquire them under very, very discreet conditions. Maybe it's for the best that this highly discreet deal that we've got lined up should go ahead. But first I want a double-check. A double-check from you. You intrigue me. I am impressed by your perseverance. If you would pay 100,000 dollars for that much lesser thing, what would you give for the big one? Maybe more than the offer we have already on the table. Most of my colleagues were in favour of eliminating you from the competition immediately. But I am more flexible. I understand the ways of the open market. I believe that competition can sometimes be healthy. So, having gone out on a limb for you, I hope you're not going to disappoint me.'

'You want to see if my offer for your merchandise is higher than the one you already have?'

'That's correct.'

'And what happens if I make a bigger offer? Can I then buy the items from you?'

'Subject to certain conditions.'

'Like what?'

'Complete confidentiality. No acknowledgement on either side as to where they came from.'

'I understand that requirement, of course. But what guarantee have I got that I can take the items out of Russia? If I can't export them, they're worthless to me.'

'If you have paid an acceptable price, you will be able to take them out of the country.'

'Even though the export of works of art from Russia is not permitted?'

Vladimir laughed and shook his head. 'There are ways and means.'

'Legal ways and means?'

'Listen, my friend. Supposing, for the sake of argument, you were to buy in Italy a Madonna by Raphael. What is the only way in which you could legally export that painting?'

'There would be no legal way. No export licence would be granted.'

'That is what you think. But supposing for a moment you had bought it from the Vatican. Then it would be possible. Because the Vatican City is not subject to Italian government export restrictions.'

'A state within a state,' murmured Parnello.

'A state within a state.'

There was silence for a few moments, then Parnello asked: 'And if my offer doesn't exceed the one you have already?'

'Then we will proceed with the existing deal.'

'And where would that leave me?'

The Russian did not reply immediately. Then he said slowly: 'In a vulnerable position.'

Parnello looked across at him. What was he hoping for? A glint of amusement in his eyes? A reassurance that what they were discussing was after all a deal like any other, to be done or walked away from? But Vladimir's expression was hard now; determined. And for the first time Parnello understood it: the full implications of his dilemma. Who would champion his right to stay alive if he did not come up with a better offer than the one already on the table? Who would go out on a limb for him then?

'In that case I think I'd better see the merchandise.'

'You are in a position to make a substantial offer? And honour it?'

Parnello thought for a moment. 'I'm in a position to do that, yes,' he said. 'If what you show me is what I think it is.'

'You will have to move quickly. There can be no delays, if you wish to be taken seriously.'

And if *you* wish to be vindicated, thought Parnello. I have gone out on a limb for you, Vladimir had told him. Parnello sensed that his own fate was obliquely intertwined with that of the man he was talking to. That if Parnello came up with a substantial counter-offer, Vladimir's judgement would be vindicated in the eyes of his colleagues. To that extent Vladimir needed him. And to that extent he must elicit Vladimir's assistance.

'I am wondering something,' said Parnello thoughtfully. 'I am wondering what sort of sum might in this case be deemed substantial.'

Vladimir said nothing, but looked across at him quizzically.

'What, for instance, would be the reaction if I were to offer thirty million dollars for the twelve pictures in the von Seitz collection?'

Vladimir frowned, and slowly shook his head.

'Thirty-two million?'

The Russian still said nothing. Once more his head shook.

'Thirty-five million?' There was something fleetingly comic about this parody of an auction.

Vladimir looked up and smiled.

'Do you know something, Mr Moran? I was once a ballet dancer.'

They had turned away from the sea and begun to walk back in the direction of the car. Parnello's two minders were following at a discreet distance. 'That accounts for your extraordinary grace of movement,' observed Parnello. 'And the quickness of your footwork.'

'Thank you. It was some years ago, of course, but the old habits remain. And you? Did you once pursue another career?'

'I once worked in an abbatoir.'

Vladimir frowned. 'I suppose that that accounts for your extraordinary ability to approach unscathed so close to violent death.'

They walked on in silence.

'A car will come for you at ten tomorrow,' said Vladimir as he took his leave. 'It will take you to see the pictures. All of them. Then we will talk again.'

TWENTY SIX

The hotel foyer in which Heinrich Stahler sat waiting was comfortingly international. There was a security in its blandness, in the copies of *Bunte* and *der Spiegel* on sale at its newsstand, in the way its decoration mirrored a hundred other expensive hotels across the world. But nonetheless Russia continued to make Stahler nervous. This was still St Petersburg, not Düsseldorf. He hid his nervousness in irritation, checking repeatedly the contents of his attaché case, looking regularly at his watch. It was seven minutes past four. It was intolerable that people could not keep to schedules.

Frau Müller had prepared his own schedule meticulously for him. There had been the morning visit to a Russian factory making cheap wooden furniture, an enterprise which boasted substantial German investment. There had been lunch followed by the press conference. Then there was the afternoon's sightseeing for the other delegates, the engagement from which he had excused himself. 'No, Frau Müller,' he had told her. 'I have my own business matters to attend to. I will need three hours at this juncture. Three hours clear.'

She had caught her breath and coloured slightly. But then she was prone to blushing. Stahler had dismissed her reaction as some female foible, as irrelevant as it was unfathomable. How could be have imagined the riot of horrified fantasy that such a gap in his schedule was unleashing in her? A Russian mistress, she had concluded. Some Siberian temptress. 'Oh, Herr Doktor!' she had been on the point of imploring him. 'Don't do it! You are too good a man to waste yourself on some Slavic slut. Don't risk yourself in some alien liaison. You are playing with fire.'

Playing with fire. That was what he was doing, he knew that: not in the way of Frau Müller's unsuspected imaginings, but with an equal imperative of secrecy. What he was embarking upon was a necessary duplicity. So he had felt no compunction about the speech he had made at this lunchtime's press conference. It did no harm to repeat the inflexibility of his position. Today of all days it did no harm, in order to deflect any hint of suspicion from himself, in order to create a necessary cover. Because the clandestine enterprise he had in prospect was delicate beyond words, and liable to grotesque misinterpretation. If his activities later this afternoon became public knowledge at this stage, he would be ruined politically, destroyed more certainly than by the revelation of any number of mistresses. But it was a risk he felt compelled to take.

A risk carefully calculated by Kracht. That knowledge sustained him, gave him confidence. And, if everything worked out right, if Kracht's judicious planning bore fruit, then it would be a risk gloriously justified by the ultimate outcome. The end justified the means. But those means must continue to be kept secret. At all costs.

'They are late,' Stahler declared. 'This is intolerable.'

He stood up impatiently. The man next to him stood up also, automatically. He was a good head taller than Stahler, thickset and expressionless. Expressionless as a mark of efficiency rather than profundity.

'Tell me something, Otto,' went on Stahler. 'Why are these hotels so ridiculously overheated?'

The bigger man shrugged. Otto did not speak unnecessarily, and this was not an issue on which he was likely to have an opinion. Stahler divested himself of his sleek cashmere overcoat and stood there with his scarf still draped about his neck, wearing the black poloneck sweater that he had calculated as being more suitable to the occasion than a shirt and tie. He was dressed for combat rather than negotiation. He might be a politician, but when the situation demanded he was a man of action too.

And at that moment they arrived. The two of them. Mikhailowsky and Hoffmann. He never saw through which door they came. whether from outside, or whether perhaps from the bar, where they had been lurking, watching, biding their time; but suddenly they were there, surrounding him, somehow bigger than he remembered them in the open air, in the woods near Düsseldorf.

'Doktor Stahler,' Mikhailowsky said softly. As if not to be overheard. 'You remember my colleague, Mr Hoffmann?'

Stahler nodded in the direction of the pockmarked face, then looked round quickly to check on Otto's proximity.

'This is Herr Reches,' he said, indicating Otto. 'Herr Reches will accompany us. He is my adviser.' Adviser. It covered many things. If the Russians chose to interpret Otto's role as that of art adviser, then that was up to them. But equally they could not fail to register his substantial frame, the way his bulk would act as ballast in the physical balance between the two groupings of protagonists setting out on this delicate enterprise.

'Excellent,' said Mikhailowsky. The small dark eyes blinked watchfully out of the sallow, puffy features. The currants sunk even deeper in the dough. 'The car is outside.'

Stahler was forced to drag on the coat that he had just this instant taken off. They stood round waiting for him. He took his time, but he sensed the exercise put him at an obscure disadvantage.

Once they got to the Volvo that was waiting for them beyond the awning at the hotel entrance, he retrieved the initiative by climbing into the seat next to the driver. That way he would not have to squash into the back close up against the Russians. Or close up against Otto, which would have been almost as bad.

As the car drove off into the slush, he was still the politician, unwilling to shed the trappings of his official role. Perhaps in order to emphasise one final time his status, and its ultimate inviolability. There was a matter that he had been meaning to bring up. And Mikhailowsky, after all, occupied some sort of rank here, possessed some sort of deliberately obscured but nonetheless potent authority. He decided to broach it with him. To make it clear that he was in this country as the senior representative of a powerful nation that was not prepared to be pushed around, not prepared to countenance the ill treatment of its citizens.

'Herr Mikhailowsky,' he began, not looking at the man but staring straight ahead out of the windscreen, 'I have this morning heard a distinctly disturbing story about the practices of your St Petersburg police force.'

'Yes?'

'A compatriot of mine who is in the city making important contributions to the development of your country's commercial infrastructure, a German businessman of the highest reputation, was last week stopped in the street by two members of the city police force who demanded to see his papers. The papers were of course in order but they looked also into his wallet, and in front of his own eyes removed two hundred-dollar bills before handing the wallet back to him. When he protested, they laughed and denied that any theft had taken place. Herr Mikhailowsky, this sort of behaviour is totally unacceptable in officers of the law.'

'Your compatriot,' said Mikhailowsky blandly, 'he should register a complaint with the appropriate authorities.'

Stahler beat his gloved hand on the dashboard and turned to confront Mikhailowsky, 'No! This is not good enough!' he exclaimed.

The other man did not reply at once. Infuriatingly, Stahler's words seemed to animate his little currant eyes with momentary amusement. 'Perhaps there is a certain irony in this situation,' he said at last. 'You speak of one German making a small donation to the authorities; and here are you, another German, about to hand over a far larger clandestine sum.'

Stahler wavered. 'But I shall be receiving in return a substantial benefit.'

'Your compatriot should then be aware of the benefit which he too will receive. He should view his two hundred dollars as an indirect contribution to the maintenance of the forces of law and order in this city.'

'That is outrageous,' declared Stahler. But he felt less inclined to argue now. He brooded on Mikhailowsky's impertinence, but said nothing. Matters were too delicately poised. For a moment he had wandered to the edge of the precipice, glimpsed the abyss. Sensed his own sudden vulnerability. So. For now he must concentrate on the business ahead. Utter discretion and total secrecy were essential. Perhaps the shortcomings of the St Petersburg police department must wait. Still, there would come a time when the smile would be wiped from Mikhailowsky's face. Provided Kracht handled matters correctly, provided his elaborate planning came to fruition. And in Kracht he had the highest confidence.

The five men inside the car settled to continue the journey in silence. The ochre palaces of St Petersburg loomed and rattled past them as the car negotiated the potholed road. For a moment, as they waited at traffic lights, they stood alongside a bus whose windows were so grimy that it was barely possible to see the mass of seething humanity within. Now Stahler looked closer, he could make out some of their faces, grey and rigid against the cold, their bodies squashed up against each other like animals. What a country. What a God-forsaken country.

And Stahler thought back to the first time he had met Mikhailowsky. To that original, extraordinary encounter six months before.

'There is a man on line two,' Frau Müller had buzzed through to tell him. 'He will not give his name but he says he must speak with you. He has some pictures to offer you. Paintings.'

'You know the procedures, Frau Müller. Refer him to Dr van Diemen.'

'I have already made this suggestion. But he says he wants to speak to you personally in the first instance, not to your art consultant. It seems there is some connection with your family in the history of these pictures.'

'What is this madman talking about? Oh, very well: put him through.'

Mikhailowsky's voice, heard for the first time. Wheedling on the telephone; pleading for the chance to show him photographs of works of art that would surely be of interest. But cunning, too. Dropping just enough hints about the pictures' provenance to whet his appetite. And as it turned out, it was as well that he took the call, that the inquiry came direct to him rather than being channeled through van Diemen. For van Diemen to have known anything about the source of these pictures would be dangerous. Van Diemen was an old woman. He would have gossiped, been unable to keep his mouth shut. Stahler himself took charge of negotiations. Discreetly. Once he understood the importance of what he was being offered.

'This man was a lunatic,' he informed Frau Müller immediately after the call. To put her off the scent. 'What he had to offer me was complete rubbish.'

'You give too much of your time to these people, Herr Doktor,' Frau Müller assured him. 'You have too kind a heart.'

'Why have you come to me?' demanded Stahler of Mikhailowsky that first time they meet, furtively, like clandestine lovers, in a coffee-house off Koenigsallee.

'It was a natural connection. There were the names inscribed on the back of these pictures. The names von Seitz and Stahler. Our inquiries revealed that while there appeared to be no-one of the von Seitz name immediately traceable who was likely to wish to acquire them, you yourself, a descendant of Friedrich Stahler, are renowned as a picture collector in your own right. Therefore we concluded that these are works likely to be of considerable interest to you.'

'You have these pictures for sale?' He gestured to the group of transparencies that he had spread out on the table between them. The transparencies that showed paintings vaguely familiar from the past; from his father's and his grandfather's past. Paintings that he had never expected to see again, only gazed at wistfully in catalogues of his great-grandfather's lost collection.

'These pictures are for sale, yes. At a price.'

'Where can they be seen?'

'Abroad.'

'In Russia, you mean?'

Mikhailowsky shrugged and stirred his coffee. But he did not deny it.

'You have control of them?'

'My people have exclusive and utterly discreet control of them.'

'Who are your people?'

'An organisation within my country. A respected and legitimate organisation.'

'Not the Mafia?'

Mikhailowsky let out a quick little exhalation of amusement. 'No, I told you. The interests I represent are entirely legitimate.'

'So what are you? KGB?'

The question hung there, unanswered. Once more Mikhailowsky shrugged and stirred his coffee. And once more he did not deny it.

'And what makes you think that I would be prepared to pay money for property that is rightfully mine by descent anyway?' In his indignation he exaggerated the narrow legal legitimacy of his personal claim to these pictures. But his moral claim on them was, he felt, perfectly valid. He had heard from his father the outrageous injustice of old Friedrich Stahler's will, which meant that all the good Stahler pictures passed into von

Seitz hands. Of course that issue had no longer been relevant so long as the collection was assumed destroyed at the end of the war. But now here was that collection resurfacing again. Here it was being offered to him under conditions of enormous secrecy in exchange for cash. In exchange for very large amounts of cash. And in the process there had been a significant addition to it: a van Gogh. A van Gogh of a wheatfield.

If there was one artist whose work Stahler desired to add to his collection, it was van Gogh. And now here was an opportunity to acquire a magnificent one. The fact that it had a von Seitz provenance even added to the attraction of the deal: here was an opportunity for the Stahlers to right the wrongs of history, to compensate themselves for Gottfried von Seitz's inheritance of their pictures by acquiring one of his.

And Stahler knew the truth about von Seitz. He had learned it from his father. 'Your cousin Gottfried?' Peter Stahler almost spat the words out to his son. 'Please do not speak to me of that man; I disown him from the family. I will never think of him as anything but a traitor. To stab his country in the back, in its hour of greatest need. It was unforgivable. And then he himself was shot by the Red Army. Excuse me if I shed no tears. It was the correct end for a man like that; one of the few good things the Soviets ever did.'

But still, the idea of paying large sums of money to the Russians, of all people, was appalling to Stahler. Was he not already on political record as having said that such negotiations were totally unacceptable? War loot should be returned unconditionally. It was as simple as that.

So it was a tribute to Mikhailowsky's powers of insidious persuasion that, between the first and second cup of coffee they drank together that first afternoon, he implanted in Stahler's mind the seeds of certain arguments in favour of doing the deal.

'Consider this,' he told Stahler. 'No-one knows that these pictures still exist. They have not been mentioned in the context of the other highly-publicised rediscoveries of recent years in Moscow and St Petersburg. So if you bought them, their history over the past half century need not become an issue. You could credibly claim that they had never left your family's possession in all that time, that you had merely been keeping them discreetly. Certainly it would not be in the interests of anyone on our side to tell a different story. Not if we have been adequately compensated. You could consider the money payable to us as being in the nature of fifty years' storage charges, if you prefer.'

'Extortionately expensive storage charges.'

'Perhaps. But I can tell you that we have done our research. Careful research. And the prices that we are asking you for these twelve pictures are by no means excessive in the context of the international market. For you we have marginally discounted them in recognition of your special status as a purchaser. We are not naive. We recognise that it would be dangerous under the circumstances for us to offer them on the open market, and therefore almost impossible for us to obtain full value for them without attracting publicity that we cannot afford. But consider this, Dr Stahler: if you buy these pictures from us at these prices, there is nothing to prevent you from selling them on yourself in a year or two, almost certainly at a significant profit. You are almost the only person in the world who has a plausible cover story for being revealed as the owner of them after all this time.'

'I see that,' Stahler mused. 'I also see that it would be impossible for you to find anyone else with such credentials as myself as a purchaser.'

'Correct. But the attraction for you is that your investment would be utterly protected. You would have acquired readily capitalisable assets.'

'So, in view of my special status, it would be necessary for me to verify that the prices being asked are sufficiently reasonable.'

'How do you wish to do that?'

'Well, it is clearly impossible to do so from these photographs. I should have to inspect the originals myself. Discreetly.'

'That can be arranged.'

'And I must emphasise that if this matter is to proceed at all between us, which I do not in any way guarantee, it must be under conditions of total secrecy. If any whisper of it gets out, if any hint of the existence of these pictures emerges, there will be no deal. Do you understand me? No deal. No money. Finished. Kaput.'

'That is understood, Dr Stahler.'

The truth of the matter was that he had already set his heart on those pictures as he left the coffee house and got into the car that Albrecht had waiting for him round the corner. They were his family, after all. And if the van Gogh was not exactly a blood relation, then he already thought of it as a very dear adopted son.

But the money rankled, nonetheless. It was not that he could not afford it. He was a very, very rich man, and he had resources set aside for the acquisition of major pictures like the van Gogh. But to pay that amount of money, a sum approaching thirty-three million dollars, to those people, that was a revolting idea. That was why he resolved to talk to Kracht. If anyone could structure a way round this problem, it was Kracht.

So negotiations had proceeded. There had been a further meeting with Mikhailowsky, this time in the woods near Düsseldorf. 'I prefer the open air,' Mikhailowsky told him. 'Business negotiations are freer, more candid in the open air.' There had been a flying visit to St Petersburg under the cover of political fact-finding. And he had seen the pictures. Pored over those old Stahler labels on the backs of the Ruysdael and the van Goyen. And he had marvelled at the van Gogh. His heart rejoiced at the subject of the wheatfield. It was so typical an image: that was what he particularly prized in his acquisitions, that the work should be typical. Even

342

his most philistine friends could not fail to recognise the famous author of this painting when they saw it hanging on his drawing room wall.

Of course at this point it had been necessary to consult with van Diemen. He told him no details of the pictures' whereabouts, but he showed him the photographs, gave him the references. A bead of perspiration appeared on the balding Dutchman's forehead when he saw the van Gogh. 'The photograph is a little out of focus,' he complained. It was true, Stahler had to admit. The transparencies the Russians had taken were not of uniform quality. Nonetheless, Stahler found van Diemen's pernicketiness tiresome. It was a form of pique at not being shown the originals, like a jealous child denied a treat.

'Very well, then,' he told him impatiently. 'Make your judgement from the entry in the de la Faille catalogue raisonné of van Gogh's works. You will find this picture perfectly well recorded.'

He watched as van Diemen took from his bookshelf the catalogue raisonné and found the entry under July 1890. The man had an annoying habit of tracing with a shaking finger particularly significant lines of print as he read them out loud. 'Look,' he had exclaimed, 'Letter 649 from Vincent van Gogh to his brother Theo refers to the series of paintings of this subject. It is dated 9th July. The artist writes: "They are vast fields of wheat under troubled skies, and I did not need to go out of my way to express sadness and extreme loneliness – I almost think that these canvases will tell you what I cannot say in words, the health and restorative forces that I see in the country . . ." '

'Yes, yes,' Stahler interrupted, 'but it is this particular version with which we are concerned.'

'Of course. See here, the provenance of the picture about which you enquire: Galerie Cassirer in Berlin. It was bought from their exhibition in 1928 by someone called von Seitz.'

'My cousin,' Stahler was unable to resist informing him.

'But it says here that this version was destroyed in the war.'

'Ah, Dr van Diemen,' Stahler laughed. 'You must not necessarily believe everything you read in your precious reference books.' It did no harm to implant the idea in van Diemen's impressionable mind that in some undefined way the picture was still under his family's control.

'But this is a magnificent example.'

Stahler shrugged, as if to suggest that he would have expected nothing less of a picture with which his family had had some connection. 'So what do you estimate the value of this van Gogh to be?'

Van Diemen prevaricated as usual, but finally he indicated that he felt a suitable insurance figure would be in the region of 40 million dollars. Stahler nodded with satisfaction. The financial negotiations that he had already conducted had led to a price being provisionally agreed of 32.5 million dollars for all twelve pictures. Thirty million for the van Gogh; and 2.5 million for the other eleven, the Stahler pictures. For the Dutch seventeenth century landscapes. For the river landscape by Dahl. For the Max Liebermann.

And there he deliberately terminated van Diemen's involvement in the enterprise. Van Diemen was not secure. The less he knew the better. Anyway, Stahler had no doubt that he could rely on his own judgement. An understanding of pictures was built into his genes. The blood of a long line of collectors coursed through his veins. He recognised outstanding paintings when he saw them. No, the only expertise he needed now was that of Kracht.

Kracht the financial genius. Kracht the accountant. Kracht, discretion personified, the man who knew how to spirit money tracelessly across borders, the man who could navigate his way through the intricate labyrinth of the Swiss banking system, penetrating its most secret places and leaving no tracks behind him. Money had been deposited in the Swiss escrow account, according to Kracht's careful instructions. Everything had been on course.

And then one day three months ago the fax had come through. Totally unexpectedly. For Stahler's sole and personal attention, from Ivexco of Liechtenstein. For a moment he wondered, annoyed, who this unknown company was. Then he remembered that it was the name Mikhailowsky had given him as his organisation's trading front. 'We regret that our transaction is unavoidably delayed,' he read, 'due to technical difficulties.'

'Technical difficulties?' he stormed on the telephone to Mikhailowsky when he had finally got through to him in Russia later that afternoon. 'What the hell does that mean?'

'A temporary postponement.' The man's tone still had the same wheedling plausibility, but Stahler's ear detected an edge of uncertainty.

'What is the problem?'

'A logistical matter. It will not take long to sort out. Please leave the matter with us, and we will come back to you.'

Stahler wondered what that logistical matter could have been that had taken ten weeks to arrange. In that period he had been telephoned once by a colleague of Mikhailowsky and asked if he would be interested in proceeding with the deal on the basis of ten rather than twelve pictures. Most certainly not, he had replied. My family collection must come back to me intact. You have no right to break it up. I shall have all those pictures which you showed me, or there will be no deal. And remember this: if one word of the existence of these pictures gets out anywhere in the world before this transaction takes place, I shall not proceed. Secrecy is the integral part of our agreement. He wasn't going to let the bastards get away with anything. That was why, once the deal was alleged to be back on the rails again, he insisted on returning to St Petersburg to recheck the twelve works of art before going ahead. He had to be sure that the pictures he was acquiring were the same ones that he had seen the first time, that there had been no substitutions, no new splits in panels hastily rejoined, no recent tears in the canvas speedily repaired. He would not have put anything past the Russians.

The first time Stahler had seen the collection, they had taken the Moscow Prospekt in the direction of the airport, and turned off some way along that interminable dual carriageway into a complex of storage buildings. At a gateway manned by security guards, they had been waved through into a courtyard, and in the confines of a semi-subterranean box room furnished with crude metal storage racks he had finally set eyes upon the pictures. Now, however, their destination was different, closer to the centre of town. They drew up in a street off Lityaeni Prospekt. Conveniently close to the big modern building by the bridge over the Neva, the building whose anonymity was betrayed only by the forest of aerials and satellite dishes on its roof. Conveniently close to KGB headquarters.

They disembarked from the car and were led towards another unmarked doorway. It was marginally warmer today, and tiny sections of the frozen snow impacted on the roofs above were thawing, leaking small drops down on to the frozen pavement below and creating a treacherous covering of water over sheet-ice. Stahler cursed the slippery surface and edged his way forward, sticking as close as possible to Otto. There must be no danger of their becoming separated.

Once inside the building they took the elevator to the fourth floor. There were guards here. Guards with Kaleshnikovs, in the hallway, and waiting for them again when they stepped out of the cabin. They passed through two doors with complicated entry-codes. And finally they were shown into a small and airless office. Against one wall leant three neat stacks of pictures.

'Here,' said Mikhailowsky. 'These are the items which you wish to acquire, I think.'

Stahler got Otto to hold each one up individually so that he could inspect the surface of the paint for scratches or abrasions, for evidence of recent restorations. Then he looked carefully at the back. Everything seemed to be in order: the van Goyen, the Ruysdael, the Liebermann, the van Gogh. None had sustained new damages. Only on the reverse of the Dahl did he find something momentarily unexpected: a newish label with a number 147 inscribed upon it, and some fresh chalk marks on the panel. He stood for a moment peering at them, perplexed. He looked back over his shoulder at the three Russians, watching him intently. Then he shook his head and told Otto to move on to the next. The atmosphere in this room was oppressive with stale perspiration. With stale Russian perspiration.

'So, Doktor Stahler, I trust that you are now satisfied?' said Mikhailowsky as Otto laid aside the final painting.

Stahler paused before he nodded. He was aware that his heart was suddenly pumping faster, and he knew that it was at the prospect of acquiring these pictures, of welcoming them back into their rightful ownership. He nodded, then frowned, because he did not want these men to guess how excited he was feeling.

'Herr Mikhailowsky,' he said quietly. 'I think we should sit down somewhere a little more comfortable in order to finalise arrangements.'

There was a little potted plant in the room into which the Russians showed him. It was the only decoration, apart from two bilious yellow leather sofas, drawn up to face each other. The plant was some sort of cactus, Stahler noticed. He had seldom seen anything so unappealing. For a moment he thought nostalgically of the opulence of the greenery in the conservatory of his own house near Essen. He thought of little Petra and Nina playing amongst the foliage, their blond hair tangling in the fronds. He was doing this for them, really, for Petra and Nina. Righting a wrong. Securing their heritage.

He sat down on one of the sofas and motioned Otto next to him. The two Russians ranged themselves opposite. Awkward. Tense.

'So,' he said, addressing them. 'We shall proceed as follows.'

Hoffmann reached into his pocket for a cigarette. He put it in his mouth and flicked flame to its tip with a lighter.

'The money,' went on Stahler distastefully, 'as you will no doubt have checked, remains in the escrow account at my bank in Switzerland ready for payment into your numbered account in Liechtenstein once certain conditions have been met.'

'Those conditions being?'

'The twelve pictures should be delivered by you into the Free Port in Geneva. As you know, this is the area beyond Swiss customs jurisdiction, where sensitive and valuable goods may safely and discreetly be stored. They should be directed by your shippers to the warehouse of Bartsch AG in the Free Port. There they will be held to our joint account. Papers will be drawn up by Bartsch allowing for the release of the pictures into my hands only upon receipt of your authorisation, such authorisation to be forthcoming once you have received from Liechtenstein confirmation of receipt of funds. Is this clear?'

'You require us to get the pictures to Switzerland?' Mikhailowsky frowned, as if calculating distances. 'You are asking a great deal.'

'I am asking a great deal because I am paying you thirty two and a half million dollars. For this substantial price I need guarantees that the pictures can indeed leave Russia. In sending them to Geneva you will be proving to my satisfaction their exportability. But I remind you that in the Free Port they will still be under your control until you have received my funds.'

Mikhailowsky regarded him thoughtfully. 'It will be necessary for our people to check the trustworthiness of this company Bartsch. Their reliability, and their true impartiality.'

'They are long-established Swiss storage and shipping agents. They are used to operating this sort of transaction. Their reputation depends on their reliability in these matters.'

'This may be so, but we will check them first. Thoroughly.'

Mikhailowsky spoke abruptly, with a sudden edge of anger to his voice.

'Do as you wish. But please act quickly. I must remind you that you have already delayed the progress of this deal an unacceptably long time.'

I'll get you, Mikhailowsky, he thought. I'll get you, with your currant eyes and your pallid unhealthy face. I'll get you for the way your country has usurped my family's property. I'll get you for the way your police force has extorted hard earned dollars from upright German businessmen. I'll get you for your absurd little cactus plant.

'You'll be hearing from us soon,' said Mikhailowsky.

Back in the hotel, Stahler put a call through to Switzerland.

'Kracht? I have been with them today. I have checked the merchandise, and it is in order. I am optimistic that we will have a deal.'

The man at the other end grunted. Stahler recognised this as a good sign. The less Kracht spoke, the more on top of the situation it meant he was.

'So arrangements are still in place in Geneva?' persisted Stahler.

'Affirmative.'

He replaced the receiver and stood up, looking at his watch. It had been a good day so far. Now it was time to change into his dinner jacket. Tonight was another official reception, the last of the visit. Stahler smiled to himself. There was a certain irony in the fact that his host at this evening's event was the Minister of Culture. He awaited with interest that gentleman's scheduled speech on the question of the restitution of German art treasures.

TWENTY SEVEN

It was dark by the time they dropped him back at the hotel. Once inside, Parnello went straight to the bar and drank three glasses of vodka. The first was to calm himself. The second was to celebrate his restored liberty. And the third was to suppress the uneasy suspicion that the liberty restored to him was only temporary. They were coming for him again at ten tomorrow morning. By that time he was going to have to work out a plan, a way of moving forward, of reaching a deal. A way of staying alive. But he reminded himself that he still had some say in what happened, that he was not entirely at their mercy. That he still had some bargaining power.

By the time he'd ordered his fourth glass, the euphoria was setting in. He was looking at it all wrong. He was on the verge of the deal of a lifetime. The sort of deal that most art dealers only dream about, that would send Shagger Parks into a haze of ecstatic reverie merely to contemplate. Acquiring just the old masters in the von Seitz collection, being able to offer to collectors such an array of distinguished, high quality pictures completely fresh to the market, that would be exciting enough; but when you added in the magnificent van Gogh, the prospect transcended all but the wildest fantasy. Short of Philip Niarchos ringing him up and giving him exclusive rights over the disposal of his family's collection, he could not think of anything to match it. The van Gogh was of the calibre to put it into that rarest of categories, the picture whose price was all but irrelevant.

It was so outstanding, the priority was simply to acquire it, to have control of it. Then there would be buyers out there who would find it irresistible, for whom money was literally no object. Suppose he managed to buy this collection for thirty-five million dollars. Then he reckoned he'd be able to ask fifty million for the van Gogh alone. And get it. Sooner or later. From the right person. From the right billionaire for whom passion was more important than prudence.

There was one immediate, practical obstacle, however, to the realisation of this dream sequence. Assuming the offer the Russians already had on the table was in the area that Vladimir had obliquely indicated to him, and supposing he came up with one that exceeded it, raising thirty-five million dollars or so at short notice would present major problems. But not insuperable ones. He finished the vodka and lit a cigarette to consider the possibilities. He had access to one or two rich speculators whose money could be available to him for a truly exceptional opportunity such as this. These speculators were that special breed of money-men with a fascination for the art market, hard-headed financiers nonetheless prepared to take the sort of punt on a painting that they wouldn't have dreamed of touching if it had involved stock in a company making plastics. Because art was glamour. Art was romance. Art was fantasy. And, if all else failed, he might have to share the spoils. There were other dealers he could call in; even auction houses. It would take a little time to put together, but as a project it wasn't impossible.

He peered into his empty vodka glass and was invigorated by a surge of anticipation, an excitement that suddenly had nothing to do with money and everything to do with the painting itself, with the lava of the imagination whose eruption prevents an earthquake. Tomorrow he was actually going to see them, all those pictures whose quest had propelled him half way round the world. He would hold in his own hands Gottfried von Seitz's paintings. The inheritance of Alexandra Hamilton. He would reclaim – briefly – his own property, too, the Dahl he had bought at auction in

New York. That seemed a hundred years ago now. And the biggest prize of them all was the van Gogh. Nature seen through that unique temperament. How good would it turn out to be? He cast his mind back to the photograph in the album that Alexandra's mother had shown him. That photograph had only been in black and white, of course, but, as if finding the colour button on a television screen, he knew intuitively how the yellows would flood across the wheatfield, how the troubled sky would be shot through with blues and whites and greens. The re-emergence of another, assumed lost, example of the wheatfield series would create a sensation. It would be a resurrection, a second coming. And he was going to witness it tomorrow.

At 1.45 a.m. he awoke, sweating. Fearful. It hit him with absolute clarity. If he did not buy the pictures he was being taken to see in the morning, they would kill him. It was as simple as that. He was only being kept alive in order to make a higher offer for them than the one they already had. If he didn't come up with that offer, he was finished. He had only to remember what had happened to Persson and Kuslov. If they had had to die, then so must he. Given what he'd seen. Given what he knew.

Maybe, indeed, they had already decided that he had to be eliminated. Maybe he was only being wheeled out tomorrow to see the pictures in order to provide a double check on the price already agreed with the existing buyer. Once that had been confirmed, he would be surplus to requirements. Unless he came up with a valuation that was conspicuously so much higher than the price agreed that they had to do business with him. But then he would truly have to dig deep to find the money. And the deal itself might finally tip over the edge of viability.

And at that point he remembered one further negative factor: the question of the pictures' provenance. Vladimir and his friends might undertake to stay silent about the paintings' Russian connection since the war. But that would still mean a fifty-year gap in their history that would be difficult to explain. The market abhors such a vacuum. There would be damaging speculation about illegal passages across borders in that time, the sort of unanswerable rumours that would render the major assets difficult to negotiate in legitimate circles. Such uncertainty might matter less with a minor picture like the Dahl. But with a work of the importance of the van Gogh, it could be fatal.

He switched on the light, got out of bed and padded over to the desk. He sat there, thinking, aware of the silence of the freezing night outside, of the city sunk into its silver torpor of cold. One by one he took up from his file the documents of his quest and considered them: the page with the illustration of the Dahl torn from the auction catalogue; the card on which he had noted Lars Persson's Stockholm telephone number; Kuslov's address hastily scribbled by Aronsky on to a scrap of paper; the print from Persson's developed film that showed the first thrilling image of the van Gogh. Finally he laid them aside, took a pen and paper and began to write. He wrote hard for over an hour, stopping only to check facts from his notes: dates, names, addresses, telephone numbers. Writing it all down was some sort of comfort; offered an obscure glimpse of salvation. When he had finished, he rang through to the reception desk. Thank God this hotel was the best. The sort of request he was making did not faze them. Even in the dark hours of the night.

'Certainly sir. I will send a man up to collect it at once.'

'When will it go?'

'We have a Federal Express collection at seven a.m.'

Parnello looked at his watch. A little over three hours from now. 'OK,' he said. 'Please make sure this package doesn't miss it.'

Then he went back to sleep and dreamed of the lift in Kuslov's apartment block and the brief bitter-sweet taste of Irena's lipstick.

*　　　*　　　*

The car drew to a stop in the street not far from Lityaeni Prospekt. Parnello opened the door and stepped out into the wall of cold. The temperature had fallen several degrees overnight, freezing yesterday's inchoate thaw in mid-trickle, resolidifying the dirty snow piled up in the gutters into new shapes and creating a fresh range of icy hazards for the unwary pedestrian. One of the anonymous army of St Petersburg street workers, his head shrouded in a flapped hat, was chipping away at the sheet-ice. Parnello was ushered across the treacherous surface and in past the armed guards.

As he came out of the lift on the second floor he encountered Vladimir. Vladimir Ivanovich, waiting for him.

'Good morning. I hope you slept well.' But the man was preoccupied as he led him along the passage, like an animal caged. There was something feral about him, about the magnificent mane of hair, about the sinuous grace of his movement, about his ultimate menace. Perhaps his natural milieu was indeed the open air. In these foetid, overheated corridors he seemed oppressed. And for a moment Parnello imagined the undercurrents to his visit to this place, the hidden conflicts of influence within the Byzantine power structures of this organisation.

'I have gone out on a limb for you. I have gone out on a limb to give you this chance.' He was marked out as Vladimir's man. If he did not perform, then Vladimir would be diminished. He sensed the Russian's vulnerability. And he felt Vladimir sensing it too.

Parnello was shown into a small and airless office. Against a wall stood three neat stacks of pictures.

'Take your time,' said Vladimir, gesturing to them. He ran his hand through his hair to pull it back off his forehead, then reached for a cigarette.

Parnello turned to confront him. 'Before I look at these,' he said carefully, 'I want you to answer me some questions about them.'

'You are supposed to be the picture expert.'

'I want you to tell me what makes these pictures different.'

'Different? What do you mean?'

'I get the feeling that there was something about these pictures in 1945 that set them apart. Why did they go straight into KGB care, separated from the others, the pictures from collectors like Gerstenberg, Krebs, and Köhler, which went into storage in the Hermitage and the Pushkin?'

'That is a matter of distant history.'

'But why have they remained secret while the others have been exposed?'

'You should be grateful that they have remained secret. That is what permits you now to make a discreet financial offer for them. Had they gone in with the others in the Hermitage, there would be no chance of buying them. They would have been public. The reason for their having remained secret is a matter of distant history which is no longer relevant.'

'Look, this is relevant to my decision whether to make an offer or not. I need to know as much as possible about the history of these pictures. It affects their future negotiability. Surely it is no longer sensitive information. Not now, as it was all so long ago; all under the old regime.'

Vladimir shrugged and frowned. There was no mistaking the tension now. He took another drag on his cigarette.

'Did it have something to do with the German owner?' persisted Parnello. 'Something to do with Seitz? Was that what made it necessary to give this collection special treatment?'

Perhaps it was the overheated room, but Vladimir was sweating. 'It does not signify. It is not important.'

'But you have read the file. You must have.'

Vladimir inclined his head in a little gesture of assent, but he said nothing.

'What was it about Seitz's pictures that made them different?'

Slowly Vladimir unwound himself from the elegant position he had taken up leaning against the wall. Finally he said, 'It was not his pictures. Not as such.'

'You mean it was Seitz himself.'

Again the little silent gesture of assent.

Behind Vladimir the door opened softly. Standing there was a pallid pasty-faced man with eyes like currants. Vladimir turned and noted him; raised a hand to acknowledge his presence. It was the pallid man who spoke next:

'To answer your question, Mr Moran: the former owner of these pictures was a war criminal. He was executed for his crimes in May 1945. He was guilty of the cold-blooded murder of innocent Russian prisoners of war. I am sure you can understand that this sets him apart, makes him different. Makes him different in the attitude of this country, at least.'

Parnello nodded. Why did he feel absolutely certain that this was not the answer he would have received from Vladimir had the other man not joined them?

In the next-door room, where the bilious yellow sofas stood, Vladimir poured him coffee. Mikhailowsky, the dough-faced man, stood impassively behind him, saying nothing. But a looming check on negotiations. A silent threat.

Vladimir handed him over the cup and then spoke abruptly. As if the fencing were over. As if time had run out and now all the debts must be called in.

'So what will you pay for this collection of pictures, Mr Moran?'

Parnello could not yet answer him. He was in a state of shock. A state of aesthetic shock. A state of physical shock.

He had gone into the room with the von Seitz pictures anticipating one of the greatest art-historical discoveries of his life. As a prelude, he had started by picking up the Dahl. His Dahl. He had felt it then, holding it in his hands again: the stab of resentment, of outrage. They had stolen this picture from him, this exquisite sunset reflected in the waters of the river, the smoking bonfires in the fading light. But then they had stolen it from Alexandra's grandfather, too. Hadn't they?

But that anger had passed. What had overwhelmed him

had been the shock that had come a moment or two later. The extraordinary discovery he had made as he went through the other paintings. The revelation that changed everything.

Now he sat on the bilious yellow sofa sipping the coffee, pretending to make notes of the pictures he had listed on his piece of paper, pretending to be absorbed in adding up their values. He needed time to make sense of what he had seen. To sort himself out, to decide how to play it.

Of one thing he was absolutely sure: he was not going to buy this collection. He was not going to make a serious offer. What he had just seen had made that impossible.

'Do you have a proposal for us, Mr Moran?' It was no longer Vladimir speaking. It was the man called Mikhailowsky now. Impatient. Mistrustful. Glancing quickly at Vladimir. Challenging him in his challenge to Parnello.

Parnello sighed, and stood up. He folded his paper and put it away carefully into the breast pocket of his jacket.

'No,' he said quietly. 'I am not interested in these pictures. I have already bought one of them in fair and open competition at auction in New York. I don't intend to do so again.'

He watched Vladimir. He could see the disbelief, then the anger in the man's eyes. 'You are not making it easy for yourself,' Vladimir told him.

Parnello shrugged. 'There is something else you should know,' he continued slowly but very clearly, so that there should be no misunderstanding. 'Last night I sent by courier a sealed letter to my lawyer in London, with instructions that should anything happen to me its contents should immediately be made public to the world's press. That letter contains everything I know about the von Seitz collection, specifies exactly what it comprises. It also contains everything I know about you people and your attempts to sell it clandestinely. It will make a sensational story, I can assure you. I have even indicated to my lawyer which magazines, journalists and TV stations in Britain, Germany and America will do it best. You see, I know about these things. So if anything happens to me, you can kiss goodbye to your other buyer. That I can promise you.'

Vladimir unwound his body from its pose against the wall. He reached for his cigarette packet, found it was empty, and crumpled it abruptly. That action was the only outward betrayal of his anger. 'You are foolish,' he said. 'You are missing an excellent opportunity.'

'That's not my opinion,' said Parnello.

Mikhailowsky interrupted impatiently: 'I think this has gone on long enough.' Parnello realised the remark was addressed less to him than to Vladimir. Vladimir Ivanovich shrugged, tossed his head and walked out of the room. He still moved with exceptional grace. As if making his exit from the stage at the end of a particularly demanding *pas de deux*.

Mikhailowsky turned to Parnello. He was not smiling. 'Explain one thing to me, Mr Moran. Even if what you say about the letter to your lawyer is true, what guarantee would we have that you wouldn't anyway exploit your knowledge once you got home?'

'No guarantee, beyond the fact that I'm not a fool. I realise that you have a vested interest in keeping me alive only so long as I'm the only one who knows the secret of these pictures. Once I share it, then I lose that security. But look at it this way: one thing you do have an absolutely certain guarantee of is that my knowledge will be exploited to the full if anything happens to me.'

Mikhailowsky considered him thoughtfully. 'And if we proceed with our other buyer? Go through with a discreet sale to him? What would be your reaction then?'

'I would say good luck to you, if you have a buyer who's prepared to proceed with the deal. I want no more to do with it. I just want to forget it. Leave Russia, go home.'

Mikhailowsky nodded. When he spoke again, his voice barely contained his anger. 'I think you'd better leave. Get out. Now.'

As Parnello reached the front door of the building and the wind hit him, fresh air had never tasted so sweet.

But the elation was only temporary. He reached the hotel unmolested and booked a flight in the name of Sorensen to London, via that afternoon's Lufthansa connection to Frankfurt.

Before he checked out he rang Dobiachowsky. He had to do something, make some sort of gesture. To show that, despite his bemusement, he wasn't entirely defeated.

'Off already, Dr Parnello?'

'I think it's wisest. My presence seems to have become unwelcome in certain circles.'

'I am sorry to hear it. Have you at least found what you were looking for?'

'Not really. That's why I'm calling you now. To ask another favour.'

'Of course. At your service.'

'You said you were going to Moscow soon, to give your lecture?'

'Tomorrow already. Tomorrow I entrust my fragile frame to the care of our fabled national airline.'

'Look, I'm only asking you this because if anyone's the master of the archives, you are. I realise it's next to impossible, but if you have a spare moment do you think you could try to get access to the KGB records? To look one thing up for me?'

'What do you want to know?'

'I want you to see if there's a file on Gottfried von Seitz.' He paused, remembering Vladimir. Vladimir had known the truth. A couple of hours ago he might even have been about to divulge it, if Mikhailowsky hadn't come into the room. 'Obviously it would be an old file, from 1945. But it's important to me to know if there's anything on record. About him or his pictures. It would relieve my curiosity.'

'Leave it with me, Dr Parnello. I believe the older files

are sometimes more accessible. I can promise nothing, but I will try.'

He took a taxi to Pulkovo. The darkened sky lay very close to the earth. There would be more snow soon. He took a last look round at the desolate landscape which separated the city from the airport. It gave the impression of having been washed in very dirty water, then frozen solid. He was not sorry to turn his back on it. He felt oddly fatalistic as he negotiated passport control and the boarding formalities. Numb. As if half concussed by the impact of the morning's extraordinary discovery.

There was nothing more for him here in Russia. Nothing more he could do. But he was leaving frustrated, impotent. Diminished. Nothing was really solved, was it? He was leaving having failed in what he had set out to do. He had climbed to the top of the rock, and found himself unable to achieve the jump into the water below upon which he had set his heart. As the plane took off, he realised he had escaped; or rather that they had decided to let him go. But all he felt now was an odd indifference to his personal safety. A despondency settled upon him, a sense of anti-climax.

And a need for solitude.

At Frankfurt he booked another ticket, this time in the name of Moran, this time for Lisbon. The destination was another capricious decision. Partly to put any followers off the scent. But mostly because of his craving to be alone for a while.

The last thing he did before going to the new boarding gate was to call Alex in New York. She was preoccupied. Her mother was still in hospital. Better, but still under observation.

'I've given up,' he told her. 'I couldn't get any further. I've come away empty-handed.'

'And the pictures?'

'No joy.' He didn't feel like elaborating. Not as long as things were so confused in his mind. Even now he was still in shock. Perhaps he'd be able to explain it all to her a little later, when he'd made more sense of it. 'I'm sorry.'

'Don't apologise. It's kind of a relief in a way. Just tell me you're OK.'

'I'm fine.'

'Thank God for that.'

'Alex?'

'Yes?'

'I'd like to see you again sometime.'

'Me too.'

'I'll ring you soon,' he told her. And then they were calling the flight and he couldn't think of anything more to say.

Lisbon. Marseilles. Valparaiso. He liked ports. He liked their implicit adventure, their anonymity, their state of constant flux. He could sit for hours watching ships as they came and went. Knowing no-one. No-one knowing him. He could spend whole days hearing nothing but the crying of the gulls.

He remembered a hotel high up above the Tagus, a sleepy, unremarkable hotel where people did not ask you questions. It was dark when the taxi dropped him, but he was grateful for the warmth that still lingered in the air here after the relentless chill of the northern winter.

Late that night, up in his bedroom smoking Ducados and drinking a bottle of duty-free vodka, he thought about them. The ones who'd died. Persson, in his leather jacket; Kuslov, the trader; the poor hopeless husband of the tearful Ludmilla with her bag of torches, the small-time thief whose body had been pulled frozen from the canal. They'd all died to protect a secret. Died so that Mikhailowsky and his shadowy colleagues could do their deal.

Three brutal killings. And the most shocking thing of all was that what he'd found out this morning invalidated the whole sequence. Their deaths had been unnecessary, based on a misapprehension. At least so it seemed to Parnello on the evening of that endless day, lying exhausted in his silent room on the edge of the Atlantic, listening to the distant ships hooting in the estuary.

PART FIVE

The soldier in the wheatfield

TWENTY EIGHT

———◆———

Alphonse Baugniet eased the document from the file marked 'Ivexco' and held it in the illumination thrown through the window by the security lights in the yard outside. Part of him was horrified by what he was doing, appalled by the betrayal. And yet as he ran his eye urgently down the text and found the two pieces of information he had suspected might be there, he was suddenly overwhelmed with relief. He stood completely still, soundless, listening to the solitude of the empty office, gazing up and down the line of unmanned computer terminals whose empty screens stared out blindly into the night. And hearing his own heartbeat.

'No-one need ever know,' Corbière had told him. 'OK, they'll realise there's been a leak. But there will be nothing to pin down where the leak occurred. Provided you are careful. Provided you take simple precautions.'

'What do you mean, simple precautions?'

'You have access to the information system, I take it?'

'Yes.'

'For the purposes of this particular enterprise, always enter under someone else's password. And if you're handling original documents, make sure you're wearing gloves. It's straightforward. Only commonsense.'

'And you're sure it won't be traceable? Where the leak comes from?'

'No way.'

Baugniet had nodded eagerly, believing it because he

wanted it to be true, absurdly grateful to the man whose demands offered him a lifeline. A way out. An expiation.

So he had told them at work that he was staying late this evening. To sort out Madame Bernier's problem. Madame Bernier had sent in a list of twenty-five pieces of Japanese jade that she was consigning to Bartsch for storage, but the list did not appear to tally with the objects that had actually arrived that morning.

'You'll drive yourself crazy with that bloody list,' Ricki advised him. 'Why don't you give it a rest for the night?'

'No,' he'd replied, 'I want to get this property straight once and for all. I'll work through them one by one in peace and quiet.'

Ricki had shrugged. 'I guess that's why you're the bloody foreman and I'm just the bloody porter,' he muttered. The distance between them was widening, anyway. Widening as Alphonse sunk deeper and deeper into himself. Widening with every Friday that Alphonse no longer joined them at the Antelope.

Fernet, the managing director, had been the last to leave. He pushed his bald head round the door of Baugniet's office and said, 'Still here, Alphonse? Burning the old midnight oil?'

Baugniet looked up from the jade and repeated to him the details of the Bernier problem.

'Family all right?' Fernet had inquired. He prided himself on maintaining touch with his employees, knowing their domestic backgrounds. One Friday evening he'd even spent an uneasy half-hour with Baugniet and his friends drinking wine in the Antelope Bar. 'How's that boy of yours? In the Olympic skiing squad yet?'

'Fine, thanks. Give him a year or two.'

'Hope he's inherited some of your dedication,' Fernet told him. He had stood there, framed in the doorway. Then, as he turned to go, he had added, 'Believe me, Alphonse, I appreciate what you do for this company.'

Why had Fernet had to say that? Why couldn't he just have gone home silently? Put on his hat and coat and slid out wordless into his sleek BMW, leaving him untormented by praise?

Still shrouded in the shadows of the darkened office, Baugniet edged softly over to the photocopying machine, inserted the document, and pressed the start button. It whirred into life, the sound of its workings unexpectedly magnified by the silence, the flash of its photomechanism suddenly washing the interior of the whole room in light. Irrational panic seized him. He extracted the original and replaced it hastily in the file. Then he pocketed the copy and hurried out.

He was doing it for them, wasn't he? He was doing it for his children.

Corbière met him, as arranged, in the buffet of the Central Station. Alphonse handed him the photocopy. Corbière inspected it, casually, there in amongst the coffee cups, as if it was just a page torn from a newspaper, or a piece of junk mail.

'Good, good,' he said, pursing his thin lips as he read it. 'Bank, yes. Contact name, yes.'

Baugniet watched as he laid the paper flat on the table, staining the corner in a half-dried spillage of coffee. Corbière ran a stubby finger along the lines of text and stopped with a little jabbing motion. He looked up at Baugniet.

'That's what we're looking for, isn't it? This sequence of letters and numbers here.'

Baugniet swallowed and nodded. 'That's what has to be quoted, yes. To confirm receipt of funds and validate the release.'

Corbière folded the paper and put it in his wallet. 'I don't need you any more, then. You can go. I'll get the check for the coffees.'

'What about my photographs? The negatives, I mean?'

'Which negatives?'

'The ones you were going to give me in return for . . . for what I've brought you.'

'Don't be in such a hurry, my friend.'

'But you said . . .'

'You'll get those negatives once the shipment's safely released into my client's hands. Not before, OK?'

The fax confirming receipt of funds into Ivexco's bank came through the next day. Baugniet knew, because he saw it there, attached to the paperwork that was handed to him just after lunch.

'Ivexco property,' Paul told him. 'Going this afternoon. Being picked up by Reuterman of Cologne. Get Ricki and the lads to have it ready.'

Baugniet nodded, running his eye casually over the document stapled to the top of the file. It was convincing enough: it had come through by fax on headed Bank paper, quoting the property number and the confidential code sequence that was the trigger to the consignment's release. Everything was in order, you couldn't have told that anything was wrong.

'And Alphonse.'

'Yes?'

'Try not to drop the cases,' quipped Paul. Paul was always a joker. 'Some bright spark's just gone and paid 32 million dollars for them.'

'It's not theft. It's a case of disputed ownership. That's something very different.'

As Stahler listened to Kracht on the telephone, he could sense a rare note of exultancy in the man's voice. Of satisfaction in a job well done.

'What if Ivexco bring in the police?'

'They won't.'

'Why not?'

'It's not a police matter any more.'

'Since when?'

'As of half an hour ago it's entered the domain of civil law. That was when I sent Ivexco a fax, informing them that the pictures are now in your possession, and that you are prepared to go to court to assert your rights to their ownership. To show that they were illegally removed from a German private collection in 1945, and that they have now returned to the rightful heirs of that collection.'

'They won't like that.'

'They may not like it. But their hands will be tied. Their vulnerability is too great for them to come out into the open, to fight it in court, either in an action against you or even against the storage company. The publicity would be fatal for them. They would be blown out of the water, both at home and internationally: all we would have to do would be to expose to the world the identity of the organisation that has been controlling these pictures and the fact that that organisation has been offering them for sale clandestinely on the market. They know they can't risk trying to obtain legal redress from you if that's going to come out. Not now.'

'I see,' said Stahler. He paused, absorbing the information. Savouring it. 'In that case, Kracht, may I tell you what I am going to do now?'

The familiar grunt. His technical advice contributed, Kracht had relapsed into taciturnity.

'I have here on ice a bottle of Dom Perignon champagne. I am now going to open it and invite my beautiful lady wife Liselotte to join me in the drinking of several glasses.'

TWENTY NINE

On his fourth morning in Lisbon Parnello got up, looked at himself in the mirror, and decided to shave and fly home. His need for his own exclusive company was sated, his self-imposed exile over. He couldn't explain everything that had happened in St Petersburg last week, but he'd come to terms with it. Put a little distance between himself and Russia. Not just physical and temporal distance. Mental distance, too. And he was still alive. His threats seemed to have worked: Mikhailowsky and his friends had decided to leave him alone. For the first time, that struck him as a positive development.

London was absurdly normal, reassuringly familiar. It came on to rain as the taxi reached Hogarth Roundabout. Even that was reassuring. He knew he must be feeling better.

'I don't believe it,' said Brenda as he let himself into the hall. 'So you've deigned to put in an appearance at last.'

She was standing there with the inevitable fag between her lips, sorting through the letters. 'Blimey, you've got a bit of paperwork to catch up on. Mostly bills.'

'You certainly know how to make the returning traveller feel welcome,' said Parnello.

'It's been all go this morning,' continued Brenda. 'Bleeding fax just came through from Russia. Reams of the stuff.'

'From Russia?' Parnello put down his suitcase and walked over to investigate. There were six sheets; he draped his wet coat over the chair and slumped down on the sofa to read them.

> Dear Dr Parnello
>
> First I bring you good news: no more shortage of photocopiers here in Moscow. So I am sending you the material I have found for you and succeeded in copying. It is from the KGB Archive to which I gained unexpected access yesterday. You see, I remembered that the KGB deputy director of public relations (this post they never had in the bad old days) owed me a favour. When I found I had some hours to spare I asked him if I could see the file about which you inquired on your friend Major Gottfried von Seitz. He agreed. (It was a big favour which he owed me, Dr Parnello, something to do with a woman). So I am sending you the interesting extracts, with translations into English. (Also another owed favour from the translator, this time something to do with a regrettable penchant for Scottish whisky).
>
> I hope this will be of some help with your researches. Please come back to see me again soon in Peter. It was a pleasure to entertain you, and I much enjoyed our conversations. Also drinking apricot vodka with someone so congenial.
>
> I have the honour to remain your obedient friend, Dobiachowsky.

The first page from the Seitz file was in Russian. It comprised a list of the pictures in Seitz's collection, together with the itinerary of their railway journey across Eastern Europe in June 1945, a journey reaching its termination in Leningrad five weeks after their departure from Berlin. Here was confirmation of what Dobiachowsky had told him that morning in the Hermitage: the collection had reached Leningrad. But then? The clue was the stamp, heavily imprinted across the page. 'Restricted to NKVD'. These pictures were special. Too sensitive to be stored away with the other examples of Trophy art in the Hermitage. These pictures had become the responsibility of the KGB.

There followed a document in German. A short, seemingly innocuous document. Until you saw its heading: Einsatzgruppen SS, Army Group South, 2nd August 1942.

I confirm, he read, that at 19.00 hours this evening I visited Captain Gottfried von Seitz having been informed that 17 Soviet commissars had been delivered into his hands during the afternoon pending disposal. Upon arrival I discovered that Captain von Seitz had already expedited matters. He reported that he had executed the prisoners by a firing squad under his command. No further action was therefore necessary on my part. Signed, SS Sturmbannfuehrer Helmut Borg.

Parnello stared at it, stricken by its baldness, its callousness. Captain von Seitz had expedited matters. That was all there was to it. A simple matter of disposal.

He recalled what Dobiachowsky had once told him, talking of hidden archives. The Soviets had removed the entire body of SS records from Berlin to Moscow at the end of the war. That material must have been combed very thoroughly in order to seek out this document. Once found, it had been added to von Seitz's KGB file. Why? As evidence, presumably. As damning evidence of Major von Seitz's guilt.

He leafed on mechanically. He thought of Alexandra. He thought of her mother. They were not responsible. How could you blame children for their father? But this was the very digging they had striven to prevent. And it had unearthed just exactly what they dreaded. What they had asked him not to find.

And then he came across the third, longer document. Dobiachowsky's note told him that it existed in both German and Russian, but he had sent just the German original and its English translation. Typed neatly on three sheets of paper and signed at the bottom in a meticulous and scholarly hand, it was headed Report and Recommendations of Comrade Werner Garbrecht. Garbrecht. The name meant nothing to Parnello, but he read on, curious as to this report's connection with Seitz, wondering what it could be doing in his file. It was dated Moscow, April 1945.

It dealt initially with the conditions which the liberating Red Army would encounter in Berlin, making accurate predictions about the extent of the destruction and the chaos into which the city's infrastructure would have sunk. It set out the practical details of re-establishing order and instituting an immediate socialist administration under the leadership of Comrade Walter Olbricht. In this administration Comrade Werner Garbrecht was apparently to play a key role as some sort of Minister for the embryonic socialist economy of Berlin. It continued:

'Of the utmost importance will be to identify within the population at the earliest possible stage reliable and trust-worthy elements who can be given immediate responsibility in the fight to eliminate all fascistic tendencies from the German people. A list has been prepared of opponents of Hitler who are assumed still to live in Berlin. These include Communist and Social Democratic former members of the Reichstag, as well as leaders of the bourgeois opposition to Hitler.

'In connection with this last-named group, I must, however, counsel some measure of caution. Those bourgeois elements who resisted Hitler will not necessarily prove immediately sympathetic to the new socialist order which we will institute. Their ultimate support, however, will be important in the securing of a sound base for socialism. They must therefore be won over gradually. This means eliminating in advance potential stumbling blocks. Attention should be drawn to one particularly sensitive potential problem, which could affect this group's perception of both the new Soviet-controlled administration, and of my own personal position in it. This is the case of Major Gottfried von Seitz. The exceptional circumstances of his case have been discussed in detail previously. It may well be that the security forces of the Nazi regime have already executed him in punishment for his role in the insurrection of 20th July 1944. However, if he is by any chance still alive, it is essential that he be eliminated forthwith.

'Certain events which took place south of Kharkov on 2nd August 1942 during the German Army's advance through Eastern Ukraine are relevant in this connection. Von Seitz has himself given me details of the order to execute 17 Soviet Prisoners of War which he received on that occasion. This demonstrable war-crime will provide justification for von Seitz's own summary execution, which I urge should take place immediately the city has been liberated.

'Finally, in a spirit of fraternal socialist co-operation, I take the opportunity to direct the attention of the Soviet Trophy Brigades to the art collection of Major von Seitz contained in the cellar of his villa in the suburb of Wannsee. This collection contains several items of outstanding quality and would constitute property of a sufficient stature to be suitable for confiscation as war reparation.'

A later stamp was appended in Russian: Restricted to NKVD.

After that, a hand-written note: Seitz eliminated 9.5.45

And then, even more chillingly, in a different hand: Garbrecht eliminated 23.4.46.

Parnello laid aside the papers on the sofa next to him. It was horrific. And yet at the same time what he had just read had a compelling, nightmarish fascination. Here was one of those rare, intensely personal insights into history which he had become more used to experiencing pictorially. Just occasionally, an image painted – a face, an action, even the play of light on an inanimate object – could shock you with the truth of its observation, inject something alive from the past into your imagination. My God, you would think: that's exactly how it must have been. He felt that sensation now. But this time the medium was the written word. Reading this document projected him back vividly into that riveting nexus of the political and the military which was Soviet-liberated Berlin in the first days of May 1945. It transported him momentarily into close and unsought contact with this long-dead German called Garbrecht. And all at once he understood what he was about; did not like or sympathise with it, but knew it intuitively from reading what he wrote. Here was a man driven by political idealism, compelled into political compromise. Compelled into subterfuge and manoeuvring in order to make something that he believed in work. Perhaps in order to save his own skin, too. Here was a man who would ultimately justify everything by the subservience of the means to the end. Most significant, here was a man in some way obstructed by Seitz; a man who therefore demanded Seitz's elimination. And – irony of ironies – a man who ended up suffering himself the same fate as his prey.

Parnello sat there on the sofa in Jermyn Street, crouched forward in thought, his long legs bunched up to support his elbows, his hands in turn supporting his chin. He stared at the carpet. Assimilating what he had just read. Trying to analyse what it was which did not quite hang together. What it was that roused his suspicion.

And therefore, absurdly, his hope.

He went back over the pages of the fax: Comrade Garbrecht was worried by something, something which made Seitz's case sensitive. It wasn't the war-crime Seitz had been revealed as having committed which constituted that sensitivity. No, it was a quite different concern: Garbrecht was fearful that Seitz's continued existence represented a threat to the viability of the Soviet-backed Socialist regime envisaged for Germany, and particularly to Garbrecht's own role in it. The war crime had been deployed simply as the justification for Seitz's elimination; but the necessity of his elimination had arisen from something quite different. Something previously discussed, but not elucidated here. A hidden agenda. A secret imperative.

What was that secret imperative which drove Garbrecht, gave him this compelling fear of Seitz? So long as that mystery remained unrevealed, then there remained also some small particle of doubt in the case against Seitz. It seemed increasingly likely that without the secret imperative to convict Seitz of something, history might well never have heard again of his brush with the seventeen Soviet commissars. That selectivity made Parnello suspicious. That manipulation made him want to know more.

He ran his eyes repeatedly over the document, first in the English translation, and then in the original German. Not that his command of the German language was faultless, but it was serviceable. His instinct told him there was something here. Something wrong. The key was in here somewhere. Perhaps in a use of words. A nuance. In his experience Russian translators were inordinately proficient; but the one that Dobiachowsky had so helpfully employed to render the document into English, seamlessly though his prose flowed, had presumably been working from the Russian translation of the German. Thus German prose had first been forced through the decompression chamber of Russian before re-emerging in English. Therefore, even without the man's admitted fondness for Scotch whisky, the transition through an extra language meant at the very least a blunting of precision; a greater susceptibility not so much to outright error, but to misreadings of nuance. Tiny misinterpretations with disproportionately significant distortions of ultimate effect.

Yes: suddenly there they were.

In the penultimate paragraph of the original text. Two words: two small differences in the passage from German into English. But telling ones. Choices of vocabulary in the original German that confirmed the doubt already growing in his mind. Garbrecht was a twister, a manipulator. An opportunist. The translator had not understood. But Parnello had. Because across the generations, Parnello understood the way that Garbrecht's mind worked. Parnello had caught the nuance the translator had missed.

And now there was hope.

Brenda came in with a cup of coffee and a foul toasted

cheese sandwich that she had just put together in the kitchen. She had many merits, but she was unquestionably one of the worst cooks he had ever come across.

'There,' she said maternally. 'Get yourself outside this lot. You need building up.' He had noticed it before, her tendency to treat him with uncharacteristic solicitousness when he came back from abroad. The truth of the matter was that Brenda didn't trust foreigners. She could not believe that you could undergo extended contact with them without suffering some sort of physical diminishment.

'You're an angel,' said Parnello. 'In an unlikely disguise, I agree, but an angel nonetheless.'

'Cut it out,' said Brenda fondly.

'Could you do one other thing for me?'

'Give us a try.'

'Book me a seat on the British Airways flight to New York tomorrow afternoon.'

'I don't believe it! What's got into you? Are you on the run from the law or something?'

'Business, darling. Business.'

'It's a bloody woman, isn't it?' Brenda brightened perceptibly. 'An affair of the heart.'

Parnello stood up, stretching his long frame languorously.

'You're an incurable romantic,' he told her.

'Probably the one that rang a couple of times this week,' mused Brenda. 'American bit.'

'Alexandra Hamilton?' He knew as he said her name that he'd jumped in too quickly.

'There! What did I tell you?' Brenda was triumphant. 'I can hear Cupid's little wings fluttering.'

At least he could allow himself to think of her again. Now he had something to work with. Now he had something to offer her.

THIRTY

It was extraordinarily warm for a March day in Düsseldorf, nearly twenty degrees. The sun radiated in a clear blue sky, rewakening the senses and presaging the forgotten pleasures of summer. Frau Müller paused for a moment to luxuriate in the view from the office window, to run her eye over the immaculate patch of green grass below with its profusions of budding daffodils. The world seemed good to her, suddenly fresh and full of promise. Best of all, the Doctor had just arrived back after his trip abroad relaxed and in excellent spirits, apparently relieved of the anxieties that had clouded his manner for the past week or two. Not that he had revealed to her the nature of those anxieties; but she, who knew him so well, had sensed them, and tortured herself with speculation about what might be distracting him, to what sensual temptations a red-blooded male like the doctor might have succumbed, blessed as he was with such giant gifts of energy, creativity and dynamism.

But something told her now that the crisis was past, that there had been some magnificent triumph achieved over his secret difficulties. She had sensed it the moment he came in and opened up the file of press-cuttings which she prepared for him, always the first ritual in his office day. He had run his eye over the article in the *Frankfurter Allgemeine*, so snidely critical of the inflexibility of his position on immigration, so meanly abusive of his talents, the piece that she had toyed with the idea of keeping from him; but, having run his eye over it, he had laid it aside and responded only with a brief laugh. She wished his political opponents could have seen that laugh, witnessed how effortlessly he rose above their petty barbs. This was true magnanimity, she told herself. This was the stuff of greatness.

She waited at the Doctor's door for a moment, patting her blond hair back into place, then went in, carrying the file he had requested.

He looked up from his desk and smiled at her as she made her way across the carpet towards him. His affability was wonderful, and yet a little frightening, too, because it was so unfamiliar; awesome, like an eclipse of the sun.

'So Frau Müller, and how is life at home?'

She was momentarily perplexed. She was not prepared for such a personal question, for such unexpected evidence of the Doctor's awareness of her private life, let alone for such an intrusion into it.

'Good, Herr Doktor, thank you.'

'And your husband, he is well, I hope?'

'Erich? Good, yes. He is good, too.'

'Excellent,' nodded Stahler. 'Summer holidays all fixed up? Where are you going this year?'

'To the Island of Sylt, Herr Doktor.'

'So. To the beautiful sands of Sylt.' And then the Doctor added roguishly, 'You will go textilfrei?'

Frau Müller, thrown into confusion by this unexpected reference to the nudist beach, tried to reply but no words would come out.

'Excellent,' repeated Stahler. He returned his spectacles to his nose and took the proffered file. 'Tell me, have you added to these papers the fax of yesterday from the museum confirming receipt of the twelve paintings that I am lending to them?'

'You will find it on the top there. They were safely delivered by the shippers Reuterman yesterday morning.'

'Your efficiency does you credit, as always, Frau Müller.'

'It is nothing, Herr Doktor.' The blush again. She wished

she could repress it. Textilfrei. The word kept reverberating about her head.

'And Professor Weisman is expecting me at 2.30?'

'The Museum Director's Office confirmed the appointment this morning.'

'Good.' There was a pause while Stahler leafed through further papers in the file. 'That seems to be in order.'

'Please, one question, Herr Doktor,' she ventured. 'These twelve pictures from your collection going on loan to the museum: I cannot find them on the insurance schedule. But surely they are not recently acquired?'

'Most certainly not,' declared Stahler with unexpected vehemence. 'These are works which have been in store for a number of years in Switzerland. They are from my old family collection. There are separate insurance arrangements in force to cover them. You see, Frau Müller, I have chosen this moment to put them on public view at the museum. For the benefit of the community. I do not approve of works of art mouldering in store-rooms when the public could be enjoying them in a gallery.'

Get them on view immediately, Kracht had advised. Get them out into the public domain, show them off as items that have been in your possession since before the war. Once that perception is officially established, your position will be secure.

Get them on show in a museum, you mean? Stahler had demanded.

Exactly, Kracht had replied. This was Kracht at his best, his eyes narrowing as he held the problem mercilessly in his gaze, probed it, analysed it, and coolly drew the sting from it. Ideally it should be a high-profile museum, whose acceptance of your loan will generate maximum publicity. As I have already indicated, I do not believe that the controllers of Ivexco will dare to expose themselves in the international lawcourts to challenge your claim to ownership, now you have asserted it. The political implications are much too sensitive. In this instance possession is even more than nine-tenths of the law. But there is always the danger that they may make a clandestine attempt to reclaim the pictures by force. This manoeuvre will forestall them, you see. While theft might be attempted if the pictures remained secret in your private residence, it would not be worth their while to steal them from a public museum. The subsequent publicity would make the pictures completely non-negotiable thereafter.

Frau Müller nodded approvingly. She was dealing with a giant. She was unspeakably privileged to be working for him. A man of the world, of course, one who knew the textilfrei beaches of Sylt. And a public benefactor of prodigious stature, a Maecenas who thought nothing of making available his family treasures for the enjoyment of the common people. 'The community should be enormously grateful for your generosity,' she said.

Professor Weisman was a small, nervous man, who compensated for his lack of stature with an abundance of body-hair. His head was thatched with straw-like layers of it, and it sprouted in tufts from his nostrils and ears. His eyebrows were particularly copious and unkempt. Flecks of dandruff lodged in them like litter caught in a thicket of brambles. Stahler regarded him with distaste, noting his dark grey shirt and his brown knitted tie, the awkward way in which he moved his feet.

'Won't you sit?' said Weisman, indicating a chair. He positioned himself behind his desk, like a defence against his visitor.

'So, Professor, you have now had an opportunity to inspect my little family collection, I think?'

'Yes. Yes, indeed.' Weisman was playing distractedly with an elastic band, winding it round his fingers, ensnaring them in contorted patterns of imprisonment.

'What is your verdict? Are they up to standard?' Stahler asked the question playfully, confident in the knowledge of their quality. The man needed putting at his ease. Stahler reminded himself that he was prone to underestimating the debilitating effect that his own eminence sometimes had on the people with whom he dealt.

'There are . . . there are some excellent examples,' agreed Weisman. But his manner was still edgy, distracted.

'You would be happy to expose them in the museum? In a special show, perhaps?'

'I . . . Well, the offer is of course most generous.'

'I thought that a well-illustrated catalogue would be appropriate, entitled something like *Pictures from the Stahler Collection*. This would emphasise the paintings' long line of German provenance, the fact that they have been in the same German family for most of this century.' He paused, then recalling some ingratiating words of van Diemen about the Stahlers' collecting activities, offered as a clinching argument: 'This makes them, of course, an important document in the history of taste.'

Weisman had abandoned his elastic band now and was fingering a pencil, examining it with the same intensity as if it had been some minute Brancusi sculpture. 'Perhaps we could show a . . . a selection,' he said in a low voice.

'A selection?' The affront was instantly perceptible in Stahler's tone. 'You would not include every piece?'

Weisman's forehead puckered. He looked close to tears. He said: 'There are certain questions about – er – specific pictures which need to be fully investigated.'

'What questions?' Stahler saw no reason to suppress the threat in his tone.

Weisman looked about him, running his gaze about the extremities of the room. Looking for some refuge. Anywhere out of the line of Stahler's own angry eyes. He made a little helpless gesture with his hands. 'This is very difficult, Herr Doktor. I hope you will not misunderstand me or take offence, because absolutely none is intended, I assure you. Absolutely none.'

'There are questions about my family's pictures?'

'No questions at all about most of them. Most of them are impeccable. The highest standards of connoisseurship.

The van Goyen, for instance: a lovely example. Equally the Ruysdael and the Hobbema are both outstanding, and the Dahl is a beautiful thing . . .'

'So where is the problem?'

'Have you . . .' Weisman appeared to be addressing the ceiling. 'That is to say, is there any more information about the . . . the history of the van Gogh?'

'The history of the van Gogh is absolutely clearcut. It was acquired by a member of my family at the Berlin dealer Paul Cassirer in 1928.'

'Has it been recently examined by the van Gogh committee in Holland? To establish its authenticity?'

'My dear Professor, this would be totally redundant. The picture is listed in de la Faille's catalogue raisonné with the name of a member of my family recorded as its last owner.'

Weisman looked miserable. He ran a despairing hand through the tangled layers of his hair, setting free a small cloudburst of dandruff. 'I agree that such a picture is listed. But I regret that serious doubts must be entertained as to whether this picture which you have generously loaned to us is that painting.'

'What are you saying?'

'That this picture is a copy.'

The room was very still and silent. In the far distance it was possible to hear the bell on a passing tram.

'A copy?' repeated Stahler. For a moment incredulity robbed him of further speech. Finally he added in a strangled voice: 'That is an outrageous suggestion.'

'Naturally that was my own reaction also when the idea was originally put to me by my colleagues.' Weisman was talking faster now, almost gabbling. 'The composition is of course entirely van Gogh's. But when I myself inspected the canvas I too was struck by certain weaknesses in the execution. We therefore sent the picture to our conservation department for careful examination. We have a very good man there, one of the best in the country: he conducted the pigment analysis himself. Then he ran the whole process again as a double-check. I am afraid the results are conclusive.'

'What do you mean, conclusive?'

Wordlessly Weisman handed over to him a sheet of paper headed 'Conservator's Report'. Stahler reached out to take it, reluctantly, as if by refusing to absorb it he could deny its validity. Then he read it, slowly. With mounting horror as he reached the section marked 'Pigment'.

'. . . The most conclusive evidence is provided by EDX analysis under the scanning electron microscope which confirms the presence in the pure whites and paler colours of titanium white, a variant not available before 1916.'

'What does this mean?' Seidler's voice was hoarser now. Strained. His belligerence was underscored by doubt. 'What is all this technical mumbo-jumbo about titanium white?'

'Titanium white was a pigment compound not invented until 1916. Therefore any oil painting that contains it cannot have been executed before that year. It is as simple as that.'

'Oh, my God.'

'Van Gogh, you will remember, took his own life in the month of August 1890.'

'So this painting cannot have been painted by him.'

Weisman shook his head. A single flake of dandruff, caught in the sharp March sunlight, fluttered down from his eyebrow to the desktop like a minute petal of blossom.

'The bastards,' breathed Stahler.

'I am sorry: of whom do you speak?'

Stahler closed his eyes. 'No-one,' he replied. 'No-one at all.'

THIRTY ONE

———— ◦◦◦◦ ————

It was six in the evening when Parnello arrived at the Onslows' apartment on East 68th Street. He'd called Ryder from the airport to say that he had something to show him. A document on which he'd value his advice.

'Come on over. Nancy's out at some Benefit Committee meeting. I could use a drink.'

Ryder opened the door to him wearing an open-neck shirt and a voluminous sweater that could not entirely conceal his comfortable rotundity. His face was still well-scrubbed, his eyes behind their spectacles intelligent and animated. 'I got to admit, I'm curious about what you're bringing to show me.'

Parnello took the vodka he was offered. It had suddenly seemed imperative to come here first. To test his theory. To submit it to Ryder's rigorous scrutiny. But now he stood in Ryder's drawing room, he felt strangely nervous. Like a PhD student whose thesis was about to be assessed.

'Do you remember I asked you about Gottfried von Seitz?' he said.

'Sure I do. The guy in Bendlerstrasse on 20th July.'

'I got access to his file in the KGB archive in Moscow.'

Ryder whistled. 'Wow!' he exclaimed. 'You've got some influential friends. Is this your little bit of idle art-historical research?'

Too much had happened since he'd last seen Ryder to start explaining the events of his unscheduled trip to Russia. A week on, and he was still trying to make sense of it himself. So he kept it simple. He told him that this document extracted from the Moscow file had been written by someone called Werner Garbrecht. A German who'd apparently gone over to the Soviets before the end of the war. 'Garbrecht knew Seitz and this is what he writes about him. Read it. Then I'd like your opinion on the translation of one particular short paragraph.'

'What's this? Textual criticism?'

'You could put it like that.'

'Hand it over,' said Ryder. He set his Scotch down on the table.

Parnello gave him the copy of Garbrecht's report. He'd highlighted the penultimate paragraph.

For perhaps ten minutes, Ryder read in silence. Absorbed. Watchful of the words, vigilant, as if to prevent any nuance of their meaning elude him.

Parnello sat waiting, upright in his chair, swaying slightly. Running his eyes over the apartment. Book-lined. Opulent. Its style was a marriage of Ryder's scholarship and his wife's wealth. The pictures were good: a portrait by Vigee-Lebrun, a drawing by Degas. Perhaps these were purchases from Marvel? In that case they wouldn't have been cheap. He contrasted his present surroundings with the cramped and squalid quarters of another academic he knew, half way across the world. In St Petersburg. No chance of books and files spilling on to the kitchen sink here. Not so long as the estimable Nancy was around. And he felt it unlikely that Nancy would ever run off with a ballet dancer.

Finally Ryder looked up and shook his head in wonder. 'This is quite a piece of history, you know that?' he said. 'I'm familiar with this Garbrecht. He was the one conspirator from the 20th July plot who escaped to Moscow. The guy was a crypto-red in the Bendlerstrasse bed. He got out through Sweden.'

'What do you make of the paragraph I've marked? How do you translate it?'

'What, this one? The one that deals with the execution of the prisoners of war?'

Parnello nodded. Sitting in the soft comfort of Manhattan, where it was difficult to envisage such brutalities.

'OK. Here we go now.' Deliberately, precisely, with enormous care, Ryder went through it out loud. Word by word. This was the way he lectured his students, thought Parnello, the way he conducted his seminars: terse, inquiring, meticulous.

' "Certain events which took place on 2nd August 1942 south of Kharkov during the German army's advance through Eastern Ukraine are relevant in connection with this matter. Seitz himself has described to me details of the order to execute seventeen Soviet prisoners of war which he received on this occasion. This *scheinbar* war-crime" –' he paused thoughtfully, narrowing his eyes, '*Scheinbar* – now that's an interesting adjective to use here: at first sight you might be tempted to translate it as "evident", but actually it means "apparent but not real", "illusory" maybe. And then it goes on: "this illusory war-crime will provide a *Vorwand*" – now that means "pretext", "cover": almost "a cover-up" if you like. Right, so this is how the sentence runs then: "This illusory war-crime will provide a cover for Seitz's own summary execution which I urge should take place immediately the city has been liberated." '

Parnello sighed, and nodded. His instinct had been right. 'The translation I got read rather differently,' he said. 'The last sentence starts, "This demonstrable war-crime will provide a justification for Seitz's own summary execution . . ." '

Ryder raised his eyebrows. 'I think my version's the correct one.'

'And what would you say about Seitz's guilt on the strength of this document?'

'I'd have to say that it raises serious doubts. When you take everything into account. That word *scheinbar* suggests the executions never actually took place.'

'And the sentence before is revealing too, if you look at

the way it's phrased. Seitz gives Garbrecht details only of the order he received to execute the prisoners, not of the execution itself.' Garbrecht the opportunist. Twisting the facts, turning them to his advantage. And in so doing leaving little linguistic traces of his manipulations.

Ryder took his spectacles off and rubbed his eyes. 'It seems to me that your friend Seitz may have been the victim of some kind of Soviet frame-up.'

'Why would they have done that?'

'God knows. Some secret political expediency? Some private revenge? One can only guess at this distance in time. I'd be inclined to suspect it was something Seitz knew about Garbrecht that was in some way compromising.'

Parnello shrugged. 'Anyway, you'd agree Seitz comes out of this less black than white, after all?'

'A whiter shade of grey, certainly.'

Parnello left it at that.

Perhaps it was wrong of him not to have shown Ryder the other document from the file: the copy of SS Sturmbannfuehrer Borg's report from Einsatzgruppe HQ. The one which recorded Seitz as having confessed to the executions by firing squad. As having expedited matters. Its suppression was intellectually dishonest, at the very least. But producing it would only have clouded the issue. Shaded the grey towards black again.

He had enough now. Enough, as things stood, to present to Alexandra and her mother. Enough of the positive about Seitz's personal history to counter the terrible disappointment of what he had discovered when he finally laid eyes on his picture collection.

'It was a fake. A copy, anyway.'

'A copy?' It was Alexandra asking the question. Two hours later, in her mother's apartment.

'Yes. Definitely not by van Gogh.' He had said it. Put into words the devastating shock that he had sustained in that oppressive little office in the faceless grey building near Lityaeni Prospekt. He remembered picking the picture up, running his eye over the expanse of yellow wheat and the rolling clouds of the sky, and knowing at once that something was wrong. The brush strokes were limp where they should have been tense; the colours calculated rather than highly-charged. There was too much deliberation and not enough spontaneity.

'A copy made by the Russians, do you think?'

'We'll never know. But I suspect it was older than that. If I'd had to put money on it, I'd have said the canvas was pre-war.'

There was a pause, then Ella Hamilton said: 'Mr Moran, I guess you've just been on one heck of a long wild goose chase on my family's behalf.' She sat there on the sofa, one day out of hospital, even thinner and frailer than when he'd last seen her. The windows were closed and the curtains drawn against the cold March night, but still there was a hint of the launderette in the air, little pervasive humidities wafting up from the street below.

'Not simply on your behalf.' He smiled at her. 'On my behalf, too.'

'I am sorry for you, then. But I'm truly grateful to you for this.' She gave a little wave of the document she had just read. Comrade Werner Garbrecht's report. She was smiling back at him, but she had cried when she'd first read it. 'I guess you can imagine, this has considerably eased my mind.'

Parnello allowed his glance to rest on Alexandra. He had forgotten the physical details of her, the way she spoke and moved. She leant across to put her hand on her mother's arm. 'It's good news, isn't it, Mom?'

'Good news,' agreed Ella thoughtfully. 'And you know something? For me it really doesn't matter about the collection. I have this one picture.' She gestured over her shoulder at the floral still life. The Lindemann. 'That's enough. That's my link.'

'How did you actually get hold of this one?' Parnello asked.

They all looked up at it. The flowers. The ugly, thick impasto of their execution.

'She found me. In the camp.' For a moment the old woman's eyes swam; her attention seemed to wander.

'Who did, Mom?'

'Clara.'

'Who was Clara?'

It seemed as though Ella had lost the thread, had sunk too far back into the past to be able to achieve coherence. But then she visibly took strength, and the words came out, suddenly undammed. 'Clara was the housekeeper, in Berlin. I was twelve. I guess you could say I was confused, I didn't know anyone any more. You see, they'd taken me away from Morwald after my father was arrested. Split us up. My mother and brother were put in another camp that winter. That was where my brother died.' She paused, wavered, then took a grip on herself again. 'Clara found me, in my camp, soon after the end of the war. She turned up, this little bent old woman a bit like the witch in Hansel and Gretel, clutching this picture and the photo album. They were all that she had been able to retrieve from the house, apparently. She told me that my father had given her the picture, just before the Gestapo took him away. I remember telling her she should keep it, then, it was hers if Papa had given it to her, but she insisted I should have it. So I took it. She was a wonderful old girl, Clara, although I guess I was always a tiny bit scared of her. She was very determined. She had her heart set on getting me that picture.'

That picture. An insignificant thing, a passing fancy, the sort of purchase that a collector makes on a wet afternoon because he's bored, because he has nothing better to do, and afterwards wonders why he bothered. A spare bedroom picture; no, not even that – a maid's bedroom picture. And that's where it had ended up, of course, given to Clara, thrust into her hands minutes before the Gestapo came for Seitz, apparently, as if in payment of a suddenly-remembered debt, a last-minute acknowledgement of the service of a faithful retainer.

'A week or two later I was reunited with my mother. Then it emerged that some distant cousins who had emigrated to America before the first world war were prepared to take us in. So finally we set sail from Hamburg. It was the biggest ship I had ever seen. I never let the picture out of my sight. It was wrapped in brown paper. It's always been my link. I've always hung it close to me, wherever I've been. Even as a new bride I insisted on that picture hanging. Joe didn't like it much. He used to say, Ella, those damn flowers bring on my hay fever. But I stood up to him.' She shook her head and laughed, her haggard eyes animated by the memory of a rare assertion of will over her husband. 'It hung in the hall in Park Avenue.'

'I could probably tell you where it hung in your family's house in Berlin, too,' said Parnello softly.

'How could you do that?'

'I noticed that every single picture in your father's collection had a location written very meticulously on its reverse in pencil.'

'That sounds like Clara. It's the sort of thing she would have done. I guess she did it when all the pictures were taken down and stacked in the cellar because the bombing got so bad. She was a stickler for that sort of detail. She probably made a note of where everything had been hanging for when they went back up. Except they never did.'

'Let's have a look,' said Alexandra. Parnello reached up to help her lift the picture off its hook, conscious of the action's ritual symbolism of a rapprochement between past and present.

It was dusty. Together they turned it round to look at the stretcher, the wooden structure at the back which held the canvas taut. A variety of labels had been torn off the reverse. Nothing was legible except the pencil inscription in the same handwriting as all the others that Parnello had seen. This was all that was left: 'Uber dem Kamin im Arbeitszimmer.' Above the study fireplace.

Perplexed, Parnello stared at it. That could not be right.

This picture had never hung in the study above the fireplace. They had all seen the photograph. The van Gogh had been in that position.

Then things happened very quickly. Galvanised, feverish, he laid the picture flat on the carpet, face down, and began working on the nails that held it in its frame, pulling at them with his fingers to release the painting.

'What are you looking for?' Alexandra had caught the sudden urgency.

'It may be nothing.'

'I'll get you some pliers,' she said, hurrying off into the kitchen. 'Before you do yourself an injury.'

When she came back with them, he attacked the remaining constrictions that he had not been able to move with his bare hands.

Now Alexandra knelt on the floor next to him. Her mother hovered behind them, leaning her frail body anxiously forward from her chair.

The moment the picture was free from its frame, Parnello held it up to study the edges of the canvas, where those edges were tacked on to the flanks of the stretcher. Prising up a corner, he found what he was looking for: beneath the outer canvas, on which the flower-piece was painted, another canvas was nailed to the stretcher, the original one. The one to which this stretcher really belonged. The painting that had actually hung above the fireplace in von Seitz's study.

Using the pliers again, he eased up the tacks holding the outer canvas. Bit by bit it came away. And there it was, revealed beneath: the wheatfield, infinite yellow, boundless as a sea. The wheatfield with the distant trees and hills, and the troubled skies. And the paint swirling across the surface in the most distinctive handwriting in the history of art.

'Oh, my God!' breathed Alexandra. 'It's not! Is it?'

He nodded, and took her hand.

There could be no mistake. They were looking at Gottfried von Seitz's van Gogh.

Something else came away as Parnello pulled off Emil

Lindemann's flower picture to reveal the stupendous resurrection beneath. Two sheets of paper fluttered free, two sheets of yellowing paper held flat between the canvases, secreted there as part of the original concealment for more than fifty years. There was writing on the paper, in pen and ink, a fluent stream of lines in a handwriting distinct from the tight efficiencies of Clara's style.

It was Ella Hamilton whose bony hand reached out. Her attention was no longer held by the miraculous painting before them. Her face was simultaneously illuminated by hope and lacerated by anguish as she picked the pieces of paper from the floor. Parnello watched her, suddenly realising that she had recognised it as something more important to her than the thirty million dollars embodied in the painting.

'What's that, Mom? What have you found?'

She did not speak for a moment as she ran her eyes quickly over the writing. When she looked up there was an expression of unalloyed delight in her eyes. For a transcendently vivid moment her youth was returned to her. 'It's a letter written by my father,' she said.

Her eyes returned to the page, then she looked up again and murmured: 'It's so terribly sad: he explains he's inserted it in this hiding place because he can't think of anyone he can send it to who won't be compromised by receiving it.'

'When is it dated?'

'On 21st July 1944.'

'In the dead hours of the night,' said Parnello softly.

THIRTY TWO

To whom should I write this letter? It would be to my wife if it wasn't that the information it contains will be compromising, perhaps fatal, to its recipient. Such is the state to which evil men have reduced our country. Such is the moral twilight in which we are forced to exist. And I have anyway already written to Waltraud a separate 'husbandly' letter which I shall ask Carla to get delivered to her. It must be faced: there is no-one in Germany today to whom I can direct this missive who will be in any position to act on its contents, no-one who won't be rendered vulnerable by their knowledge. But still I must write down everything, because the truth must not be lost to the world. If there is to be an honourable future for my country, then these things must be known.

I have very little time left. But first I must explain in more detail the reasons why I now find myself sitting here in Wannsee awaiting my own arrest on charges of treason. Why it was that I felt compelled to take up arms against the leadership of my own country. How I came to the realisation that there was a higher imperative than obedience to oaths of loyalty sworn to a leader of the Fatherland who was manifestly evil. Resistance became a duty. And with it the risk of being perceived as a traitor in some men's eyes. So be it if I betrayed my country's leadership in the hour of its greatest need. I had to do it, in order not to betray my country.

The moment when I first became aware of the evil at the heart of the Nazi regime was in Russia in the summer of

1942. It was then that the full implications of the Fuehrer's despicable Commissars' Order were made clear to me. Enemy prisoners of war were to be ruthlessly executed. We the frontline troops who thought we were fighting an honourable war that would add lustre to our tradition of military prowess were brutally compelled into crimes for which we felt only horror and revulsion.

On the afternoon of 2nd August I was encamped with my company behind the front line on a seventy-two hour stand-down from action. Captain Seidler delivered to me seventeen Russians together with an order from Battalion HQ that I should supervise their immediate elimination. I queried this order, which was demanding something to which no self-respecting Wehrmacht soldier could possibly agree. I was told by Colonel Diederich that the order stood; and that if I did not carry it out, then the SS most certainly would without any compunction. Einsatzgruppen units were due to join us later in the day for mopping-up operations. I was horrified. I began to think about the appalling situation in which I found myself. It was not merely that I could never be party to such an act. It suddenly became imperative to do what I could to save some small particle of German honour by preventing these men who had been consigned to me from suffering death unjustly at our hands. It was the least I could do.

I therefore conceived a plan. I marched the prisoners out under guard to the area decided upon as the execution ground. It was on the edge of a wheatfield. I drew aside my junior officer, Lieutenant Ebers, and told him what I proposed. Having done so, I ordered the prisoners to dig a trench to the prescribed depth of one metre. It was pitiful to watch them working, increasingly fearful as to what was to follow.

They had all but finished when I walked forward and motioned them to lay down their spades. Then I told them, quite simply, to run for it. That they were free. That I was letting them go. They stood there, incredulous and mistrustful.

Looking back, I realise that they must have suspected a trick, that they feared we would use their flight as an excuse to shoot them down as they ran. Then all at once one of them – he had ginger hair and wore a green tunic – shouted something and turned and sprinted off down the margin of field and forest, finally ducking into the wheat itself and disappearing from view. When the others saw that my men had not lifted their weapons against him, they too dropped their spades and turned and ran. Within not much more than thirty seconds there was no more sign of them.

I ordered my own men to pick up the spades and refill the trench with the freshly exhumed soil, so that, should official enquiries be made, it would look as though there had been bodies recently buried here. Then I marched my own men back to the encampment. I made them no explanation of what had happened. But I think they understood. They were fine German soldiers.

I filed a false report that the order I had received had been carried out. It seemed the best way of achieving what I wanted. And I went back to the front line a changed man, in the sense that I knew my allegiance to the Fuehrer had been undermined, that the validity of my oath of loyalty to my country's leader had been fatally weakened. It is important to me now, standing as I do on the verge of a terrible retribution which may take everything from me, even my life, to make clear once and for all what happened that afternoon south of Kharkov. No executions were carried out and the so-called commissars were released. But the very fact of the command being given to me to behave in such a dishonourable way made me feel unclean. It was the root of my later willingness to stand up to the evil of Hitler. From that moment nothing was the same any more.

There is not time to record the stages through which I went in my conversion to the belief that only direct action against Hitler would offer Germany salvation. Suffice it to say that I fell into the company of a group of brave and honourable men, men whose utter probity will in the end act as its own defence against biggotted accusations of betrayal and treason. I have to turn at once to the tragic events of today, and specifically to one highly significant incident which it is beyond anything essential that I should record for posterity.

Major Werner Garbrecht is the central figure in this incident. Major Garbrecht is an officer in whom, up till today, I had learned to place my trust. As one of my co-conspirators in the plot to overthrow the Fuehrer, he was someone on whom I had come implicitly to rely. In the event, that confidence has proved uniquely and tragically misplaced. I am still trying to understand the full extent of his duplicity, the motivation behind his utterly unexpected conduct in the course of the day's events. Even as I think over now, a few hours later, what happened, I still react with disbelief. But I will attempt to set down the facts without comment or adornment.

At a time not long after 5.30 p.m. this afternoon, when the outcome of our attempted coup was in the balance, when in my judgement there was still every cause for optimism about the ultimate outcome, I had occasion to enter Major Garbrecht's office. He cannot have heard me come in, because he was engaged on a telephone conversation with his back to me. I stood there listening for perhaps a minute or a minute and a half. I here recount that conversation, or rather Major Garbrecht's part in it, as clearly as I can recall it.

'Listen to me. This is urgent. Can you connect me with Major Remer?'

. . . 'Can you get a message to him, then?'

. . . 'The message is top priority. There is an insurrection taking place in Bendlerstrasse. Yes, in Reserve Army Headquarters. There has been an attempt on the Fuehrer's life. A considerable number of disloyal officers here are attempting to overthrow the government under the cover of the Valkyrie Order. Major Remer should therefore disregard all orders emanating from Bendlerstrasse. Repeat, disregard all orders. Specifically, it is of crucial importance that he should not proceed as instructed to arrest or in any way restrict the

THE SOLDIER IN THE WHEATFIELD

movement of Reichsminister Goebbels. Instead he should go immediately to the Propaganda Ministry and take instructions only from him. I repeat, it is crucially important that Major Remer should accept instructions only from Reichsminister Goebbels and no-one else. Is that understood?'

'. . . That's correct. The safety of the Fatherland is now in your hands. Make sure the message gets through immediately. That's all now.'

There is no doubt in my mind that Major Garbrecht thereby betrayed the resistance at this crucial juncture and was thereby instrumental in its ultimate failure. It was not till later in the evening, however, after the conspiracy had lost all chance of success that I had the opportunity to confront him with his staggering treachery and demand an explanation.

Why, I asked him, had he taken this unforgivable action when I had believed him as implacably set against the evil of Hitler as the rest of us?

He replied that his detestation of the Fuehrer was as strong as ever, but that it had become necessary to ensure the failure of the coup as a means to a greater end.

A means to what greater end? I demanded, still uncomprehending.

Germany had no future under the old order, he assured me. The whole structure must be razed to the ground and then rebuilt from the beginning. The new rebuilding must be socialist. That was the only way ahead. The only true socialism came from Russia. He had reached that conclusion pretty early on, apparently, well before the war. And as the war itself progressed and defeat became increasingly likely, it became clearer and clearer to him that Germany's salvation could only be achieved under Soviet influence rather than under that of the western allies. That meant ensuring that Germany submitted to Soviet military domination rather than conquest by the west. The intention of our conspiracy, if successful, to sue for peace with the western allies once Hitler had been overthrown, was unacceptable to him. It would have limited Soviet territorial advancement; and it would have meant Germany being reconstructed on a western rather than a socialist model.

Did he mean to say that he was in contact with Moscow? I could not believe what I was hearing.

Of course, he said. From the earliest days, when our two nations were joined by the pact, he had had contact with our then allies. It had continued, grown, even when the alliance collapsed and Russia was invaded. He was Moscow's secret agent, took his orders clandestinely from the Soviet Union. And it was not in Moscow's interest for such an uprising as ours today to have succeeded. Not at this delicate juncture of the war.

I do not understand, I repeated. You betrayed your friends.

Of course you do not understand, he told me. He said people like me would never understand, that I was a dinosaur, someone utterly irrelevant for the future of Germany. My day was done.

So this is what it has come to. Incomparably brave men like Stauffenberg and Mertz, Olbricht and Haeften have already been gunned down. Others will surely die, quite possibly myself among them. And the man responsible for our betrayal from within has fled like a rat. Presumably via Sweden to Moscow, his mission accomplished.

I am impotent to broadcast the extent of this man's treachery. Who will listen to me now? But I write these words in the hope that some day they may be read sympathetically, so that some day it may become clear how lamentably and callously Major Werner Garbrecht altered the course of history.

I began by wondering to whom this letter should be addressed. I think I see it now: it is for my children, perhaps even for my children's children. I write these words for their benefit. May they understand the horrific nature of the evil I battled against, how I tried to act always according to the dictates of honour. How our failure today, and therefore my personal failure, too, was the result of having to operate against insuperable odds: to combat a force whose evil has become deeply embedded in our country, and then, at the moment of crisis in our struggle to displace it, to suffer an inconceivable betrayal from within.

I have done my duty. God save Germany. Now He is the only one who can.

THIRTY THREE

'I showed your grandfather's letter to Ryder,' he told her at dinner the next evening. 'Ryder Onslow, a historian at Columbia. He's very excited. He's talking about significant reappraisals of the German Resistance to Hitler, and particularly the events of 20th July. Gottfried von Seitz is in for a little rehabilitation.'

'Just explain to me again why this guy Garbrecht had it in for my grandfather,' she said. 'Why was he so set on eliminating him even though the war was over?'

'Because Seitz was the only one left alive who knew the full extent of Garbrecht's betrayal of the 20th July plot. And, even more important, the only one left alive who knew why Garbrecht had done it: on Moscow's orders. On Moscow's orders, so as to prevent the Western allies gaining advantage from the coup, as they would have done had it succeeded. If Moscow's machinations in 1944 had come out when Berlin was liberated, Soviet postwar relations with Britain and America would have soured even further. And it wouldn't exactly have helped Garbrecht personally in his new role in the whiter-than-white socialist government, to have been revealed as the man whose actions propped up Nazism for an extra nine months.'

'So the KGB stepped in and silenced my grandfather.'

He nodded. 'And because of the sensitivity of his case, when his pictures were appropriated by the Trophy Brigades, the KGB diverted them into their own care.'

She was silent for a moment, as if in awe at the scale of the injustice. Then she asked: 'How much difference do you think it made to the coup, the way that Garbrecht betrayed them?'

'They were up against enormous odds that day, of course.' Parnello paused to imagine them. Ryder's 'toffs' of Bendlerstrasse, holed up there in the hot Berlin afternoon, striving to trigger an uprising across the Reich. To light a fire. 'But Garbrecht's treachery was certainly a turning point. If Major Remer had continued to obey orders a little longer and taken out Goebbels, who knows? The Wehrmacht had already arrested the entire SS in Paris, don't forget. It could have spread.'

He spoke the last sentence with such wistfulness that Alex looked up at him and smiled. 'You're one of them really, Parnello, aren't you? You're one of the freedom fighters. That's how you'd be happy, taking some glorious, crazy stand, against all the odds. Having a cause to believe in.'

'Perhaps,' he said.

He was thinking about the way small actions could have such disproportionately far-reaching effects. Garbrecht's brief telephone call arguably altered history; it certainly consigned Seitz to half a century as a war criminal. And then again, that small-time thief in St Petersburg, the pathetic Ludmilla's husband: if he hadn't chanced upon that pair of so-called icons, Parnello would not be here now. Would never have known of the existence of Seitz. Would never have met Alexandra.

'You know you're an heiress, now, don't you?' he told her a little later. 'There's really no need for you to go on working at that clothes shop. Your mother's worth thirty million dollars.'

'The thought had crossed my mind.' That giggle again.

'How is she, your mother?'

'She's got to go back into hospital again next month, but the good news is her condition's treatable.' She laughed.

'I guess paying for the best medical care won't be a problem now.'

Parnello nodded. He watched her as she took a mouthful of pasta, then laid her fork down on her plate. He thought he'd never seen her look so beautiful. He remembered the moment when he'd first glimpsed her, standing in front of the Dahl in the saleroom, and he felt a fleeting twinge of sadness. Not for her. But for the enchanting evening light in the landscape that he'd briefly owned.

'We wanted to ask you something, Mom and I,' she went on. 'The van Gogh's in the bank for safekeeping. But she's going to have to sell it. There's no way we can hang on to it. How should we go about that? Could you do it for us?'

He wavered briefly, seduced by the sheer weight of dollars that the transaction involved. He was a dealer, wasn't he, after all? Of course he could sell it for them, could sell it many times over. But in the end, it wouldn't be right. How could she be sure he'd achieved them the highest possible price? Even if he got forty million for it, the little nagging doubt would remain. He wasn't prepared to risk that uncertainty clouding things between them. Still, it was a tough decision to have to take. Shagger Parks would have despaired of him.

'No,' he said. 'Not me. Look, the market's pretty strong now. Do it at auction.'

'At auction?' She regarded him doubtfully. Perhaps she had caught a quick glimpse of the professional sacrifice he was making on her behalf.

'Yes, go for it.' He laughed, to reassure her. The essential irony of life again. 'Just contact the two major houses and ask for their sale proposals. Then sit back and prepare to be courted and flattered to within an inch of your lives.'

'How do you mean?'

'You'll be offering those sharks at Sotheby's and Christie's one of their most desirable pieces of business of the year. That picture's sensational by any standards. Both sides will kill to secure it for sale. They'll pursue you relentlessly until you make a decision. You'll be wined and dined, pampered and cosseted. Flowers will arrive by every delivery, from one side or the other. You may even be lucky enough to get another dinner invitation from Humphrey Gardener.'

'And will you be on hand to save me from that fate?'

'If you want me to,' he said.

'I guess I do,' she said softly, and reached out to take his hand.

For a moment he closed his eyes and wondered why, at the very height of desire and human pleasure, he felt a mingled sense of doubt and sorrow. Occasionally the poet spoke to him. Whispered personally in his ear. 'I know not,' said Byron, 'except that on a pinnacle we are most susceptible of giddiness, and we never fear falling except from a precipice – the higher, the more awful, and the more sublime . . . In my own experience, it is odd that I never set myself to wishing without attaining it – and repenting.'

'Just so long as you remember one thing,' she added, as if their touching enabled her to read his thoughts. 'That guy Byron was a selfish bum, always wanting to have it both ways. A menace. Olympic class at self-delusion.'